PRAISE FOR JAMES SHEEHAN'S LEGAL THRILLERS

"If you like South Florida crime novels, legal thrillers, and court-room dramas, then you'll love THE MAYOR OF LEXINGTON AVENUE...This is a debut novel, but it reads like it was written by a master of the genre."

—Nelson DeMille on *The Mayor of Lexington Avenue*

"Sheehan writes with bleak clarity when he's sharing the dirty tricks of his trade in the harrowing trial scenes, but there's a touch of the poet in his voice."

—Marilyn Stasio, *The New York Times Book Review* on *The Mayor of Lexington Avenue*

"Powerful...reads like *To Kill a Mockingbird* on steroids."
—*Chicago Tribune* on *The Mayor of Lexington Avenue*

"Not only is this a top-notch legal thriller, it's also a moving story about love, guilt, personal redemption, and friendship. Sheehan is a truly gifted storyteller, and the novel's format is fresh and clever... This is a terrific novel, a genuine literary achievement."

—*Booklist* (starred review) on *The Mayor of Lexington Avenue*

"Fast moving and tightly written...boasts a gripping story and char-acters who will make the reader care. All in all, a stylish and engaging novel." —Richard North Patterson on *The Law of Second Chances*

"An assured, elegant, suspenseful cou[...]—*Kirkus Reviews* [...] *Second Chances*

"Sheehan creates an involving thriller that is also a moving meditation on love and friendship."   *—Booklist* on *The Law of Second Chances*

"[Sheehan] is especially good whenever he takes us into a courtroom.... Sheehan brings the three-way jousting of a criminal trial... to blazing life."   *—The Washington Post* on *The Lawyer's Lawyer*

"As a writer, Sheehan, a former trial lawyer, bears comparison to Scott Turow: his books are noteworthy not just for their intricate plotting but also for their literary finesse."   *—Booklist* on *The Lawyer's Lawyer*

"James Sheehan delivers an intricately plotted, fast-paced read with more than enough thrilling plot twists to satisfy the most dedicated Grisham and Connelly fan."
   —Bookreporter.com on *The Lawyer's Lawyer*

"The plot is well crafted, the characters are authentic, gritty and sympathetic... This story moves the heart as you identify with Jack, the 'lawyer's lawyer' and root for him in his biggest case yet."
   —RT Book Reviews Top Pick on *The Lawyer's Lawyer*

"Sheehan has written another thriller with some great courtroom scenes."   *—The Oklahoman* on *The Lawyer's Lawyer*

"THE LAWYER'S LAWYER keeps the tension high as it delivers a thoughtful look at the law and how an attorney has a duty to his client, no matter the cost.... [Sheehan] shows his affinity for making the intricacies of a police investigation and the resulting trial exciting."
   —South Florida Sun Sentinel on *The Lawyer's Lawyer*

"Exciting...Sheehan...keep(s) the tension high..."
   —Publishers Weekly on *The Lawyer's Lawyer*

"THE LAWYER'S LAWYER grabbed me from the beginning, and kept me ensnared the entire time. Full of engrossing characters, touching friendships, heart shaking twists and high stakes courtroom action, THE LAWYER'S LAWYER sets the bar quite high for this year's batch of Legal Thrillers."

—*The Guilded Earlobe* on *The Lawyer's Lawyer* (audiobook)

"THE LAWYER'S LAWYER is a book worth reading just for its exposure to the talent of James Sheehan. Once I opened its pages I was hooked. The book reads like something Grisham would have written in his earlier days."

—*The Huffington Post* on *The Lawyer's Lawyer*

"James Sheehan, a trial lawyer with 30 years of experience, presents a tightly-woven, fast-paced legal thriller. His experiences in the courtroom help create some of the best trial scenes in contemporary fiction...Sheehan's third book lands him a spot on the list of great legal thrillers alongside Grisham and Connelly."

—The Celebrity Café on *The Lawyer's Lawyer*

"Wow—I just finished reading THE LAWYER'S LAWYER and I was completely blown away by this relatively new voice in legal thrillers!"

—*The Marco Eagle* on *The Lawyer's Lawyer*

"THE LAWYER'S LAWYER is a truly riveting thriller, one not to be missed."

—Mysterious Reviews on *The Lawyer's Lawyer*

THE
LAW
of SECOND
CHANCES

ALSO BY JAMES SHEEHAN

The Mayor of Lexington Avenue
The Lawyer's Lawyer

THE
LAW
of SECOND
CHANCES

JAMES SHEEHAN

**CENTER
STREET**

New York Nashville Boston

Center Street
Hachette Book Group
237 Park Avenue
New York, NY 10017

www.CenterStreet.com

Printed in the United States of America

RRD-C

First ebook edition: August 2013
First trade paperback edition: September 2013
Originally published by St. Martin's Press, March 2008
10 9 8 7 6 5 4 3 2 1

Center Street is a division of Hachette Book Group, Inc.
The Center Street name and logo are trademarks of Hachette Book Group, Inc.

The Hachette Speakers Bureau provides a wide range of authors for speaking events. To find out more, go to www.HachetteSpeakersBureau.com or call (866) 376-6591.

The publisher is not responsible for websites (or their content) that are not owned by the publisher.

Library of Congress Control Number: 2013941545

ISBN: 978-1-4555-7452-0 (pbk.)

To my sweet sister Kate, whose boundless energy, knowledge, enthusiasm, faith, and love are so responsible for my success as a writer.

PART ONE

ONE

Benny Avrile wasn't a bad guy. He just looked for the easy way out of things—like every major obligation in life. Consequently, he had to steal a little to eat and sell a little to get something for himself. Cocaine, marijuana, liquor—it didn't matter to Benny. Whatever he could get his hands on. He steered clear of heroin and crack, though. The boy knew his limitations. He wasn't an addict—at least, that's what he told himself. He simply needed some help to deal with the stress of living on the street. People didn't understand the mental strain involved in not working, in not supporting a family, in not being responsible for a household. It was almost too much.

Another Saturday night found Benny at the Crooked Fence, a bar on the Upper East Side. The Crooked Fence had the perfect setup for a man with Benny's talents. It had a long bar near the front door with tables in the back. The place always rocked on Saturday nights. Benny would position himself at the bar, usually in the middle somewhere, and start talking—to anyone and everyone about anything and everything. He might be homeless, and at twenty-eight he might have abused his body more than the average fifty-year-old, but on a Saturday night, with a little shower, a little gel, and a little Kenneth Cole, in the dark shadows of the bar, Benny looked okay.

"Nice necklace," he said to the blonde on his left, who appeared to be in her mid-thirties, the optimum age for Benny's conquests or, as was normally the case, his attempted conquests.

"Thanks," she replied and then turned her back to him.

It was so perfect and he had it down to such a science. As she turned away, Benny, knowing exactly where her purse was, reached in and slipped her wallet out. Almost without looking—he had to take a little peek to be sure—he found the credit cards and put one of them in his pocket. If he took them all, she might realize too soon that she'd been robbed. With only one gone, she would probably think that she'd left it at home. Benny could do as much damage with one credit card as he could with ten, and it usually bought him more time because the victim might not report the card missing for hours, or even until the next day. He was very proud of himself for developing this system—he was a real thinking man's thief.

A minute or two later, he tapped the blonde, who was talking to another woman, on the shoulder. She looked over her shoulder at him.

"Can I buy you ladies a drink?" Benny asked, giving her his fabled Li'l Abner–I'm–a–hick expression.

"Listen, stupid," she began, turning more toward him to make her point. By the word "stupid" Benny had the wallet back in her purse. "You don't take a hint, do you? Get lost! Do you understand that? *Get lost!*"

"Okay, okay. Geez, I'm sorry." Benny was already off his stool and headed for the door. "I didn't mean to offend you," he yelled back over the din of the crowd and the music as he retreated. Then he was out the door and walking down Second Avenue. "I just needed your credit card," he said to nobody in particular as he patted his back pocket.

Half a block down the street he felt something hard shoved into his lower back.

"Don't turn around. Just keep walking." It was a woman's voice, and she was behind him just to his left. Benny assumed the hard thing was a gun, and he had no intentions of trying anything. If there was going to be any negotiation, she would have to start. He could counter from there.

"I'd been working her for two days before you showed up," the voice behind him said.

Benny breathed an imperceptible sigh of relief. It wasn't the cops, and he wasn't going to jail. Another thief he could deal with. It didn't happen often, but sometimes he crossed paths with another member of the profession and they got in each other's way. Benny was the guy who always deferred. It was easier that way.

This was probably the woman who had been talking to the blonde. He'd never run into a woman before during this kind of gig. *They can get money a lot easier than that*, Benny thought. At least, it seemed easier to him.

"I didn't know," he replied to the voice. "I only got a credit card and you can have it, with my apologies."

"Where is it?"

"My back pocket, right side."

"Turn left at the corner," she told him, still jabbing the gun into his back. They turned left onto Seventy-seventh Street. It was much darker off the avenue. They walked halfway down the block before she told him to stop.

"I'm going to remove this gun from your back and I don't want you to move."

"I won't," Benny replied emphatically.

"Then I'm going to slip that credit card out of those tight pants of yours, so don't get excited."

"I'll try not to," he said, relaxing just a little. She'd noticed his tight pants. *Maybe once we get past the credit card issue...*

"Good." She abruptly interrupted his thoughts, reached in, and deftly removed the credit card from his trousers.

Not bad, Benny thought, *but I'm a much better pickpocket. With me, you don't feel a thing.* He was starting to feel more comfortable.

"Turn around," she ordered.

Benny turned around. He could instantly tell she knew what she was doing. Her right hand, her gun hand, was in her pocket and she stood far enough away from him so that she had ample time to react to any aggressive move on his part. One other thing he noticed: she was a very good-looking thief—tall and dark with thick black hair that rested comfortably on her shoulders and brown eyes that at that moment were glaring at him in a menacing way.

"We're not even," she told him. "You still owe me. You fucked up my mark."

"Like I said, I didn't mean to. What can I do?" Benny was now sure she wasn't going to shoot him. Besides, she was sharp. Maybe there was something in it for him.

"I'd studied her, gotten everything I needed to know—and then you showed up."

Benny was starting to realize that he had fucked up a big score. He didn't know what to say, but he knew that he wanted to be a part of the next one. "Maybe I can make it up to you."

"You? What could I possibly do with a loser like you?"

"People like you always got another score set up. Maybe I can help. You can always use a second hand. Besides, I wouldn't want much, just a little to keep me going."

"What do you mean, people like me?" she snapped.

"You're smart. You set things up. You think about things. Me—I do the same stupid shit every Saturday night."

She started to smile. "You did all right," she said. "I almost missed you lifting the wallet, and I'm in the business."

Benny nearly blushed at the compliment. "Can I buy you a drink?" he asked her, even though he was down to subway fare for his ride back to the South Bronx.

"No," she replied firmly, but then something changed. The tone of her voice became somewhat softer, her expression more congenial. It was a subtle change, but Benny noticed. "On second thought, I'll buy you a drink," she said. "I've got the credit card, remember? And by the way, it works a lot better when a woman uses another woman's credit card."

Benny just smiled. "A minor inconvenience. I say it's my wife's and that usually works."

"Walk on my right side," she told him.

They grabbed a cab on First Avenue and went to Kettle of Fish, a place in the West Village, where they had drinks for a couple of hours. Benny would have been all over any other woman by that point, but he kept his distance with this one. He played that movie scene over and over in his mind—the one where the woman shoots the guy in the balls. *I ain't making that mistake*, Benny told himself.

A little after twelve, she finished her drink, paid the bill, and stood up to leave. They'd been having a nice conversation about nothing in particular. He still didn't know her name. Now she was looking at him intently.

"If you want to make a score that will last you a while, be here Tuesday night at nine. And don't be dressed like a pimp," she said, gesturing at his Saturday-night outfit. Then she was gone.

Carl Robertson was a creature of habit. He found comfort in ritual, and success in doing things right over and over again. Carl had started his career as an economist in an oil exploration business and ended up as the CEO. In "retirement," Carl continued his habit of doing things right over and over again, and as a consequence his financial status had increased to the point that he was one of the quietly growing number of multibillionaires in the world.

But Carl wasn't happy. He and his wife of forty years barely spoke. His three children saw him as a bank and nothing more. Carl knew he bore most of the responsibility for that and for many other things in his life. But the past was the past, and now in his early seventies he was just looking for peace and a little happiness.

He met Angie at a bar five years ago in New York. Carl and his wife lived in Washington, DC, but he spent most of his recreational time in New York City. Angie was young and beautiful with long legs, supple, round breasts, and silky long blond hair that shimmered. She didn't even talk to him that first night. He was almost forty years older than she was. He remembered the look she gave him when the bartender told her that he wanted to buy her a drink—like he was some kind of a whack job. But he had his people find out where she lived, and he sent her flowers the next day. By the time he came back to the same club the next week, she had found out who he was, and this time she accepted his drink offer. From there it was a matter of negotiation. He offered to set her up in her own luxury apartment and give her a monthly stipend. All she'd have to do was be "available" two nights a week and occasionally on weekends if *her* schedule permitted it. The rest of her time would be her own.

Angie didn't jump at the deal right away. He knew she wouldn't. But while she was making up her mind, he took her to the best places in New York and one time flew her to London for the weekend. Angie was from Omaha, Nebraska, and worked as a waitress while waiting to be "discovered" as an actress. Four weeks after meeting Carl, while her landlord was standing outside her door screaming at the top of his lungs because she was once again late with her rent, she picked up the phone, called the number Carl had given her, and, as Carl had instructed her, told the person on the other end of the line that she had changed her mind. She had never regretted it in the five years since.

Every Tuesday and Thursday night, Carl would fly in from Washington on his private jet and drive himself to "Angie's place" in a car he left at the airport for just that purpose.

Carl was good to her—never asked her any questions about her personal life and gave her ten thousand dollars in cash every month in addition to her all-expenses-paid luxury apartment on East End Avenue. It was spacious, and it had a doorman who opened the door when she went in or out and greeted her as if she was someone special. Carl even paid for her to decorate it. It wasn't just about money either. Carl was obviously a lot older than Angie, but he was a vigorous, healthy, handsome man who, at six feet four, still stood out in a crowd. Six months after their arrangement began, Angie told her girlfriend Carol, "I hope he never dies. I can't go back to living like I did before."

It was love, of a sort.

Benny arrived at Kettle of Fish on Tuesday night at 8:30 sharp. He didn't want to be late for his first big score. He had on a pair of black jeans, a black T-shirt, and his boots. He'd been doing a second-story job one night when he saw the boots. Normally, he was strictly after money and jewelry—in and out in no time, traveling light. But the boots he couldn't resist. They were leather and black and shiny and they looked very rich. After he tried them on and they fit, he had to have them.

What's-her-name arrived exactly at nine dressed in black jeans, black silk shirt, black leather jacket, black silk gloves, and stilettos.

You don't want me looking like a pimp! Benny said to himself. *You ain't exactly incognito in that outfit. And how the hell you gonna run from anybody with those fuck-me pumps on? Hell, most people would have a hard time walking in those shoes.*

But he kept his thoughts to himself. He still wanted—*needed*—a piece of the action.

"You guys back again?" the bartender said to them after they'd ordered drinks. The Kettle was a rundown little place and not one of the more frequented establishments in the Village. Showing up twice in the same week almost made you a regular and certainly caused Rick the bartender—whose living depended on the tips he could squeeze out of the paltry clientele—to take notice. Benny's companion did not appreciate the attention, however.

"Let's walk," she said after they had finished their first drink.

As they walked, she talked. "The mark is going to be on East End Avenue and Seventy-eighth Street. He'll arrive at ten o'clock sharp in a black Mercedes. I'll show you where he parks the car. When he gets out, we'll be there hiding in the shadows. I'll do the talking and hold the gun on him. He'll have ten thousand dollars in his inside suit pocket. You get the money while I keep him covered. You hand me the cash, then we take off in different directions. I'll meet you on the corner of Ninety-fifth and Lexington exactly one half hour later. Don't be late."

She stuck her finger in Benny's face to emphasize the importance of timeliness, and as she stepped closer to him she appeared to catch her heel in a crack in the sidewalk and fell hard to the pavement.

"What the hell—are you okay?" Benny asked as he started to bend down to her.

"Does it look like I'm okay?" she yelled. "I twisted my ankle."

I'm not the one wearing those stilts, Benny wanted to shout, but he held it in. "Let me see," he said instead and bent down to look.

She put her arm out to stop him. "I don't need you to examine me. I know when I've twisted my own ankle. I can move it, so it's not broken."

"Okay, okay. I'm just trying to help."

"Then hail a cab. We gotta get moving."

He hailed a cab while she slowly got up and hobbled over to get in. She kept rubbing at her ankle during the ride, and when they got out at Seventy-eighth and York, Benny noticed that she wasn't putting any weight on it.

"I don't know if I can do this tonight," she said, grimacing as she leaned against a wall. "Maybe we'll have to put it off until next month."

"No, no, no!" Benny told her, unaware of how desperate he sounded. "I can do this alone! You just stay off in the shadows."

"No way. I'm not letting you fuck this one up on me. I need that money."

"I won't fuck it up, I swear."

"I'm supposed to trust you? I don't even know you, for Christ's sake."

"I ain't gonna cheat you. I need the score too. I won't take off without you, I promise." Benny was giving it his all, even though he had no intention of sharing one thin dime with her.

"All right, all right," she finally relented. "I'll let you do it. But if you fuck me, I'll search the ends of the earth to find you, and then you don't want to even think about what I'll do to you." Benny couldn't believe such venom was coming from this beautiful creature.

She reached into her jacket pocket and pulled out a revolver and handed it to him. "Here, take this," she said.

Benny took the gun and held it in his hand, pretending to look it over while he tried to feel comfortable with it. He hated guns, hated being around them at all.

"Do you even know how to fire it?" she asked.

"Sure, I do," he blustered. "You just aim and pull the trigger." He started to point the gun at an imaginary target.

"Be careful with that. It's got a hair trigger and there's no safety on it," she told him. "Don't even think about using it. He'll give you the money. Ten thousand to him is like pennies to you and me. Just point the gun at him and tell him to hand the cash over."

Benny lowered the gun. "Okay, okay. I got it. So what's the split?" he asked.

"What split?"

"The money. I figure it should be fifty-fifty since I'm doing everything now."

"You'd be doing nothing if it wasn't for me, shithead. It's a seventy-thirty split, that's it. Take it or leave it."

Benny was a bit surprised she hadn't brought the subject up herself. Anyway, he had his answer. She was going to fuck him, so it was okay for him to fuck her first. He felt a lot better now.

"I'll take it," he replied.

She then pulled what appeared to be a makeup case out of her jacket pocket. She found a stoop nearby, hobbled up the steps with the aid of the banister, and sat down.

"C'mere," she said. "I've got something to give you a little confidence." Benny walked up the steps and saw she was laying out a few lines of coke on the mirror of her makeup case. She offered it to him and he gratefully accepted. The lines of coke disappeared up his nose in an instant.

"One more," she said and repeated the ritual. Benny had smoked a ton of dope before he'd left for Kettle of Fish for the same reason—to work up some courage. Now he was flying so high he barely knew what planet he was on.

"I'll be up the block waiting," she said "We'll get a cab. And remember what I said—don't even think about fucking me over."

Benny gave her his best Li'l Abner, innocently shaking his head back and forth. His own mother would have believed him.

Carl arrived promptly at ten and parked in his parking spot, the one he had paid the city a fortune for. The one that had its own sign: "No Parking Anytime. Violators will be prosecuted to the full extent of the law." Carl knew that for the right amount of money you could get anything, including your own parking space.

As he emerged from the car, he was surprised to see a wide-eyed young man in front of him holding a gun. No need to panic. He'd been in this situation before. It was surely about money and, therefore, negotiable.

"What can I do for you, young man?" he asked, looking down at Benny, who stood five feet eight inches tall *with his boots on*.

Carl never got an answer. Instead, he heard a sharp *crack* and felt a stinging pain in his head, a pain so severe it caused him to lean forward over the open car door so far that his head crashed into the outside of the door's window. Then he slid to the ground beside the door. While he was lying there in shock, he felt the man's hands reach into his inside jacket pocket and pull out his cash—the money he had brought for Angie. Carl wanted to stop him but couldn't move. Then everything went black.

TWO

Mary Walsh never answered the phone after ten o'clock. With thirty years of marriage to a cop, the last twenty of which he'd been a homicide detective, she was used to the late-night—sometimes middle-of-the-night—calls, and she wanted no part of them. The hairs on the back of her neck always stood up when that damn phone rang past ten and her husband Nick answered it.

"The murder has already been committed," he'd invariably tell her. "I'm just mop-up duty." But Mary never bought it. Every time he walked out that door, she was afraid that he might not come back. All she had to do was read the papers to be assured of that possibility.

This night was no different. When the phone rang at a few minutes to eleven, Mary wouldn't go near it.

"Can you get that?" Nick yelled from his seat in the bathroom. Mary picked up the phone without answering it and walked it to the bathroom. She opened the door and extended her arm and the phone to her husband without looking in.

"Here," she said. Nick was able to reach out and grab the phone while maintaining his seat on the throne.

"Walsh," he answered, just like he was in the squad room. That frosted Mary. The man was never off duty, even at home—even on the toilet.

"Nick, this is Severino." Anthony Severino was Nick's latest part-ner in homicide. They'd been together for almost a year. Nick was the senior man by about ten years.

"Yeah, Tony, whaddaya got?"

"Some high-powered guy got whacked about an hour ago on Seventy-eighth and East End. The captain wants us down there right away."

"All right, I'll be there in fifteen minutes."

Nick and Mary lived in the same rent-controlled apartment on Ninety-seventh and Park where Nick had grown up with his parents and two younger brothers. It was the only way they could afford to live in the city. Mary's dream was a house upstate, or in New Jersey or Rockaway Beach—they could never afford Long Island—but Nick wouldn't hear of it.

"People get murdered all over the city at all hours of the day and night," he told her. "I can't be driving in from the suburbs like some commuter. I gotta be there right away. Besides, you're living on Park Avenue." It was a quip that had always made Mary laugh in the early years. The real Park Avenue ended at the imaginary line south of Ninety-sixth Street. Nowadays, after all the years of being a cop's wife and making the necessary sacrifices, she simply ignored the remark.

Twenty minutes later Nick was standing over the body of Carl Robertson, his eyes exploring every detail of the dead man's body—searching for the obscure clue. It was one of the things that separated him from the run-of-the-mill homicide detective. In this case, there was nothing subtle about the fact that Carl had met his demise as a result of a gunshot wound to the head.

The place was swarming with uniformed police officers, gawkers, and reporters from both print and television. Nick was the guy in charge, and he looked the part. He was a big man, a few inches over six feet, with broad shoulders and an ample waistline that he carried well, even though it seemed to be growing an inch or two each year. He was constantly telling himself that he was going to start working out "one of these days." Tony Severino, on the other hand, worked out like a madman, but in some respects it did him no good. At the end of the day, Tony was still short and stocky.

A perimeter had been set up with tape before the two detectives arrived. The perimeter was supposed to secure the crime scene, but too often everybody—cops included—just walked through like it was Disneyland. That wasn't going to happen on Nick Walsh's watch.

"Get those uniforms outside the tape line," he told Tony. "I don't want the crime scene destroyed. Have them do crowd control or something." Technically, uniforms and detectives were the same rank, but at a homicide scene the detectives were in control. "And get the fuckin' press as far away from here as you can," Nick added. He hated the press. They had a tendency to report what they wanted to report, regardless of the facts—although Nick wasn't above using a reporter from time to time to put out a story.

Tony set about giving the uniforms assignments outside the lines and moving the press and everybody else out of the way.

When he had finished his initial investigation of the corpse and the immediate area surrounding it, Nick strode over to the assistant medical examiner on the scene, Dan Jenkins, who was standing just a few feet away directing his people and making notes.

"Whaddaya got so far, Dan?"

"It seems open-and-shut, Nick, although you and I both know it's never open-and-shut." Nick nodded. They both had been doing this long enough to know that nothing was as it seemed. "It looks like death was caused by a single bullet to the brain. I don't know if you have this yet, but the woman who called this in said she heard a noise that sounded like a gunshot a few minutes after ten. She looked out her window and saw the deceased there lying on the ground. She also saw a man—apparently the shooter—kneel over the deceased while he was on the ground, then get up and run away. She was too far away to give a description and she didn't know if he took anything from the deceased or not."

"What about time of death?" Nick asked.

"It's a little early to say definitely"—it was a disclaimer Nick always expected and usually received—"but rigor mortis has not set in yet, and from the coagulation of the blood in the ankles I'd say offhand that everything shut down about ten o'clock."

Coroners, Nick thought. *They have such an interesting way of describing death.*

"Thanks, Dan. I'm sure we'll be seeing a lot of each other in the next few days and weeks."

"Yeah," Dan groaned. "You know, Nick, I was scheduled to be off tonight. Just my luck to get one of these high-profile cases where everybody is breathing down your neck."

"I'm with you," Nick replied. "Who the fuck was this guy anyway?"

"Some super-rich oil guy."

"Jesus. Let's see if we can put this to bed as quickly as possible."

"Sure thing, Nick. Okay if I take the body? I want to get it out of here before the reporters start sticking their heads down his shorts looking for a scoop."

Nick laughed. It wasn't far from the truth. "He's all yours."

"Thanks, Nick."

As Nick watched Dan Jenkins assemble his people and equipment to transport the body to the morgue, the assistant chief, Ralph Hitchens, sidled up next to him.

"Looks like a robbery gone bad," he said, trying to sound like he knew what he was talking about. In twenty years in homicide, Nick had never seen Ralph Hitchens at a murder scene before.

Nick stifled the urge to say, *No, Sherlock, it looks like a murder.* Instead, he just nodded in agreement as he watched Dan Jenkins's young assistant load the body onto a stretcher. He didn't like to miss any of the details, especially in a high-profile case like this.

"Any thoughts so far, Detective?" Hitchens asked.

Nick couldn't bring himself to ignore the question. The assistant chief was nothing more than a glorified pencil pusher: they had entered the academy together and graduated at the same time, but while Nick went directly to the street, old Ralphie boy became some captain's clerk. Nobody who knew Ralph Hitchens back then would ever have picked him as a leader of men. They might have picked him as the guy most likely to piss his pants in a gun battle, but that was about it. He rose in rank the way most of them did, sticking their nose up enough asses until they were rewarded for the endeavor. *Politics*, Nick thought with that exact picture in his mind. *No wonder it stinks!*

"Well, it's definitely a homicide, Chief. Bullet wound to the head," Nick deadpanned. Over to his left, Nick noticed that Tony Severino, recently returned from his crowd-management duties, was fighting to keep from laughing out loud.

Ralph Hitchens's jaw tensed. He clearly was not amused by the remark.

"I want this case wrapped up quickly, Walsh. You've got an eye-witness."

Is this shithead for real? Nick fumed to himself. *Yeah, Chief, there's an eyewitness who saw someone next to the body. That narrows it down to eight million people, you schmuck!* He decided to pull the prick's chain a little longer. *What the hell, I'm vested.*

"I'll get right on it, Chief. An unidentified male shouldn't be too hard to find."

As he said the words, Nick realized all he needed was a description to solve the case. Whoever did this crime was probably in the system somewhere.

Thanks, Chief! he said to himself. *I wouldn't have thought of that right away if I hadn't been busting your balls.*

THREE

Clang! The gates of the maximum-security state prison in Starke, Florida, slammed shut behind Jack Tobin as he entered. It wasn't an unfamiliar sound. This had been his work for the last two years—representing people on death row. There were aspects of the endeavor that he loved and aspects that he hated. One of the things he hated most was entering the prison, with its dank odors and its chaotic sounds bouncing off the bare walls and steel bars and ricocheting up and down the corridors. The racket reminded him of the Central Park Zoo when he was a kid, when it was the sounds of animals that rang in his ears and the smells of their excrement that filled his nostrils. Zoos had changed since then. Apparently, some experts decided that animals thrived in a more open, natural environment. *Maybe someday a lightbulb will go off somewhere and they'll realize that a better environment might work for human beings as well,* Jack thought as he walked down the corridor and into the visiting room accompanied by a uniformed guard.

He was visiting an inmate named Henry Wilson. Jack did not know the complete details of the case. He knew that Wilson, who was black, had a rap sheet about six miles long, that he had been a criminal and a drug addict his entire adult life, and that he'd been convicted seventeen years ago of murdering a drug dealer named Clarence Waterman.

Jack had been a very successful civil trial lawyer in Miami for twenty years. He had started his own firm, and when it grew to one hundred lawyers and he could no longer stand it, he had negotiated a twenty-million-dollar buyout of his interest. He had planned on retiring to the little town of Bass Creek near Lake Okeechobee and becoming a part-time country lawyer and a full-time fisherman. Other matters intervened, however. First, the governor offered him the position of state's attorney for that county. Even though he didn't want the job, he couldn't say no. And then he learned that his best friend from his childhood years in New York, Mike Kelly, had died, and that Mike's son, Rudy, was on death row in Florida. Thus began a quest to save Rudy from the electric chair. It was through the process of representing Rudy that Jack realized he had a calling and that his particular calling was to represent death-row inmates.

The visiting room was as stark and uninviting as the rest of the facility, with nothing in it but a steel table and steel chairs bolted to the ground. Jack took his seat and waited for the sound of Henry Wilson coming down the hall. It was always the same. You heard them long before you saw them: chains clanging, feet shuffling. Still, Jack was shocked when Henry Wilson walked in the room. He was an imposing figure, standing at least six feet, five inches tall with a wide, thick, muscular frame. His brown eyes were dark and inset, and the corners of his lips turned downward in a perpetual scowl. He looked like he could break his shackles, overpower the guards, and walk through the walls to freedom anytime he wanted.

Jack also noticed that there were three guards with Henry Wilson instead of the usual two and they were watching Wilson's every move. Jack took his cue from them.

Henry shuffled in and stood in front of the bolted chair on the opposite side of the table. "Hello, Mr. Wilson, I'm Jack Tobin," he said rising from his seat. He did not offer his hand because he noticed that Henry's cuffs were shackled to a waist belt. "I'm a lawyer."

Henry Wilson looked across at the man standing on the opposite side of the table. He appeared to be in his late forties, early fifties, and he had a tough, weathered look about him—kind of like an old marine. At six-two, Jack was not quite as tall as Henry; his thinning gray hair was short and he looked fit, even muscular. Henry Wilson said nothing in reply to Jack's introduction. He simply gave the lawyer a bored look.

They both sat down, Henry filling his chair and then some. Jack could feel his disdain.

"I'm with Exoneration. It's a death penalty advocacy group located here in the state of Florida," Jack continued. The mention of Exoneration seemed to strike a chord with Henry. He finally spoke.

"I've dealt with your organization before, Mr. Tobin. They handled my second appeal approximately six years ago. I guess my name has come up because my execution date is two months away, am I right?"

"I expect so," Jack replied, somewhat surprised. The man was articulate. "No matter what the reason, they've asked me to look at your case again. I haven't really reviewed your file. I wanted to meet you first."

"I see," Henry said. "You're trying to get your own read on me."

"Something like that," Jack replied. That was certainly part of it. He wanted to see and feel the man's own commitment to his innocence. It wouldn't affect whether he took the case or not. The evidence, or lack of it, would make that decision.

"Well, you do what you gotta do."

"You don't sound too enthused," Jack said.

Henry smiled at Jack like he was a schoolboy about to learn a valuable new lesson.

"It's like this, Counselor. I've been here for seventeen years. I've talked to more lawyers than I care to remember. I've heard more promises than a priest in the confessional. And only one thing remains constant: I'm still here."

Jack had heard a version of that line a time or two in the recent past. Anybody who had been in prison that many years had long ago lost any realistic hope of release. "Let me tell you this, Mr. Wilson: I will make no promises to you—ever. I will review your file thoroughly after this conversation and I will conduct my own investigation. If

I believe there is a basis for requesting a new trial, I will discuss that with you, and we'll decide together whether to move forward or not. If I don't think there is a basis, I will tell you that as well. Fair enough?"

Henry didn't respond. He just stared at Jack as if he was trying to see inside him.

"Have you read my rap sheet? Did you get a feel for who I was before I landed in here?"

Jack stared back into Henry Wilson's cold eyes. "Yes, I read it."

"That usually stops most of them. They go through the motions, but they're pretty sure I'm guilty by the time they're done reading my history. Why should it be any different for you?"

Their eyes were still locked on each other. "It's not," Jack replied. "My first inclination is that you're probably guilty. But the law isn't about inclinations—it's about evidence. And I'm going to make my decisions based on the evidence. Do you want to tell me why you're innocent?"

Henry continued to stare for almost a minute before answering.

"I'm going to make this short and sweet. I was convicted based on the testimony of one man, a snitch named David Hawke. I was supposed to have killed this drug dealer who I didn't know. I bought drugs from him a few times and that was the extent of it. Hawke testified that he drove me *and his cousin* to the guy's house and that I slit his throat and watched him bleed to death.

"Hawke was a convicted felon on probation. I guess I don't need to tell you that cops can pull one of those guys off the shelf anytime they want, to say anything they want, because they own them."

"Maybe so, but why would a guy testify that he drove you there if he didn't actually do it?" Jack asked. "That would make him an accomplice and as guilty as you under the felony murder rule."

"And why would someone implicate his own cousin in a murder if he wasn't involved?" Wilson added. "It doesn't make sense. I think the jury asked those same two questions and that's why they convicted me of first-degree murder and sentenced me to death. There was no other evidence linking me to the murder. And here's the kicker,

Counselor: neither David Hawke nor his cousin was ever charged with the crime."

Wilson had certainly gotten his point across. Jack had not heard of a case where known accomplices were never even arrested. Still, he also knew that this was not a basis for a new trial, especially seventeen years later. Something else was bothering him, though. It didn't become clear until he was in the car on the way back to his home in Bass Creek. A picture kept forming in his mind—Henry Wilson was holding a normal-size man by the hair of his head like a rag doll. The man's throat was cut from ear to ear and the blood was roaring down the front of his torso.

The three-hour drive back to Bass Creek wore Jack out. When he arrived home, Pat, his wife, was cooking in the kitchen in her jogging clothes.

"Hi, honey. How was your day?" she asked while standing over the stove. She had only to look at him and smile, and Jack felt good. That smile was all that he needed.

"It was a long day. Have you gone running yet?" he asked as he came over and kissed her on the cheek.

"No, I thought I'd wait for you. If you're too tired, I'll go by myself."

"I'll go with you," he called back as he bounded up the stairs to get changed. "I could use a good run."

Pat knew he would say that. Jack's first meeting with a client on death row was always stressful, and he needed a little commune with nature and his wife to get his balance back.

Bass Creek was a backwater little town located on the northwest tip of Lake Okeechobee. It was bordered on the south by the Okalatchee River. Pat and Jack's house was right on the river, and they headed out on their run along the north bank between two lines of weeping willows. It was a cool autumn night and a gentle breeze was blowing—perfect running weather. The river was calm, the fishing boats asleep for the night. Pelicans were floating lazily atop the glasslike surface, spent after a day of flying and fishing. Two squirrels were chasing each other in the thicket up ahead; the crickets and cicadas were in full chorus—all was right in Bass Creek.

They didn't speak for the first few minutes as their bodies warmed to the task and settled into a rhythm. Finally Jack broke the silence.

"Henry Wilson is a very angry man."

Pat had been through enough of these conversations that she could usually tell before he said a word whether he was optimistic about the case or not. Henry Wilson did not seem like a man Jack wanted to defend.

Jack was a passionate opponent of the death penalty for many reasons but primarily because he felt that the criminal justice system was flawed. DNA testing had unmasked some of those flaws by revealing that a vast number of people had been wrongfully convicted in all types of criminal cases, especially rape. Unfortunately, however, the general public now believed that DNA had solved all the problems. In fact, it had just scraped the surface. Eyewitness identification, the worst type of evidence, was still sending many people to death row, and the use of prison "snitches" and convicted felons made that process even more troubling. Add to the mix incompetent counsel, aggressive prosecutors, and cops willing to hide evidence or worse, and the true picture started to emerge.

In Jack's mind, the defeat of the death penalty would only come by proving, one case at a time, that innocent people were still on death row. That was why he had to make sure he was spending his time representing innocent people.

Pat pressed the issue. "Is that all you can say about him?"

"Well, he's a giant of a man—very, very intimidating. And he's got a rap sheet a mile long. The guy exudes danger. He looks like a killer."

"Well, then I guess he must be guilty," Pat replied somewhat sarcastically.

"I'm not saying that. However, if I was going to put money on it, I'd wager that Henry Wilson could kill somebody in a heartbeat with his bare hands."

"Did he kill the man he's accused of killing?"

"I don't know, Pat. My gut feeling is yes. However, he did raise a few points today that, if they are true, might mean he is innocent of this murder. Even so, I don't know if I want to put a guy like that back on the street."

"I see." Pat winced slightly as she spoke and put her hand to her right side like she was getting a runner's stitch.

"That gallbladder pain still bothering you?" Jack asked. She'd been having a dull ache in her abdomen for some time. Her doctor had said it was just a natural aftermath of the gallbladder surgery she'd had the year before.

"Yeah, just a little. But I'm fine."

"Good," Jack said, taking a deep gulp of the night air. "God, it's great out here, isn't it?"

"It sure is," Pat replied. "It's perfect."

Henry Wilson's case faded into the background as they took in the night air and simply enjoyed the moment together.

Patty Morgan had met Johnny Tobin, as he was called in his younger days, in a playground in Central Park when she was three years old. He was a few years older, but his mother and Patty's were good friends, and they took their kids to the park together to play. The families lived in the same apartment building just off Third Avenue. Over the years, Patty and Johnny and Mikey Kelly, who also lived in the building, became great friends. They played stickball and punchball and all kinds of sports together. Patty was just one of the gang until she started wearing dresses and putting on makeup and dating other boys. After that, things changed. Johnny and Mikey liked girls as much as the next guy. They just didn't see Patty that way.

Jack and Mike lost touch when they were seventeen and eighteen, respectively. They had stolen a car, and only Mike had been caught: he eventually went to prison. They had never spoken after that. Jack went on to college upstate, then law school in Florida, where he decided to settle. Jack and Pat kept up sporadic contact, but they only saw each other a few times, at weddings and funerals and such. The last funeral had been Mike Kelly's. Pat was the one who told Jack about Mike's son, Rudy, being on death row in Florida.

Jack remembered that day, walking into John Mahoney's funeral home and seeing her across the room. After all those years she still looked spectacular. It was almost as if the aging process had missed her altogether. She was still tall and slim and beautiful. He was smitten right away but didn't acknowledge it at the time, even to himself. Pat was a CPA and about to retire from her firm. When Jack decided that he had to represent Rudy, that he owed it to Mike to do so, Pat moved to Florida to help. She didn't foresee it as a permanent move although she, more than Jack, understood that something had clicked for them at the funeral home that day.

They fell in love and eventually made their partnership permanent. Pat came out of retirement to pursue a passion of her own—teaching. Now she was the new fourth-grade teacher at Bass Creek Elementary School.

When their run was over, Jack headed for the lap pool in the backyard and a quick half-mile swim while Pat finished cooking the chicken parmesan she'd started earlier that evening.

After his swim, Jack lingered in the backyard, plucking a tangerine from a nearby tree and eating it under the stars in the fresh night air. *It doesn't get any better than this*, he said to himself.

He was right about that.

FOUR

Just after seven on the morning after the murder, Nick Walsh and Tony Severino headed over to the luxury apartment building at Seventy-eighth Street and East End Avenue. The uniforms had learned from several of the tenants that the deceased, Carl Robertson, had been a frequent visitor to the apartment of a young woman named Angie Vincent.

"Sounds like a high-class hooker setup to me," Tony opined from the passenger seat. Nick looked across at him. Tony looked like shit—unshaven face, rumpled, slept-in suit, raging coffee breath. He was still half asleep. He'd been sitting at his desk writing the preliminary report on their crime scene investigation and had woken up two hours later. The Styrofoam cup of black coffee he was now holding, probably his twentieth of the night, was the only thing keeping his brain ticking.

Nick, on the other hand, who was ten years older than Tony, looked almost as fresh as a daisy.

"Don't jump to conclusions," Nick responded. "He could have been visiting a sick relative, or his dentist." He paused for a moment, then continued in the same serious tone: "Or his weenie and testicle cleaner." It was perfect timing, honed over many years of telling stories to the same audience—cops. Tony laughed, spitting out a mouthful of coffee.

When they got to the building, they flashed their badges to the doorman, who told them Angie was home. Minutes later they were at her door.

Angie answered on the second knock. The two detectives could tell with one look that she had had a rough night. Her eyes were red and had charcoal half-moons under them. She was still in her nightgown, yet, despite the circumstances, she looked good. The nightgown was one of those flimsy jobs that left little to the imagination, and Tony was finding it hard to concentrate. He had an eye for the ladies, regardless of the situation.

Nick, on the other hand, was the consummate professional.

"Ma'am, I'm Detective Walsh, and this is Detective Severino. We'd like to talk to you for a few minutes."

Angie opened the door and let them walk in, not even bothering to excuse herself to put on a robe. She sat on the couch in the living room. The two detectives sat facing her in the leather chairs on the other side of the coffee table.

"What is your name?" Nick asked softly.

"Angela Vincent." Nick could tell she was aware of the events of the previous evening.

"Angela, did you know the deceased?" Nick maintained the same soft tone.

"Yes."

"And how did you know him?"

"We were lovers."

It didn't take Nick long to get the entire story from her—right down to the ten thousand dollars a month.

"Do you know why anyone would want to kill Carl?"

"No, I have no idea."

"When did he bring you the money?"

"Usually the first week of the month, either Tuesday or Thursday."

"Yesterday was the first Tuesday of the month. Were you expecting him to bring you the money last night?"

"Yeah. He usually brought it on Tuesday."

"Did you tell anyone—maybe a boyfriend or a girlfriend—that he was bringing you the money that night?" Nick noticed her pause. Perhaps she was just searching her memory, but she clearly hesitated before answering.

"No, I didn't tell anybody."

"You're sure?"

"Positive." This time there was no hesitation. Nick made a mental note to follow up on that detail.

"Did he keep any personal effects here at the apartment?"

"I'm not sure what you mean."

"Clothing, personal papers—anything at all?"

"No. Carl was very meticulous. He never left anything here—not even a toothbrush."

"Did he ever receive any telephone calls here or make any telephone calls?"

"No." Nick was about to move on when Angie interrupted him. "Wait. He did get a call here about two weeks ago, maybe three."

"Who was it from?" Tony interrupted, his first words of the interview. Nick glared at him, a cue not to butt in.

"I don't know. Carl was very agitated about being disturbed. I could tell, though, that it was an important call, so I put a notepad and a pen on the table in front of him." She looked at Nick, hoping he would understand it wasn't just about sex for her. *She wants to be helpful*, Nick thought as he gave her an understanding, fatherly nod. "As the conversation continued he picked up the pen and almost absentmindedly wrote something down. He inadvertently left the note behind. Now that's the only little piece of him that I have."

Nick hated to break the news to her that she wasn't going to have that little piece for long.

"May I see the notepad?" he asked. Three days before, Nick had punched a 250-pound brute in the mouth while simultaneously calling him a motherfucker. Now, as he talked to Angie, he seemed like a cross between Ward Cleaver and Mother Teresa. Angie handed over the notepad.

Nick looked at the pad as Tony leaned over his shoulder. Two words were scribbled haphazardly on the sheet: *Gainesville* and *breakthrough*. Nick looked at Tony, who shrugged his shoulders. Neither of them had any idea what the words meant.

*　*　*

"Whaddaya think?" Nick asked Tony when they were in the car on the way back to the station.

"She's worth maybe two hundred a pop but not ten thousand a month."

Nick went with it. "One man's two hundred is another man's ten thousand."

"I guess you're right. If you're a billionaire, why not pay for what you want? If I were a woman I think I'd be a hooker."

"No you wouldn't," Nick replied. "We've both rousted enough hookers in our day to know very few make it to the big leagues."

Tony thought about it for a second. "Yeah, I guess you're right about that, too."

"That wasn't my question to begin with. Whaddaya think about the notes?"

"I don't know. They make no sense to me. Maybe he was doodling and just wrote a few random words on the notepad. Hell, it could have been his bookie."

"Could be," Nick replied. "We'll have to check and see if there were any horses with the names Gainesville or Breakthrough running that day." He gave a sideways glance at his partner just to let him know that he thought he was nuts.

"What?" Tony shrugged. "I was just thinking out loud. What do the shrinks call that—free associating? I was free associating with you, Nick."

"Good," Nick replied. "I hope it cures you of whatever fucking psychosis you have. In the meantime, I think I'll check out his cellphone records and find out where the call came from. What about her? What did you think of her?"

"Nice tits," Tony answered.

"I noticed that you noticed. She probably saw you staring at them too. My question is, do you believe her story?"

"Yeah, she seemed pretty sincere. And pretty devastated too."

"I agree," Nick said. "I think she cared about the guy. But there's more to the story. She seemed uncomfortable when I asked if anyone knew about Carl bringing money that night. I'll bet she told somebody, and I'll bet it was recently. I'm gonna go back there tonight and talk to the doorman on duty then and see if she's had any other visitors recently."

"I'll go with you," Tony offered. "By the way, was I really staring?"

Nick just looked at his partner and smiled. "I'm just grateful you didn't have your mouth open and your tongue hanging out."

FIVE

New York City, August 1965

*S*ometimes just living in the neighborhood was stressful. At least, it was for fifteen-year-old Johnny Tobin. He'd be sixteen in another month. He was sure it wasn't the same for his best friend Mikey, who was just a year older; Mikey was liked by everybody and always got invited everywhere.

Frankie O'Connor had a poker game at his family's apartment on Friday nights. Frankie was two years older than Johnny, and most of the guys who went were in his age group. Mikey always got an invite and he was a year younger than Frankie. So did Norman Martin, who was the same age as Johnny. They both had older brothers—maybe that was the difference. Johnny and Mikey never talked about it, but Mikey knew Johnny wanted to go. Hell, they did everything else together.

Mikey was the one who delivered the invitation.

"Why don't you come to Frankie's on Friday night?" he asked on Thursday afternoon, knowing that Johnny would need some time to come up with an excuse to get out of the house. His parents were real strict.

Johnny wanted to make sure the invite was legit and not just Mikey trying to squeeze him in. There would have been nothing more embarrassing for him than to show up and then be kicked out.

"Did Frankie tell you to ask me?"

"Yeah, he did. He also said he wanted to talk to you."

Jesus, what the hell was that about? Frankie O'Connor wanted to talk to him—in front of everybody. Maybe things had been better when he wasn't getting invited.

Frankie O'Connor lived on the "other side" of Ninety-sixth and Lexington. The painted line running down the middle of Ninety-sixth was the unofficial demarcation separating Manhattan to the south from Spanish Harlem immediately to the north and Harlem itself beyond that. So Frankie O'Connor unofficially lived in Spanish Harlem.

Frankie had a comeback whenever anybody brought it up. "Hey, Jimmy Cagney lived on my block." The mention of the most famous Irishman to come from the neighborhood usually shut them up.

Frankie lived with his father and brother; his mother had passed years before. The apartment was much bigger than Johnny's four-room railroad flat, all of which would fit nicely inside Frankie's living room. The bathroom was big enough to hold two or three people, and it had a shower. Johnny could only dream about someday living in a place that had a shower.

Frankie's father always went out on Friday night and came home Saturday morning. His boys never knew where he went and they never asked. One day about two years earlier, the old man had simply said to Frankie, "I'm going out. I won't be back until tomorrow. Keep an eye on your brother." The card party hadn't started for another year after that, when Frankie was sure that his father's overnight excursions were a permanent thing.

There were two card tables set up in the living room and the games were already under way when Johnny arrived with Mikey and his two brothers, Danny and Eddie. Johnny brought money to play, but he had decided beforehand to be inconspicuous on his first night—just hang out and watch, get people beers, that kind of stuff. As it happened, Marty Russell lost big and cashed out early, so Johnny was drafted into one of the games.

"Hey, Tobin, get me a beer and sit in here in Marty's place. We need your money." The voice belonged to Doug Kline, a big, burly guy two years ahead of Johnny in school.

Johnny got the beer, put his money up, and sat down. Part of being accepted was acting like you belonged.

He won his second hand and Doug Kline pushed him good-naturedly as *he raked in the pot. "We're supposed to take your money, kid, not the other way around."*

Johnny just smiled sheepishly. He was having a great time smoking cig-arettes and drinking beer.

He had only played a few hands when Frankie called him over.

"Johnny, sit out a hand or two. I want to talk to you."

Johnny didn't hesitate. You didn't say no to Frankie. Not that he would beat you up or anything—Frankie wasn't like that. He was just one of those guys you didn't say no to.

Johnny followed Frankie into the kitchen. He was glad they were away from the others. If he had done something wrong he didn't want the whole world to know about it.

"What's up?" he asked as nonchalantly as he could, his knees knocking.

"I've been watching you play football over at the Hamilton on Saturday mornings." The Hamilton was a clearing in Central Park where the younger guys in the neighborhood would get together to play tackle foot-ball. All the older guys had played there at one time or another. It was like a rite of passage before you hit the bigger field. One of the sideline mark-ers just happened to be a statue of Alexander Hamilton. You had to be very careful not to run into it while running an out pattern.

"Yeah," Johnny replied. "So?"

"So," Frankie said, "I think it's time you think about coming out for the Lexingtons."

"Me?"

"Yeah, you. Tryouts start next week. I wanna see you there."

"Sure thing, Frankie. I'll be there."

Johnny was so excited he almost couldn't contain himself. The Lexing-tons were the neighborhood football team. All the great athletes from the neighborhood had played on the team. Frankie was one of the present stars and was the unofficial captain. Now it was Johnny's turn to play with the big boys. Of course, Frankie had only invited him to try out. There was no guarantee he was going to make the team. And what if he got cut? He'd be a laughingstock.

Yeah, Johnny thought as he walked home that evening, living in the neighborhood certainly was stressful.

SIX

Jack began working on Henry Wilson's case by reading volumes of material: trial transcripts, appellate briefs, and the investigative files from both the state's attorney's and the public defender's offices. It took him two weeks to finish. If he decided to take the case, he had six weeks before Henry's scheduled execution to file a motion for a new trial, set an evidentiary hearing before a circuit judge, and put forward enough newly discovered evidence to convince the judge to grant a new trial. Time certainly weighed against them, but it was not the biggest hurdle. In order to meet the "newly discovered evidence" standard, Jack would have to produce some evidence that no other counsel representing Wilson in the past *could have* discovered; evidence that had been available back then but inadvertently overlooked didn't pass the "newly discovered evidence" test. It was a next-to-impossible standard, and so far he had nothing to go on.

He did confirm, however, that Wilson had told him the truth: there was no physical evidence linking him to the murder of Clarence Waterman. His conviction rested solely on the testimony of one man, David Hawke, and neither the snitch nor his cousin was ever charged with Waterman's murder. Those facts alone lent credibility to Wilson's claim of innocence.

He hashed it all out with Pat one night after dinner. Pat was reading a book in the living room while Jack had Wilson's file spread out on the dining room table nearby.

"I don't think this is worth it," he told her. "I'd be okay getting Henry Wilson off death row, but not out of prison."

"Is that your decision to make, Jack? Aren't you supposed to simply determine whether the evidence was sufficient to prove he committed the murder?"

"It's a little more complicated than that. My feelings about the case are always part of my decisions, Pat. They have to be. This isn't an intellectual exercise for me—or an economic one. I have to believe I'm doing the right thing."

"I understand," Pat replied. "But you've always said that the evidence should decide a person's guilt or innocence and nothing else. Aren't you getting away from that?"

"I guess I am. This guy is so angry, though. I just don't know if I want to make the effort to put him back on the street."

"You only met him once. Why don't you give him the benefit of the doubt for now and make your decision based on the evidence? If it's not the right decision then you probably won't succeed."

"What does that mean?"

Pat smiled at him. "Things happen for a reason. All you can do is your part."

Jack thought about it for a minute or two. "Maybe you're right," he admitted. "There is already a question in my mind about whether Wilson is guilty or not. I'll continue the investigation. If there is enough evidence to move for a new trial, I'll file the motion. After that it's in God's hands."

Jack decided to continue his investigation by talking with Henry's original lawyer, a distinguished Southern gentleman named Wofford Benton who was now a sitting circuit judge in Bartow, Florida.

Wofford Benton was an old Florida cracker born and raised in Bartow, a cozy little town in the central part of the state. He loved to tell folks that he never wore shoes until he was five years old. He spent his youth hunting and fishing and riding horses and herding cattle. When he graduated from high school, Wofford, like his daddy before him, moseyed on up to the University of Florida to get his college education. He stayed for seven years and left with a law degree.

Wofford's first job was in the public defender's office in Miami. Although it was a successful career move, Wofford never felt comfortable in the big city, and after twenty years he quit and went home to Bartow to run for judge.

They met for lunch at the Log Cabin Inn, an upscale steak house just outside of town where the local businessmen hung out. Inside, it looked like a real log cabin, complete with a fireplace that was hardly ever used. Among the concessions to modernity were the plush, dark blue carpeting and the seats upholstered in black leather. Judge Benton was already seated at his favorite table when Jack arrived. He was in his mid-sixties now, with a bald pate and a stomach that looked like it didn't miss too many meals. He had a big cigar wedged in the right side of his mouth, although it wasn't lit. The waitress came over to take Jack's drink order as soon as the lawyer sat down. She also had a message for the judge.

"Judge," she started with a thick Southern accent, "Walter suggests you try the prime rib sandwich today. He says it's real good."

Wofford smiled at Jack. "Walter's the chef. They treat me right here," he said proudly. "All right, Sally, you tell Walter to fix me one of those sandwiches. He knows how I like it. How about you, Jack?"

Jack wasn't much of a red-meat eater, but he was looking for information.

"I'll have the same," he replied. "Medium. And a glass of water."

"So what can I do for you, son?" Wofford asked when Sally had left.

"Well, Judge, as I told you over the phone, I'm looking into the Henry Wilson case to see if there is any basis to file a motion for a new trial."

Henry's trial had been almost eighteen years ago, and the judge had been a little sketchy on the details when Jack had called him initially.

"I didn't remember the case when you first called, but I do now. I can't see his face, but I remember Henry Wilson was a big, imposing man and he was a career criminal. I don't know if I can help you any more than that."

"Did you have any active participation in his subsequent appeals?"

"No. Once the trial was over I was out of the picture. I talked to some of the appellate people over the years, but I can't remember the conversations."

"Do you remember anything about the trial?" Jack persisted.

"Not really. I can't tell you how many cases I've had since then, both as a lawyer and a judge. I've sentenced a number of men to death myself. It is something I don't take lightly. I'd like to help you, but I don't think I can."

The waitress arrived with the prime rib sandwiches, each with a side of steak fries. She filled the judge's coffee cup and gave Jack a large glass of water before leaving the men to continue their conversation. The break enabled Jack to collect his thoughts.

"I'd like to ask you some specific questions about the trial itself," Jack told him.

"I'm not sure I'll be able to answer them. You refresh my memory about the details and we'll go from there."

"Your defense," Jack began, "was that someone else had committed the crime, a man named James Vernon. You put Vernon—who was in prison at the time for another drug-related crime—on the stand, and he took the Fifth. Then you called up his cellmate, a fellow named Willie Smith, to testify that Vernon had confessed to him the Friday before, do you remember that?"

"Vaguely," the judge replied. "The prosecutor tore Willie Smith a new asshole. James Vernon supposedly confessed to him the Friday before trial. It was so convenient that it was laughable, but it was all we had."

"Something seems to be missing," said Jack. "I've read the appellate attorneys' notes—and somewhere you told one of them that you actually talked to James Vernon while he was in prison, is that correct?"

"I don't recall. I'll tell you this, though I wouldn't have called him to the stand without knowing what he was going to say. So either I talked to him or my investigator did."

"How did you find him?"

"Again, I have no idea. I imagine somebody gave me his name as a possible suspect."

"And I guess you don't recall what he told you when either you or your investigator interviewed him?"

"No. It would have had to exonerate Wilson in some way though, otherwise I wouldn't have called him."

"But when you put him on the stand, he took the Fifth and refused to testify?"

"Yeah. And when he did, I wanted to wring his neck and snap it like a chicken's. I remember that." Benton paused, put his index finger to his lips, and seemed to stare off into space for a few moments. "You know, there's got to be a record somewhere of my interview with him. I recorded witness interviews when I was with the public defender's office in Miami. I had to because we had so many cases. It wasn't under oath, so I couldn't use it in the trial or anything, but it would at least tell you what he said."

This was news to Jack. He had meticulously combed through the appellate files and never saw a reference to a recorded statement by James Vernon. Perhaps it was nothing, perhaps it was everything. He decided to think about this for a minute while he and the judge worked on their prime rib sandwiches, which were amazingly good.

"Judge, I never heard about this recorded statement before. Did you tell the appellate attorneys about it?"

Judge Benton furrowed his brow. He seemed to Jack to be getting a little irritated with these questions about what he did or maybe failed to do seventeen years ago.

"The reason I ask is because there is no reference anywhere in any of the appellate files to a transcript of an interview with James Vernon."

Benton put another piece of prime rib in his mouth and took his time chewing. He then took a sip of his coffee.

"If there was a transcript, wouldn't it have been in the public defender's file?" Jack persisted.

"Obviously not, if you and the other appellate attorneys have never come across it," Benton answered testily. "I had my own files. I left the public defender's office soon after the Wilson trial and took them with me—boxes and boxes. I rented a U-Haul, packed 'em all up and put 'em in my barn. Haven't looked at them since. It's possible it's in one of those boxes if the rats haven't eaten it."

"Can you check and see?" Jack asked.

Wofford Benton took another sip of his coffee and stared at Jack.

"Now I'm angry at myself for even telling you about my personal files. I guess I didn't think you'd be so persistent. I might have as many as fifty boxes in that barn, Counselor, so the answer to your question is no—I can't check. I don't have the time. I'm a judge. I've got work to do and I'm coming up for reelection."

Jack wondered himself why the judge brought up the boxes in his barn if he had no intention of looking through them.

"How about if I went through them?" he asked. The waitress came to the table and started to remove their empty plates.

Benton sighed. "Counselor, I think I might be violating some ethics rules if I let you just rummage through my files. There are a lot of other people in those files besides your Mr. Wilson, you know."

"Most of it would be public record by now, Judge. Besides, a man's life is at stake."

"A man who was found to be guilty and deserving of death by the state of Florida," the judge replied.

"You have a point. However, his execution is less than six weeks away—he's entitled to have every stone unturned before that time."

Judge Benton leaned back from the table, looked up at the ceiling, and let out another deep sigh. He then picked up the unlit cigar he had set on the table and twirled it in his fingers while staring at it.

"Okay, Counselor," he finally said. "You can take a look. I'll give you a day. When do you want to do it?"

"First thing tomorrow."

"All right. Be at my ranch at seven tomorrow morning and I'll get you set up." He put the cigar in his mouth. "Now I'm going to go outside and have a good smoke."

The next day, Jack drove east out of town for about two miles, as the judge had instructed, made a right on Benton Road, and drove another three miles until he saw a sign for the Benton ranch. Since he hadn't planned on spending the night in Bartow, he had on the same clothes from the day before, although he discarded the tie and jacket and rolled his shirtsleeves up.

Wofford's ranch was out in the middle of nowhere—flat grassland for as far as the eye could see. Jack could smell the cattle before he saw them as he drove down the dirt road. Wofford was sitting on the porch in his bathrobe, waiting for Jack. The house was a modest two-story with a three-car garage. The barn was several hundred yards behind it to the southeast. It was almost as big as the house.

Wofford was much more pleasant this morning. As Jack got out of his car, the judge slipped into a pair of cowboy boots that were sitting on the porch, right by the front door. Jack thought Wofford looked quite distinguished standing there in his bathrobe and boots.

"I don't do any of the ranching here anymore," he told Jack as they walked toward the barn. "I have a foreman who does everything. I like being out here though. It's where I grew up."

The barn doors were open, indicating that work for the day had already begun. A few chickens were squawking and running around in the front, along with two cats and a rooster. As they walked in, Jack noticed some horses' stalls off to the left, although they were empty. The loft was full of hay, but the place had a foul smell, probably from the animals and their excrement. Wofford apparently noticed that Jack had caught a whiff.

"You'll smell good after spending a day in here, Counselor. It's a little bit different than a day at the office. The files are over here."

He brought Jack to a door leading to a separate room in the right rear of the barn. The door had to be opened with a key, and when Wofford did so, Jack saw stacks and stacks of boxes in racks. The room was dark and obviously musty.

"There's no electricity in here," Wofford told him. "I'll get you a lantern, a chair, and a cup of coffee. After that, you're on your own. Just be careful opening boxes—you never know what's living in there.

"I've got a meeting tonight in town, so I won't be back until late. There's a restaurant called Rooster's right on Main Street. Maybe we can meet there first thing in the morning for breakfast."

Jack hadn't planned on staying another night. Hell, it was possible he'd be done in an hour. He didn't want to bring any of that up with the judge, however, so he agreed with Wofford's suggestion.

"That'll be fine—about seven?"

"Make it seven-thirty," the judge told him. "As you've probably noticed, I don't get going as quick as I used to."

Jack's optimism was misplaced. Although the boxes were neatly placed on racks, the files inside were a mess. Cases were not separated or labeled. He had to go through every folder and every piece of paper. He had no idea how many pages were in the transcript or if the pages were stapled together—or if the document even existed. The lighting was terrible, and, as Wofford had predicted, from time to time a mouse scurried out of the box when Jack lifted the top. Jack was just glad that he hadn't encountered a rat—yet.

The hours ticked past and the light outside was beginning to fade when he finally opened a box and saw a large folder labeled "Wilson." He hesitated before opening it and said a little prayer. Another hour of this place and he'd be ready for a straightjacket. He opened his eyes and looked down. Within the folder, in a jacketed cover, was the transcript of Wofford's recorded interview with James Vernon.

SEVEN

The next morning, Jack was a very conspicuous visitor at Rooster's, sitting among the farmers as he waited for the judge to arrive. He'd taken a shower at the hotel that morning, but for the third day in a row he had to don the same clothes—clothes that had spent the previous day in Wofford Benton's barn. That, however, actually made him fit in with the breakfast group. He stood out because he was a stranger.

Wofford came in about ten minutes after Jack and made the rounds of each table, shaking hands with everybody in the place.

"You can never stop politicking," he said as he sat down at Jack's table. "You forget to shake one hand and it could cost you a hundred votes in this town. Word travels like lightning."

Ruthie, the waitress, came over and simply inquired if the judge was going to have "the usual." Wofford nodded that he was. Jack had already given his order.

"Did you find anything interesting?" Wofford asked when Ruthie had left.

"I did," Jack replied. "I found the transcript of your interview with James Vernon."

"Well…?"

"Well, Vernon told you that he was there when Clarence Waterman was murdered. Vernon claimed to have been there with two other guys he wouldn't name, neither of whom was Henry Wilson. One of those other two guys supposedly slit Clarence Waterman's throat."

Wofford thought about what Jack had said for a moment. "It makes sense," he finally said. "That's why I called Vernon to the stand. I hope you noticed something though. Vernon told me he was there at the scene. He told Willie Smith, the prison snitch I called to the stand at trial, that he *actually committed* the murder. One of those statements is a lie, and James Vernon supposedly made both of them. Of course, Willie Smith could have been lying. It's a problem with these criminals—they never tell the whole truth and nothing but the truth."

"There was something else, Judge."

"Really?"

"Vernon said that he also told Ted Griffin, his lawyer on the case he was in jail for, about the Waterman murder. Did you know Ted Griffin?"

"Yeah, I knew him." Ruthie arrived with the food, and both men were quiet for a moment. Jack was careful not to press the judge. He wanted Wofford to stew over the information and come to his own conclusions.

"I guess I should have anticipated that Vernon might take the Fifth and should have had Ted Griffin ready to testify at trial. He'd have made a much better witness than that snitch I had to use—Willie Smith," he said finally.

Jack was glad Wofford had seen the problem on his own. It didn't matter what version of the story James Vernon gave Ted Griffin. It would have been dramatic and compelling testimony to have a lawyer on the stand telling the story after Vernon refused to testify, and it might have made the difference in the outcome of the trial. Jack had another issue he wanted to address, however, before coming back to the judge's mistake.

"Judge, did you know that neither David Hawke nor his cousin was ever prosecuted?" he asked.

"Who are they?" the judge asked.

"David Hawke was the only witness who testified against Henry Wilson. There was no other evidence to connect Wilson to the crime. Hawke was a convicted felon, and he testified that he drove his cousin and Henry to Clarence Waterman's house and waited outside while they went in and killed him."

"I vaguely recall that now," Benton admitted.

"So you didn't know that Hawke and his cousin were never prosecuted?"

"No, I didn't."

"What I don't understand is why Hawke would testify that he drove his cousin and Henry to Waterman's house and waited while they killed him. It doesn't make sense—Hawke implicating himself like that in the crime if he was actually innocent."

Benton looked at Jack quizzically. "Are you a criminal defense attorney?"

"No, sir. I spent my career representing insurance companies. I've only taken up representing death-row inmates in the last couple of years."

"I see—your personal penance for representing those insurance companies for so long?"

Jack smiled. "I guess that's part of it."

"Well, let me tell you something, son. In criminal law, sometimes you don't have any proof and yet you know something's there. You get a whiff of it in the wind." Benton leaned forward and lowered his voice. "As I remember, David Hawke was a career criminal, a druggie—kind of like Henry, if you want to know the truth. The state had something on David Hawke, something we'll never know about. They probably made a deal. That's how he came to testify at Henry Wilson's trial."

"Would the state put on false testimony?"

"It's never that clear-cut, Jack. They may have nabbed Hawke for something. He finds out about this murder case—there's a grapevine in the criminal world that you wouldn't believe—so he concocts a story to make himself a valuable witness. He implicates Henry and starts to negotiate with the authorities. The state looks at Henry's record and sees that he's a pimple on the ass of society, sees that he bought drugs from the deceased—and they run with Hawke's testimony. Should they pause and say, 'Wait a minute, this guy is a lowlife piece of shit—we shouldn't use him to convict somebody else, especially in a death penalty case, without other corroborating evidence'? Yes, they should. Do they? Not usually. Prosecutors have agendas too, Jack. It's just the way of the world."

"About this transcript of your interview with James Vernon, Judge—what do you think I should do with it?"

"Don't be coy with me, Counselor. You know what you're going to do with it. You're going to claim incompetence of counsel because I didn't call Ted Griffin to the stand."

Jack didn't respond to the judge's charge. He hadn't made any decisions yet. "Did you talk to Griffin about this?" he asked.

"I don't remember."

"Maybe Griffin refused to talk to you since he represented James Vernon in the past?" Jack offered.

"He may have, but I don't remember."

They talked a little more before Jack got up to leave. His head was spinning from all that he had learned, and he was anxious to get back to his office in Bass Creek and sort it out. The judge continued to surprise him right up to the end of his visit.

"Do what you have to do, Counselor. I'm not anxious to have my record besmirched, but I understand a man's life is at stake. I'm still not convinced Wilson is innocent, but if he is, I've got some responsibility for him being where he is at. Keep me posted on this, will you? And call me if you need a sounding board."

"I sure will, Judge."

During their run that evening Jack told Pat all about what he had learned in the past three days. They took a different path, bypassing the river and heading directly into the woods. The crickets were already chattering.

"God, it's good to be out here," he said. "I felt like I was swimming in a cesspool today."

"Why's that?" Pat asked.

"I'll tell you in a minute. First, tell me about your day."

"What's to tell? I've got thirty ten-year-olds all with Mexican jumping beans in their pants."

"That's got to be the hardest job in the world. I could never do it."

"Well, you do have to be a certain type of person. But I love it, I really do. And I'll tell you what, Jack. I can see how the future criminals of America get started. Kids in foster care, kids who are neglected by their parents—those are the ones with severe emotional problems. These kids don't have a chance.

"They don't get lost as adults, Jack. They get lost as children." She paused, and they both concentrated on their running for a moment. "Enough about me—why did you feel you were in a cesspool today?"

"Because I learned some valuable lessons about how the criminal justice system really works. Do you ever wonder how it is that when you drop a piece of food on the ground, a thousand ants suddenly appear out of nowhere?"

"What does that have to do with your client on death row?"

"Well, apparently when a crime occurs, a similar phenomenon takes place. Eyewitnesses pop out of the woodwork. Criminals with information to sell about other criminals."

"True information?" Pat asked.

"Who knows? Truth is what a prosecutor thinks he can sell to a jury."

"Really? Is that what happened in Henry's case?"

"Wofford Benton thinks it's possible, and he was Henry's trial lawyer. The state had no physical evidence against Henry. This guy David Hawke gave them a credible story and they went with it.

"Listen to this. I found a transcript of a conversation Wofford Benton had with a guy named James Vernon, who said he was at the murder scene with two other guys, neither of whom was Henry Wilson. And one of those two other guys slit Clarence Williams's throat."

"If that's the case, how did Henry get convicted?"

"Well, Wofford called Vernon to the stand, and Vernon took the Fifth. There was another witness Vernon had told the story to, a lawyer named Ted Griffin, and Wofford never called him to the stand."

"Why not?"

"He just forgot, I guess. He doesn't remember ever talking to Griffin."

"You're kidding me!" Pat said. "Is this Wofford Benton who *forgot about the other witness* still practicing?"

"Practicing? He's a circuit judge! That's the guy I went to see. And by the way, none of this evidence means that Wilson is innocent."

"You're losing me, Jack."

"James Vernon told two people two different stories, so he could have been lying."

"So what are you going to do?"

"I'm going to keep on working and see how it all shakes out. I'll talk to the other witness, Ted Griffin, the lawyer, and listen to what he has to say."

Later that evening, as they both lay in bed, Pat revisited their earlier conversation.

"Has your gut feeling about Henry changed?"

"I don't know. I'm still a little too confused."

"Well, it'll come to you, Jack." She kissed him softly. Then they made love. As they moved slowly, rhythmically, Pat felt a sudden stabbing pain in her abdomen. Her body went into spasm and their lovemaking ended abruptly.

"What's the matter?" Jack asked. "Did I hurt you?"

"No, no, honey—nothing like that. I think it's that stomach pain from the gallbladder surgery. It's never been this severe, though. Maybe it's just the position we were in. I'm sure it will go away."

"The same pain you've told Dr. Hawthorne about for almost a year now?"

"Well, it's never been this bad. He says it can take up to a year for these things to heal. I have some pain medication but I just don't like to take it."

"Has Hawthorne given you a CT scan?"

"No."

"Well, don't take this the wrong way, honey: Hawthorne may be a good doctor, but he's a primary-care guy. Let me set up an appointment with somebody I know in Miami, okay?"

"Jack, it's not necessary. It's just a minor pain."

"I'm probably overreacting, but humor me, okay? Let me set up the appointment?"

"All right," she said and nestled her head in his chest and went to sleep.

Jack stayed awake for a very long time.

EIGHT

Melvin Gertz was short and slight, and he had a huge nose that took over his small, narrow face, making him look a little lop-sided. He also had a permanent five o'clock shadow, and to make matters worse, his blue doorman's uniform always looked like he'd slept in it the night before. *No wonder this guy works the night shift,* Nick Walsh thought as Melvin opened the front door of the apartment building for him and Tony Severino.

Melvin wasn't exactly overjoyed at seeing the two detectives either.

"I told the cop last night I don't know nothing. People come and go. I open the door for them. That's it."

This was a guy who needed Nick's special brand of persuasion. Nick didn't need any prompting.

"Melvin, you think you don't know anything, but you may have a valuable piece of information. You could give us something that could help us solve the whole case."

"Me? Really? You guys are pulling my leg."

"No we're not," said Nick. "It happens all the time. Remember the cabbie who delivered the baby in the backseat just last week in the Bronx? It was all over the news."

Melvin was confused. "Yeah, I remember that, but what's that got to do with me?"

"You give us information that blows open this case, you're going to be a hero just like that cabdriver."

"I already told ya, I don't know nothing."

"You let us be the judge of that. You just tell us everything you've seen. And when the TV cameras are on you and the news reporters are fighting for a quote, put in a good word for Tony and me, will you?"

"Sure thing," Melvin said as he took a pen and pad from his uniform pocket. "What's your names again?"

Nick noticed that Tony Severino had turned his back to them. His partner couldn't keep from laughing at Melvin's gullibility. Nick handed the doorman a card with both his and Tony's name on it.

"That's me, Detective Nicholas Walsh. You can call me Nick."

"And you can call me Philly," Melvin told Nick. "That's what everybody calls me."

"How come?" Nick asked.

"Well, when I was a kid, I loved Philly cheesesteaks. Everybody in the neighborhood started calling me Philly and the name stuck. And I kinda like it too. I never liked Melvin—never forgave my mother for that one."

Nick knew what Melvin-Philly was talking about. A lot of guys in his neighborhood had nicknames that had stuck for life.

Once Philly got to feeling good and started talking, he was a treasure trove of information, as Nick knew he would be.

"Two nights before the murder, she comes home with this beautiful woman—tall, dark hair, a knockout."

Nick interrupted. "You're talking about Angie coming home with a woman?"

"Yeah, Angie. I didn't think anything of it, you know. I figured they were just friends or something. Anyway, when I came on the next night, I was telling the day guy about how good-looking this broad was when the two of them come walking out dressed to the nines. They weren't holding hands or anything like that but—what am I trying to say—they looked like they were together, if you know what I mean. Then the day guy tells me he didn't see them all day. I don't want to say anything bad about anybody, you know what I mean— I'm just telling you what I saw."

"Great, Philly. It's exactly what we want—your observations."

That was when Philly laid the big bombshell on Nick and Tony.

"Speaking of seeing things—there's two gay guys on the first floor here who saw the guy who did it. They say he ran right by their window, stopped, and practically posed for them. They were pretty surprised that nobody came by to talk to them."

Nick looked at Tony, who shrugged his shoulders, letting Nick know he didn't have a clue.

"See what I mean, Philly?" Nick said. "We didn't even know about those guys. This is the kind of stuff that's gonna get you in the newspapers."

"Well, I better get my uniform clean and get a haircut. My wife won't believe this."

Nick was trying to get a picture in his mind of the woman who was married to Melvin "Philly" Gertz. *Probably an old battle-axe who leads him around by the nose*, he thought as he looked at that nose again. *She's certainly got a lot to work with.*

"Those two guys," he asked, "would they happen to be in right now?"

"They sure are, and they'll want to talk to you. I know you guys are macho cops and everything, but Paul and David, they're really great."

"I'll take your word for that, Philly. Why don't you give them a buzz and see if we can talk to them right now."

"I sure will." Philly picked up the telephone receiver on the wall. Before he started dialing the number, Nick slipped in another request.

"Do you think you could come down to the station when you get off and maybe look at a few pictures? See if you can identify this woman from some photographs we have at the station?" That lie always rolled off the tongue so easily:

"Maybe look at a few pictures"—actually, it's several books full of pictures, and you may be there for a few hours!

"Sure thing," Philly replied. "Whatever you guys want."

Paul and David were both in their mid-thirties, clean-cut and very fit. Paul worked at home and had converted one of the two bedrooms into an office. Tony questioned Paul in his office while Nick and David chatted in the living room.

"We were sitting in the living room watching TV—I can't remember what show it was. I think it was *NYPD Blue*," Paul told Tony. "We heard this noise. It sounded like a blasting cap or a firecracker. You know, you don't normally think, hey that's a gunshot, because frankly I never heard a gunshot before except on TV. We both went to the window. We didn't rush or anything—just kind of curious. The sound had been pretty close."

"Did you see anything?" Tony asked.

"Yeah. We look out and to the left we see this car with the driver's door open, and there's a man lying on the ground. And there's this other man leaning over him—he could have been checking him out to see if he was okay. I'm not saying he's the person who shot the man—I couldn't say that. I didn't even know he was shot at the time. I found that out later. Anyway, the man who was leaning gets up and he walks toward us and then he sees us at the front window. He's looking at us and we're looking at him—and then he takes off. I wrote a description down right away. So did David. And we didn't compare our descriptions. Nobody came to talk to us, so we figured you must have caught the guy."

Paul handed Tony the description he'd written. Tony took a couple of minutes to read it, then looked up at Paul. "How far away from you was this man when you saw him?"

"Well, when we first saw him he was maybe twenty, thirty feet, but when he came closer, he was six or eight feet from us."

"What about the lighting? Was it light enough for you to get a good look at him?"

"Oh yeah, I'll show you before you leave. We have security lights on the side of the building. It's like daylight out there."

"Could you see if he had a gun on him?"

"I didn't see a gun."

"Did you see him take anything off the deceased, like a wallet or something?"

"No."

At about the same time, in the living room, David was at the window showing Nick exactly where the man was standing when they spotted each other.

The two men agreed to come to the station the next day to give a sworn statement and "look at a few pictures."

After the interviews, Tony had wanted to quiz Angie about her mysterious girlfriend right away. "If we go to her apartment right now we may catch her before she goes to bed," he told Nick.

Nick suspected that Tony simply wanted to catch Angie in her negligee again.

"Let's go tomorrow," he said. "We'll call first, so she's not surprised and defensive. We'll tell her we're trying to tie up some loose ends."

Nick saw the disappointment on Tony's face, but his partner didn't argue with his decision.

"Did you tell Philly not to say anything?" Tony asked when they were in the car and driving back to the station.

"Oh yeah. When I got through with him, he was only going to talk to movie producers after he and I solve the case together."

Tony chuckled. "I gotta admit, Nick, you certainly have a good line of bullshit."

Nick ignored the compliment. "What did you think of David and Paul?" he asked.

"Well, they're very credible. Their descriptions are consistent and so detailed. I can't believe we have people scouring the neighborhood for witnesses, and they miss the two guys who had front-row seats to the action."

"It happens. At least we found them and now we have something to go on."

Tony glanced again at the two descriptions. Both David and Paul had written that the man leaning over Carl Robertson had been about five-seven or five-eight, with somewhat unruly or greasy hair. He was thin and dressed totally in black. Paul wrote that the man appeared to be Latin, perhaps Puerto Rican or Cuban, based solely on his skin color. David noted that he wore no jewelry and that his eyes appeared to be brown and glassy.

"How about Angie's girlfriend?" Tony asked. "Any possible connection to the murder?"

"I don't know," Nick replied. "It may be a red herring but we gotta check it out."

"If Angie is a switch hitter and this woman looks as good as Philly says, I think we should set up a surveillance."

Nick looked at him and smiled. "I'll let you handle that."

NINE

*J*ohnny made the team that first year, but there were times he wished he *hadn't. Practices were two nights a week and on Saturdays until the season started. Then the games were on Saturday mornings. Johnny had just turned sixteen and was by far the youngest person on the team. He barely saw any playing time.*

There were eighteen teams in the Greater Metropolitan League, and they were equally divided into Eastern and Western divisions. The season was eight games long, and the winner of each division made it to the championship game. The Lexingtons were the only team from Manhattan. Four or five were from Brooklyn, and the rest were from the Bronx.

The Lexingtons didn't have a home field; every game was an away game for them. They also didn't have a sponsor to pay for uniforms and transportation and things like that. So they wore white shirts and white pants that each player had to supply for himself, along with his own equipment. And they had to find their own way to the football fields in the Bronx and Brooklyn. For Johnny that meant lugging his equipment on the subway. It was okay, though. He usually went with Mikey and his brothers.

You had to be at least sixteen and not older than nineteen to play, and everyone had to submit a copy of his birth certificate at the beginning of the season to prove it. The age requirements were the biggest joke in the league. You could change the date on the copy of your birth certificate pretty easily if you wanted, but it was even easier than that to beat the system. All you had to do was borrow a younger guy's birth certificate; nobody ever bothered to check whether it was really yours.

As a result, ringers were rampant. That first year, Johnny saw guys showing up to play games with their wives—and kids! The referees never batted an eye.

Late in a game if the score was lopsided, Johnny would be sent in to play—usually at a position that required no skill, like defensive tackle. Johnny, who was six feet tall and maybe 170 pounds soaking wet, would often line up against a 250-pound, thirty-something man.

"When that ball is snapped I'm gonna kick your fucking ass, kid," was not an uncommon line for Johnny to hear. It was a far cry from high school football, where he should have been playing. But Johnny, like everybody else on his team, was a street kid. He knew bullshit and bluster had to be ignored. He also knew that Frankie O'Connor, who played middle linebacker, expected him to do the job when he was in there, no matter what the score or who he was up against. Even though he was scared, he was not going to be intimidated in front of Frankie. He might not be stronger than the guy on the other side of the scrimmage line, but he was usually faster and he was definitely tough enough. Late in the season, after he had made some tackles for losses and recovered a couple of fumbles, the coach started to play him more—probably at the suggestion of Frankie.

I'll be starting next year, *he told himself.* I've just got to show them I'm an athlete and I'm tough.

TEN

Jack called Dr. Erica Gardner early the next morning after Pat left for work. In his previous life as an insurance company defense attorney, Jack had represented many physicians in medical malpractice cases and had used the services of some of the most prominent physicians in the United States to testify as expert witnesses on behalf of his clients. Erica Gardner was one of those experts. She was from St. Louis and had graduated magna cum laude from Harvard Medical School, one of the relatively few African American women to do so. She was board-certified as a specialist in internal medicine and had a very successful and busy practice in Miami. Jack hoped he could get Pat in for an appointment within the next month.

He gave his name to the receptionist and was on hold waiting for the scheduling secretary when he heard Erica's voice on the other end of the line. "Is that really you, Jack Tobin? I heard a rumor that you had moved to Tibet and become a monk."

"Not quite, Erica, but close. I'm living in a small town called Bass Creek."

"I've heard of Bass Creek. It's a lovely town over by Lake Okeechobee."

"That's the one."

The small talk was now out of the way. "What can I do for you, Jack?" Erica asked.

"It's my wife, Erica." Jack explained that Pat had had stomach pains for some nine months and her local physician kept telling her it was related to her gallbladder operation and would get better.

"Did he do a CT scan, do you know?"

"No, he hasn't. That's one of the reasons I'm calling you."

"How about a pelvic ultrasound?"

"Nope. No tests of that nature."

"Let's get her in here right away."

That afternoon Jack called on Ted Griffin in Miami. His office was in a run-down two-story masonry building in a seedy part of town. The inside didn't look much better.

Ted Griffin was as tall as Jack and much heavier, with big hands and big feet. His attire was as sloppy as his office. He reached out affably to shake hands and then put his arm around Jack's shoulders.

"You probably don't remember me, Jack," he said in a deep Southern drawl. "I had a few personal injury cases about twenty years ago when you were on the other side. You pasted my behind so bad that I convinced myself to stay with criminal law."

Jack honestly couldn't remember ever meeting the guy. He was certain they'd never tried a case against each other. He never forgot lawyers he litigated against. "I'm sure that's an exaggeration, Ted. I'll bet we settled."

"We sure did, Jack—for a pittance."

Jack detected a little resentment in the tone, yet when he looked at Ted, the man was smiling from ear to ear. He was certainly not like the typical criminal lawyers Jack had known over the years.

"What can I do for you, Jack?" Ted asked as he cleared papers off one of two client chairs in front of his desk and motioned for Jack to sit. Ted sat in the other chair next to Jack. He would have been invisible behind the desk, which was stacked almost two feet high with files.

"Well, Ted, I want to ask you some questions about an old client of yours, a man named James Vernon."

"I remember James, all right," Ted said quickly. "He was one of my regulars until he got himself killed a few years back. He was a slippery, slimy son-of-a-bitch. The kind of guy you could never be comfortable around. He was cold and edgy and dangerous. What do you want to know about him? Whatever it is, I'm sure he did it."

"I'm investigating the murder of Clarence Waterman."

Ted leaned back in his chair and looked at the ceiling for a moment before answering. "Did I represent James on that one?"

"No, he was never charged. Somebody else was, a man named Henry Wilson. Clarence Waterman was a drug dealer and a hairdresser as well, and somebody slit his throat."

"The hairdresser. Oh yeah, I remember the hairdresser," Ted said, almost as if he was recalling a fond vision from the past.

"You do?"

"Oh yeah."

"I'm surprised."

"About what?"

"I'm surprised you answered so quickly," said Jack. "I mean, the murder happened seventeen years ago. Yet as soon as I mentioned he was a hairdresser, you recalled it. Why?"

"Because James told me he slit the hairdresser's throat. It's not every day your client tells you something like that."

Jack almost fell off his seat. At best, he'd expected Ted to confirm the story James Vernon had told Wofford Benton. Instead, he confirmed that Vernon had told him exactly what the snitch, Willie Smith, had testified to at trial.

"James Vernon told you he killed Clarence Waterman?"

"Yeah." Ted said it nonchalantly, like he was talking about the score of a baseball game or what he'd had for dinner the night before.

Jack wanted to grab the man by the throat and ask him if he understood that another man was on death row for this murder. But he restrained himself. He was going to need Ted Griffin's help in the not-too-distant future.

"What exactly did Vernon tell you?"

"He said he went to Waterman's house to buy drugs. He said Waterman started to come on to him in a homosexual way and he took out his knife and cut his throat."

"Was anybody else with him?"

"Two other guys, I believe. I'm a little fuzzy on that part."

"Do you know if either one of those two other men was Henry Wilson?"

"Who is Henry Wilson?"

"My client. The man who is on death row for this murder."

"Oh yeah, I see. That's why you're here. You told me that already, didn't you? That's the part I'm not sure about. I don't know if your client was one of the two men with James or not."

"Why didn't you go to the authorities with this confession?"

"Counselor, you know I couldn't do that. That's privileged information."

Jack didn't want to argue the legalities of the attorney-client privilege with the man. He did feel compelled to inquire a little further.

"How long ago did James Vernon die?"

"About five years ago. It was some kind of a drug deal gone bad."

"Well, if he died five years ago, the privilege died with him. Why didn't you tell somebody then?"

"Because, first of all, I didn't know that James was telling me the truth—I mean, he told Anthony Webster somebody else killed Waterman. Second, I didn't know if your client was one of the other two men. I don't know much about Henry Wilson's case. I don't know why they convicted him."

"Who is Anthony Webster?"

"He was the investigator for the state. He's retired now."

"The prosecutor's investigator? You mean the prosecutor was aware that James Vernon said he was at the murder scene?"

"I believe so. At least, that's what James told me."

"Where's Anthony Webster now?"

"I think he moved to Lake City. I'm not sure he's still alive."

"Would you be willing to put what you told me today in an affidavit?"

"Go ahead and prepare it. If it's accurate, I'll sign it."

Ted Griffin was an affable enough guy, but it was obvious to Jack that he wasn't going out of his way for anybody.

*   *   *

On the drive back to Bass Creek later that afternoon Jack started adding all this new information to the other evidence he had uncovered. James Vernon had told both Henry's lawyer, Wofford Benton, and the prosecutor's investigator, Anthony Webster, that he, Vernon, was at the scene of the murder and Henry wasn't there; he told his own lawyer, Ted Griffin, and the jailhouse snitch, Willie Smith, that he *committed* the murder. Unbelievably, only Willie Smith's testimony was brought out at Henry's trial and his two subsequent appeals. Could these recent revelations pass the "newly discovered evidence" standard? And if so, would they be enough to get Henry a new trial?

He was getting ahead of himself. He needed to contact Anthony Webster—if the man was still alive—and find out what he remembered. And then Jack needed to talk to Henry.

ELEVEN

Philly Gertz, the doorman, was at the Twenty-third Precinct the next morning to "look at a few pictures." He actually made a better appearance in slacks and a sports shirt than he did in his doorman's uniform. Nick set him up at a table with a cup of hot coffee and several thick photo books.

Nick made Philly feel like a million bucks. "If there's anything you need, Philly, you just let me know. If any of these uniforms ask you what you're doing here, you just tell them you're working for Manhattan Homicide and give them my name."

"Sure thing, Nick."

Philly was a little freaked out by the station. People were coming and going, talking and shouting. He was in a big room with a bunch of desks. Uniforms and plainclothes cops were everywhere. There was a little cell in the middle of the room, and a guy in the cell was yelling at a plainclothes cop.

"I gotta go to the fuckin' bathroom," he was saying. Philly noticed there was no toilet in the cell.

"You shut the fuck up or I'll come in there and shut you up. You understand?" said the cop, pointing his finger. The man did shut up but started holding his groin area and jumping up and down.

Nick seemed to have vanished. He had just walked out among the desks and cops and disappeared. Philly opened his photo book for the first time and started looking at female mug shots.

Half an hour later, Paul and David arrived at the station and were led to separate rooms where Nick and Tony took their sworn statements. There were no new revelations. Everything was totally consistent with what they had said the night before.

As Philly was finishing up his first book and starting to feel a little more comfortable, Nick returned with Paul and David and several more thick photo books.

"I'm going to slide Paul here next to you, Philly, so you'll have some company. How's that coffee? You need a refill?"

"No, I'm okay, Nick. Thanks," said Philly.

"We still have to keep you two apart while you look at these pictures," Nick told Paul and David, "because you can't talk to each other about them. David, I'm going to set you up somewhere else and we'll split the books up. If you see someone who looks familiar, just make a note of it and let me know. Then we'll switch books. I want your identifications to be totally independent. You understand?" Both men nodded. Nick took David to another table on the other side of the room.

Two hours later, the three men still had not picked out anybody from the photo albums. "This is a little more than looking at a few pictures," Philly whined to Nick.

"Well, Philly, if you want to be a star you've got to work hard," Nick replied. Paul and David didn't complain, but Nick could tell they were done looking at the books as well. He decided to change gears and bring the police sketch artist in to see if they could help him come up with a composite of the suspected murderer and the woman.

Later that day, Benny Avrile was hiding in the corner of his favorite bar, Tillie's, having a glass of beer. It was his first venture into the public since the murder two days before. It had taken him a while to come to grips with what happened that night. He'd spent most of the last two days smoking a lot of weed to calm his nerves and doing a little coke to keep his spirits up. Benny lived on the street— actually in a vacant condemned building—in a very rough section of the South Bronx, but he had never even witnessed a shooting before. He'd never seen a dead person close up—at least not before the makeup, the powder, and the formaldehyde. Seeing Carl Robertson lying there dead had truly flipped him out.

The story had been all over the *Post* and the *Daily News*, but so far the police didn't seem to have any leads. Benny was fervently praying that they would continue to remain in the dark.

Tillie's was a small place and it was empty except for Tillie, who was working behind the bar. Tillie was half Puerto Rican and half Italian and about forty-five years old, and he enjoyed his own booze a little too much. "I can't go to the party and not play," he'd told Benny one night after they'd both had a few too many. Tillie's compromise with his demons was to work the day shift. It was usually slow, and he had no desire to drink during the day.

Benny was not in a talkative mood, so Tillie stayed at the other end of the bar catching up on some paperwork, approaching only when Benny called for a refill. They were in their respective positions when she walked through the door.

Benny didn't notice her right away—he was too busy praying to his beer. Tillie hardly noticed her either. He just walked over to where she'd sat down and waited for her order. There were no solicitous greetings in this place.

"Vodka and tonic," she said, and Benny looked up. She had dark glasses on, her hair was pulled back in a ponytail, and she was wearing a tight white tank top with jeans and sneakers, but there was no mistaking—it was definitely her.

Benny looked back down at his beer and tried to appear as inconspicuous as possible—no easy feat in an empty bar. After Tillie put her drink on the bar, she picked it up and started walking toward him. Benny didn't budge.

"How ya doin'!" he said, turning toward her. "I'm glad you finally showed up. You know, I still don't know your name."

"Never mind," she said as she came closer.

Benny snuck a glance at Tillie to make sure he was watching and listening. Tillie had a sixth sense about trouble—you didn't last as a barkeep in this neighborhood for long if you didn't. Benny knew he had a gun under the bar as well.

"Pull up a stool," he said. "You're making me nervous standing over me like that."

"You should be nervous." He could tell she was angry. "You should be real nervous. Is there someplace we can go to talk?"

"This is it. I don't have a place. It's okay, though. Tillie's almost deaf," he said, nodding toward the far end of the bar. That would have been news to Tillie if he had heard the remark.

Benny figured this was the safest place to be at the moment. He and Tillie weren't great friends, but he knew Tillie would blow this woman away in a heartbeat if she pulled a gun. She clearly wasn't from the neighborhood.

"Where's my fucking money?" she demanded.

"I've got it, I've got it. I've been saving it for you," Benny said quickly. He wasn't lying. He'd been afraid that she might find him, so he hadn't spent her share yet.

"Give it to me."

"It's not here. It's hidden. You wait here and I'll go get it."

She laughed, causing Tillie to look up.

"I've got a better idea," she told him. "We'll go together."

Benny had known she'd say this, but he hadn't yet worked up an appropriate response, so he decided to be truthful.

"I don't want to go anywhere with you. I don't want to get my head blown off."

"I'm not the shooter in this group, Benny. Besides, I don't have a gun. I'll let you search me before we leave."

As afraid as he was, Benny relished the thought of running his hands up and down that body, even if it was just to check for a weapon. And maybe, just maybe, she'd like it. It might have been wishful thinking, but Benny had always been an optimist.

"Well," she interrupted his thoughts, "are we going to do this peacefully or not?"

"What if I say okay? What happens when I give you the money?"

"And my gun."

"And your gun. What happens to me?"

"Nothing. You have my word. Why did you run off that night?"

"I got freaked out," Benny said. "When the old man went down, I didn't know what to do. I just ran and ran and ran. Then I hopped the subway and ended up back here."

She looked around the bar uneasily. "Come on, search me," she said. "We can talk while we go get my money and my gun."

She put her arms out and Benny patted her down. He ran his hands up the inside of her legs and checked her crotch, lingering a moment. She didn't say anything. Then he ran them up the side of her torso and across her breasts, again taking his time. "If you don't move those hands, I'm going to break your neck," she said calmly. But she didn't do anything to stop him. It was almost as if she was letting Benny have his feel.

"What?" Benny said as he withdrew his hands. "I had to make sure you're not hiding anything in your bra."

Benny saw Tillie watching the patdown with a puzzled expression on his face. He decided to confuse him a little more. "I left a ten-spot on the bar," he said over his shoulder as the two of them walked out.

Benny led the woman down a side street to an abandoned building. He pushed open the front door, and they started climbing the stairs.

"I'm up on the fifth floor," he said. "The rats don't like to come up here and neither do the junkies. It's too far a walk."

Most of the walls on the fifth floor had been knocked out, but Benny had found one intact room. There was a mattress on the floor with sheets and covers on it, and there was even a dresser. Some dress clothes on hangers were dangling from a pipe—obviously Benny's weekend attire.

Her eyes scanned the room as if she was looking for something. Benny thought it might be the john and felt the need to explain. "There's a hotel at the end of the block. It's a pretty seedy joint but I bring the desk guy some goodies once a week—things I find, you know? And he lets me use the facilities in the empty rooms. They're never full so I don't have a problem. I've even got electricity when I need it. I run a wire across the roof to the next building and hook up. I gotta be careful, though. I only do it when it's cold—for my portable heater, you know?"

"I'm happy for you, Benny. Now where's my money and my gun?"

"They're here, don't worry. I just thought maybe we could relax, you know?" Benny casually glanced over at his mattress.

"Are you out of your fucking mind?" she said. "You're lucky I'm letting you live."

"Okay, okay." Benny could tell from her eyes and the tone of her voice that her patience was wearing thin. He walked to the far end of the room to a bare brick wall and started working one of the bricks until it came loose. He reached into the wall and pulled out a wad of bills and the gun. He put the brick back and walked over to where she was standing and handed her the money and the gun.

She paused for a moment as she looked down at the gun, then she handed it back to him. "Keep it," she said. "You may need it—especially in this neighborhood."

Benny didn't want the gun but he never turned anything down. He could sell it down the road if he needed to.

"Tell me something," she asked as she stashed the money in her overcoat. "Why did you shoot the old man?"

"I don't know. I don't know," said Benny, his words spilling out. "I haven't thought about it. I put it out of my mind. I don't even remember it." He closed his eyes as he spoke.

"I told you not to shoot. I told you he'd give you the money."

Benny put his hands over his ears. "I know, I know. I was so fucking high I don't even remember what I did. You shouldn't have given me a gun with a hair trigger. And that wasn't coke you gave me either because I didn't come down for two days."

"Don't blame your fuckups on me," she said.

"I'm not blaming you, I'm just saying."

"Yeah, well, don't say any more. This is the end of our brief love affair. When I walk out of this room you and I are finished. Got it?"

"Got it." As hot as she was, he had no desire to ever set eyes on her again.

He watched her as she walked down the stairs. Something was bothering him. He had only given her five thousand dollars—instead of the seven she'd insisted on—and she hadn't checked the amount.

Why didn't she count the money? he asked himself. *And why did she decide to leave the gun with me?*

TWELVE

New York City, September 1966

Johnny was bigger, stronger, and faster when the next football season rolled around. He worked out for weeks before the start of practice; he even stopped smoking. He took his cue on that from Frankie, who was one of the few guys in the neighborhood who didn't smoke. Johnny hoped like hell Frankie didn't stop drinking beer.

Ever since he'd become a member of the Lexingtons, his status in the neighborhood had changed. Johnny wasn't just an obscure punk anymore—he was one of the guys. And he was part of everything they did, whether it was playing cards at Frankie's on Friday night, going to Rockaway Beach for the weekend during the summer, or stealing cases of beer from the basement of Fellino's Market—Mikey had figured out a way to slip through the basement bars. One night they took two cases out and stored them up at Frankie's apartment.

The next day Sonny Fellino, the owner's son, a twenty-something-year-old who was big and tough as nails, lined four of them up against the wall in front of the store and grilled them—Johnny and Mikey, Norman Martin and Frankie. Sonny was sure they were the thieves.

"You guys are gonna tell me who did it!" Sonny was yelling at the top of his lungs. "And if it was one of youse and you tell me right now, I'll go easy on you."

Nobody believed a word of it. Sonny was a bully. He wore a tight white T-shirt with his Marlboros stuck inside his rolled-up right sleeve. His

*hair was greased up and combed straight back except for the front, which
fell over into his eyes. Admitting to anything was going to get you beaten
unmercifully, and then you'd become Sonny's slave at Fellino's until he decided the debt had been paid.*

*They all held tough, however, and Sonny let them go—all except
Johnny. Sonny knew he'd never get anything out of Frankie. Hell, Frankie
might give him a run for his money if he tried. Same with Mikey—he was
young, but he had a reputation of never backing down from anyone. Norman had two older brothers, and Sonny did not want to mess with them.
That left Johnny—the weak link.*

*"C'mere, Johnny, I wanna talk to you," Sonny said as he motioned him
to come away from the wall. Johnny watched the others walk away, each
one catching his eye and giving him a look that told him what would happen if he ever talked. He was between a rock and a hard place. He decided
he needed to give Sonny something.*

*"You know who did it, don't you, Johnny?" Sonny said, his left arm
around Johnny's shoulder. He was so close Johnny could smell his body
odor. Johnny knew he would have to make his story good.*

*"Yeah, I do, Sonny. I mean, I wasn't involved last night or nothing. Nei-
ther were the other guys. I should have told you this when it happened. I'm
sorry I didn't."*

*"Told me what?" Sonny asked impatiently. He was in the mood to beat
somebody's ass, not to talk.*

"I saw Billy Reynolds checking out your cellar the other day."

*Johnny instinctively knew that a good story had to have some truth to
it, and he had come up with a beauty. Billy Reynolds was the local junkie.
Heroin had not yet hit the neighborhood like it eventually would, and Billy
stuck out like a sore thumb.*

*It was not uncommon to see Billy, wild-eyed, walking down the street
in the middle of the day carrying a TV he'd stolen or a window fan he'd
probably taken right out of somebody's window. Billy used to go to the local pizza shop on Lexington Avenue, pull wads of jewelry out of his pockets
that he'd stolen from who knows where, and try to sell it to Rocco, the
owner. Rocco would take a piece of jewelry and ask Billy how much, Billy
would start at some outrageous price, and Rocco would have him down*

to pennies in minutes. Johnny and Mikey were often there to witness the negotiation. It was fun to watch, but it was sad too. Billy stole from the neighborhood, and Rocco and others stole from Billy.

One of those "others" was Sonny. Billy often included Fellino's on his rounds to sell his goods, and Sonny had bought a TV from him once, among other things. Johnny's story had struck just the right note of believability with Sonny.

"That was some quick thinking," Frankie told Johnny after he'd described what happened. "Mikey, you were right. Johnny is the Mayor of Lexington Avenue. A mayor's gotta think on his feet. Only a mayor could come up with a tale like that."

Johnny and Mikey had recently secured jobs as ushers at St. Francis, the local Catholic Church. Father Burke, the pastor, had dubbed Mikey the Mayor of Lexington Avenue because, as he told Mikey's mother, Mikey knew more people than he did, even though he had the pulpit. Mikey, in turn, had passed the moniker on to Johnny, telling him that a mayor was smart and knew how to run things and that the description fit Johnny more than himself. The nickname hadn't caught on in the neighborhood yet. Johnny's story to Sonny gave it fresh legs.

Something else happened that third week of practice that changed the course of the season. Some boys from north of the unofficial Ninety-sixth Street boundary line came to join the team. There were eight of them: one white guy, one Puerto Rican, and six blacks.

Johnny never knew for sure how they ever found out there was a team called the Lexingtons that practiced in Central Park, but he had his suspicions. Frankie O'Connor lived in that neighborhood, and Frankie made a point of walking up and shaking hands with each one of these new guys. It was a message to everybody else. The coach had to be in on it, too, because the new guys were on the team from the moment they arrived.

Johnny would soon find out why.

THIRTEEN

Anthony Webster, the prosecutor's investigator in Henry Wilson's case, did not live in Lake City—as Ted Griffin had surmised—but in Live Oak, a small community in north central Florida that was in the same general vicinity as Lake City. Jack figured that was probably the story of Ted Griffin's life: he got things *almost* right.

It didn't take Jack long to get the correct information. Like most investigators, Anthony Webster had been a retired cop before going to the state's attorney's office and starting to work on his second pension. Jack called his good friend Joaquin Sanchez, a retired homicide detective with the Miami Police Department, and told him his predicament. Twenty minutes later Joaquin called back with the address and number.

"You know the rules, Jack," Joaquin said. "You don't know where you got the information from, and you and Pat are going to have to take Maria and me out to dinner soon."

"Gotcha, Joaquin. We need to get together anyway—it's been too long. I'll call you next week."

Joaquin and his wife, Maria, had worked closely with Jack and Pat and another retired Miami homicide detective, Dick Radek, on Rudy Kelly's case. They had all lived in the same house for a time and become close friends.

"Where did you get this number?" was the first question Anthony Webster asked after Jack introduced himself on the telephone.

"It's not important," Jack answered. It was the wrong thing to say.

"Hell it's not! I don't like people knowing where I am and snooping around in my business."

"I know somebody you know, Mr. Webster." It was a lie but a plausible one. "I had to convince that person that I would only use this number once. I also had to convince that person there was an important enough reason for me to have the number."

There was a long pause on the other end of the line. For a moment Jack wasn't sure if Webster was still there.

"So what is it that's so important?" Webster finally asked.

"A man's life."

"Oh shit, you're not one of those DNA activists, are you? 'Everybody in jail is innocent! Everybody was wrongfully convicted!'"

Jack could tell this was going to be a challenging interview.

"No, nothing like that. DNA isn't involved. It's about a death-row case though, a man named Henry Wilson. He was convicted seventeen years ago based solely on the testimony of a convicted felon, David Hawke. Do you remember that case at all?"

"Not at all," Webster replied.

Jack refused to be deterred by Webster's faulty memory. "The deceased was a guy named Clarence Waterman, a drug dealer who also worked as a hairdresser. David Hawke said he drove Henry Wilson and Hawke's cousin to Waterman's place and waited while they killed him and then drove them away."

"Doesn't ring a bell."

"Neither David Hawke nor his cousin were ever charged with the crime, even though by Hawke's own testimony they were both guilty."

That last remark finally hit pay dirt. "That kind of shit happened all the time. Who was the prosecutor?"

Jack thought back to the records he had reviewed but couldn't come up with the name. "I'm not sure. It was Man-something."

"Mancuso?"

"That's it."

"It figures," Webster replied. "Mancuso was famous for shit like that. I'll never testify to that though, so I'm afraid I can't help you."

"Hang on a second, Mr. Webster. An attorney named Ted Griffin represented a guy named James Vernon—"

"Ted Griffin," Webster interrupted Jack again. "Now, there's a piece of shit." Jack had him interested again—at least momentarily.

"Yeah, I'm with you on that one," Jack replied, feeding right into the negativity. "Anyway, Vernon was a possible suspect in this murder. At least, that's what the defense thought, and Griffin says that Vernon told him he'd talked to you. Do you remember that?"

"Do you have any idea how many thousands of people I've talked to? No way can I remember one particular interview."

Jack was at his wit's end. Of course Webster couldn't remember. The murder happened seventeen years ago. He kept talking though.

"Would you have taken any notes? Where would they be?"

Jack was never to know why Anthony Webster gave him anything. Maybe the man had it in for the prosecutor, Mancuso. Maybe he simply didn't like the system that allowed a man to be convicted on a felon's word. But something Jack said flipped a switch in the former investigator.

"I always suspected that somebody was going to get caught with their tit in the wringer one day for using convicted felons as prosecution witnesses in cases like this. Don't get me wrong—most of the prosecutors were hard-working, honest guys. Every barrel always has a few rotten apples, you know what I mean?"

Jack took his cue. "I sure do."

"I don't know if any notes exist, Mr. Tobin. I always made notes of my interviews, so if I interviewed this guy, there is a record of it. Prosecutors, especially guys like Mancuso, never produced those notes to the defense. They claimed they were work-product or some other bullshit terminology lawyers use when they don't want to produce something. Anyway, those notes would probably be considered a public record by now. If you make a written request for the investigator's notes in the prosecutor's file for Henry Wilson, they should produce them, if they exist. You can call too. Ask for Margo Drake—she's the records custodian. She can help you. Just tell her it's a public record—

those are the magic words. You didn't get this information from me though. Understood?"

"Understood," Jack replied, crossing his fingers.

Webster hung up the phone before Jack had an opportunity to thank him.

Jack got Margo Drake's number and called her right away. He told her who he was and what he was looking for. He didn't have the faith Anthony Webster did that the magic words *public record* were going to do the trick, so he added a few extra.

"Anthony Webster was the investigator on that case and he instructed me to give you a call and to tell you his notes were now a public record."

"Oh, I'm glad you told me that," Margo Drake told Jack. "Because we don't usually give out anything in the prosecutor's separate file. That file contains all the prosecutor's notes and everything. However, since this case is so old—and you just want Mr. Webster's notes and not the prosecutor's and Mr. Webster instructed you to call to tell me it is a public record—we'll have to comply. It will take me a few days because those files are in storage."

Jack thanked her and told her a few days would be fine. He then sent her a letter confirming their telephone conversation.

The notes arrived five days later. Anthony Webster had indeed interviewed James Vernon, and Vernon had told him essentially the same story he told Wofford Benton—that he was just a witness to the murder.

Jack's dilemma still remained the same. James Vernon had told two different stories to four different people. He had no credibility, and therefore, in Jack's mind, the question of Henry Wilson's innocence was still very much in doubt. On the other hand, Anthony Webster's notes changed the legal ball game entirely. If Wofford Benton had been able to call the prosecutor's investigator to the stand instead of a prison snitch to talk about what James Vernon told him after the state had put on its case and rested and after Vernon had taken the Fifth, Henry Wilson might not have been convicted. Jack's burden was now clear: he would have to convince a judge that Anthony Webster's testimony was newly discovered evidence.

He sent a copy of the notes to Webster, along with an affidavit confirming under oath that the notes were indeed his and that the interview took place during the prosecution's investigation of the case, a month before Henry Wilson's trial.

When he received the signed affidavit back in the mail, Jack called Wofford Benton. The judge was in the middle of a hearing. To Jack's surprise, he recessed his hearing temporarily to take the call.

"What's up, Jack?"

"Well, Judge, I just want to update you on the case. You asked me to do that."

"Yes, I did. Thank you."

"I just received an affidavit from Anthony Webster. He was an investigator at the state's attorney's office."

"Yeah, I vaguely remember him. He was wound a little tight as I recall."

"That's the guy. Anyway, I found notes of an interview between Webster and James Vernon in which Vernon told Webster the same thing that he told you. Did you know that Vernon had spoken to the prosecutor's man a month before the trial?"

"Of course not. How did you find out?"

"Ted Griffin told me when I talked to him."

"Dammit!" the judge swore. In the silence that followed, Jack could hear Wofford breathing heavily on the other end of the line. He was processing the information, and it didn't take him long to arrive at the same conclusion Jack had reached.

"Let me ask you this, Jack. Do you think Henry would have been convicted if I had been able to put the state's chief investigator on the stand to testify on his behalf rather than that jailhouse snitch, Willie Smith?"

"I don't think so, Judge."

"Neither do I. I'll go ahead and prepare my own affidavit, and you use it however you need to. Even though I don't think you will be successful with the 'incompetence of counsel' defense, I understand that you have to raise the issue."

Wofford Benton no longer appeared to be a disinterested observer. He had joined the appellate team.

Jack's next call was to the Florida State Prison at Starke to set up an interview with Henry for that Friday. He now had some news for him.

That evening Pat and Jack took their treasured run along the river. "This is so boring," Pat said as they jogged along together. "Every night the same thing—starry skies, peaceful waters, weeping willows, pelicans, owls.... I miss the action of the big city—the robberies, the murders, the rapes. You know what I mean, Jack?"

"I'm with you, honey." She was always content, and she made him feel the same way no matter how his day had gone.

"So tell me about all this new evidence that you've uncovered."

"Well, I talked to Ted Griffin, the lawyer, and Anthony Webster, the prosecutor's investigator, and I got the notes of his interview with James Vernon. The bottom line is that James Vernon told the prosecutor's investigator that he was at the scene of the murder and Henry Wilson wasn't there, and Wofford Benton never knew about that conversation."

"Would it have made a difference if he did?"

"Absolutely. When Vernon took the Fifth at trial and refused to testify, Benton called a prison snitch to the stand. If he had known about Anthony Webster and called him instead, Henry Wilson might have walked."

"So Henry is innocent."

"Not necessarily. The original source of all this new information was James Vernon and he may have been lying like a rug."

Just then Pat saw something rise in the river. "Look!" she pointed.

"What is it?" Jack asked as they stopped to look.

"It's a manatee!" she said gleefully. "I was just telling the kids about them the other day. Oh, I wish I had a camera." They stood and watched as the big hulking thing lazily drifted down the river with not a care in the world. They only resumed their run when it was out of sight.

"Have you tried to locate James Vernon and what's that other guy's name—the witness against Henry?"

"David Hawke?"

"Yeah, that's the one I was thinking of. Have you tried to find them and talk to them?"

"I did. They're both dead. Vernon was killed five years ago in a drug deal gone bad and Hawke was also murdered—I don't know when."

"Is that good or bad for Henry?"

"It's good if he gets a new trial. With Hawke dead, there'll be no evidence to convict him. It won't help him get a new trial though."

"It sounds like you've got the evidence to do that."

"Maybe. I don't know if I can meet the legal standard, and I'm still not sure that he's innocent."

"Well, Jack, as I said before, present the evidence and leave the rest to fate. What's the standard you need to meet—new evidence?"

"Newly discovered evidence."

"Well, this is newly discovered evidence, isn't it? How was anybody to know that the prosecutor's investigator did this interview?"

"Wofford would have known if he had talked to Ted Griffin. Wofford didn't talk to him, and he should have. Ted Griffin would have told him about Anthony Webster."

"Wait a minute! You mean the prosecutor finds evidence that the person he or she is prosecuting may be innocent and they can hide it?"

"Something like that."

"No, Jack. No. I won't accept that. That can't be the law. How can a prosecutor who represents all of us hide evidence of a person's innocence? It doesn't make sense."

"It's just an evidentiary rule."

"Well, if that's the rule, whoever said the law is an ass is right. That is asinine."

Jack smiled to himself. Pat certainly had a way of getting to the heart of the matter.

FOURTEEN

It took about an hour for Ralph Giglio, the police sketch artist, to come up with a detailed picture of the man Paul and David had seen outside their window on the night of Carl Robertson's murder. Nick and Tony were both impressed.

"We need to get this picture in the neighborhood—stores, shops, apartment buildings—everywhere," Nick told Tony.

"How about the *Post* and the *News*?" Tony offered. "They've been following this case pretty closely. I'll bet they'll put something like this on the front page."

"You're probably right, but let's wait. The last thing we want is for this guy to see his picture in the paper and skip town."

Tony took another look at the sketch. "You know, this guy looks familiar to me. I think I've run across him in my travels."

"Well, if you have, it will come to you probably when you least expect it—like in the shower or something," Nick said. "Take a copy of the sketch with you and start thinking about all the different places you've worked in your career. If you know him, he'll pop up."

"All right, I'll give it a shot," Tony said as he stuffed a copy of the sketch in his inside jacket pocket.

Meanwhile, Philly Gertz was getting his turn with Ralph. Their attempt to come up with a sketch of the woman who'd been with Angie was a little less successful. Ralph could draw the black hair, but the rest of Philly's description just didn't make it.

"She was beautiful."

"In what way, Philly?"

"She was hot, you know what I mean? Legs up to her neck—man, I'm telling you, she was hot."

"Can you give me any specifics about what she looked like?"

"I just did."

"Can you describe her in any other way—her facial features, for instance?"

"All I can tell you is that they were like grapefruits. Not too big, just the right size. You know what I mean?"

"This guy's impossible," Ralph told Nick a half hour later. "If he tells me she had nice grapefruits one more time I'm going to club him."

Nick shook his head knowingly. There were people who just couldn't manage to provide an accurate description. It didn't surprise him that Philly Gertz was one of them.

"Thanks, Ralph. I'll let him go."

Nick walked out into the waiting area where Philly was sitting.

"Ralph says you were a great help, Philly."

"Really?"

"Yep."

"Because I'm kind of a big-picture guy, you know? I'm not much for details."

"Well, Ralph says he got the big picture."

"Good, 'cause I was a little worried there."

"No, you did fine. We'll be in touch. Thanks again."

"My pleasure, Nick. I won't forget you guys, either—you know, when the press comes around."

"Thanks, Philly."

Nick had gotten in touch with Angie, and the next morning he and Tony arrived at her apartment to tie up some loose ends.

Angie looked much better this time. The dark circles under her eyes were gone and she appeared well rested. She was dressed in a pair of jeans and a T-shirt, her blond hair pulled back in a ponytail. Nick could see the disappointment on Tony's face. Tony had wanted to see Angie one more time in that nightgown. The man was hopeless. It wasn't an entire disaster for Tony, however. Angie was just plain beautiful any way you cut it, and she looked especially sexy in jeans and a T-shirt.

"Won't you come in, gentlemen?" She motioned to them with a polite smile on her face.

The apartment had changed quite a bit since their last visit. There were boxes everywhere, some of them half-filled, some already sealed.

"I'm not waiting for Carl's family to get a court order. I'm getting my things and I'm getting out," she told them before they could ask.

Tony and Nick both knew the operative part of that statement was "getting my things." Once an executor was appointed, the apartment would be locked and all assets would be frozen. Angie was taking possession of what she could before that happened.

The couch and chairs were still there, however, and the three of them sat in the same seats as they had two days before.

"So what can I do for you?" Angie asked, her voice much stronger and more confident.

"We just want to ask a few more questions," said Nick. "First of all, are you going to be okay? Do you have a place to stay?"

"Yes, I'll be staying with my girlfriend in Queens. It's not far, but it's light-years away from here." Both men nodded to let her know they understood. Queens was a blue-collar borough. Working people could no longer afford to live in Manhattan.

"We're going to need that address and your friend's telephone number," Nick said as nonchalantly as he could.

"Fine. I'll write them down. Anything else?" Nick noticed that her demeanor changed after he asked for the address. She sounded anxious, almost rude.

"What's your friend's name?"

"Barbara Verbinski."

"Could you write her address and telephone number down for me now?"

"It's Fifteen Demeter Avenue," she said while writing on a piece of paper. "And this is her telephone number." She handed the paper to Nick.

"You must know her pretty well—you didn't have to look up her number."

"I'm good with numbers. Now are we done?"

"Just a few more things," Nick told her. He leaned forward in his chair. "During the course of our investigation we've learned that you had a woman staying with you a few days before Carl was murdered. Would that have been Ms. Verbinski?"

She hesitated momentarily. "No, it wasn't Barbara."

"Was this somebody else another friend, or a companion—"

"Just what are you implying, Detective?"

"I'm not implying anything, ma'am. I'm just asking a question."

"Well then, yes, she was a friend."

Nick had the commitment he needed. Now he could go to work. "Okay, she was a friend. What was her name?"

Angie didn't hesitate. Nick knew she wouldn't. Not yet. "Lois," she replied.

"Lois what?"

"Barton. Lois Barton."

"And how long have you and Lois known each other?"

"A while."

"What does that mean—months, years?"

"Years, we've known each other for years. We're good friends. Now if you two will just leave me alone, I need to get finished with my packing and get out of here."

"I understand," Nick said. "Just a couple more questions. Where does Lois live?"

Angie hesitated for the second time. Nick caught it right away. So did Tony, even though he didn't seem to be concentrating all that hard on what she was saying. He was still trying to figure out if she was wearing a bra or not.

"Queens," Angie finally replied.

"Where in Queens?"

"I don't know. I can't remember her address."

"I guess she's not as good a friend as Barbara?"

"No, she's not."

"How about her telephone number?"

"I don't remember that either."

"Do you have it written down?"

"Somewhere."

"Could you get it for us?"

"Not right now." Angie stood up abruptly. "Look, I've got work to do here. I'd like to sit around and chat but I don't have time."

Neither Nick nor Tony moved. "We'll be leaving in a minute," Nick said, maintaining his soft, calm tone. "Where does Lois work?"

Angie slumped back on the couch. "I don't know. I don't know," she replied, and then she started to cry.

Nick waited a minute or so, then continued in the same tone.

"Angie, Tony and I are professionals. We're not here to judge you. We're investigating a murder and you are a witness in that murder investigation. We're going to find the truth eventually, and if you don't give it to us you may subject yourself to criminal penalties. I know you were not involved in this murder. So I'm advising you for your own good—tell us everything."

Angie stared at her lap, silently crying. Tony, the other professional in the room, waited anxiously to hear the exotic details of Angie and Lois Barton's relationship. Nick had broken her down very quickly and very skillfully. Most cops would have tried to intimidate her and would have gotten nowhere.

"You have no idea what it's like being alone all the time," Angie began when she had composed herself somewhat. "I couldn't bring another man into the picture. That wouldn't work. I met Lois at a local bar a couple of weeks before Carl's murder. We went out a few times together before I invited her home. It was nice—much nicer than I thought it was going to be. I'd never been with a woman before. It seemed to be going so well. Then she just disappeared a few days before Carl was killed."

"When was the last time you saw her?" Nick asked.

"It was at a bar called the Crooked Fence. It's not far from here. I yelled at some creep who was trying to come on to me, and he left the bar and she left the bar right after him. I never saw her again."

"Did she go after him?"

"I don't know. She just said, 'I'll be right back' and left."

Nick took Ralph Giglio's sketch out of his pocket and placed it in front of Angie. "Do you recognize this man at all?"

Angie looked at the sketch and shrugged her shoulders. "No, not offhand."

"Could he have been the man at the bar that you yelled at?"

"He could have been. To tell you the truth, I never really looked at the guy. I just told him to get lost. If he walked in this room right now, I probably wouldn't recognize him."

"Anything else that you can tell us that might help us in this investigation?"

"No, I don't think so." She seemed calmer now. "Wait a minute." She sat up straight. "There was one other thing. I didn't realize it until the next afternoon when I went shopping, but one of my credit cards was missing. I immediately called the credit card company and canceled it."

Nick stole a glance at Tony to see if he'd caught the significance.

"Can you give us an old bill so we can get the card number?" he asked.

"Sure, I have it right here." She started shuffling through some papers on the coffee table in front of her. "Here it is." She handed a single piece of paper to Nick, who passed it over to Tony.

Nick turned back to her. "Angie, just one more question, I promise. Did you ever tell Lois about Carl?"

Angie hesitated once more. Nick waited. There was no need to go through his criminal penalties speech again. She was a sharp girl. She got it.

"I think I may have," she finally told him.

"Did you tell her about the money and how he brought it?"

"I think so. She'd asked me how I could afford such a nice place. I was trying to be honest."

Nick thanked her for her time as he and Tony stood up to leave. He needed to go back to the office and methodically fit the puzzle pieces together, but it appeared that Angie's female lover might have been an accomplice in Carl Robertson's death. He brought it up with Tony once they were in the car and moving.

"Run that credit card as soon as we get back."

"Will do," Tony replied. "How come you didn't ask her to come down to the station to look at some pictures—see if she could identify the broad?"

"I figured it could wait a day or two. We pressured her enough today."

"I guess you're right."

"So they were a team—the woman and this guy Paul and David identified."

"It seems that way," said Tony. "She got the information, he pulled the job. But why kill Robertson?"

"I don't know. Maybe he tried to grab the gun?"

"There was no evidence of a struggle."

"We'll probably never know exactly what happened. Things just don't add up, though. If they were a team, and if the shooter and the guy at the bar are the same person, what the hell was all that about at the bar—her running out after him? It doesn't make sense."

Tony didn't have an answer for that one. And clearly, at the moment, neither did Nick.

FIFTEEN

*G*regory Brown, one of the new black guys from north of the Ninety-sixth Street line of demarcation, was the fastest player on the team—maybe the fastest player the Lexingtons had ever had. Joe Sheffield, the coach, installed him as running back after his very first practice. Floyd Peters, another black kid, and Luis "Rico" Melendez, the Puerto Rican, were neck and neck in the sprints and a close second to Gregory. The next fastest was the biggest surprise—Johnny Tobin. Johnny had grown into his body in the last year, going from a gangly youth to a more coordinated, muscular athlete. As a consequence, his reflexes were quicker and he was a lot faster.

After three weeks of practicing and scrimmaging, the positions were set. Johnny secured a starting spot in the defensive backfield with Floyd Peters and Rico Melendez. Although he was speedy enough to stay with most receivers, Johnny initially had no idea how to play defensive back. Rico and Floyd took him under their wing.

"You gotta practice differently than the rest of the team," Floyd told him. "You gotta practice running backwards and sideways without looking where you're going."

The three of them would go off by themselves and practice running backward on their toes and sideways with cross steps at full speed. They didn't have the luxury of a defensive backfield coach so they coached themselves—at least, Rico and Floyd coached Johnny. He didn't know where they'd learned their skills, but Rico and Floyd knew how to play. Floyd was Johnny's height but thin and wiry. He could twist and turn his body in fluid motions like a ballet dancer. Rico was short, quick, and tough.

Rico was the tactician, and he worked Johnny every day on the fundamentals of playing defensive back. Floyd taught him how to make plays without getting hurt.

"If you want to last in this league, don't meet everybody head on like that maniac," Floyd said one day, pointing at Rico. "Catch them at an angle. If you hit a man from the side he goes down a lot easier and it's a lot easier on you. Just don't forget to wrap your arms—that's the key. You gotta play tough but you gotta be smart about it too."

Rico constantly pushed Johnny to be more aggressive.

"You got a nickname?" Rico asked him the Thursday before the first game.

"Kinda."

"What is it?"

"They sometimes call me the Mayor of Lexington Avenue."

"You? Why do they do that?"

"It's a long story."

Rico didn't have time for a story. He was too busy teaching. "I call myself the Rico Kid. You know why?"

"Why?" Johnny asked.

"Because I have my turf, and nobody's coming into the Rico Kid's territory without getting hurt. You understand?"

Johnny nodded hesitantly. Rico filled in the blanks. "When we line up in the game on Saturday, you'll be on the right side—you'll always be on the right side. I'll be on the left and Floyd will be in the middle. When you're out there on that right side, you look at that field in front of you right up to the line of scrimmage and you say to yourself, 'This is the Mayor's turf. I own this place. Nobody's catching a ball in here. Nobody's coming in here without getting hurt.' You got that?"

Johnny nodded. "I got it. But you're not going to call me the Mayor from now on, are you? It's a little embarrassing."

"I hear you, man. I'll tell you what. Off the field I'll call you Johnny, but on the field you're the Mayor. Fair enough?"

"Fair enough."

*   *   *

The first game was at McCombs Dam Park across from Yankee Stadium. Their opponents were the Bronx Bears, whose uniforms matched those of the Chicago Bears—black shirts and white pants. They were big, and Johnny could tell they weren't sticklers for the rules. They were all grown men in their late twenties and thirties.

The Lexingtons won the toss and elected to receive. Johnny was on the kick return team. Gregory Brown and Floyd stood back by the end zone ready to catch the ball, and Johnny and Rico were ten yards in front of them with Mikey and his brother Eddie; ten yards ahead of them were the linemen. It was a formation they had practiced for the first time on Thursday, for about five minutes. Johnny's assignment was to find somebody to block after either Gregory or Floyd caught the ball. He was standing out there in his clean white jersey, nervous as hell, butterflies in his stomach, waiting for the referee to start the game. He tried to think about nothing else but finding a man to block.

The referee blew the whistle, the Bears kicker started toward the ball, and his teammates in unison began running downfield. Then the ball was in the air. At first Johnny kept his eyes on the wave of players coming down the field. He was supposed to pick up the ball's line of flight so he could set up his block, so he briefly glanced up. But something was wrong: the ball wasn't going over his head to the two guys back by the end zone. The kick was short, way short, and it was coming right at him. And so was everybody on the other team.

There was no time to think. He concentrated first on catching the ball, something Floyd had drilled into his head: "Catch it first, then look to see where you're gonna run. If you don't catch it, running is not going to be your problem." Keeping his eyes glued to the ball, Johnny extended his hands and pulled it into his gut. Only then did he shift his gaze to the field in front of him.

The sideline looked open so he headed straight up the field. Johnny saw Doug Kline and Frankie O'Connor ahead of him, watched as they threw their blocks and then cut the opposite way into the hole they had cleared. Johnny got through, but there was nobody to block the next wave of tack-

lers. He tried to outrun them and did for another ten yards before he was brought down hard. In the pile, somebody punched him in the stomach. Somebody else welcomed him to opening day in the city league: "Pull that shit again, kid, and we'll break your leg." Johnny smiled to himself. Last year he would have been scared shitless. This year he was amused. The butterflies were gone.

He had gained thirty yards on the play. Everybody slapped him on the pads when he reached the sideline. "Way to go, Johnny." "Good run, man!" It was a nice feeling. Rico and Floyd were the most excited. "The Mayor owns this turf!" Rico shouted.

On the next play, Gregory Brown sprinted around the left end for a touchdown. The game turned out to be a defensive struggle after that. The Lexingtons held the Bears scoreless and won six to nothing.

They celebrated that night at the Carlow East, one of the neighborhood bars. Johnny was the only one on the team who wasn't eighteen. In fact, he had just turned seventeen that month.

"We can't go drinking without the Mayor," Frankie said when Johnny pointed out that he wasn't legal. "Hell, he set up the winning touchdown." Johnny felt like a million bucks.

The Carlow had a long bar to the right as you walked in the door. Halfway down the bar on the left was the men's room. They walked in as a group and headed for the far end of the bar. As they passed the men's room, Johnny slipped in. He stayed there while Mary McKenna, the bar owner, checked everybody's identification. Ten minutes later, Jimmy Walsh, the white kid from north of Ninety-sixth Street, came in and handed Johnny his driver's license. The hope was that Mary wouldn't notice that she hadn't proofed Johnny, but if she did, he'd have Jimmy's license; they looked enough alike for it to work.

The plan worked. Mary never did card Johnny, probably because she was too distracted by the makeup of the group and the reaction it was receiving from the other patrons. Even though the whole team didn't show up, there were still three blacks and a Puerto Rican in an Irish bar. The regular patrons didn't take kindly to that, and there were some grumblings down the bar soon after the boys arrived. Johnny watched as Frankie O'Connor took over. He walked up and down the bar telling everybody *about how the Lexingtons, the neighborhood team, had just won their first game and how they were going to make the neighborhood proud by winning the city championship.*

Pretty soon the whole bar was laughing and toasting the Lexingtons. The Carlow East had gone color-blind.

SIXTEEN

Hope was not something that flourished in the dim gray atmosphere of Florida's death row. Hope could be as painful as execution itself. But that was exactly what Jack brought to Henry Wilson as they sat across from each other in the same room where they first met with the two guards in the corners behind Henry. Hope came in the form of a rough draft of a motion for a new trial and copies of the affidavits of Wofford Benton, Ted Griffin, and Anthony Webster. Henry pored over the documents, leaving Jack to sit, wait, and wonder if Henry was going to grab that last ray of hope that he was offering. Finally Henry spoke.

"This is very good work, Counselor. In no time, you have uncovered evidence that nobody else could find—in seventeen years. But there are problems, aren't there?"

"Yes," Jack replied. He felt that Henry was baiting him a little.

"Let's talk about the problems," Henry began. "You're not going to win on ineffective assistance of counsel. Nor are you going to win on newly discovered evidence."

Jack wasn't totally shocked. He knew death-row inmates had a lot of time on their hands, and many of them read court cases. It was the analysis—the direct, incisive pinpointing of the problems—that was surprising. "You're right," he replied. "We're not going to win on ineffective assistance of counsel because—"

Henry interrupted him. "Because the case law is against you. This kind of mistake by defense counsel isn't going to do it."

"That's right. And it's probably not newly discovered evidence because—"

"—because my attorney could have found all of this evidence seventeen years ago if he had done his job correctly."

Jack reluctantly had to agree. "You're right again. So what we have left is…" Jack paused to see if Henry Wilson could answer the most important question.

"A *Brady* violation," Henry said without hesitation. Jack looked at him in disbelief. In 1963, the Supreme Court of the United States had decided the case of *Brady v. Maryland*, which held that the state had a duty to disclose evidence favorable to the accused, and if the failure to disclose such evidence deprived the accused of a fair trial, then the accused was entitled to a new trial. It had taken Jack days of research to find the *Brady* decision and to realize it was Henry's only realistic hope.

"What?" Henry finally asked Jack. "You're speechless? What do you think I've been doing here for the last seventeen years, twiddling my thumbs? I knew the prosecutor held back stuff. I just needed somebody to find that evidence. I've read *Brady* so many times the ink on the pages is worn. I knew as the years rolled by that a *Brady* violation was going to be my only shot."

"It's still a long shot," Jack warned. "A judge has to determine that you were deprived of a fair trial, and that's a subjective evaluation."

"Well, I guess we'll just have to get the right judge," he replied, and Jack knew that Henry had grabbed onto that tiny strand of hope with both hands.

On Wednesday afternoon, Jack and Pat were in Dr. Erica Gardner's empty waiting room.

"Jack, why don't you just leave me here and go do something? Check in at the hotel. Visit your friends. Anything," Pat said.

"We can't check in at the hotel until four o'clock and there is nobody I want to see in this town. Besides, I want to be here with you."

"I know, honey, but they're just going to examine me today and take tests. They won't talk about the results until tomorrow. You can be with me tomorrow."

Reinforcements for Pat came in the form of Dr. Gardner, who appeared in the waiting room a few minutes later. She greeted Jack first, kissing him on the cheek. "It's good to see you again, Jack." She waited while he introduced Pat, then turned her attention back to him. "Jack, your wife and I need to get acquainted. It's going to take some time to chat, do an examination, and have these diagnostic tests performed. Why don't you go do what you men do with your free time and check back here in about three hours?"

Pat was standing behind Dr. Gardner looking at Jack with a big smile on her face. "All right, I can see I'm outnumbered," he muttered and retreated toward the front door. "I'll go check us in at the hotel and be back at five."

They were staying at the Windmar Hotel in South Beach. Anxious and unable to settle down, Jack spent the next couple of hours walking the beach and sightseeing. He made a reservation for them that evening at a restaurant on the main drag, specifically telling the maitre d' that he wanted a table on the patio overlooking the street.

Pat was waiting when he arrived back at Dr. Gardner's office at five. "How was it?" he asked.

"Great. Dr. Gardner is very nice and very professional. She had somebody from her staff drive me to the hospital for the CT scan and the ultrasound, and I didn't have to wait at all. Everything was all arranged beforehand. She's going to read the reports tonight."

"Good," Jack replied. "I got us all set up at the hotel and I made us dinner reservations."

"Oh, where are we going?"

"Right on Ocean Avenue. We can watch the show while we eat."

The show was the other people who walked up and down Ocean Avenue to see and be seen and the exotic cars that took their turn driving up and down the same runway.

"This *is* quite a scene," Pat marveled after they'd settled in at their table.

"It never changes," Jack told her. "Some of the buildings around here get redone and the styles change a bit, but the people are as wacky as ever."

They went dancing after dinner at the Windmar nightclub. The music was a little loud, but after a few drinks they didn't notice.

"I think this is the first time you've ever taken me dancing," Pat shouted to him over the music. "You're pretty good."

The liquor had removed Jack's usual inhibitions on the dance floor. He was flailing his arms and gyrating and laughing and having a grand old time. "It's not the first time," he shouted back. "I danced with you at one of Father O'Pray's dances when you were fourteen."

"I remember." She laughed. "You stepped on my foot."

Later, in their room, they opened the sliding glass doors and made love to the continuous roar of the ocean smashing up against the shore. Their lovemaking was slow and sweet, and Pat didn't have any pain this time. When it was over they lay there silently, listening to the waves and thinking about the news they would receive the next day.

At ten a.m., they were back in Erica Gardner's waiting room holding hands. Finally the receptionist ushered them into the doctor's office.

Erica motioned them to sit. "I'm afraid I have bad news," she said, leaning forward on her desk.

Pat spoke first. "How bad is it?"

"There is a mass in your uterus, which by its size and shape I strongly suspect is malignant. That's not the worst part, however." Pat squeezed Jack's hand. He felt like he was in a dream—a nightmare. "There are other tumors in your lungs and liver."

They were both stunned. Jack was normally a realist, yet he could make no sense of Erica Gardner's words. He wanted to protest, to tell the good doctor there was some kind of mistake, that other than a little pain once in a while Pat was the picture of health—hell, they ran every night. All you had to do was look at her. Instead, he sat there silently, his arm around his wife, wishing they were someplace—anyplace—else.

"What does this mean?" Pat asked after a long silence.

Dr. Gardner took a deep breath. "The outlook isn't good," she began. "But there is always hope. Miracles happen every day."

Miracles? Jack thought. *Pat's life is dependent on miracles?*

"My cousin, Estelle," Dr. Gardner continued, "is a gynecological oncologist here in Miami. I have already called her and made an appointment for you to see her this afternoon. I've discussed your case with her and I'm sending your films over right away. She will discuss all available options for treatment with you."

Jack could not say anything. Pat, on the other hand, was able to focus on the doctor's words and question them.

"I'm not sure I understand what you mean by 'the outlook isn't good,'" she said.

"You have what we call stage four cancer, which means that in most cases it is terminal," Erica told her. "That doesn't necessarily mean that your case is terminal. You're young and you're healthy. Your chances of tolerating heavy doses of chemotherapy are better than most. If your tumors can be reduced and controlled, they can possibly be removed. But the cancer has spread through your system and it's already in three places. That is not good."

They left in a daze, stopping for lunch before heading over to Estelle Wright's office, although neither of them was the slightest bit hungry. Jack was devastated. Pat was his rock, his world. He couldn't remember his life before she'd come into it, and he certainly couldn't contemplate a future without her.

Estelle Wright was very nice, but she didn't have any better news for them. She took a needle biopsy of the tumor in Pat's uterus and explained to her the joys of Carboplatin and Taxol, the two drugs that were going to be used in her chemotherapy regimen.

"We haven't confirmed the diagnosis, but I'm going to go ahead and schedule you for chemotherapy based upon an educated assumption that you do, in fact, have cancer," Dr. Wright explained matter-of-factly. "You'll come in once a week. The chemo will be administered intravenously. It's not a traumatic process at all."

Jack could tell from her use of just the right words that Dr. Wright had given this little speech quite a few times in the past. He tried to concentrate as she continued with her description of what lay ahead. "You may become very tired and listless," she said, looking directly at Pat. "Some people don't. You may experience nausea, constipation, diarrhea—and your hair may fall out. You may have a loss of appetite. You may develop sores inside your mouth. You may need a blood transfusion from time to time. If anything gets too bad, call us immediately and we will admit you to the hospital. Do not hesitate to call. Someone is available twenty-four hours a day. I will meet with you every six weeks so we can discuss your progress."

They didn't say much to each other on the ride back home, partly because they didn't have the energy to talk. Jack drove with one hand and held Pat's with the other. Ever since they'd first heard the news, he hadn't let go of her—not even through lunch. He wanted to tell her everything was going to be all right, but he couldn't. This was out of his control. What he could do was be with her every moment of her fight.

"You're not going to quit Henry's case," Pat suddenly said to him after many minutes of silence.

"What are you talking about?" he asked, refusing to acknowledge that she had read his thoughts.

"I'm talking about what you're spinning in your mind right now."

"I'm just thinking that I don't want to be away from you for one second. They can get somebody else to pick up Henry's appeal."

"Jack, honey, it's three weeks to Henry's execution. You can't drop his case. You will never forgive yourself. I don't want you to."

"Sweetheart, I'm going to be with you. We're going to fight this together. That's the end of it."

"No it's not, Jack. We're going to fight this together, but you are *not* going to let Henry go, and neither am I. His fight is our fight. That's the way it has always been with us, and we're not changing now."

He looked across at her in the darkness as they drove along the back road that led to Bass Creek. Even now, with all they had been through this day, maybe now more than ever, she was magnificent.

"Okay," he said quietly.

SEVENTEEN

Tony Severino was lost in that world between deep sleep and first waking—the world of light dreams. He and his old partner Joe Fogarty were rousting some lowlife in the South Bronx for information. He was in Narcotics at the time, and this particular lowlife sometimes—though not very often—had information to give or sell. They found him in a bar in the middle of the afternoon, the only customer in the place.

Joe Fogarty walked up to the man, put his arm around him, and cuffed his neck in a pseudo headlock. "How ya doin', Benny?" he asked. "Got anything for us?" Benny looked at the two of them. Tony saw his face, his eyes. Reality penetrated through his dream state. He sat up in bed.

"That's him! Benny—what the hell was his last name? Joe Fogarty will know."

"What are you talking about? Who's him?" his startled wife, Frances, exclaimed from her side of the bed.

"Our murderer—I just remembered where I've seen him before."

"Well, I'm happy for you, honey. Just try to be a little quieter the next time you find a murderer in your dreams. Some of us are still sleeping."

Tony ignored the remark as he pulled off the covers and stepped out of bed. He checked the clock. It was 6:10 in the morning. There was no need to call Nick; he'd see him soon enough. He decided to get dressed and head for the office, then call Joe Fogarty at eight to see if he remembered Benny's last name.

Tony caught Joe Fogarty at his precinct before he headed out for the day.

"Joe, I'm going to fax you up an artist's sketch of a perp we're looking for. Call me right away and let me know if you recognize him."

Joe called him back immediately. "That's Benny Avrile. You remember him, don't you? He was one of our snitches. He's still one of mine, although I haven't seen the skinny little bastard in a while. Benny has these brief periods when he tries to go straight. Unfortunately, nobody will hire the poor son-of-a-bitch."

When Tony told Joe why they were looking for Benny, Joe didn't believe it.

"Benny a murderer? C'mon. Is there something in the water down there in Manhattan? This guy is harmless. I don't think he even knows how to shoot a gun. Don't get me wrong. Benny's a lot of things, but he's not vicious or violent."

"I'll keep your thoughts in mind, Joe, in case we need a character witness for Benny. Right now we just need your help finding him."

"What I wouldn't do if I were you is show up here and start asking questions in the neighborhood. If word gets out that you're looking for him, Benny will disappear. If we see him, we'll nab him and I'll give you a call."

"Fine, Joe. Just remember he's a priority. This case is in the paper every day and you know what that means."

"Yeah, I know. The powers that be are crawling up your asshole. I'll get the word out around here. We'll get him, Tony."

Benny was maintaining a low profile. At first, he had a tremendous desire to run, but he had no idea where to go, and gradually the urge to flee dissipated. He started to believe that somehow he had gotten away with it all.

Even though he had run into the Bitch from Hell, as he liked to call her, on his first venture out, that didn't deter him from continuing to stop at Tillie's now and then for an afternoon beer. There was always the possibility that she would show up again, especially since he had shortchanged her, but that was a risk Benny was willing to take. *Shit, she knows where I live anyway*, he thought. *If she's coming back, she's coming back. Nothing I can do about it. The money's almost gone anyway.*

Benny didn't talk to anybody at the bar except Tillie, and he never stayed for more than a couple of hours. Usually it was just the two of them, and they shot pool or smoked a joint in the back. Tillie was just starting to get used to Benny buying his own drinks. Now, wonder of all wonders, Benny was supplying the pot as well.

One week after Tony Severino's call to the Bronx, on a quiet, pleasant afternoon when Benny and Tillie, high as kites, were playing eight ball at the pool table in the back of the bar, Joe Fogarty walked into Tillie's. He went right up to Benny, put his arm around him, and cuffed his neck in a pseudo headlock. Joe Fogarty had obviously not bought into the dangerous-desperado routine they were selling downtown.

"Benny, Benny, where've you been? You don't call, you don't write. Old Joe is starting to think you don't like him."

"I've been right here where I've always been, Joe. You can ask Tillie."

Joe ignored Tillie for the moment. Benny was the star of the show today. "I've got bad news for you, Benny. I've got to take you in."

"For what?"

"Never mind. You're in big trouble though, so just keep your mouth shut until they give you a public defender. Now turn around and put your hands behind your back."

Benny turned around and did what he was told. "I didn't do anything, Joe."

"Oh, you've done shit, Benny, but that's not what I'm locking you up for. Like I said, just keep your mouth shut until you get a public defender. Don't go pissing on people's legs and making up stories, you understand me? Shut up until you get a lawyer."

"All right, Joe." Joe was a good guy. Benny almost wanted to tell him what happened, how it all went down, but he decided to take Joe's advice and say nothing.

Joe checked Benny's pockets after he locked the handcuffs in place and pulled out two tens and two joints. He threw the joints on the pool table. "You better hold these for him until he comes back, Tillie." Then, taking Benny by the arm, he led him out of the bar and into his car.

Tony Severino put the phone down and spoke to Nick, who was on the other side of the desk, typing a report.

"They got him."

"Good," Nick replied. "Has he said anything?"

"Joe said he hasn't talked. That surprises me, because Benny is a flapper."

"Maybe we can get him to talk when we get him down here. Let's go pick him up."

They brought Benny back to Manhattan and put him in a cell on the second floor.

"Let's just hold him for now," Nick suggested. "Let him wonder what's going on. In the meantime, we can finish our investigation. We'll talk to him when we know what we need, if anything."

Tony disagreed. "I think we should do it right away, Nick. If we get him to confess, we can short-circuit the rest of this investigation."

"Think about it, Tony. If we put him through a lineup and tell him he's been fingered already, isn't he more likely to confess?"

"I guess you're right," Tony conceded, although he was irritated. He had located Benny and he knew he could wrap this case up if he got a shot at interrogating him.

With Benny in custody things started to move, although not as fast or as smoothly as Nick would have liked. They did two lineups, one each for Paul and David, who both identified Benny within seconds.

Angie came to the station to look at a few pictures. When she was unsuccessful in that regard, Nick took her to see Ralph Giglio to try and come up with a sketch of Lois Barton. However, she proved to be as bad in the description department as Philly Gertz: after describing Lois's long black hair, she came up blank. Ralph prompted her for almost an hour but got nowhere. Nick suspected that Angie was holding back again. He knew he'd have to have another heart-to-heart with her, but not right away. He'd talk to Benny first. Maybe Benny would give him something that he could use to make Angie open up about Lois Barton.

Something else troubled him as well. Tony had contacted the credit card company, who told them there had been no charges on Angie's credit card after it had been stolen. That didn't make sense if Benny had actually stolen Angie's credit card at the bar that night. A guy like Benny should have charged thousands of dollars by now. Yet there was nothing.

It was just like Dan Jenkins, the coroner, had said the night of the murder: *it's never open-and-shut.*

EIGHTEEN

*A*t mid-season the Lexingtons were three and one and tied for first place. Johnny Tobin, the hero of game one, had allowed a receiver to get by him for a long touchdown pass in game four. Even though the team pulled the game out, Johnny felt terrible. That evening they were having a few beers at their usual spot, the Carlow East. Johnny was huddled with Rico and Floyd. Floyd was consoling him.

"Everybody gets beat once in a while, Johnny. You just gotta shake it off."

Rico, however, was still coaching. "What happened on the play, Johnny?" he asked.

"I don't know. He just beat me, I guess," Johnny said, looking down into his beer.

"Look at me," Rico said sharply. Johnny looked at Rico, who stared into his eyes. "You're gonna continue to get beat until you figure out why. That's the way it is, Johnny. You don't let things pass. You correct them."

"Man, leave the guy alone, he feels bad enough," Floyd told Rico. Rico and Floyd were best friends although they were polar opposites.

"I'm not trying to make him feel bad," Rico replied. "I just want to go over the play and find out what went wrong. Take me through it, Johnny."

"Well, he came off the line and ran out about five yards, then turned to do a buttonhook. I saw the quarterback look at him and raise his arm to throw. That's when I made my move toward him. I remember thinking I could intercept. He just turned and went right past me."

"Did he give you a fake before he did his buttonhook?" They were on their third beer, but Rico was just as intense as he had been on the field that day.

"No, he didn't."

"Do you remember back in practice before the season started and we were talking about fakes?"

"Yeah."

"And what did I tell you to be careful about if a guy doesn't give you a fake before he makes his cut or turns for the ball?"

Johnny didn't answer right away. His head was a little fuzzy from the beer. Rico had drilled the fundamentals into him, however, and eventually they started surfacing.

"If a guy doesn't give you at least one fake before making his cut, then watch for him to go long."

"That's what happened, isn't it?"

"Yeah." Johnny felt as if a lightbulb had just gone on in his brain. "The buttonhook was really the first fake and I went for it."

"Exactly!" Rico shouted. "So if he doesn't fake before he turns, don't charge until the ball is released, got it?"

"Got it," Johnny told him. He and Rico smacked hands—the lesson was over. Johnny took a swig of his beer while Rico went to get another.

"Man, Rico is intense, isn't he?" Floyd observed.

"Yeah," Johnny said, "but he's right. That's the way you become a champion."

Just then Frankie O'Connor yelled over to Floyd. He'd been talking to one of the regulars who had been upset when the team first came into the Carlow East weeks before. Frankie never stopped politicking.

"Hey, Pink Floyd, come on over here. I want you to meet someone."

Floyd had earned his nickname only recently. At practice the week before, he'd opened his equipment bag and found that his white practice jersey and pants had changed color. His mother had washed them with something red and forgot to tell him about it. So Floyd had to dress for practice in a pink jersey and pink pants. The jeering was unmerciful; even Joe Sheffield got into it. Floyd laughed along with everybody else. Most guys would have gotten mad or at least embarrassed, but not Floyd. He had that rare ability to laugh at himself.

Floyd walked over to Frankie.

"Pink Floyd, I want you to meet Vinny Gaines." They shook hands.

"That was a great story Frankie just told me about how you got your nickname," said Vinny. "Man, you must have been surprised when you opened your equipment bag. I would have just gone home."

Before Floyd could respond, he was interrupted by Joe Meeley, another regular, who had been eavesdropping on the story. "We outta be thankful the son-of-a-bitch washed his clothes at all. Most of them don't."

Nobody could say for sure what happened next because it happened so fast. As best as anyone could recollect, there was a brief awkward moment after Joe Meeley's remark when nobody said anything, then Frankie hauled off and punched Joe Meeley right in the nose.

Joe flew off his bar stool and hit the ground hard, although he wasn't knocked out. All conversation in the bar stopped as everybody braced themselves for a brawl.

Mary McKenna came out from behind the bar almost before Joe hit the floor.

"Joe Meeley, get the hell out of here!" she yelled.

"But Mary!" Meeley protested. He was on his feet now but going nowhere near Frankie O'Connor. "He hit me and I'm a regular customer here."

"I heard what you said," Mary told him. "He had a right to hit you. You won't come back in here until you apologize to this young man." She pointed at Floyd. "And anybody else who feels the same way Joe does, you can leave too. Now get going, Joe."

Mary was taking a big risk. Her regulars came in every day. They paid the rent. With the Lexingtons it was once a week at best, and then only during the season. But there was something about the exuberance and the casual camaraderie of the young men that had caused her to change her opinion about them. She was gambling that many of her regular patrons had similar feelings, and she was about to find out if she was right.

Joe Meeley walked out of the Carlow East alone.

Ten minutes later everybody was laughing and talking like the incident had never happened. Frankie O'Connor's punch, however, would become a part of the neighborhood folklore forever.

NINETEEN

Night still lingered on the river when Jack and Pat jumped into their dinghy and headed out on the Okalatchee. At its widest point the river extended only a hundred yards from bank to bank, and at this time in the early morning it was teeming with fishing boats heading out to the big lake. Their dinghy had no lights, so they had to hug the shoreline and be extra careful. Twenty minutes out, Jack made a right turn, and they both ducked as the boat meandered under a thicket of brush and foliage for several minutes until they emerged in a narrow inlet bordered on both sides by mangroves, cypress trees, and tall pines.

Pat had been here many times, but she never ceased to be amazed by the dramatic transformation that occurred in those few minutes. They went from the hustle-bustle of the river—with motors roaring and waves from the bigger boats buffeting the dinghy—to total calm and a chorus of crickets that blended with the peacefulness of the dark.

Jack steered to the middle of the inlet, cut the engine, and let the boat drift. They sat there breathing in the early morning air, neither one of them saying a word. Gradually the sky started to lighten, although they could not see the rising sun through the thick foliage. The droning of the crickets ceased and all was quiet. A slight mist hung just above the smooth surface of the water. Nothing moved.

Minutes later everything began to change again. One bird sang a note, then another joined in. Before long it was a symphony. A deer appeared on the far bank, dipping its head to the morning water. A heron and two egrets ventured past the edge of the shoreline, studying the shallow water intently for signs of breakfast. A gator surfaced not far away, the shore-birds taking notice. Robins and blue jays glided overhead while above them, atop the highest tree, lording over his realm, sat a lone osprey.

Jack remembered the first time he had brought Pat here. He remembered the wonder in her eyes, the astonished smile on her face, and the satisfaction he felt giving her this gift for the first time. It had been a cool morning, unlike this day, but Pat had shed her warm clothes *and* her bikini and plunged into the brisk water. He smiled to himself at the memory. He had almost tipped the boat that day following her lead.

Pat was having the same memory at the same time. *What better way*, she thought, *to relieve the burdens of yesterday*. She unzipped the light jacket she had worn, slipped out of her bikini, and dove joyfully into the water—again.

As she stood to jump off the boat, Jack kept his eyes on her. She was so beautiful. Admittedly she had been losing weight steadily for the last six months, but she still looked great. *How could anyone who looks that good be so sick?* he thought, but he didn't dwell on it. Instead, he pulled off his bathing trunks and jumped overboard.

They came up together not fifty yards from the gator. Jack put his arms around her.

"Are you afraid?" he asked.

"Of what, the gator? No. And I'm not afraid of the rest either, Jack. We'll get through it one way or the other. Remember this—no matter what happens, we'll always have this place and these moments to cherish."

She kissed him and Jack held her tight there in the water. He wished that he could squeeze her so hard that she would become a part of him and he could take up the battle with her. The gator eyed them cautiously.

Later, as they swam together in that narrow cove, they seemed to blend seamlessly with the mangroves, the shore-birds, the gator, and the osprey.

*   *   *

Jack had filed his motion for new trial the day after he met with Henry. He also filed a request for an evidentiary hearing, knowing that the court would have to first hear testimony from both sides and allow for cross-examination before deciding the motion for new trial. The motion would have to state a basis for the court to even consider an evidentiary hearing. Jack attached with it the affidavits of Wofford, Ted Griffin, and Anthony Webster, along with Webster's notes. He hoped that was enough.

The case was assigned to Judge Arthur Hendrick, a circuit judge in Dade County. Jack called every day to check on the status of his pleadings—something he normally wouldn't do, because it might irritate the judge, but he couldn't afford to adhere to the typical niceties of practice. Henry's time was running out.

Jack never found out whether it was his constant nagging or a lack of merit in his legal arguments, but five days later the judge denied both the motion for new trial and the request for evidentiary hearing. Jack didn't even have time to be disappointed—he had less than two weeks left. He called Wofford Benton to see if he had any ideas on how to handle this latest setback.

"Everything's been denied," he told Wofford. "I'm not sure whether I should file an appeal directly to the Florida Supreme Court or a motion for rehearing and ask the circuit judge to take another look at it. What do you think?"

A motion for rehearing was a request for the court—in most cases the same judge—to reconsider the original motion for new trial on the basis that it may have overlooked something. It was rarely granted.

"Did the judge give any reason for the denial?" Wofford asked.

"None. It was just a summary denial."

"A summary denial," Wofford mused. "The last bastion of cowards. Who was the judge?"

"Arthur Hendrick."

"Damn, I could have told you going in that Artie would deny

the motion. I've known him a long time. We went to law school together and we've maintained a pretty good friendship over the years,
although our politics are on opposite ends of the spectrum. He's a
wonderful guy in a lot of ways but he's a law-and-order man. It's all
black-and-white in Artie's world—no gray areas whatsoever. You'd
better just file your appeal, Jack. You won't get anywhere on rehearing."

Jack didn't respond right away. He was mulling over Wofford's advice when the judge spoke again. "Hang on, I've got a better idea—
move to recuse him. I'll give you another affidavit stating the nature
of our friendship over the years, including the fact that we room together at all the judicial conferences. Artie would die before he'd enter
an order finding me incompetent as an attorney, even if it was seventeen years ago. He simply shouldn't be on this case."

"Do you really think he would recuse himself?" Jack asked.

"He has to, especially if I put it in my affidavit, which I will, that
he could not be fair and impartial when it comes to me. I've even got
a case for you right here in Polk County—a similar situation. The attorney was a sitting circuit judge at the time of the motion, and all
the circuit judges in Polk County recused themselves from hearing the
case. You have an even stronger basis because of my close friendship
with Artie. Either he recuses himself or you have a winnable issue on
appeal."

"I'm running out of time, Wofford. Am I better off getting another
judge or just appealing this denial?" Jack favored an immediate appeal, but he wanted to hear what Wofford had to say.

"Think about it, Jack. You got a flat denial from Artie—no reason-
ing, nothing. Your chances on appeal with an order like that are slim
at best. On the other hand, if you get a new judge, you've got another
shot and you still have an appeal."

Wofford's analysis made perfect sense. "You're right," Jack said.
"I'll get started on both motions today."

"Take the recusal motion over yourself to his office and bring an
order for him to sign, and then wait for him to sign it. I'll fax you my
affidavit within the hour."

"You guys aren't going to be rooming together anymore," Jack told him. "He probably won't ever talk to you again."

"I don't give a shit, Jack. We've got more important fish to fry."

Jack was a little surprised at Wofford Benton's colorful language but not his message. Something had changed in the judge, and Jack thought he knew why: Wofford Benton had made a mistake seventeen years ago and he wanted to rectify it. The judge was committed to doing whatever was necessary to get Henry a new trial.

TWENTY

After Paul and David picked Benny out in separate lineups, Nick and Tony had him brought down to the basement of the station house for questioning. A uniform cop led him into a rectangular room with mirrors on both sides, one door, and no windows.

Benny had seen enough television shows to know what the mirrors were for and what was going to happen next. He remembered what Joe Fogarty told him: "Shut up and ask for a lawyer."

The cop sat him down in one of four chairs clustered around a steel table and left him with his hands still cuffed behind his back.

Nick Walsh and Tony Severino were standing in a separate room behind one of the mirrors when Benny and the cop walked into the interrogation room. Their lieutenant, Angelo Amato, was with them. Amato had already determined that Nick would do the questioning alone, and Nick could tell that Tony didn't take too well to that decision. Tony had found Benny, and Nick knew that Tony thought he should get the honors. At that point, it didn't matter to Nick who did the questioning. His thinking was about to change.

"The brass upstairs wants this case over yesterday," Lieutenant Amato told Nick before the detective left to enter the interrogation room.

Nick Walsh was a planner about most things. A good homicide detective had to be able to patiently and methodically build a case, often starting from the minutest details. However, when he walked into a room to question a suspect, Nick did not have a set agenda, a certain style, or even a specific list of questions. He learned in advance everything there was to possibly know about the man he was going to interrogate, and, of course, he knew every detail of the criminal investigation.

Nick's plan, if someone wanted to call it that, was to start a conversation with the suspect—about anything under the sun—and gradually, when a rapport had been established, get around to the crime at hand. It was a time-consuming process that required a lot of patience, although Nick could be forceful when necessary and was not above making threats. He simply let the circumstances dictate who he was going to be on any particular day.

Benny was a little guy, almost emaciated. There was quite a contrast between Nick with his huge hands and thick forearms and little Benny. Nick knew he had to soften his appearance if he was going to get Benny to open up. He rolled up the sleeves of his white shirt and opened his shirt collar, letting his tie hang loosely around his neck like an unwanted appendage. He walked in the room with his hands in his pockets and a slight smile on his face, although he didn't overdo it. This was a criminal investigation, after all.

"Mr. Avrile, I'm Detective Nick Walsh," he said to Benny, who was sitting uncomfortably on the edge of a chair with his hands still cuffed. Before Benny could answer, Nick approached him. "Let me get those cuffs off you," he said, "so you can be comfortable when we talk." He reached behind Benny and deftly removed the cuffs. Then he shook Benny's hand.

"Nice touch," Tony said to Lieutenant Amato on the other side of the mirror.

"You can call me Nick," Nick said to Benny.

The last thing Benny expected was to be shaking hands with his interrogator. He had envisoned the room darkening, the overhead lamp being pulled close to the table, and somebody knocking him around the place with body shots until he started talking.

"You can call me Benny," he said to Nick.

"How are you doing, Benny? Are they treating you okay?"

Benny thought he would ask for the moon right away since Nick was being so pleasant. "Not bad. Can you get me out of here, Nick?"

"Sorry, Benny. I can't do that, but we'll talk about what I can do for you in a few minutes. Why don't you tell me a little bit about yourself—where are you from?"

"Well, I was born in Spanish Harlem."

"Really? So was I—Ninety-seventh and Park."

"How about that," Benny replied. "I was born on Ninety-ninth between Third and Lex. My father grew up there but I didn't live there too long. My mother and father were drug addicts and she split from him after a couple of years, and we lived all over the city until she got strung out and I got put in a foster home."

"Sounds like an all-American childhood."

"Yeah. I guess the best I can say is, I survived."

Something happened at that point in the conversation that Nick Walsh had not and could not have anticipated. For some strange reason, as he looked at this skinny little Puerto Rican sitting in that chair trying to pretend he wasn't scared, he thought of his younger brother Jimmy, and a feeling of both empathy and sorrow for Benny and his plight rushed over him like a tidal wave.

They didn't look alike at all—Jimmy had been tall and fair-skinned. If anything, Jimmy had been more like Benny's father—he found his courage and his pleasure at the end of a needle. He was younger than Benny when he died of an overdose.

Nick had interrogated hundreds of drug addicts since Jimmy's death. *Why does this Benny conjure up memories of my brother?* he asked himself. *Why do I care about this guy?* Maybe it was the neighborhood connection, he didn't know for sure. He tried to put it from his mind.

"Benny, listen to me. You're not in a strong bargaining position here. I've got two eyewitnesses who have picked you out of a lineup and identified you as the person they saw leaning over a man who had just been shot on Seventy-eighth Street and East End Avenue on August twenty-ninth of this year."

Behind the mirror Angelo Amato and Tony Severino looked at

each other in surprise. Nick Walsh did not usually cut to the chase that quickly.

Benny didn't reply, so Nick continued.

"Which means you are the prime suspect in the murder. You may not know this, but we now have the death penalty in New York and our good governor was elected in part because of his sworn promise to use it. I can't get you out of here but if you work with me—if you tell me who the woman was who was your accomplice—maybe I can get you life imprisonment."

Nick watched as the words *death penalty* and *life imprisonment* hit Benny like a torpedo to the chest. The little man lost his breath for a minute and started hyperventilating. It wouldn't be long before he was spilling his guts. But Benny surprised Nick, although he couldn't keep his mouth shut totally, as Joe Fogarty had advised.

"I'm sorry Nick, I can't talk to you. I need to see a lawyer. This woman you're talking about. I don't know her name or where she came from."

Nick now had his opening with Benny's half answer about the woman, and he could easily drive a steel tank through that opening with a barrage of questions. Nobody was better at it than he was. He took one last look at Benny—and saw Jimmy again.

"All right, Benny. If that's what you want, we'll get you a lawyer." Nick stood up and walked out of the room.

Behind the two-way mirror, Tony and Angelo looked at each other in shock.

TWENTY-ONE

*E*verybody started to walk with an air of confidence, a swagger, after the team won their fourth game. They felt unbeatable. But it didn't last long. They lost the very next week to the Redskins by a score of thirteen to twelve. They missed both extra points, and that had cost them the game. They hadn't made an extra point all season.

"If we could have made just one kick we could have tied the game," the coach, Joe Sheffield, reminded the team several times afterward. Joe was angry at himself, not the team. He knew he should have worked harder on the kicking game before the season started. Normally he was just trying to field a decent team, not vie for a championship. This year was different. He shared that thought with the team.

"Now, we're going to have to win every game if we want to make the championship," he told them. It was the first time that he had mentioned the championship game since the season started—and it certainly got the boys' attention.

They won the next two games and were tied for the lead going into the last game of the season, against the Tremont Avenue Vikings.

Two teams in the league were consistent winners—the Tremont Avenue Vikings and the Mount Vernon Navajos. Both had great organizations and money behind them. Every year they got new jerseys and their equipment was updated. They leased a team bus for all their away games. The Navajos were tearing up the other division as they usually did. Both teams had that arrogance about them that comes with a winning tradition.

The odds were stacked against a motley crew like the Lexingtons beating both teams in back-to-back games in a three-week period.

The Vikings game started off slow. The Vikings were a running team, and they liked to pound it up the middle. They were finding it hard to run against the heart of the Lexingtons' run defense, however. It was only a matter of time before they changed their plan of attack.

"Watch the ends," Frankie O'Connor told everybody in the huddle. "They'll be testing us outside real soon."

Sure enough, on the very next play the Vikings halfback came around the left side. He got past Mikey, who was playing outside linebacker, but Rico and Floyd converged on him, catching him at the same time from opposite angles. The hits were clean and hard, but everybody in the vicinity heard a loud snap as the man went down.

"Oh shit, shit, shit," the guy shrieked. "Get off! Get the fuck off!"

Both Rico and Floyd scrambled to get off, but it was too late. One of the bones in the man's right leg had snapped just below the knee and was protruding from the skin. It hurt just to look at, and Johnny winced at the sight. Blood was everywhere, and the man lay on the field groaning. The referees stopped the game to call an ambulance.

Meanwhile, somebody brought the guy with the broken leg a beer and a cigarette, and as the wait extended from ten minutes to twenty, another beer and then another. Pretty soon the guy was sitting up talking to his buddies—despite the fact that one part of his leg was going one way and the other part the other way. The bone was still sticking out, but the blood had slowed to a trickle even though nobody had thought to apply a tourniquet.

When the ambulance pulled onto the field, everybody turned to look—except Johnny, whose eyes were riveted on the man with the broken leg. Johnny had seen him drop the cigarette and slump over.

Johnny ran to him. The man was not moving. "He's unconscious!" Johnny yelled at the top of his lungs. "Tell them to hurry up!"

The emergency guys tried to revive him on the field but couldn't. They transferred him to a stretcher, put him in the ambulance, and drove off. Before the sound of the siren had faded and the lights were out of sight, the referee blew his whistle and yelled, "Play ball!"

Johnny was bewildered. Football was the last thing on his mind, but he did what everybody else did. He huddled up and got ready for the next play.

"Stay focused," Frankie told them in the huddle. "They just lost their best guy."

Even though they had lost their best guy, the Vikings didn't give up. The game the Lexingtons absolutely needed to win ended in a tie.

They were standing on the sideline listening dejectedly to Joe Sheffield tell them they had "played a hell of a game" when a cop came up to the coach. There were three other cops on the far sideline talking to the Vikings players.

"Hey, Coach, can I talk to you for a minute?" the cop asked, motioning Joe Sheffield to step to the side. Joe looked at him and then at his nameplate, Dan Gillette. Dan was very fat, his face was purple and bloated, and he was breathing heavily from his walk across the field.

"Sure," Joe said, but he didn't move away from the team. If something was going to be said, it was going to be said in front of his players

"A player on the other team—I don't know his name—is dead," Officer Gillette said casually, like the kid had merely left the field to get a hamburger. He pointed to the other sideline. "Some of his teammates say he died because two of your people hit him illegally."

"Bullshit!" someone shouted angrily. Joe Sheffield stuck his hand up to quiet them.

"Whoever's making that accusation is wrong, Officer. It was a clean hit."

"Maybe so," Gillette replied. "But I gotta take the two involved in for questioning." He turned to the team. "Who were the two guys who tackled the dead kid?" If the incident hadn't been so tragic, Dan Gillette's attitude and choice of words would have been funny.

Nobody responded.

"I got no takers, huh?" Dan said, looking around at their faces. "Okay, we'll play it a different way." He turned toward the far sideline and whistled. Two Viking players came across the field.

"Can you guys pick those two tacklers out?" the fat cop asked when they arrived.

The taller, heavier one pointed right at Floyd. "That nigger back there is definitely one of them."

"*Watch your mouth,*" *Frankie O'Connor snapped at him.* "*That cop is gonna be gone in a minute and you're gonna be dealing with me.*" *The Vikings player didn't react to Frankie's words, although he had to have heard them.*

"*You!*" *Gillette yelled, pointing at Floyd.* "*Come up here. What about the other one?*" *he said, turning back to the two Vikings as Floyd slowly made his way out of the pack.*

They scanned the faces of the Lexingtons. One of them fixed right on Rico. Johnny saw it.

"*It was me,*" *Johnny said, stepping in front of Rico before the Vikings player could say anything. He didn't know why he did it. Maybe deep down he knew things would go better if he, rather than Rico, went to the station with Floyd.*

"*No it wasn't,*" *Rico said.* "*It was me.*"

"*No!*" *Johnny protested.*

Rico grabbed Johnny by the shirt with both hands and pulled him close. "*Listen,*" *he said.* "*Me and Floyd deal with cops all the time. We know how to get out of this. You—they'll have you feeling so guilty about this guy dying, you'll sign a full confession and still be apologizing as they cart you off to prison. Just shut up and let us handle this, okay?*"

Rico didn't wait for a reply. He turned and walked straight up to the cop.

"*All right, let's go down to the station,*" *Gillette said, motioning to Floyd and Rico.* "*You boys have some questions to answer.*"

TWENTY-TWO

Charlene Pope—Charlie—had been a certified public accountant at the firm of Harrel and Jackson in New York City for twenty years. She was one of those strange people who truly found the tax code interesting. She loved her work, and she especially loved the firm she was with. All her significant relationships were at Harrel. She'd met her ex-husband there. When they divorced, there was no question that he would be the one who would have to go. Charlie would never leave the firm. She also met her best friend at Harrel—Pat Morgan.

Pat was ten years older than Charlie, but they had common interests. They liked concerts and sports, good books and men—not necessarily in that order. Pat was a runner, Charlie was a swimmer, and both of them were in great shape. Pat was the taller of the two, although Charlie was almost five-six. She had large green eyes that complemented her auburn hair and a smile so warm it could melt an iceberg.

They took long walks together accompanied by Charlie's dog, Tinkerbell. Charlie was crushed when Pat moved to Florida but made frequent visits. As a senior member of the firm, she had plenty of vacation time stored up. And she loved Bass Creek.

"This place is like going back in time," Charlie had exclaimed on her initiation morning at Jack and Pat's special place on the river. "I feel like I'm part of it all—nature, I mean." She caught the way Jack and Pat smiled at each other. "What? What did I say?"

"You said what we all say," Pat told her. "That's why it's funny. Of course, if you didn't say it, Jack and I would have to drop you as a friend." Pat and Jack laughed, but they were half-serious.

Charlie felt like somebody had kicked her in the stomach the day she learned about Pat's cancer. Denise Nichols, another friend of Pat's and Charlie's, worked in Human Resources at Pat's old accounting firm, and Pat had called to check on her insurance coverage and to make sure the bills would be paid. Even though Pat had been working full-time as a teacher in Bass Creek, she was still considered a "substitute" because she had not received her certification from the state Department of Education. Consequently, she received no benefits from her teaching job.

Pat told Denise she was going to have some major bills but she was fuzzy on the details. Denise suggested Pat send the initial bills to her so she could personally verify the necessity, put them in line for payment, and make sure there were no glitches. When Denise saw the test results, she was shocked. She was almost in tears reading them when Charlie walked into her office to find out if she wanted to go to lunch.

"What's wrong?" Charlie asked, noticing Denise's teary eyes. Charlie had to do a little prying and persuading, but finally she got Denise to spill the beans. Try as she might, Denise could not keep the news from Charlie at that moment. Charlie was on the phone with Pat that night.

"I'll be on the plane tomorrow," she told Pat. "I just called to let you know I'm coming."

"Charlie, I'm fine. There's no need to come."

"Are you doing chemo?"

"Yeah."

"When does it start?"

"Monday."

"Okay, I'll be there Tuesday. How's Jack doing?"

"He's fine. We're both fine. Really we are."

"I'll just have to see for myself. I'll see you on Tuesday."

Charlie's pushiness was a godsend for Jack, who had been faced with a dilemma. He had to file the motion for recusal personally in Miami and wait for the judge to sign the order, no matter how long it took. But he also didn't dare leave Pat. Even though she looked okay, he knew she wasn't, and he refused to leave her alone under any circumstances. Charlie's arrival solved the problem. She was someone he trusted.

He stayed for an hour after Charlie arrived, to visit and catch up. He knew what a private person Pat was and that she hadn't wanted anybody to know about her illness. Now that Charlie was here, he could tell that she was delighted. They could sit and have tea and talk and maybe take a walk—so far, Pat was feeling no ill effects from her first chemo treatment. And she could tell Charlie her fears—things that he knew she might hide from him. As the two women cheerfully waved good-bye, he felt his burden of concern lighten a little. They seemed to want to get rid of him.

Jack handed the motions for rehearing and recusal and the order of recusal to Judge Hendrick's secretary and told her he was going to wait until the order of recusal was signed.

"I wouldn't suggest you do that," she lectured him, as only a judge's secretary could do. "He's got a busy day. He may not even get to it."

"Well, ma'am, I have a client on death row who is scheduled to be executed in a week, so I'm not going anywhere until the judge looks at these pleadings. You tell him that."

The judge's secretary looked taken aback by Jack's tone. She wasn't used to being talked to that way by attorneys. It wasn't Jack's way either, but he didn't have time to be polite. "I'll tell him what you said," she replied coldly.

"Thank you. I'll be in the waiting room."

Every half hour he walked into the judge's outer office just to let her know he was still there and to remind her, in case she'd forgotten, that this was a pressing matter. Jack suspected that the judge had already looked at the motion, heard from his secretary how rude Jack had been, and was making him wait until the last minute. Some things were just so predictable, even when a man's life was at stake.

Judge Hendrick called him in at 4:30.

"What is this, Mr. Tobin, some kind of joke? You don't like my ruling so you move to have me recused?"

"Judge, I waited all afternoon because I need an answer now as to whether you're going to sign this order or not. I didn't expect to talk to you, and I'm uncomfortable stating my position on this matter when the state is not present."

The judge ignored him. "I think your actions are despicable, Counselor. There is a finality to the law, and death-row inmates are not going to get out of their just deserts with shenanigans like this on your part."

Jack had had just about enough. "Look, there is a motion in front of you and an order. I've attached a case from Polk County that is right on point where ten judges recused themselves when a colleague's competence was questioned. I've got a wife at home sick with cancer and a client who is scheduled to be executed next week. With all due respect, Judge, I don't have time to listen to your petty insults. Now make a decision: either sign the order or don't."

Judge Hendrick glared at Jack. There was a long silence while he appeared to be weighing his options. Then he turned toward his office door.

"Martha!" he yelled to his secretary in the other room. His door had remained open during the entire conversation: the judge had wanted a witness. "Get Wofford Benton on the phone."

Wofford was waiting for the call. Jack had phoned earlier to say he was at the judge's office, and Wofford had assured him that he would take the call no matter what he was doing.

"He's on line one," Martha shouted back to the judge a few moments later.

"Wofford, Arthur Hendrick here. I've got a motion for recusal on my desk and an affidavit from you. Mr. Tobin has been here all afternoon and he has been rather insistent. I would say rather insolent as well."

"Well, Arthur, he's insistent and probably insolent because a man that I once represented is about to die," Wofford told his colleague, his voice booming on the loudspeaker phone. "Frankly, it was my idea to file the recusal motion. I made mistakes in that case, and I know you wouldn't grant a motion for a new trial on that basis. So sign the order and let Mr. Tobin get on his way."

Five minutes earlier, Arthur Hendrick had no intention of signing the order of recusal. Now he had Jack Tobin standing over him and Wofford Benton—whom he had called—telling him to sign it. He was boxed in pretty good.

Arthur Hendrick sighed heavily. "If you insist…and because you insist, Wofford, I'm going to sign this order."

He hung up the phone, signed the order, and handed it to Jack without ever looking up.

Jack left Judge Hendrick's office on the run. He had barely enough time to take the order to the clerk of court, file it, get another judge assigned, and take the court file and the motion for rehearing to her office—only to learn that Judge Susan Fletcher had already left for the day.

"Much better!" Wofford told him later that evening. "Susan Fletcher has a good mind and she's fair. The problem with her is that she's disorganized and we've only got a week. Sometimes it takes her a week to tie her shoes. You've got to call her office every day, Jack."

"Will do, Wofford. I'll keep you posted."

Pat and Charlie were having a grand old time back in Bass Creek while Jack was having it out with Arthur Hendrick. Their walk was short, mainly because Pat was tired. Then they sat out on the back porch by the pool drinking tea and catching up.

"How is that new guy you were dating—Ted?" Pat asked.

"Oh, he's history," Charlie replied. "It's a shame how people who really seem promising end up disappointing you. I thought Ted was the real deal—handsome, generous, caring—everything you look for in a man but never seem to find. About week five, the whining started. He had to have everything his own way. And he was so tight his ass squeaked."

Pat laughed. Charlie had a way with words. "Oh, that's too bad. With your looks you've never been without suitors. Any new prospects since then?"

"None that have passed the initial sniff test. I guess I'm getting jaded. I just can't stand to go out with a man who wants to do nothing all night but talk about himself. Ninety percent of them are like that, you know. The other ten percent are whiners like Ted."

Charlie had succeeded in one of her goals: Pat was laughing. It was time to get serious for a moment.

"What are they telling you, by the way?"

"It's not good. They say I have stage four cancer, which is usually terminal, but then they tell me I'm young and strong and don't give up hope."

"I didn't know it was that advanced, Pat."

"Yeah, it is. We haven't given up, though. I can't give up. I couldn't do that to Jack."

"I'm sure he's a mess, the way he adores you. I've never had a man feel that way about me."

"Yeah, I'm very lucky, Charlie. Jack is special."

Charlie leaned across the table and took her best friend's hands in hers.

"So is his partner."

TWENTY-THREE

A few days after he had cut short his interview with Benny Avrile, Nick Walsh was called downtown to the office of Assistant Chief Ralph Hitchens. Tony Severino was with him when he got the call.

"I wonder what the fuck that asshole wants," Nick said out loud.

"It's probably nothing," Tony replied, although Nick could tell from his tone of voice that Tony knew something.

"They could at least wait until the investigation is over," Nick continued, now trying to feel out his partner.

"Well, you know the brass on the big ones—the ones where their ass is hanging out there on the line with the rest of us," Tony quipped. "They want to declare victory at the earliest possible moment."

There were more surprises awaiting Nick when he arrived downtown. He was ushered right into the assistant chief's office, something that had never happened before in all his years on the force.

Ralph Hitchens was sitting behind his massive mahogany desk looking like an overnourished, stuffed turkey. He wasn't alone. Another gentleman, dressed in a dark blue suit, was with him. As Nick walked in, Hitchens accomplished the very arduous task of getting out of his chair and shaking hands with him as if they were old friends. Nick instinctively tightened up. He knew something bad was coming.

"Nick, I want you to meet Spencer Taylor from the district attorney's office. He's going to be trying this case." Taylor extended his hand and Nick shook it. He and Taylor had never met, but he had seen Taylor on television. Taylor was the chief assistant district attorney. He was not only their premier trial attorney, he was often the spokesman for the DA's office when Warren Jacobs, the district attorney, didn't deem the issue important enough to merit his personal appearance. To Nick Walsh, Taylor was a peacock— impeccably dressed, with a silky smooth voice that instantly made you want to check your pockets and tighten the belt holding your pants up. *Well, they obviously think this is an important case*, Nick thought to himself. *They're bringing out the big gun. But why am I meeting him now? The investigation isn't over.* Nick's question would be answered momentarily.

Hitchens started on a congratulatory note. "Nick, you and Tony did a real good job on this Benny Avrile case."

But... Nick was thinking.

"But," Hitchens continued, "we want you to shut it down. In fact, I'm taking you off the case. It's got nothing to do with the work you did—the detective work was great. I just want to shut it down."

"Can I at least ask why?"

Spencer Taylor cut in at that point. "You see, Nick—and don't take this as a criticism because it's not—you think like a cop. You want to run every thread down until every aspect of the case makes sense. Me, I think like a lawyer. I've got a suspect and I've got two eyewitnesses that put him at the scene at the time of the murder. And I've got a motive—robbery. It doesn't get any better than that. If you keep snooping around you may dig up enough dirt to give a good attorney a defense that at present doesn't exist."

"I don't understand," Nick said.

"Let's take this Lois woman, for instance," Taylor continued. Nick could tell from that remark alone that Taylor had studied his investigative file in great detail. "Right now there is just a vague reference to her as being a friend of Angie's. There's no concrete tie between her and Benny. There's no evidence that they even knew each other. She wasn't at the scene, as far as we know, and we don't even know what she looks like, other than she has long black hair like a million other people."

"And your point is, Counselor?" Nick knew where Taylor was going; he just wanted to hear him say it.

"My point is, I can live with that evidence. You start filling in some of those blanks, however, and my case starts getting weaker. You see what I mean?"

"Yeah, I see what you mean. Benny might have had a female accomplice, but you don't want me to continue to look for her because it might weaken your case, is that right?"

"Exactly," Taylor responded.

"So we just let a murder suspect go because we caught somebody else?"

Nick could instantly tell he'd struck a nerve. Taylor's warm smile turned to a sneer.

"Look, Walsh, I've tried to be nice about this. I heard about your interrogation of Avrile the other day. You treated him with kid gloves. Worse, you raised the issue of the woman and you didn't follow up. It's that kind of police work that fucks up a prosecution's case, so don't start talking to me about letting a suspect go. If I leave it up to you, both of them will walk."

Nick made a move toward Taylor who took a step back. "I ought to smack you in the fuckin' head, asshole," Nick said. "I was solving murder cases when you were still sucking on your mother's tit."

Hitchens butted in at that point and stood between the two men. "All right, that's it—end of discussion. Nick, the investigation is officially over at this point. We may reopen it down the road when Benny is convicted. For now it's over—got it?"

"Sure thing, Chief. You're the boss," Nick replied, still looking directly at Taylor who wasn't saying a word.

Nick was still seething as he walked out of the building. It never ceased to amaze him: somebody with money and a little fame gets killed and shitheads like Taylor start coming out of the woodwork and throwing their weight around. He was also sure that Tony Severino had broken the sacred code between partners and talked to the state attorney's office behind his back. He didn't have any hard evidence to support that suspicion but somebody had filled Taylor in on the particulars of Benny's interview and Nick remembered the guilt in Severino's voice earlier in the day.

What else did he tell them and why? Nick asked himself.

Maybe it is time to retire.

TWENTY-FOUR

*R*ico called Johnny at home on Sunday, the day after the Vikings game.
   "What happened?" Johnny asked.

"Piece of cake," Rico told him. "Floyd clammed up and I started ranting and raving about the ambulance drivers—how it took them forever to show up. Well, city cops don't wanna hear that, so after about an hour they let us go. It ain't over yet, but they ain't got shit on us."

"Rico, I don't think that's going to work. You get the wrong people mad at you and it usually backfires. Listen. Let me come down with you the next time they call you. I've got an uncle who's a cop. Maybe he'll help us."

"Don't worry about it, Johnny. Floyd and I can handle it. I appreciate the offer, though. I really do."

The team didn't find out until the following Tuesday that because of the common opponents they had beaten and the margins of victory, they had won a tiebreaker with the Vikings. They were going to the championship game after all. Joe Sheffield called every player personally to let him know. Practice was as usual on Thursday night, and there would be a full practice on Saturday. The championship would be the following Saturday.

On Thursday night, the coach opened auditions for a long snapper and a holder. It was a little late in the season, but Joe figured he had nothing to lose. Rico grabbed Johnny.

"C'mon, we're gonna volunteer."

"I don't know anything about that stuff!"

"There's nothing to know. You've got good hands. I'll be the long snapper and I'll teach you what to do."

Nobody else volunteered, so Joe Sheffield let Rico and Johnny go off
with Jimmy Walsh and practice kicking. He figured they knew their regular jobs pretty well.

For the next hour and a half they practiced extra points.

"It's all about timing," Rico told them. "Jimmy, when the ball hits
Johnny's hands, you gotta start moving toward it. You gotta trust that
Johnny is gonna get it down in time. Mayor, you just concentrate on catching the ball and getting it set. You don't even look at Jimmy." Johnny
wondered how Rico knew so much.

Rico had taken three balls from the equipment bag, so they got plenty of
repetitions in. It wasn't working too well at the start. Gradually, however,
Jimmy Walsh got Johnny's rhythm down and adjusted his approach to the
ball. Rico was remarkably good at the long snap. By the end of the hour
and a half, Jimmy was kicking four out of five balls through the uprights.
He was stoked.

"I knew I was a good kicker," he told them. "We just had no timing."

"Yeah, well, you don't get timing in one practice," Rico said. "Timing
comes from repetition. The timing you have now will be gone by next week."

"So what are we gonna do?" Jimmy Walsh asked.

"Can you get to the park at four o'clock every day next week?" Rico
asked him.

"Yeah," Jimmy replied.

"How about you, Johnny?"

"I think I can, yeah."

"All right, it's settled. We'll meet at the Hamilton statue every day next
week at four o'clock and then go to the big field and practice extra points."

They shook hands on it.

By the last practice on the Thursday before the championship game, the
new kicking team was very consistent. Jimmy Walsh was getting almost every ball through the uprights. Joe Sheffield was impressed. He announced
to the rest of the team at the end of practice that Rico, Johnny, and Jimmy
were the official new extra-point team. He had another announcement for
them as well.

"We're going to meet at 8:30 in the morning on Saturday in front of the Carlow East. The regulars at the Carlow chipped in and rented a bus so we can travel together to the game."

Everybody cheered. They wouldn't have to lug their equipment on the subway to the Bronx. They'd be traveling in style.

Joe Sheffield saved the final surprise for Saturday morning when they were all assembled in front of the big yellow school bus. Mary McKenna was there. She opened the bar up and Joe ushered everybody into the back of the room. He stood next to Mary, who was smiling from ear to ear. They were standing behind a table with two cardboard boxes in front of them.

"Mary called me the other night," Joe said, scanning their faces. "She didn't want you guys going up to the Bronx to represent this neighborhood looking like a bunch of ragamuffins. So we had some jerseys made." Joe pulled a jersey out of one of the boxes. It was white with short sleeves, kelly-green trim around the shoulders, and a shamrock on each sleeve. It had a big number ten in kelly green on the front and back. Everybody cheered when they saw it.

"Everybody has to have a number for the championship game," Joe went on. "I have already handed in a roster with your name and number on it. There's a program they'll hand out today, and each of you will be in it." More cheers. "So come up here when I call your name, pick up your jersey, and get on the bus. We've got to get moving."

Johnny watched Floyd as he took his jersey and walked over to Mary McKenna and gave her a big hug. Ever since the night Mary kicked Joe Meeley out of the bar they had developed a special relationship.

Joe Sheffield called Johnny's name. He got his jersey, number thirty-three, put it on over his T-shirt and headed for the bus. After a send-off like this, he was sure they were going to bring the championship trophy back to the Carlow.

Johnny sat next to Floyd on the bus ride to Mount Vernon.

"What happened with that police thing?" he asked. "Rico keeps saying nothing happened."

"It's over," Floyd told him.

"That's it? They just dropped it?"

"They didn't just drop it. They didn't have anything on us, really. I mean, it was just a tackle. Rico kept talking about the ambulance guys not showing up and I think it made them mad—you know, like he was trying to use it as an excuse even though it was absolutely true. If they had showed up in five minutes instead of twenty-five, that guy would still be alive. Anyway, the last time they called us down to the station they had an Army recruiter there. They told us they would drop all the charges if we agreed to sign up for four years. If we didn't, they were going to charge us with manslaughter."

"So you signed up?"

"Yeah. We had no choice."

"You could have fought it and won."

"Johnny, where we come from, getting rousted by the cops is a daily occurrence. Fighting with them only makes it worse. Part of me thinks that if they'd nabbed you instead of Rico, this wouldn't have happened. They don't have the balls to railroad a white kid from a nice neighborhood."

"I can change that. I can still say it was me."

"It's too late now. It's done."

Johnny was silent. Floyd was right. There was nothing either of them could do about it.

TWENTY-FIVE

Charlie decided to stay an extra week when she heard about Henry. Jack and Pat initially protested, but Charlie dismissed their objections.

"I'm staying. You've got things to do, Jack, and so do Pat and I. We're going to spend all your hard-earned money."

That was the end of it. Charlie's presence freed Jack up to concentrate on Henry's situation. Pat was always on his mind—but he could see that Pat was having a lot more fun with Charlie than she would have with him.

He called Susan Fletcher's office every day that week about the motion for rehearing, but he never managed to speak to her.

"She knows about your motion, Mr. Tobin," her secretary told him. "I give her your message every day. She's very busy. She's in court right now."

With just three days to go before the execution, Jack called Wofford.

"I can't get through to Judge Fletcher. I don't think she wants to overturn a decision of one of her colleagues, so she's just ignoring it and letting the time run out."

"You're probably right," Wofford told him. "Have you talked to Henry?"

"Every day for about two minutes. I've kept him informed, but I need to see him in person. I've got a federal habeas corpus action prepared, but I need his permission to file it."

"You have to talk him into it?" Wofford asked.

"He's a stubborn man. It was a chore to get him to agree to the original motion. He's just sick of the system."

"I'll tell you what, Jack. You go see Henry, and I'll take care of the Susan Fletcher problem. Trust me. One way or another, you are going to have an order."

"Okay, Wofford, I'll leave Susan Fletcher in your hands."

The next morning, Jack left for Starke, where he planned to stay until Henry either got a stay or was executed. The last time he'd taken such a trip, Pat went with him. She knew the ordeal he was in for. She held his face in her hands as she kissed him good-bye.

"Remember that I'm with you in this, right next to you. I know that you will do everything for Henry that is humanly possible because that is who you are. I'll be praying for both of you."

Henry doesn't know how lucky he is, Jack thought as he set out on his long journey to North Florida. *Having Pat as an advocate before the Almighty is as good as you can get.* He was hopeful suddenly that the Almighty, seeing the sorry shape that he was in, would give Pat a little more time before He called her home.

On the eve of his execution, Henry's handlers were giving him all kinds of special treatment. He was allowed to be with Jack in their special meeting room unfettered by handcuffs and shackles. The two men shook hands for the first time.

"You did a good job, Counselor. You did everything you possibly could for me. Remember that."

"We're not done yet, Henry. Not by a long shot. I've got a habeas corpus petition to file in federal court. There's a study that says the lethal injection method is cruel and unusual. I just need your permission to file it."

"The answer is no, Jack. You may not be done, but I am. I'm not going to let them strap me on that gurney tomorrow night just to release me at the last minute so they can do it again a month from now."

"Why do you say that?"

"Do you honestly think they're going to stop executing people because there might be a flaw in the lethal injection process? They've gone from the noose to the electric chair to lethal injection—which, by the way, is optional. They still have Old Sparky. What I'm saying, Jack, is if I don't get a new trial and I'm not found innocent, I don't want to play their game. Let's get it over with."

Jack didn't know what to say, so he said nothing. Henry had a right to decide when enough was enough. It was now up to Judge Susan Fletcher whether Henry would live or die.

Wofford Benton had thought that because he was a judge Susan Fletcher would take his calls. After trying every hour on the hour for a day and a half, he realized he was sorely mistaken.

On Thursday, October 29, 1998, the day Henry Wilson was scheduled to die, Judge Susan Fletcher was in her courtroom in downtown Miami presiding over preliminary hearings when an overweight, balding man in his mid-sixties walked in and came straight down the middle aisle. He strode deliberately past the bar that separated the people from the judge, her staff, and the attorneys. The courtroom was full with those who were being brought before the court, their attorneys, the state's attorneys, sheriff's deputies, and numerous other spectators and court personnel.

An attorney was standing at the podium arguing on behalf of his client when the intruder interrupted him in mid-sentence.

"Excuse me, sir. I'll just be a minute," the man said to the attorney, turning to the judge, who had not yet recognized him. "Your Honor, I am Judge Wofford Benton from Polk County and I have been trying to get in touch with you for two days. I want to talk to you about a motion that is pending before you regarding a man who is about to be executed today—Henry Wilson. I would like to know why you have not addressed that motion."

There was dead silence in the courtroom. All eyes were on Judge Fletcher.

Wofford had learned a long time ago that transparency created its own pressure. He knew that he would not have gotten anywhere if he had gone to the judge's chambers and tried to see her. Now that he had stated his position in open court, she would have to address the issue. He wasn't just another lawyer that she could tell to sit down. He was her peer.

Susan Fletcher glared at Wofford. They knew each other, although not very well.

"We're going to take a ten-minute recess," she announced as she stood up. "Judge Benton, if you will follow me, we'll discuss this matter in my chambers."

As soon as they were in chambers and the door was closed, Judge Fletcher erupted.

"How dare you walk in my courtroom and make an accusation like that?"

"I didn't make an accusation. I made a statement that is true. You have not addressed the motion and today is the last day."

"What's your stake in this, Wofford? Arthur Hendrick has already denied the motion. The tactics this Tobin guy has used—and I understand he has a very good reputation on the civil side here in Miami—these tactics border on the unethical. He's forum-shopping and I don't want to be part of it."

"Wait a minute, Susan. He moved to recuse a judge for a valid reason. Artie Hendrick signed the order because he had to. That's not forum-shopping. Why the hell do you think they have the rule? It was my suggestion, by the way. And you shouldn't be prejudging his motives without reading the damn motion."

"Your suggestion? You still haven't told me what your stake in this is. No matter—you are way out of bounds. Coaching a lawyer on a pending case? The Judicial Qualifications Commission will have your ass, Wofford."

"I represented the man on death row seventeen years ago.

He's there because of my incompetence. I'm having a difficult time with that, Susan, so I'm now going to see that he gets justice no matter what it costs me."

"It might cost you your seat on the bench."

"So be it. This man may be innocent, and I'm not going to sit idly by and watch him die because of something I neglected to do seventeen years ago."

Susan sighed. "Even if I look at this motion, I might not think it merits an evidentiary hearing or a new trial. Seventeen years is a long time. I'm sure every stone has been turned over."

"Just look with an open mind, that's all I ask. Don't think about the seventeen years. Don't think about Artie Hendrick's recusal. Just read the motion. If you think the facts merit an evidentiary hearing, then enter an order setting one. That will stop the execution. Here is the number to call." Wofford handed her a card. "If you don't think it merits an evidentiary hearing, then enter an order denying the motion."

Susan Fletcher looked at him.

"All right, Wofford. I'll read the motion this afternoon. I make no promises, however. If there is no new evidence that warrants a hearing, I'm going to deny it. What time is the execution scheduled for?"

"Six o'clock."

"All right. Now if you'll excuse me, I've got a courtroom full of people I've got to get through before this afternoon."

TWENTY-SIX

Sal Paglia's American dream was pretty much like everybody else's—a good career, a nice car, a big house, and a loving family. And he'd almost made it. His criminal law practice had been going fairly well, he drove a Cadillac, and he owned—along with the bank, of course—his own two-story home in the Bronx not too far from his office. He'd made a mess of the family part, however.

Sal was a little guy and part of his Napoleon complex was his perceived sexual prowess. He represented a boatload of hookers, so blow jobs were a regular component of his fee. Every now and then, when a high-class hooker got busted—it wasn't every day because *high-class hooker* and *the Bronx* were words that usually didn't go in the same sentence—Sal would require the whole enchilada, and then some. He was collecting the "then some" one night at his office from Brigitte Babcock—aka Amy Stevens, originally from Peoria, Illinois—when his wife, Cynthia, showed up unexpectedly.

Cynthia Paglia had been suspecting Sal of infidelity for some time. The clue was always the same—a late night at the office, followed by Sal dragging his ass through the door smelling of alcohol and perfume. One thing about Sal—even though they had been married for ten years, he was still as horny as a teenager on his first date. All she had to do was express an interest in sex and he was ready—except on those nights he worked late at the office. Then he was dead to her in every way.

Cynthia desperately needed to resolve her suspicions and she decided to do it personally. She had an office key made early one Saturday morning while Sal was sleeping. The very next time he called to say he'd be working late—the night he was with Brigitte Babcock—Cynthia hung up the phone, jumped in the car, and drove directly to his office on Webster Avenue about twenty minutes from the house. Slipping in very quietly, she tiptoed past the vacant secretary's desk and cracked open the door of Sal's inner sanctum. Her eyes scanned the room. She smelled the pot first. Then she saw the half-empty bottle of Chivas Regal on the corner of the desk and a woman all decked out in a beautiful black leather outfit—complete with boots, garter belt, stockings, and one of those designer whips with the little tassels on the end. She was standing over a nude male who had his head in the seat of an upholstered high-back chair and his buttocks raised toward the whip.

Although the man's face was completely obscured, Cynthia instantly recognized her husband. She could no longer control herself. Bolting into the room, she pushed the surprised Brigitte out of the way, raised her right leg high in the air, swung it forward and kicked Sal right in the ass.

"Oooh!" Sal moaned. This infuriated Cynthia even more. She reared back and kicked him again.

"Oh my God!" Sal screamed in ecstasy. "Do it again, Brigitte."

Cynthia stood there for a moment looking at him with disgust. Then she turned to Brigitte, who was cowering in a corner of the room.

"He's all yours," Cynthia said and headed for the door.

Somewhere in the recesses of his brain, beyond the booze and the dope, Sal heard his wife's voice and—even though his mind fought against the reality of the circumstances—realized his predicament. But he didn't move. He simply peered through his legs at Brigitte and noticed that his dick had gone limp.

When he returned home the next day with a story about how some client had slipped a tab of acid into his coffee, his wife and two kids were already gone. A few weeks later, Cynthia's lawyer filed an emergency motion with the court, and Sal was tossed out of his two-story home. He still got to pay the mortgage, however, which meant that he could only afford to rent a cheap one-bedroom flat in a high-rise not far from the office. Part of Sal's dream had slipped away forever.

Luckily for Sal and his clients, he was a somewhat better lawyer than he was a husband. He did mostly small-time stuff, but over the course of fifteen years he had handled several murder cases, all of them court-appointed except for the Russell O'Reilly case, the one that had finally brought him some notoriety. Russell O'Reilly was accused of the heinous murder of a blind girl. The case and Russell's lawyer, Sal Paglia, were in the news every day for six months. In the end, Russell was exonerated because the DNA of the skin found under the blind girl's nails—skin which came from her scratching her assailant—did not belong to Russell O'Reilly.

The O'Reilly case had brought Sal a steady stream of clients, but it was now three years old and had lost its legs. Sal was starting to have problems meeting his monthly obligations at the office. He had also taken up two new hobbies to fill the void caused by the absence of his wife and children—drinking and gambling—and he was doing a poor job controlling either of them. He was in to Beano Moffit, the local loan shark, for thirty thousand dollars when fortune seemed to smile on him once again.

A short, stocky Latin man with muscular forearms and calloused hands walked into his office early on a Wednesday morning.

"I'd like to see Mr. Paglia," he told Sal's secretary, Hazel.

"Do you have an appointment?" Hazel asked without looking away from the game of solitaire she was playing on her computer.

"No, I don't," the man replied. "I live a couple of blocks away. I thought I'd just stop in."

"Sorry," Hazel told him, her eyes still glued to the computer. "Mr. Paglia is a busy man. He can't see you without an appointment."

The man didn't go quietly as most of them did. He stood his ground. "I've got cash," he said, "and I'm willing to pay today. It's a matter of life and death."

Those words meant nothing to Hazel, who was unaware of the dismal financial status of her boss. But to Sal—who was sitting in his office with the door slightly ajar throwing paper airplanes at the trash can and wondering how he was going to pay the rent, make payroll, and keep his legs from getting broken—they sounded like sweet music.

"Send him in, Hazel," Sal shouted.

"But he doesn't have an appointment," Hazel protested.

"Send him in," Sal shouted back.

Hazel gave the man a dirty look but ushered him in to Sal's office before returning to her game.

Sal came rushing from behind his desk, his right hand extended and a huge smile on his face. "Sal Paglia. Nice to meet you."

The man shook his hand. "Luis Melendez," he replied. "Nice to meet you too." He did not smile.

Sal motioned Luis to one of his upholstered high-back chairs, the same one where, not many moons ago, his wife had caught him in a very awkward position. Luis sat down. His eyes roamed the room as Sal went back behind his desk.

Sal knew that his building was not much to look at from the outside and the neighborhood was, to put it kindly, a little seedy—a good place to find criminal clients but with few other redeeming values. His inner sanctum, however—the place where he coaxed the money from the clients, among other things—was top-shelf: plush maroon carpeting, rich mahogany paneling, a massive desk so large that Sal looked a little puny sitting behind it in his equally large and impressive burgundy leather lawyer chair.

"So what can I do for you?" Sal asked, changing his expression to one of pleasant, professional concern.

"My son is in jail and he's been charged with murder."

Dollar signs flashed in Sal's eyes but he maintained his composure. "How long has he been there?"

"Not too long—a couple of months," Luis replied. "He's had several minor hearings about one thing or another. The public defender is representing him."

"What's your son's name?"

"Benny Avrile."

Sal noted that father and son did not have the same last name, but there was something else. He'd heard that name before, although he couldn't remember where. Then it came to him. The case had been on the front page of all the papers and was still getting coverage months later. The trial for sure would be big news, maybe even international. Sal started to salivate.

Benny Avrile had killed some rich guy. *What the hell was his name?* Ah, it didn't matter. What mattered was that little Benny's father was sitting in front of him, offering the case up to him on a silver platter. The publicity alone would guarantee him another three years in the black, win or lose. He could pay off Beano, who was starting to pressure him a bit. Sal wanted to kiss Luis Melendez on the spot, but he had to play it close to the vest. After all, there was money to be had *right now*.

"Why are you coming to me?" Sal asked, the words slipping out of his mouth before he could catch them.

"I don't want the public defender representing my son. He's already had three different lawyers in two months. I'm afraid he'll get assigned to somebody new on the day of trial who won't know anything about his case. I remember you got a guy off a few years back—the one who was accused of killing the blind girl. Some people in the neighborhood say you're pretty good, too."

Sal wondered who had recommended him. Sometimes he paid people in the neighborhood to talk him up in criminal circles—maybe it was one of those guys. He'd find out soon enough. Somebody would be sniffing around, looking for a bonus.

But now it was time to talk about the money. "You know, my services don't come cheap. It's expensive to try a murder case. Very expensive."

"I've got five thousand dollars in cash," Luis said without hesitating.

"That's not even a third of what I would require up front."

"It's all I got."

Sal had heard that line a million times. If this guy had five grand in cash, he could come up with fifteen, no problem. It was just a case of helping him find it. It didn't matter, though. Sal was taking the case regardless. He just needed to squeeze Luis for as much as he could.

"Do you own a home?"

"Yes."

"Do you have any equity in it?"

"I'm not sure I understand what you're talking about."

"How long have you owned your home?"

"Seven years."

"Do you have a mortgage?"

"Yes."

"How long have you had that?"

"Since I bought the place."

Those answers told Sal all he needed to know. Luis was not a sophisticated businessman. He didn't know that he had equity in his home and that he could refinance and pull cash out to pay for the legal services of Sal Paglia.

"Luis, I've got great news for you. I'm going to take your son's case, and I'm going to take it for the initial five thousand. And I'm also going to help you with the paperwork to refinance your house so you can get the additional twenty thousand dollars you're going to need to pay me through the trial."

Sal said the words in such a way that Luis felt like thanking him for being so helpful and kind. He promptly took five thousand dollars out of the front right-hand pocket of his pants and handed it to Sal, who stashed it in a desk drawer.

"I'll file a notice of appearance first thing in the morning," Sal told him, handing him a receipt for the cash. Luis thanked him several times before heading for the door, but stopped just as he reached it.

"One other thing," Luis said before Sal ushered him out.

"What's that?" Sal asked.

"Don't tell Benny you got the money from me. He must never know I'm involved."

That was okay with Sal. He could put ethical considerations aside for the greater good—at least, for *his* greater good. It wasn't going to fly with the court, however. Benny was the client. He needed to approve of the arrangement. Technically, Benny could agree that he didn't want to know who was paying, but Sal didn't want to go down that road unless he had to.

"Sit," Sal said, steering Luis back to the infamous chair again. "Tell me why you don't want your own son to know that you're paying for his lawyer."

Luis sat down again. He took out a cigarette. "Mind if I smoke?" he asked.

Sal was a smoker himself. He took his own pack out of his pocket. "I'll join you," he said, handing Luis an ashtray.

"He doesn't know me. I never married his mother." Luis took a long drag on his Marlboro. "We lived together for about two years after Benny was born. We were both on drugs. She left. I didn't see her after that. Years later, when I got clean, I couldn't find them. That's it. That's the story."

"So you assume he doesn't want to hear from you?"

"Yeah."

"But you don't know?"

"No, I don't."

"How do you know that this Benny Avrile is your kid?"

"The name, the age, and the picture in the paper. He's a dead ringer for me. Benny's my kid, all right."

"And you want to do this because you feel you owe it to him?"

"Yeah. It's a little bit more complicated than that, but that's essentially what it's about."

Sal thought about his own kids for a minute. He hadn't seen them since his wife left. *Maybe*, he said to himself, shrugging his shoulders.

"Here's the deal, Luis. You need to talk to Benny about this. It's a legal requirement and I can't have it blow up in my face. I've got a reputation to uphold." Those who really knew Sal would have gagged at that last remark.

"I don't think that's such a good idea," Luis replied. "It's not that I don't want to talk to him. It just might be better coming from somebody else."

There was no way Sal was giving the five thousand back. "Well, it's going to be either you or me, Luis. I assure you, if Benny's reluctant after talking to you and finding out the money's from you, I will eventually convince him that it is in his best interests to have me represent him. But I think you should talk to him first."

"All right, I'll give it a shot," Luis said reluctantly.

Benny was lying on his cot in his cell feeling downright miserable. He'd been in jail before, but the charges had never stuck and he was always out in a day or so. This time it was different. He'd been here for two months already, and the prospects didn't look good. Hell, they weren't even trying to reduce his bail. His stomach was in a perpetual state of violent upheaval from the swill that masqueraded as food, not to mention the ever-present smell of ammonia, which they used to mop the floors. After the first few days he'd refused to eat, but then he got so dehydrated and hungry he had to—his body demanded it. When he did, the churning in his stomach started all over again.

Why do guys say they want to come back here after they get out? he asked himself on one of the many days he had absolutely nothing to do. *Man, I was homeless and I lived a lot better than this.*

While Benny was contemplating death as a pleasant alternative to his present condition, two guards approached his cell.

"You've got a visitor," one of them shouted at Benny.

"Who?" Benny asked.

"How the hell should I know?" the guard responded. "What am I, your press secretary or something? I want you to stand up and turn around and face the wall. Now."

Benny immediately did as instructed. There was no percentage in playing games with these guys.

"Now I want you to kneel down and put your hands behind your back." Benny again did as instructed. He'd never had to follow this procedure before when the public defender visited. *This must be special treatment reserved for murderers who have visitors*, he concluded.

"Now we're going to open this cell door and handcuff you, but I don't want you to move until I tell you to. Do you understand?" Benny just nodded. "I need a verbal response," the guard told him.

"Yes, sir," Benny replied.

"That's better."

As they led him handcuffed out of the cell and down a long corridor, Benny wondered who the hell it was that was coming to visit him. He knew it wasn't his public defender. They only showed up a few minutes before a scheduled hearing, and he had no hearings coming up. There was nobody else. *Maybe it's Tillie*, he thought. *Maybe he misses me.*

TWENTY-SEVEN

*T*he Navajos had won the Greater Metropolitan League Championship four years in a row, and they appeared to be on their way to
another one. They were undefeated, and their average margin of victory was
twenty-one points. They didn't like to merely defeat their opponents—they
liked to crush them. They wore the Green Bay Packers colors—not just
shirts like the Lexingtons, but everything: shirts, pants, socks, helmets. Hell,
they even had their own cheerleaders. To top matters off, the Mount Vernon
field was their home field. The deck was certainly stacked in their favor.

Frankie O'Connor huddled the team up before the opening kickoff.

"All right, guys, this is what all the sweat all year was about. Let's show
these blowhards how to play football."

The Navajos took the opening kickoff and marched down the field for
a touchdown. Their kicker made the routine extra point, and on the ensu-
ing change of possession, they forced the Lexingtons to punt. A twenty-yard
punt return gave them excellent field position, and they scored again. After
the second extra point was made, the score stood at fourteen to nothing and
the game was only five minutes old. The defense stiffened up after that.
Still, at halftime, with the score fourteen to nothing, the Lexingtons looked
like a defeated team.

Frankie O'Connor gave an impassioned speech in the locker room at
halftime.

"Those guys are a bunch of prima donnas!" he told them. "Yet they're
playing like a team. We fought hard to get to this game. We've had each
other's backs the entire season. Now let's go out there and show it!"

It was a short speech, but it had the desired effect. Everybody ran out of the locker room with fire in his eyes.

They fought back in the second half, and with three minutes left in the game the score was fourteen to twelve. Even with their new kicking team, the Lexingtons had missed both extra points. Jimmy Walsh was kicking well and they had their timing down, but Rico was too small to play center and the middle linebacker was blowing by him every time and blocking the kicks.

It didn't look like the team would have another opportunity either. The Navajos had the ball, and they weren't about to give it up. It was third down and four yards to go. A first down would seal the victory.

The next play was like slow motion for Johnny. He watched the quarterback take the ball from the center and set up for the pass. The wide receiver came off the line and ran five yards downfield, then gave his first fake and planted his opposite foot. Johnny reacted instinctively, moving toward the area where he expected the ball to be thrown. He cut right in front of the receiver and caught the ball in full stride. There were two linemen to avoid, and then it was off to the races. He got past the first one, but the second one caught him by the ankles, slowing him down just enough to allow the quarterback to make a game-saving tackle on the twenty-yard line.

All the Lexingtons went crazy when Johnny intercepted, and they were still going crazy when he ran to the sideline after the play was over. Rico slapped him on the helmet. "Way to protect that turf, Mayor." Johnny laughed and slapped his hand.

The ball was now on the Navajos' twenty-yard line: there was less than two minutes left, and they were down by two. However, they only gained three yards on the next three plays. With ten seconds left, there was only time for one more play. The euphoria of minutes ago had vanished. The Lexingtons' sideline was hushed. Joe Sheffield called a time-out and summoned the entire offensive team over to the sideline.

"What do you suggest?" he asked Bobby Schmidt, his quarterback. They both knew there was only one call—a long pass into the end zone. Standing behind the coach, Johnny looked over at Rico, who was about ten feet away. Rico didn't say a word. He knew exactly what Johnny was thinking. Before the quarterback could respond, Johnny broke in. He hadn't said ten

words to Joe Sheffield all year, but now, at the most important moment of the most important game of the season, he was interrupting the coach and his quarterback.

"Coach, we can do it."

"Do what?" Joe asked, agitated by the interruption.

"Kick a field goal. Doug can help Rico block the middle linebacker and Jimmy can kick it through." Doug Kline was the left guard.

It was an absurd suggestion. They hadn't made an extra point all year and hadn't even attempted a field goal. Joe Sheffield looked out on the field and saw the Navajo defensive backs positioned well back near the end zone. A long pass was almost futile. He looked at Bobby Schmidt, who shrugged his shoulders. "It's as good a shot as any, Coach," he said.

"Doug, are you sure you can get that middle linebacker?" Joe asked.

"Don't worry, Coach. He's mine," Doug replied.

Still Joe Sheffield hesitated. "Aw, what the hell. Let's give it a shot. Jimmy, get in there and kick that ball through the uprights."

Johnny, Rico, and Jimmy raced onto the field with the rest of the offensive team and huddled up. "Just like we did in practice," Rico calmly told them. They broke the huddle and lined up.

"Hike!" Johnny shouted. Rico hiked the ball. As he did, the middle linebacker headed straight toward him. Off to the left, Doug Kline went airborne. As the linebacker reached Rico, Doug blindsided him.

Rico's hike was a perfect spiral. Johnny caught the ball and set it in one fluid motion. As he put the ball on the ground, Jimmy Walsh took a step forward and swung his right leg back and then threw the ball. It sailed off the turf. All eyes stayed on the football as it turned end over end toward the goalposts. The referees hesitated a moment as the ball passed the uprights before raising their hands and signaling that the kick was good. Just then the clock ran out.

Johnny, Rico, and Jimmy were hugging each other, jumping up and down.

"We did it! We did it!" Rico was yelling at them.

The rest of the team caught them on the field in mid-jump, and they were buried in a swarm of white and green jerseys. Joe Sheffield stayed on the sidelines and took it all in. It was a moment he would remember forever.

*   *   *

Coach Sheffield came to the Carlow East that night with the championship trophy. The Carlow regulars were as excited as the team, and nobody more so than Mary McKenna.

"Three cheers for Mary!" Frankie yelled out. And everybody cheered.

"Coach!" Frankie said when the cheers had died somewhat. "Will you say a few words?"

They got a chair for him and he stood on it with the trophy in his right hand. The place went dead silent.

"As you guys know, I'm not much for words. I just want to say that this might be a small league and an insignificant victory to the outside world, but I could not be prouder of a group of guys than I am of this team, and I would have said the same thing to you had you lost today. You are a team. You are so much of a team that I'll bet none of you noticed throughout the entire season that you were the only integrated team in this league. That's right. Some of you are colored." Everybody in the bar laughed. Joe put his hands up to quiet them.

"There are leaders on this team who I assure you will be leaders in life. And there were friendships made that will also last a lifetime. For me, I will always cherish this trophy."

Everybody clapped as Frankie helped Joe off the stool. There were more than a few misty eyes in the place. Johnny was standing with his buddies, Rico and Floyd.

"I'm with the coach," Johnny told them. "I'll never forget this season. And you guys are two of the leaders he was talking about."

Floyd hoisted his glass. "To friendships that will last a lifetime," he said, and all three tapped their glasses together before draining them.

They went their separate ways after that night, assembling only one more time as a team—six months after the Navajos game. They met at the Carlow East before heading to the funeral up in Harlem. Mary McKenna went with them. Her good friend Pink Floyd had been killed in Vietnam.

TWENTY-EIGHT

Jack spent several hours with Henry on his execution day.

He arrived around noon. As six o'clock came closer and closer, Henry's treatment got better and better. He and Jack were taken to a room with a couch and two comfortable chairs. All Henry's shackles were removed. He seemed unusually calm for a man about to die. Jack had not heard anything from Wofford, so they had no idea whether Judge Fletcher was going to intervene or not.

"Henry," Jack asked after a few minutes of awkward silence, "tell me how you have come to be so articulate." They were sitting in the two chairs facing each other. Of course, the chair Henry was sitting in was too small for him.

"I surprised you, didn't I?"

"You sure did."

"Well, I've had a lot of time in this prison. After a while, I decided I was going to make use of it. I started reading everything I could read—educating myself. Eventually, I got a letter from an inmate—a guard had told him about me—asking for my help. I filed a petition on his behalf and got him a reduced sentence. After that, I was a jail house lawyer. I'll bet I've written over a hundred briefs."

"So how come you never filed a brief on behalf of yourself? You knew about the Brady rule."

"I'm not exactly sure. Maybe I knew I would only have one shot, and I didn't want to waste it by filing myself. The appellate hill becomes a mountain when you're representing yourself. I figured somebody would come along before they gave me that final cock-tail."

"And that somebody was me." *And I haven't been able to get it done.*

"There are some good things that are going to come from this ex-ecution, Jack," Henry told him. "I'm pretty sure I'm going to see my mother. I just have a good feeling about that. We've got a lot to talk about, her and I. The other good thing is, I'm getting out of here. Seventeen years in a six-by-nine cell is enough. I *almost* prefer death."

"You never talked about your mother before."

"There's not much to tell. She died when I was six."

"Really? From what?"

"A series of very bad decisions. My mom was a heroin addict. All her boyfriends were drug addicts who used to beat the shit out of her and me. It wasn't a model childhood."

"I can only imagine."

"No you can't, Jack. There's nothing in your universe that could help you imagine what happened to me. There was a little creek by the apartment complex where we lived. One day I couldn't find my mother anywhere. She hadn't come home the night before, which was rare even for her. I looked everywhere. I found her down by the creek. She was lying there, naked—naked and dead. Her latest boyfriend had strangled her for who knows what reason. They finally caught him, but that didn't do me any good. I went from the hell of living with my mother to the hell of foster care. From getting the shit beat out of me by drug addicts to getting the shit beat out of me by people who were paid by the government. I can't even tell you what happened to me in foster care. It was worse than anything that goes on in here."

"And you're looking forward to seeing your mom after all that?"

"Yeah. She had her own hell. Mom and I can compare notes. I'm just going to hug her and tell her I love her and she's going to tell me how sorry she is and we'll go from there. I think it's going to be lovely."

"I hope that's the way it is, Henry—I mean, if the worst happens." Jack felt awkward and a little guilty that they were having this con-versation at all.

"It will, Jack. I feel it. I'm not very religious—as a matter of fact, I think I'm going to throw that minister out on his ear when he comes to pray with me. I believe in a higher power, though, and I just feel closer to that power and to my mother lately. I can't explain it."

Henry stood up at that point. He towered over Jack, who was still seated. Henry's inner serenity at this most crucial time in his life made him seem otherworldly to Jack—larger than life itself.

"Jack, why don't you go home now? You 'on't need to hang around here and hold my hand."

"I'm not going anywhere, Henry, until we have a final decision one way or the other."

Henry's last meal was scheduled for three o'clock, and he invited Jack to be his guest. It was a little unusual, but the warden approved the request. They had broiled grouper and broccoli. Any Las Vegas bookie, looking at the size of Henry, would have taken odds that it would be a porterhouse with baked potato and sour cream.

They were mostly silent during the meal. Henry's face brightened, however, when they brought in dessert—tiramisu.

"I've been reading about this stuff in books and magazines for years, Jack. I've never actually had it before, but I've been dreaming about it."

Henry wasn't disappointed. The tiramisu was delicious.

The guards made Jack leave right after dinner. The final preparations were about to begin. As the two men said their good-byes, Henry took Jack's hand and held it.

"I just want you to know that I could never have had a better person fight for me than you. I know that you did everything that could be done, even though you weren't ever sure in your own mind whether I was innocent or not."

"How did you know?" Jack asked.

"You told me so in the beginning, and you never told me that you changed your mind. Right up to now. Why did you stick with me?"

"It was my wife. She convinced me to stay with your case—not to prejudge you."

"Well, that is one hell of a woman you've got there, Jack. Here's the truth. I'm guilty as hell—of a lot of very bad things that I never got caught for. However, I did not kill Clarence Waterman."

Jack was glad that his efforts were not in vain—that Henry was truly innocent. Unfortunately, at that particular moment, Henry's confession did not make him feel any better. Guilty or innocent, Henry was about to die.

"It's not over yet, Henry. We still have time. Something could happen. I'll be here with you right to the end."

"Jack, I don't want you sitting in that gallery when they open those curtains. I don't want any friend of mine to witness this. Promise me you won't be there."

Jack hesitated a moment before answering. Part of him felt that if he left he would be abandoning Henry. But there was nothing he could do, and it was Henry's call.

"All right, if that's your wish, Henry, I won't be there."

Even though the Florida Supreme Court had found the electric chair to be a constitutional method of execution, the Florida legislature in 1996 had passed a law making death by lethal injection a legal alternative. Unless an inmate affirmatively opted for Old Sparky, he would be killed by lethal injection. Henry was a sane man. He had not opted for Old Sparky.

The death chamber was still the same. The electric chair was simply removed and replaced by a gurney on which the prisoner lay. At the appropriate time, the curtain would be drawn, and those in attendance in the little theater adjacent to the chamber could watch as the protocol, as it was called, was administered. There were only a few people in the theater to witness Henry's execution. Normally, family members of both the accused and the victim would attend. In this case, neither the victim nor Henry had any family in attendance. A few reporters were there, as were some representatives from the state legislature and the governor's office.

After Jack left, the warden made his ceremonial visit to Henry to read him the death warrant and to ask him if he had any questions.

"They want to make sure you understand that they're killing you," Henry had told Jack earlier in the day. After that it was the chaplain's turn. Henry did not kick him out as he had threatened to. Instead, they read from scripture and talked some about the afterlife. When Henry told the preacher he was looking forward to seeing his mother, the man didn't respond. He just kept talking about the Almighty. *I was better off talking to Jack*, Henry told himself.

When the chaplain left, preparations began in earnest for Henry's demise. He was brought from the death cell to a special place where he was fitted with a heart monitor and then strapped to the gurney. Two IVs were set up in his arms and flushed with saline solution, the final preparation for the death cocktail. At the appropriate time—in Henry's case, six p.m.—the signal would be given to the executioner by the warden, and the procedure would begin. There were eight syringes in all. The first two contained no less than two grams of sodium pentothal, which was designed to make the victim unconscious. The third syringe was again a saline solution to flush the arteries. The fourth and fifth syringes contained pancuronium chloride, to paralyze the muscles. The sixth was another saline flush, and the seventh and eighth syringes contained 150 milliequivalents of potassium chloride, which would cause a massive heart attack and almost instantaneous death. The doses would be administered by the executioner; a doctor and a nurse were present to observe. Doctors did not take part in the actual execution because it violated their Hippocratic oath to "do no harm."

A special phone was set up outside the death chamber, where the warden would stand. If there was going to be a last-minute reprieve, that phone would ring. In the final minutes and seconds, while Henry was in the death chamber strapped to the gurney, his IVs prepared, all eyes would be on that phone.

Jack had followed his own procedure, the one he used when he was last at Starke awaiting word on Rudy Kelly's fate. He went outside the prison gates and stood with the death penalty protesters and sang hymns and said prayers. He felt totally helpless.

At 5:45, Henry was wheeled into the death chamber. The curtain was pulled open and the waiting began. At 5:57, Henry thanked God in advance for answering his prayer, closed his eyes, and dreamed of his mother and their joyful reunion. Jack too offered his final prayer at roughly the same time, a simple Hail Mary. At exactly six o'clock, as tears streamed down his face, Jack was singing, with all his heart and soul, the hymn "Peace Is Flowing Like a River."

Jack didn't learn what happened in the death chamber until an hour later, when a guard came to the outer gate to let him in and to give him the news. At exactly six p.m., the executioner had begun to administer the sodium pentothal just as the phone rang. He stopped immediately, but Henry was already unconscious. Somehow, Wofford had convinced Judge Susan Fletcher to read the motion for rehearing. She granted it and the request for an evidentiary hearing and entered an order stopping the execution. Henry was by no means out of the woods, but he was about to have his first real day in court with Jack Tobin as his lawyer.

Two hours later, Jack was in the prison hospital with Henry when Henry woke up. It took him a few minutes to focus and a few more to realize he wasn't dead. Although he was still quite groggy, he clearly saw Jack.

"How did you beat me here? And where's my mother?" he asked.

Jack smiled and put his hand on Henry's shoulder. "The judge signed the order, Henry, but not before they gave you a little juice."

"I guess that's as close as you come," Henry said before again closing his eyes.

Henry didn't fall right back to sleep. He lay there thinking about what had transpired in the preceding hours. He had started on a journey that had been aborted at the absolute last minute. Something, however, had irrevocably changed. He could feel it in his core. Even though the reprieve might only be temporary, Henry knew that from the moment this journey began, he had embarked on a new life.

TWENTY-NINE

Benny was escorted from the cell block by two guards. They walked for several minutes down long, narrow corridors. Eventually the guards placed him in a small room and told him to sit in a chair facing a rectangular opening with bars across it. One of the guards stayed in the room with him and stood against the back wall. *My own little private visiting room with a butler*, Benny thought. *I wonder if they have carpeting on death row.*

I'm wisecracking to myself, he decided. *I must be going crazy!*

Moments later a short, stocky Latino man came into the part of the room on the opposite side of the barred window and sat down facing Benny. Benny had never seen him before.

"Who are you?" he asked.

"Luis Melendez," the man answered.

Benny struggled for a few minutes to remember where he had heard the name before. Then it came to him from deep in the recesses of his brain, behind closed doors. As he remembered, he stiffened. His stomach started to churn. Rage began to swell. Part of him wanted to leap through the bars and grab the man by the throat. Another part wanted to bolt from the chair and run like lightning as far away from this man as he could.

Benny caught his rage before it got out. He struggled with it for several moments, acutely aware of the guard behind him. He finally concluded he had two options: ask the guard to take him back to his cell, or quietly ask Luis Melendez what he wanted. He chose the latter.

"What do you want?" he said quietly.

"I want to help."

Once again the rage began to build and once again Benny fought it down. *This needs to be said*, he told himself. He bit his lip and waited for the beast within to subside. Then he began to speak, again in a low voice so the guard would not hear.

"Where were you when I was four years old and I was taken from my mother because she was strung out on drugs? Where were you when I was dumped in a foster home with two animals who beat me every day and locked me in the closet when I cried? I called out to you every day for help. I wanted you to rescue me, to tell me everything was going to be all right. But neither of you ever came."

"I tried to find you, Benny, I did."

"Oh yeah, it's pretty hard to find foster kids, especially when you're the real parent."

"I wasn't thinking straight back then," his father protested. "I didn't think to look right away in the foster care program for you. When I finally did, you were gone."

"Whatever. You're too late now. You know, back when I was a kid, I went from fear to terror to 'I don't give a shit' to being so angry I could scream. I took it and took it and stuffed it in every day and it built and built. Eventually I dreamed of killing those two animals and then finding you and killing you *and* her." Benny was struggling to keep his voice low. "I never went near a gun my whole life, but I thought about it plenty—about putting one right between your eyes. That man stood over me and I had a gun. I killed him and now you're too late."

Luis just kept looking at his son. Then, as quietly as Benny, he said, "I'm not going to give up. I can't do anything about what's already happened, but I've found you now and I'm going to do everything I can to help you."

"Fine, you do that. You spend every fuckin' dime you have. I hope it kills you, 'cause it ain't gonna save me." Benny turned to the guard. "I'm ready," he said and stood up to leave.

THIRTY

The day after Henry's stay of execution, Jack called Wofford. It was mid-morning, so Wofford was already at work.

"Wofford, you worked a miracle. How the hell did you do it?" Jack asked.

"Well, Jack, I simply walked into Judge Fletcher's courtroom in the middle of a hearing, introduced myself, and asked her in open court, in front of a full house, what she was doing about that motion on her desk regarding the man who was scheduled to die that day."

"I'll bet that got everybody's attention."

"It did. She was pissed. She called a recess right away."

"How did she get from being pissed at you to giving us an evidentiary hearing?"

"Like I told you, she's a good judge when she puts her mind to something. We just had to get her focused. She gets a lot of credit in my book. She could have taken the easy way out and gone along with Artie Hendrick. People aren't going to like what she did, and she's going to hear about it. She knows it, too. That's why she's one of the people who actually should be a judge."

"And so are you, Wofford. So are you."

"I may not be for long, Jack. If the Judicial Qualifications Commission gets wind of half of what I've done, I'm toast."

"I'll represent you, Wofford. Count on it."

"I appreciate that, Jack, but you know, I haven't felt so good since God knows when. Knowing that I'm helping to rectify a wrong that

I was part of is all I need to sleep at night. By the way, Judge Fletcher set the evidentiary hearing for two weeks from today."

"We'll be ready. I'll get my subpoenas out right away. And you can also count on me telling Henry all about your efforts on his behalf."

"Thanks, Jack. I appreciate that too."

Henry's circumstances had certainly changed since the day before—and not all to the good. He was no longer facing imminent death—so he was back in chains, and the couch and chairs were gone. He and Jack were returned to the sterile room where everything was bolted to the ground. Jack could tell Henry was still a little groggy from the injection and still a little shocked by the turn of events.

"I was in a good place yesterday, Jack. I was ready to die—with dignity. But when they strapped me on that gurney and pressed that needle into my skin, I felt degraded, like some sort of guinea pig. Now I'm back in my little cell until they decide to do this again. What the hell do they think I am? I'll tell you this, Jack—the next time they strap me in will be the last. Everything is different now."

"I'm with you, Henry. We're going to have a hearing before Judge Fletcher in two weeks, and she's going to decide whether there's enough evidence to grant you a new trial or not. If the answer is yes, you probably won't be retried, since the state's only witnesses are dead. If the answer is no, there will be no more appeals. No more stays. The next time they strap you in will definitely be the last."

"Geez, Jack, don't sugarcoat it like that."

For a second Jack didn't know how to take Henry's last comment. It wasn't until the big man started to laugh that he followed suit.

"By the way, Henry, this reprieve was all Wofford Benton's doing." Jack told him blow-by-blow about Wofford's encounter with Judge Fletcher.

"And she still granted the motion after all that?"

"She did," Jack replied. "Which means you have a good judge hearing your case now."

"And a good lawyer defending me," Henry replied. "Give Wofford my thanks, Jack."

*　　*　　*

Jack was greeted at home as the great liberator by Pat and Charlie.

"I'm so proud of you, Jack," Pat told him. "You saved Henry's life."

"It wasn't me. It was Wofford. And besides, it's not over yet. We're going to have an evidentiary hearing in two weeks."

Pat seemed to be feeling pretty good, so Jack suggested they take Charlie out to dinner at La Taqueria, their favorite restaurant in Bass Creek, to thank her for forcing herself on them when they needed her most.

Because of its location in southern Florida, Bass Creek was home to many people from south of the border—Cuba, Mexico, Guatemala, Honduras, Colombia. Many were transients who worked in the orange groves and the sugar fields, and they formed their own barrio in the northwest part of town. La Taqueria was on the border of that barrio. Its décor reflected that boundary location, which was one of the reasons Jack loved it. Nestled between portraits of matadors and bulls and Spanish, Cuban, and Central American landscapes were stuffed deer heads, gators, and jackrabbits, together with Florida State and University of Miami pennants. There was even a rectangular sign that had no ties to any part of the community. It read: *Tips up, Aspen, Colorado.*

The menu at La Taqueria reflected its diversity as well. There were Cuban, Spanish, and Mexican dishes alongside some typical American fare. The meals were tasty and plentiful and the prices were low, so just about everybody came to partake. It was the genuine melting pot of town—busy every night, the conversation always loud and lively.

Not too many people knew that it was owned by a husband-and-wife team who were Irish and Jewish, respectively. Lisa served as the friendly, helpful hostess while Mike stayed in the back and supervised the kitchen. Since Jack and Pat were frequent patrons, they had become friends with the owners over the years. No matter how busy it was, Lisa always managed to find a table for Jack and Pat in Rose's section. Rose, a robust Cuban woman, was their favorite waitress.

"How's my favorite lawyer?" Rose would say every time as she planted a big kiss on his cheek. She always had a hug for Pat too, but both women knew that she saved her greatest affection for Jack.

"The chicken chimichanga is great tonight," she told them.

"I'll have that," Pat said. She knew she would pay for the choice later, but she didn't care. Tonight she was going to have fun. So far, Pat had avoided most of the symptoms of chemotherapy, although she had slowed down somewhat. She was nauseated from time to time, however, and Mexican food was not exactly the prescribed diet.

"I'll have that too," Charlie piped in.

"Just give me one of Mike's Cubans, Rose, with some black beans and rice," Jack said, having not even looked at the menu.

"And a pitcher of sangria," Pat added, looking at Charlie and Jack. "I'm with the man I love and my best friend and I'm feeling good. I'm going to have a good time and that's it." Jack saw the sparkle in her eye and decided not to say anything. It was best to enjoy the moment.

"I'm going home for a week and then I'm coming back," Charlie told them after Rose had brought the pitcher and filled their glasses.

"No, Charlie," Jack protested. "You've already done enough. We'll manage, won't we, honey?"

"Listen, it's not an inconvenience for me," Charlie responded quickly. "This is still the off season in the tax world, and I've got more vacation time than I know what to do with. If I don't use it, I'll lose it. Besides, I love it here. And Jack, I covet your pool. Do you know what it's like to swim in a lane with three other people every day? I know you think I'm going out of my way for you guys, but there's a lot in it for me."

Pat shrugged. "She's hard to fight, Jack. And she never takes no for an answer."

"Charlie, you should have been a used-car salesman," Jack told her. In truth, he was glad once again that Charlie was so insistent. With her there, he could devote his attention to Henry's hearing without worrying constantly about Pat.

"Then it's settled," Charlie declared. "I'm going to go home for a week, and then I'll be back. That'll give you a full week when I return to prepare for your hearing, Jack."

They had a second pitcher of sangria and talked and laughed into the evening. Jack kept one eye on Pat. He was sure this wasn't good for her, although she continued to laugh and to sparkle.

"By the way, your Uncle Bill came by every day you were gone," Pat told him.

"Really? Does he know you're sick?"

"He must. He hasn't said anything to me directly, but there's no other reason he'd be coming around so much."

Not long after he came to Bass Creek, Jack had persuaded his Uncle Bill to move from St. Petersburg, a city on the west coast of Florida. Uncle Bill was eighty-seven years young and Jack had always been close to him. He was a retired merchant marine, a salty old tar and a sharp contrast to his brother, Jack's dad, who had been an accountant. Jack had gravitated to his colorful uncle at an early age. It was only natural that he would want Uncle Bill close to him when he himself retired to Bass Creek to become a fisherman.

Uncle Bill had very quickly established his own group of friends and usually only visited Jack and Pat one night a week for dinner. "I don't like to be a bother," he'd told Jack when Jack had inquired why they saw him so seldom.

"It's really strange how word just gets out in Bass Creek," Jack said.

"It sure is," Pat agreed.

Pat paid a price for her fun night out. Although she'd only had two small glasses of sangria, she was miserable the next day. The combination of wine, food, and Taxol and Carboplatin, her chemotherapy cocktail, was simply too much for her system.

"I should have put my foot down," Jack said as he brought her a couple of aspirin and a glass of water. She was lying in bed moaning.

"It's not your fault, Jack. It's not anybody's fault. I made my own decision. I knew there would be repercussions. I'll have to remember this feeling the next time I'm tempted to stray from the straight and narrow."

*   *   *

The next time was the following Monday. Pat had her third chemotherapy treatment earlier in the day, and that night she and Jack had visitors. Jack was against having anybody over, but Pat once again convinced him it was okay.

"I usually don't feel the effects of the chemo until the next day, and we'll have them over after dinner. It'll be fine."

Jack finally relented. He could never say no to her when she wanted to do something. Besides, the visitors were old friends, and seeing them would probably be good for the both of them.

During the time that Jack represented Rudy Kelly, he had two retired homicide detectives, Dick Radek and Joaquin Sanchez, working with him on the case. An important witness in part of the litigation was a woman named Maria Lopez. For security reasons, they had all lived together for several months, initially in Jack and Pat's house in Bass Creek and later in a ranch house owned by a friend of Jack's, Steve Preston. They became very close as a result of the experience. Joaquin and Maria fell in love and were married in a joint wedding ceremony with Jack and Pat. Dick eventually bought the ranch house they had all stayed in, and he married Steve Preston's sister, Peggy. The six of them got together from time to time.

This evening, however, was different. Jack could tell from Dick's tone of voice when he called to make plans that they knew of Pat's illness. It was just another example of bad news traveling through unknown channels very quickly.

It turned out to be a wonderful evening. Although Jack could tell that Joaquin, Maria, and Dick were initially shocked that Pat had lost so much weight and appeared so pale, he could also see how happy the visit made her. They sat on the patio out by the pool and reminisced about their "commune" days. Poor Peggy, the newest member of the group, had to listen to the stories every time they got together.

"I don't know if I ever told you this one before, Peggy," Pat began. "Maria and I had to do some extra planning to make the testosterone members of the house hold feel comfortable. Do you remember, Maria?"

"I sure do," Maria replied. "We got each man his own newspaper. Every morning at breakfast, the three of them would have their noses in their own individual paper."

"And do you know," Pat continued, "they never even thanked us."

"It wasn't every morning," Dick countered. "As I recall, most mornings Maria and Joaquin and you and Jack were making goo-goo eyes at each other across the table."

"Oh yeah, I remember," Joaquin said. "That's when Dick uttered his famous line, 'I feel like a fifth wheel around here.'" They all cracked up just as they had the morning that Dick first said it— including Peggy, who had heard the story several times before.

Even though it was a great evening, Jack, the protector, made sure it ended early. As they said their good-byes, each one expressed in his or her own way how special Pat was to them. Only Maria acknowledged her illness, and then only implicitly.

"I'm an hour away," she said. "If you need anything, don't hesitate to call me. Please."

"I will, Maria," Pat replied, reaching out to touch her hand. "I promise."

On Tuesday morning, Jack and Pat loaded the big boat, the thirty-six-foot Sea Ray they had purchased the year before, and headed out for Lake Okeechobee. They brought the dinghy along as well. The plan was to stay out on the lake for a week, weather permitting, away from everyone and everything but not too far from town, and use the dinghy on daily excursions to explore the little tributaries off the Okalatchee River and the big lake itself. Mostly, though, they just wanted to be alone.

Almost immediately, Pat's condition started to deteriorate. Even though Jack did the vast majority of the work getting ready, Pat was exhausted by the first afternoon and took to her bed belowdeck before they'd even picked a spot to spend the night.

"Maybe this isn't a good idea," Jack said to her after he'd stopped and set the anchor.

"No, honey, I'll be fine. I like the water. It soothes me even when

I'm in bed. If I'm going to be tired for a couple of days, I'd rather be tired out here."

It was a good choice. She had a restful night's sleep, and in the morning Jack made breakfast and served her in bed. In the afternoon, he brought her on deck and let her relax in the shade under the canopy. She could breathe the fresh air without the harmful effects of the sun. The doctor had warned both of them about overexposure to the sun during chemotherapy.

By Thursday she was feeling better, although for the first time since she started chemo, clumps of hair were coming out in her hairbrush. She'd awakened before sunrise and gone on deck. It was peaceful and serene on the lake as the sun broke through—nothing like the stark transition in their little cove where they were surrounded by the trees and the animals, but just as stirring in its own way. Jack joined her a little later, having caught a whiff of the breakfast she was cooking for him.

"One good turn deserves another," she said jauntily. Jack didn't say anything. He was just happy to see her up and about and so full of life.

After breakfast, she undressed and jumped in the water. Jack followed right behind.

"Pat, you've got to be careful," he chastised her when they both surfaced. "You need to save your strength."

"For what? Next Monday, when it gets sapped all over again? Seize the day, Jack. Live in the moment." She proceeded to swim away from the boat. Jack could do nothing but follow.

After lunch, they took the dinghy out and explored a little. In one of the offshoots between the river and the lake—"mangrove corridors," Jack called them, because they were bordered on both sides by mangroves with an occasional tall pine here and there—they came upon a partially sunken houseboat lying on its side. The boat was two stories high and very large. Pat spied two gators resting nearby and an osprey high atop one of the pines. A cormorant was swimming close to the gators, seemingly oblivious to their presence, and Pat worried about its safety.

"I hope that cormorant doesn't get too close to the gators."

"Oh, I wouldn't worry about it," Jack said. "What's meant to be in nature is meant to be."

"I never thought about it quite that way," she replied. "I guess you're right."

"Rudy told me about this houseboat," Jack remembered. "I never thought I'd actually find it. It looks exactly as he described it."

"Don't you wonder sometimes about the stories behind wrecks like this?" Pat asked. "Just imagine, a murky swamp in the dead of night. Gator-infested waters. Maybe it was a gambling boat. Or even better, a brothel."

"Maybe so," Jack replied, leaning back in the dinghy with his feet hanging over the side, letting the boat drift aimlessly. It didn't get any better than this. "I'll bet the osprey knows the whole story. He can see everything from up there."

"I think you're right," Pat replied, looking up at the majestic bird, its proud white chest protruding, framed by dark brown wings.

They made love that night—carefully, rocking along to the rhythm of the great Okeechobee. Afterward, they both slept soundly.

On Sunday morning before dawn they took the dinghy to the cove they had adopted as their own, for their own special sunrise service. They spent the rest of the morning there as well, swimming au naturel, arriving home in the early afternoon just in time for Jack to jump in the car and drive to Fort Lauderdale to pick up Charlie.

"Thank you, God," Jack said as he drove down the two-lane road that led to the airport. "I know this week was a gift from heaven."

THIRTY-ONE

Luis Melendez called Sal Paglia the day after his visit to Benny. He'd first had to digest everything over a few scotch and sodas before he could revisit it with anyone. Luis rarely drank. He was very disciplined after the drug years of his youth. Benny's diatribe, however, had taken a toll on his psyche.

"My son has agreed to your representation," Luis told Sal after Hazel got him on the line.

"Good. Good," Sal said. "How'd the meeting go?"

"It went."

"Not good, huh?"

"No. He's got good reason to be angry."

"Well, maybe we can do something for the both of you by getting him out of jail. By the way, I've got a mortgage broker coming in here to meet with us tomorrow afternoon at four o'clock to get the paperwork done on your refinancing. Be sure to bring your tax returns and everything else on that sheet I gave you so he can get started right away."

Luis sensed a tone of desperation in Sal's voice and he was right. Sal was scared. He had already given three thousand bucks to his loan shark, Beano Moffit, who had visited him rather unexpectedly a few days before.

"Give me one reason why I don't break your legs," Beano had asked at the time. Sal loved that about shylocks—they always made it sound like it hurt them more than you when they broke your body parts into pieces. Just to be sure he remained intact, he'd given Beano three thousand reasons not to break his legs. But he knew the reprieve wouldn't last for long. He needed Luis's money. He also needed to tell somebody about the heat he was getting from Beano, so he called his good friend, Sergeant Al Borders of the NYPD.

"Al, don't ask me any questions, okay? I just want you to know that if something happens to me, Beano Moffit is behind it."

"No. Sal. Don't tell me you're into Beano."

"I'm not telling you anything, Al. I'm just saying, if I turn up missing or something, you tell the powers that be to put the heat on that prick."

"Don't say anything else, Sal. Consider it done."

After Luis had been to the office and the paperwork was completed on the refinancing, Sal took a trip downtown to see Benny. They met in the same room where Benny had spoken with his father. Sal was determined to make things go smoothly.

"Benny, I'm Sal Paglia, the lawyer Luis Melendez hired to represent you. First thing I want to tell you—Luis is paying the freight, but you are my client. I'm working for you, not him. I've got experience in this stuff and I've got a plan, which I'll tell you about in a minute. Second item—I do the talking. You don't tell me nothing unless I ask. If I ask a specific question, you give me a specific answer. The reason I tell you this is because if you tell me something, I have an ethical obligation not to put on evidence that contradicts what you told me. Understand?"

Benny nodded. At this point, he simply didn't care. Sal continued to explain, despite Benny's nod. "You see, the less you tell me, the greater leeway I have in defending you. Got it?"

"Sure," Benny replied. Trying as best he could to tune Sal out.

"Third item," Sal continued. He was on a roll now—he'd had a few cups of coffee before showing up at the prison. "Bail. I don't think I'm going to get you out of here anytime soon. That stiff you smoked—I mean, allegedly shot—was a high roller. Anytime you smoke—and I'm just talking hypothetically, you understand?"

"I understand." Benny felt the need to say something just to slow Sal down a bit. The lawyer was like a runaway freight train.

"Anytime you smoke a high roller, all hell breaks loose. So to make a long story short, that's why you ain't gettin' out of here anytime soon."

"Gotcha. Anything else?" Benny had had his fill of Sal. *This is who my old man entrusts my life to? I'm getting fucked all over again.*

"Oh yeah. I just want to tell you I've got a plan to get you out of here. I've been over the public defender's files in detail, and I see some things we can work with. I'm going to hire a world-famous medical examiner from California to testify on your behalf. I've used him before. He's great. His name is Dr. Donald Wong—you may have heard of him. So don't worry, we're working on a defense for you."

Those last words made Benny feel a little better. Sal had reviewed the files and actually had a plan. Benny's cautious optimism wasn't entirely unwarranted, either. As goofy as Sal was, he knew how to get people off.

"The thing is," Sal cautioned, "getting this guy is going to take some time. Like I said, he's a big shot. He's got to clear his calendar not only to do his investigation but also to testify at trial. So you're going to be in here for a while."

"How long?" Benny asked.

"Six months to a year."

Benny shrugged his shoulders. "I ain't got nothing better to do," he said.

Sal had Benny sign a bunch of papers before leaving, including a contract of representation and a waiver of speedy trial. The lawyer gave Benny some final words of encouragement before he left.

"And don't worry about the death penalty. They got it in New York, but they never use it."

THIRTY-TWO

Even though Charlie was back in town and he needed the time to prepare for Henry's hearing, Jack decided to make the trip to Miami for Pat's Monday morning chemotherapy treatment. Pat had not slept the night before and she was having severe pain again, which was unusual; her pain generally subsided when she started chemotherapy. Jack wanted to talk to Dr. Wright about it in person.

"This is not a good sign, Mr. Tobin," Dr. Wright told him when he described Pat's pain. "It means that the tumors are withstanding the chemotherapy and are growing again. We won't know for certain until we do the scans, which are scheduled for next week. I'm going to prescribe ten milligrams of Oxycontin for her to take once a day, and I'm going to give you a prescription for Percocet, which you can give her anytime she has pain. I'll be calling your local doctor to coordinate all this."

"We don't have a local doctor."

"I have records from a local doctor who was treating your wife."

"That would have been Dr. Hawthorne. We stopped going to him because he failed to realize that Pat had a serious problem, even though she was complaining of pain for nine months."

Dr. Wright didn't respond. Jack didn't blame her. He was a lawyer, after all, and his words could easily be taken as a prelude to a lawsuit. "I'll make a few calls today and find someone local for your wife. I think we'll also set up her chemotherapy locally after next week. She doesn't need to be making this trip. I'll call you later this afternoon with your new doctor's name."

On the way home, Pat was almost giddy as she talked and laughed up a storm. The drugs did that to her. For Jack, considering what he had heard from the doctor that day, it seemed almost surreal.

Jack maintained a separate office in Bass Creek away from home, even though he no longer had any clerical help. He still liked the ritual of going to the office. It was quiet, and he could shut everything else out and do his work. He had four days left to prepare for Henry's hearing.

On Tuesday night when he returned home, Pat was still in bed. He had come to expect this for the first couple of days after chemo, but when she was still in bed on Thursday, he began to worry.

"She's not eating either," Charlie told him. "I can barely get those protein drinks in her. She's losing more weight." By this time, all her hair had fallen out. Things were happening very fast, and Jack wasn't sure what to do. Dr. Wright had given him the name of another local doctor, but they were scheduled to be in Miami on Monday and to see Dr. Wright then anyway.

"I think we'll just do the best we can until Monday," he told Charlie. "What do you think?"

"I think you're right. She seems to be comfortable, and we probably wouldn't be able to get an appointment with the local doctor before Monday."

He called Judge Fletcher's office and told her secretary the problem.

"I can't start until Tuesday with my wife in her present condition. The judge has set aside the week for this hearing, but I don't think it will last for more than three days anyway."

"I'm sure the judge won't have a problem with the delay, Mr. Tobin. So, unless you hear different from me in the next fifteen minutes, you can notify your witnesses that we'll start on Tuesday."

Next, Jack called Henry to let him know about Pat's condition and the reason for the delay. Up to now, he had not told Henry about Pat's cancer.

"Jack, I know you've had your reasons for not telling me about your wife's condition. I even think I know what those reasons are. From now on, though, keep me abreast of everything. Pat told you to stick with me; now I'm telling you that her medical condition has priority over my hearing. I don't care if you have to delay the hearing for a year, Jack—make sure Pat gets well."

It was a long weekend. Pat did not get out of bed once, even though Charlie and Jack constantly encouraged her to do so. She wasn't eating either. It was a chore just to get her to take a few sips of her protein drink through a straw.

"We've got to change something," Jack told Charlie outside Pat's room. "This particular chemotherapy treatment doesn't seem to be working."

Charlie agreed. "We'll take it up with the doctor on Monday," she said.

On Monday morning, Pat had a CT scan and an ultrasound. In the afternoon, Dr. Wright examined her. Jack took her to both appointments in a wheelchair because she was too weak to walk.

"I'm okay, Jack. I'm just tired," she told him. It was the same thing she'd been saying to him and Charlie all week.

"I'm going to put her in the hospital for a few days," the doctor told Jack and Charlie after the examination. "She needs some IV fluids to get her stabilized and a blood transfusion. Her red blood count is low."

A blood transfusion. The words hit Jack like a sledgehammer.

"It's not unusual, Mr. Tobin," the doctor explained. "Patients on chemotherapy often have to have blood transfusions. What's troublesome is that she is not eating, she's losing weight—and she's in pain. The scans will tell us what we need to know, and we can set a game plan from there. Okay?"

Unable to say anything, Jack just nodded. "You can go in and visit her if you want. I'm having an ambulance take her to the hospital."

Jack was about to follow the doctor into Pat's room when Charlie grabbed his arm and held it.

"You can't go in there looking like that, Jack," she told him. "Pat will know the doctor gave you bad news. Get yourself together. And remember, it's our job to keep her spirits up."

THIRTY-THREE

Jack hardly slept that night worrying about his wife. Wofford could tell there was a problem as soon as he walked in the restaurant where they had arranged to meet.

"What the hell happened to you, Jack? You look terrible."

"I'm fine. I didn't get much sleep last night. My wife is in the hospital. She has cancer."

"I'm sorry, Jack. Is it real bad?"

"Yeah."

"Look, we can postpone this hearing until a better time."

"There may not be a better time, Wofford. At least now she has round-the-clock care."

"You're sure?"

"Yeah."

"Well, just ask me open-ended questions and I'll take it from there."

To the casual eye, Henry appeared to be public enemy number one when he walked into the courtroom on Tuesday morning. He was wearing handcuffs, leg irons, and a waist belt to which his handcuffs were attached, and he was accompanied by no fewer than eight sheriff's deputies, two with shotguns. Since this was a non-jury hearing, the shackles were not removed, and none of the officers left the courtroom. If Henry made the slightest unanticipated move, the possibility existed that he would be shot on the spot.

Henry sat down next to Jack and turned to look at him.

"Are you okay, Jack? You look like hell. And how's Pat?"

"Thanks for the compliment, Henry. Wofford said practically the same thing. I'm fine, but Pat's not doing so well. We had a rough night last night. She's in the hospital."

"Let's put this off, Jack. I told you I can wait."

"No, Henry. This is the best time. Really. She has twenty-four-hour care in the hospital. Her best friend Charlie is there too. And I'm ready. We need to do this right now."

"Are you sure you shouldn't put your wife first?"

"Henry, she's the one who sent me."

Moments later, Judge Fletcher took the bench. Jack hadn't even checked to see who was representing the state, but somebody was over there shuffling papers, getting ready.

"This is the evidentiary hearing to determine if Henry Wilson, who is presently on death row, is entitled to a new trial," Judge Fletcher began. "Counsel, are we ready to proceed?"

Jack stood up. "The defense is ready, your honor."

A man stood up at the state's table across the aisle. Jack saw that it was Scott Tremaine, a lawyer he had known for the past twenty years—a lawyer with a great reputation. Scott was no longer with the state's attorney's office: he had been specially appointed to represent the state in this case.

"The state is ready, your honor," Scott said.

"Then let us proceed."

In a non-jury situation with an experienced judge and experienced counsel, many procedures were short-circuited. For instance, the attorneys did not make opening statements. They both knew that the judge was going to make her decision based on testimony from the witness stand. There was no need to waste her time.

They spent most of the morning marking all the exhibits, agreeing to enter some of them into evidence and stipulating to certain facts. Jack was glad that Scott Tremaine was on the other side. Scott was not a game player. If there was a legitimate basis to exclude something, he would argue until the cows came home against its inclusion, but he wouldn't make stupid or illegitimate arguments. That tactic would backfire with this judge anyway.

By lunchtime all the exhibits that the parties agreed were admissible—including the transcript from the original trial, the previous motions for new trial, and all previous orders—had been entered into the record. All documentary evidence that the parties could not agree on had been simply marked as an exhibit. When it was time to introduce disputed exhibits, appropriate objections would be made to the judge. The parties had also stipulated that David Hawke, the main witness against Henry, was deceased, and that James Vernon, the man who Wofford had argued in the original trial was the real killer, was also deceased. Scott Tremaine produced both death certificates, which surprised Jack. He wasn't sure why the state was concerned about the precise dates of death.

The state further stipulated that neither David Hawke nor his cousin Delbert Falcon had ever been charged with any crime arising out of the death of Clarence Waterman, the man Henry was convicted of killing.

After lunch, Jack called Wofford to the stand. There were certain preliminary matters he had to establish for appellate purposes, such as Wofford's past experience as a criminal defense attorney and his present position as a judge.

Once the preliminaries were out of the way, Jack honed in on the issues. Susan Fletcher leaned forward, listening intently.

"What was your defense in Mr. Wilson's original trial?" Jack asked Wofford.

"Our defense was that someone else committed the murder and that Henry Wilson was not at the murder scene."

"Did Henry Wilson have an alibi?"

"No."

"Did he testify?"

"No."

"Were there any witnesses who placed him somewhere else?"

"No."

"So you were limited to creating a reasonable doubt as to Henry

Wilson's guilt by giving the jury evidence that someone else may have committed the crime?"

It was definitely a leading question, but Scott Tremaine didn't object.

"That's about it," Wofford answered.

"What was the evidence you put on to establish that fact?"

"The only evidence I had was a prison snitch, a fellow named Willie Smith. James Vernon was in jail at the time of this trial, and Smith was his cellmate. Smith testified that on the Friday before the trial was to begin James Vernon told him that he murdered Clarence Waterman."

"Did you think that was strong evidence?"

"Absolutely not. This guy was a convicted felon and the timing of the confession was just too convenient. But it was all I had."

"Was that the only evidence you planned on putting on when the trial began?"

"No. I planned on calling James Vernon himself."

"For what reason?"

"He had told me that he was present at the murder and that Henry wasn't. He said two other men were with him and they did the killing. He wouldn't name the other men."

"Did you call him at trial?"

"Yes."

"What happened?"

"He took the Fifth and refused to testify."

Jack picked up the transcript of James Vernon's unsworn interview with Wofford Benton, which had been marked as defendant's exhibit number 8 but not stipulated into evidence.

"Mr. Benton, I'm handing you defendant's exhibit number 8 and ask you if you can identify that document."

"Yes. It is a transcription of a recorded interview I had with James Vernon on April 13, 1980, about a month before Henry Wilson's trial began."

"Did you ever tell any of the appellate attorneys representing Mr. Wilson in his two previous appeals about the existence of this transcript?"

"No, I did not."

"Why not?"

"Nobody asked me. It wasn't really significant to me, and I actually forgot I had it."

"Since that time, have you changed your opinion on the significance of this transcript?"

"Yes."

"And why have you done so?"

"To be perfectly honest, I don't think that I ever read it before you found it in my barn a few weeks ago. In the transcript, James Vernon not only said he was at the murder scene and that Henry Wilson wasn't there, but he also said that he told the same story to his lawyer, Ted Griffin."

"Why was that significant?"

"Well, if I had anticipated James Vernon changing his mind about testifying, I could have talked to Ted Griffin and had him available to testify."

Jack introduced the transcript into evidence over the objection of Scott Tremaine, who argued that it was hearsay and that it was irrelevant. The judge let it in.

"In your opinion," Jack continued, "would Ted Griffin's testimony have made a difference in the outcome of the trial?"

Scott Tremaine was on his feet. "Objection, your honor. This is opinion testimony on one of the ultimate issues you will have to decide."

"Overruled." The judge obviously wanted to hear what Wofford had to say.

"Absolutely, it would have made a huge difference," Wofford responded. "James Vernon took the Fifth. If I could put a lawyer on, rather than the prison snitch, and have him testify as to what James Vernon told him about this murder, we would have had a much stronger case."

"You didn't do that, though—have Ted Griffin waiting in the wings in case James Vernon took the Fifth?"

"That's correct."

"When did you realize that you'd made a mistake in not having Ted Griffin waiting in the wings?"

"Just a few weeks ago, when I read the transcript again for the first time. For some reason, even at trial I did not remember that James Vernon told me he had talked to Ted Griffin. It was a huge mistake."

"Do you know who Anthony Webster is?"

"Yes. Anthony Webster was the investigator for the state in this case."

"Did you know that Anthony Webster also spoke with James Vernon?"

"I know now because you told me that a few weeks ago as well."

"The first time you knew that Anthony Webster, the prosecutor's investigator, had spoken to James Vernon was less than a month ago?"

"That's right. You told me that you obtained that information from Ted Griffin."

Jack stole a glance at the judge. She was writing copious notes.

"If you had known that Anthony Webster talked to James Vernon at the time of the original trial would you have called Webster as a witness?"

"Absolutely."

"Would that have made a difference in the outcome of the case, in your opinion?"

Scott Tremaine was on his feet again. "Objection, your honor. Mr. Tobin is trying to have Judge Benton decide this case rather than you." Jack could tell that Scott was attempting to play to the judge's vanity, but she was obviously having none of it.

"What's your legal objection, Counsel?"

"It calls for an opinion on one of the ultimate issues before this court."

"Overruled. The witness may answer the question."

"Yes," Wofford answered, "it would have made a great difference to the outcome of the case. I would have been able to put the state's investigator on the stand after the state's case was over and have him admit that there was a witness out there who said Henry Wilson didn't commit the murder. That testimony would have made the prosecution look like it was hiding something, and I would not have had to use the prison snitch. I don't think Henry would have been convicted under those circumstances."

Wofford's testimony was going well. Jack switched gears to cover the final subject matter of his direct examination.

"Was there any physical evidence to link Henry Wilson to this murder?"

"No."

"What evidence was there?"

"There was the testimony of David Hawke that he drove Henry Wilson and Hawke's cousin, Delbert Falcon, to Clarence Waterman's hairdressing salon; that he waited while they went inside to steal his money and his dope; and that they killed him when they were in there. Henry Wilson didn't have an alibi. I believe that the jury considered David Hawke's testimony and asked themselves the following question: why would a man tell a lie to voluntarily incriminate himself and his cousin? When they couldn't come up with a viable answer, they concluded that David Hawke was telling the truth and that Henry Wilson was guilty."

"Did you know at the time of trial that David Hawke was not going to be prosecuted for his role in this crime?"

"No. As a matter of fact, I asked him—and that is on page 197 of the transcript, exhibit number 1, your honor—if he was promised anything for his testimony, and he said no. I didn't find out until you told me that neither he nor his cousin was prosecuted for this crime."

"If you had known that at the time of the trial, would that have made a difference?"

Scott Tremaine felt obligated to make his objection even though by this time he knew it would do no good with this judge. He had to preserve the point for appellate purposes. "Objection," he said matter-of-factly.

"Overruled."

"It absolutely would have made a difference," Wofford replied. "The jury might have questioned the entire case if they'd known the other two men involved were walking."

"No more questions," Jack said and sat down next to Henry.

"Great job," Henry whispered in his ear.

"Don't evaluate the testimony until cross-examination is over," Jack told him. Henry may have had experience reading legal briefs and cases for years, but he didn't know what could happen to a seemingly good witness on cross-examination.

Scott Tremaine walked to the podium.

"Judge Benton, do you believe that your failure to anticipate that James Vernon would take the Fifth and to have Ted Griffin waiting in the wings to testify was incompetence and was one of the reasons Mr. Wilson was convicted of murder seventeen years ago?"

Wofford swallowed hard before answering. It wasn't easy for a sitting judge to admit incompetence on the record. "Yes, I do," he said.

"It's my understanding that you have been a circuit judge for about ten years, is that correct?"

"Yes."

"And I assume that during that time you have had to sit and decide cases just like this one, is that correct?"

"Yes."

"Many, many times?"

"Yes."

"And you have had to decide this very issue—incompetence of counsel—haven't you?"

"Yes."

"So you are thoroughly familiar with the case law?"

"Yes."

"Let me ask you this question, then. Even though you feel your mistake in Henry Wilson's case constituted incompetence, does it satisfy the legal standard for incompetence?"

It was Jack's turn to jump to his feet. "Your honor, he's asking the witness to make a legal evaluation of his own behavior."

"No, Judge," Scott responded. "I'm just asking him for an opinion on one of the ultimate issues—the same thing Mr. Tobin has been asking for the last hour or so."

Scott Tremaine had deftly turned the tables.

"Overruled," the judge declared. "The witness will answer the question."

"It should constitute incompetence," Wofford said.

Scott Tremaine looked right at Judge Fletcher. "Your honor, I request that you instruct the witness to answer the question posed."

"Answer the question, Wofford," Judge Fletcher said.

Wofford continued to hesitate. Scott Tremaine waited patiently. Finally, Wofford answered.

"I don't believe the incompetence satisfies the test of *Strickland v. Washington*. As this court knows, it's a very high standard. The level of incompetence must be such that the accused is, in effect, denied counsel."

"Thank you, Judge. Just to be a little clearer, is it your opinion that your representation and the errors that you made did not constitute incompetence as a matter of law?"

"That's correct," Wofford admitted.

Jack could now see how the rest of the cross-examination was going to go. Tremaine had succeeded in turning Wofford into his own expert. Through Wofford, he was going to try to prove that Henry had not met any of the legal criteria for a new trial. It was a brilliant tactic. *Just hang in there, Wofford*, Jack thought. *You've been here before.*

Meanwhile, Scott Tremaine continued his assault on Henry's case.

"Is it accurate that besides not having Mr. Griffin available for trial, you never spoke to Mr. Griffin after interviewing Mr. Vernon?"

"That's correct."

"And if you had talked to Mr. Griffin back then, if you had done your job, you would have learned that James Vernon had also spoken to Mr. Webster, the prosecution's investigator, and told Mr. Webster he was at the crime scene at the time of the murder, correct?"

"Possibly."

"Possibly? I don't understand."

"He could have refused to talk to me based on the attorney-client privilege."

"In any event, you didn't bring Ted Griffin into court back then and ask the question and test the privilege issue before a judge, did you?"

"No."

"As a circuit judge, you are familiar with the law on newly discovered evidence, correct?"

"Yes, I am."

"And you have had to decide what constitutes newly discovered evidence in cases just like this?"

"That's correct."

"What James Vernon told Ted Griffin seventeen years ago cannot be considered newly discovered evidence, can it?"

Jack was on his feet. "Objection, your honor."

"Overruled."

"No," Wofford answered.

"And that's because you knew about the conversation seventeen years ago, even though you never asked Ted Griffin what was said, correct?"

"That's correct."

"And even if what James Vernon told Ted Griffin was privileged, the privilege died with Mr. Vernon five years ago, correct?"

"That's correct."

"How long do you have to file a motion for new trial when you learn, or should have learned, of newly discovered evidence?"

"One year."

"So even if what James Vernon told Ted Griffin was privileged, this motion is still four years too late, correct?"

"Objection."

"Overruled."

"That's correct," Wofford answered.

"And since the information about Anthony Webster's interview with James Vernon came from Mr. Griffin, that's something that could have and should have been discovered at least four years ago as well, correct?"

"That's correct."

"So that's not newly discovered evidence either?"

"It may not be newly discovered evidence, but it still may provide a basis for a new trial." It was the answer Jack had hoped to hear. "I believe that a prosecutor has an affirmative duty to disclose exculpatory evidence under *Brady v. Maryland*. If the prosecution does not disclose that evidence, it cannot hide behind the argument that the defendant's counsel could have and should have found out anyway."

"Do you have any case law to support that opinion?"

"No, but that is my interpretation of *Brady*."

Yes! Jack was saying to himself. *Hang tough, Wofford.*

"But you do agree that you could have learned about Anthony Webster if you had talked to Mr. Griffin seventeen years ago or four years ago?"

"Yes."

"And would it be fair to say that if David Hawke and his cousin Delbert Falcon were not prosecuted for two years after Henry Wilson's conviction, that was enough time to put you on notice that they weren't going to be prosecuted, correct?"

"Yes."

Scott Tremaine should have stopped there, but he didn't.

"So the fact that they were not prosecuted is not a basis for a new trial, is it?"

"If the prosecutor affirmatively kept this information from the defense at the trial, I think that too is a *Brady* violation and could form the basis for a new trial."

Jack looked at Henry, who was taking it all in. He saw Henry mouth the word *yes* when Wofford gave his last answer. Jack had two more witnesses to put on, but he and Henry and probably Scott Tremaine all knew that it now came down to Judge Fletcher's interpretation of *Brady v. Maryland*.

Scott Tremaine did not want to end his cross-examination on such a sour note, but he had nothing else to ask, and he knew that any further questions of this witness about the *Brady* decision would get him nowhere but into further trouble. "I have no further questions, your honor," he said and sat down.

It had been a long day, so the judge decided to wrap it up at that point. Jack had a few words with Henry before his personal army took him back to jail. Jack met with Wofford in the hallway outside the courtroom. The man was beside himself.

"I'm sorry, Jack. I didn't realize that I was going to hurt Henry."

"How do you think you hurt him, Wofford?"

"Hell, I gave opinions against your case."

"Look, Wofford, we all knew this was a *Brady* case going in. We knew we couldn't win on those other arguments. Your truthfulness and the way Scott had to pull the opinions out of you are going to work in our favor. You have narrowed the issue and framed it just the way we want it."

"It's funny. I've been doing this for so many years as an attorney and a judge. It was a totally different experience being a witness. I thought he blew me away."

"He almost did. It was a very effective cross, but you hung tough. I think we are exactly where we want to be."

"Thanks, Jack. I don't know if you're telling me the truth, but I feel better."

"The truth will be in the decision. I'm going to be done tomorrow, in case you want to stick around."

"Really?"

"Yeah. The judge has all she needs right now, I think. I'm going to put Griffin and Webster on for five minutes apiece."

"Watch out for Webster. He could be a tricky witness."

"You know the old mantra, Wofford. If you're going to try cases, you have to be fearless."

"Or crazy," Wofford replied.

THIRTY-FOUR

Soon after filing his notice of appearance, Benny's lawyer, Sal Paglia, filed a motion to set bond. He knew he had no possibility of getting Benny out, but that wasn't his goal. Sal knew how to manipulate the media and how to gather them together in a heartbeat to make a dramatic pronouncement about nothing. It was better advertising than money could buy.

So Sal called a press conference right after his motion was denied.

"This is a travesty of justice!" he told all the broadcast networks, plus CNN and a few others. "My client is being denied his constitutional right to bail." Sal blustered on for about ten minutes, which he figured was the maximum attention span of any television reporter. Then he stopped. He had earned a significant spot on the evening news.

"Sal, my boy, you've still got it!" he proclaimed in his rented apartment that evening as he watched himself on TV. "Keep stoking that fire and you're back in business."

He filed another motion two weeks later, seeking more of the same free publicity. This time, however, he also had a legitimate purpose.

The courtroom was full of lawyers waiting to have their motions heard. Sal wasn't shy. "Judge, I have here the affidavit of Dr. Donald Wong saying he has been retained on this case but that he will not be available until the last two weeks of October next year. I've discussed this with my client, and I'm waiving speedy trial and requesting that you set a date certain for this trial in the last two weeks of October of next year."

It was an unusual request. Most defendants who were incarcerated wanted to get out as soon as possible. Sal was trying to keep his client in jail for almost a year before he even had a trial. It didn't make sense. On the other hand, Sal had a legitimate problem with his expert. Judge Franklin Harrison was handling the motion calendar that day: he had heard of Dr. Donald Wong and knew him to be a famous pathologist who wrote books and testified all over the world. Harrison didn't understand why Wong had been retained in this case, but that was the lawyer's decision. The judge never suspected that Sal's real motive was to milk the case for all it was worth before finally taking it to trial.

"What says the state?" the judge asked.

Ellen Curry was a rather new deputy district attorney who had been on the job only six months, working misdemeanors. She was handling the hearing for a big shot who couldn't make it. She knew nothing about the case, having seen the file for the first time five minutes before walking into court. She did know, however, that if she agreed to this outlandish delay there would be hell to pay when she returned to the office. "Judge, this is a ridiculous request. Do the wheels of justice come to a halt because of the schedule of one man? There are other experts. Mr. Paglia can find somebody else who doesn't sell his soul so often. The citizens of New York have a right to have this case heard within a reasonable time."

Judge Harrison liked that about young lawyers—they spoke of justice and the rights of citizens and selling your soul. Nobody did that in a motion hearing. Those were words that were saved for juries, because only jurors would swallow that stuff. The other lawyers in the courtroom were probably gagging. They all knew from experience what the still-idealistic Curry had not yet figured out—paid experts all over the country were selling their souls every day. The judge didn't need to be told that. Every once in a while, though, it was refreshing to hear.

Sal stood to counter the argument, but the judge stopped him.

"I've heard enough, Mr. Paglia. I agree with Ms. Curry. This court cannot revolve around the calendar of one man. I'll give you six months to get another expert and be ready for trial. We're going to put this case on the docket for June 14th of next year. Next case."

On the courthouse steps, Sal ranted and raved for precisely ten minutes about the injustice done to his client that day. Actually, he had gotten just what he wanted—six months.

"When you want six months, you ask for a year," Sal told the TV set as he watched his performance on the six o'clock news.

Benny was also watching that night from prison. *This guy is some kind of nut*, he thought. *But he does have balls. Maybe that's what you need in that business.* Benny didn't realize that his thoughts about Sal were pretty much in line with those of his father, Luis.

THIRTY-FIVE

Pat was sitting up in bed talking and laughing with Charlie when Jack got to the hospital that night. A little bit of color had returned to her cheeks.

She beamed when she saw him. "Hi, honey. How did it go today?"

"Pretty good, sweetheart. How are you doing? You look a whole lot better." He gave her a big kiss.

"I feel better." She was slurring her words a little, which Jack attributed to the medication. They were giving her morphine.

"She had the blood transfusion this afternoon," Charlie told him when Jack sat down next to her. "That and the IVs have made a world of difference."

"What does the doctor say?"

"She hasn't said anything yet. The test results still aren't back. Maybe tomorrow."

"How is Henry?" Pat asked. It was a funny thing. Pat always asked about Henry and Henry was now always asking about Pat—and the two had never met.

"Henry is doing fine."

"Are you proving to the judge that he's innocent?" Charlie asked.

"Innocence has very little to do with it at this point," Jack replied.

"Yeah," Pat added. "It's about whether they can prove the lawyer screwed up or the evidence is new. Right, Jack?"

"That's pretty much it."

"Wait a minute, I'm lost," Charlie said. "Why has innocence got nothing to do with it?"

"I don't really want to talk about this," Jack responded.

"We do," Pat told him. "Charlie and I have talked about everything under the sun. We need something new, don't we, Charlie?"

"We sure do—something with substance."

Jack looked at the two of them. In the midst of all this, they were still having a good time with each other.

"All right, I'll explain it to you, Charlie, but the peanut gallery," Jack said pointing at Pat, "has to refrain from making editorial comments."

Pat put her hand to her lips and mimicked zippering them shut.

"At this stage of the game, Charlie, to get a new trial you have to show that your lawyer was either totally incompetent, or that there is some new piece of evidence out there that nobody could have found before, or that the prosecutor hid evidence. If you can't demonstrate any of those three things, it doesn't matter whether you're innocent or not."

"That's really the way it works?"

"Yeah."

"And there are no other avenues?"

"Essentially that's it. You can go to the governor for clemency, but that's a political issue and our governor has never granted clemency."

Jack slept well that night knowing that his wife was doing so much better. *Maybe she and Henry will both get a reprieve*, he thought before nodding off.

The next morning in court, Jack put Ted Griffin on the witness stand and had him tell the judge about his conversation with James Vernon, which Griffin did in essentially the same nonchalant manner as when he first told Jack.

"He told me he cut Clarence Waterman's throat."

"Why did he tell you that?" Jack asked.

"I'm not sure."

"And you never told anybody?"

"Not until I told you a few weeks ago."

Jack left it right there. Let Scott wade into unknown waters if he wanted to.

"Did you believe him?" Scott Tremaine asked on cross.

"I didn't really think about it one way or another. James Vernon was certainly not an honest fellow. On the other hand, what was his motivation to lie?"

"In the seventeen years since this murder happened, did anybody ever ask you if James Vernon talked to you about this murder?"

"No. Not until Mr. Tobin did a few weeks ago."

"No further questions, your honor."

"Call your next witness, Mr. Tobin."

As usual, the second day of trial moved a lot faster than the first. Anthony Webster took the stand. He reluctantly admitted that he'd interviewed James Vernon and that Vernon had told him he was at the murder scene with two other men, neither of whom was Henry.

"I really didn't put much stock in what this guy had to say," Webster told Jack. "He might have been a friend of Henry Wilson's or something. As I recall, they both bought drugs from the victim."

Jack was sure that last line had been recently rehearsed. Webster had no independent recollection when Jack had interviewed him.

"In any event, you told the prosecutor about that interview, correct?"

"That's correct."

"Did you take notes of that interview?"

"I did."

Jack handed him a document. "I've handed you defendant's exhibit number 10 and ask you to identify that document."

"These are the notes of my interview with James Vernon."

"The same notes that you provided to the prosecutor?"

"Yes."

"No further questions."

Scott Tremaine had no cross.

"Call your next witness," the judge told Jack.

"I have no other witnesses, your honor."

"Mr. Tremaine, do you have any rebuttal?"

"No, your honor."

"Let's break for lunch," the judge announced. "I'll hear closing arguments when you come back."

"You handled Webster just right," Wofford told Jack over lunch. "You kept it tight so he couldn't give any opinions, although he managed to stick one in—that crap about Henry knowing Vernon. But it didn't make sense anyway. Just because you know a guy doesn't mean you're going to confess to a murder to save him."

"The only thing that mattered with Webster was that he interviewed Vernon and told the prosecutor about it. That made it a *Brady* case."

"Let's hope the judge sees it the same way we do."

After lunch, Jack argued every point, even though he knew the only viable one left was the *Brady* disclosure. He tried to anticipate Scott Tremaine's argument on that issue.

"Judge, in a moment Mr. Tremaine is going to tell you that the nondisclosure by the state's attorney is irrelevant because Wofford Benton could have and should have learned of the Webster interview from other sources. I ask you not to accept that argument. It would, in effect, emasculate the *Brady* rule. It would say to prosecutors, you can still withhold information and get away with it. I do not believe that is the law."

When Scott Tremaine rose to speak, he had no choice but to make the arguments Jack had already addressed: that the information about Anthony Webster's interview should have been discovered by Wofford Benton or any other attorney representing Henry Wilson at least four years ago; and that it had been a known fact for fifteen years that David Hawke and his cousin were not prosecuted. He threw something else in as well—something Jack had been worried about throughout the entire case.

"Finally, Judge, in order for you to grant a new trial, you would have to determine that the outcome of the original trial would have been different. The only new evidence was what James Vernon told three people. If James Vernon was lying, then all that new evidence is meaningless. The evidence is undisputed that James Vernon told three different people two different stories. That's pretty good evidence he was lying."

Henry's fate was now in the hands of Judge Fletcher.

"I'm going to prepare a detailed written order," Judge Fletcher began, "but I am going to announce my decision at this time." She proceeded to shoot down the ineffective-assistance-of-counsel argument and all the newly-discovered-evidence arguments before getting to the part Jack was really waiting for.

"With regard to the fact that David Hawke and his cousin were never prosecuted, I don't believe that that is a *Brady* violation. Mr. Hawke testified at trial that no deal was struck beforehand. However implausible that testimony might be, there is simply no evidence to contradict it."

Jack tensed. Henry's options were running out. They now had one issue left—Anthony Webster's interview.

"But I do believe," Judge Fletcher continued, "that Mr. Webster's interview of James Vernon was *Brady* material, because Mr. Vernon told Mr. Webster that Henry Wilson did not commit this crime. I believe such testimony would have affected the outcome of this trial, and I say that particularly because there was no physical evidence connecting Mr. Wilson to this murder. His conviction was based solely on the testimony of one man. Yes, Mr. Benton should have talked to Mr. Griffin, and if he had, he probably would have learned of the Webster interview. However, that is not the issue. In my opinion, a prosecutor who fails to disclose exculpatory evidence to the defense, whether intentionally or not, must suffer the consequences if that failure to disclose is prejudicial.

"As to the argument that Mr. Vernon may have been lying, that's an issue that the jury should have been allowed to decide." She paused, then looked directly at Henry.

"Therefore, I am granting the motion for new trial."

Henry sat in his chair, stunned. The only spectator in the gallery was Wofford Benton, who gave an audible sigh of relief.

"Did she just say what I thought she said?" Henry asked Jack.

Jack put his hand on Henry's shoulder. "Yes she did, Henry. You are getting a new trial."

It wasn't over yet, though. Scott Tremaine stood to address the court.

"Your honor, it is my duty to inform you that the state does not intend to appeal your decision. Nor does it intend to retry this case."

It was Jack's turn to be stunned. He wondered whether Henry had any idea of what was about to happen. The judge addressed Henry directly.

"Mr. Wilson, would you stand up?" Henry pushed himself out of his chair. His hands were visibly shaking. "In light of the pronouncement by the state, it is my duty to advise you that you are a free man. If you choose, you can be transported back to prison to pick up your belongings and clean out your cell, or I can enter an order right now releasing you and you can send for your things when you get settled. The choice is yours."

Henry very calmly addressed the judge.

"I'd like to be released right now."

The judge looked at the sheriff's deputies. "Release this man," she ordered.

It took a few minutes for all the shackles to be removed, during which time Henry's hands continued to shake and tears started to run down his cheeks. Finally, he was freed, and he and Jack embraced.

"I never thought this day would come," Henry told Jack through his tears. "And I will never forget what you did for me."

Jack had to clear his throat to speak. He was in almost as bad an emotional state as Henry. "I had a lot of help, Henry—from the man standing in the back of this courtroom." They looked to the back of the courtroom where Wofford Benton was standing, and Jack motioned him to come forward.

Wofford walked hesitantly to the defense counsel's table. He and

Henry had not spoken in seventeen years. Henry wrapped the small, pudgy man in his arms. Both men cried.

"Thank you, Wofford."

"Thank you, Henry, and thank God for giving me this opportunity to redeem myself."

Nobody had anticipated that Henry would be released that day. The only clothes he had were his prison clothes, and the state was not about to let him walk away with those. Wofford volunteered to buy him a new outfit, so Henry and Jack waited in the courtroom for another hour with the sheriff's deputies while Wofford went shopping.

Jack took the opportunity to have a brief conversation with Scott Tremaine.

"That was a great cross-examination of Wofford," Jack said, trying to soothe the sting of the judge's ruling.

"Thanks, Jack. I want you to know I agreed to take the case before I reviewed the entire file," Scott said. "After I reviewed it, I told the state's attorney that I would argue the legal points but if the judge ruled against us, I wanted to be able to tell her that there would be no appeal and no retrial. Otherwise, I was off the case."

"That answers a bunch of questions, Scott, thanks. I wish there were more prosecutors around like you."

Wofford had done a good job picking out Henry's new wardrobe, at least in one respect: everything fit. Henry felt a little awkward, but he looked good. Wofford had bought him a blue oxford shirt, a pair of gray slacks, black socks, and black loafers—size fourteen.

"You look like an Ivy Leaguer," Jack told him when he emerged from the courthouse bathroom in his new ensemble. Henry gave him an embarrassed smile. He was a little nervous about everything.

The three of them went across the street to have a cup of coffee. "Where are you going to go?" Wofford asked when they were seated.

"He's coming home with me," Jack jumped in.

"No, Jack," Henry objected. "You've got too much going on with Pat being sick and all."

"Exactly, Henry. I'm going to be needing some help. We've got plenty of room, and Pat's been looking forward to meeting you for quite some time."

"I don't know what to say."

"Don't say anything, Henry," Wofford suggested. "Just go with it."

THIRTY-SIX

Pat was doing even better when Jack arrived at the hospital that afternoon.

"Hi, honey," she said as he walked in the door. "You're here early. How'd it go in court today?"

"It went very well," Jack told her and Charlie.

A smile cut across Pat's face. Charlie's too. "Really? You got Henry a new trial?"

"Better than that," Jack offered teasingly.

"Better?"

"Yup." He turned to look at the doorway where he had just entered. "Come on in." He gestured to someone in the hallway as he spoke. "I want you to meet some people."

Henry walked into Pat's private room, which immediately got a lot smaller.

"Wow!" Pat exclaimed when she saw Henry. "This is unbelievable. You have to be Henry. I'm Pat, and this is my best friend, Charlie. You're actually free! I'm sorry, Henry, I feel like I know you already." Her words came rapid-fire, a combination of the medication and her true happiness for Henry. She extended her hand, and Henry took it in his.

"I feel like I know you too," he said. "And I'm so glad you're feeling better."

"Yeah, the doctor is coming in soon. I feel great. Jack, come over here and give me a kiss, and then the two of you can tell us all about this absolutely remarkable day. Henry, I still can't believe you're here."

"I can't either," Henry said, his smile widening.

Jack sat on the edge of Pat's bed and, holding her hand, proceeded to fill her and Charlie in on the events in the courtroom. "I wasn't surprised when the judge granted Henry a new trial. I can't say I expected it, but I wasn't surprised by it. I was absolutely floored, though, when the state dropped the case."

"So it's completely over?" Charlie asked.

"Yeah," Jack replied. "It's completely over."

"Where do you go from here, Henry?" Pat asked. "Do you have any family or anything?"

Jack answered before Henry could say anything. "I've invited Henry to come home and stay with us for a while until we figure things out."

"Absolutely!" Pat replied. "We've got plenty of room."

"I don't want to be a bother," Henry told her. "With your illness and all."

"Nonsense, Henry," she scolded. "The world isn't going to stop because I'm sick. Besides, Jack and I could use the company. We've worn poor Charlie out."

"Yeah, I've got to go home soon," said Charlie. "And somebody has to look after these two."

While they were talking, Dr. Wright came into the room.

"It looks like there's a party going on in here," she said.

"Of sorts," Jack replied. "Do you have anything to tell us?"

"I do. Do you and Pat want to talk to me in private?"

"No," Pat said firmly. "Charlie here is my best friend, and Jack and Henry have just been through a life-and-death struggle together. They can hear whatever you've got to say."

Dr. Wright looked at Jack, who nodded his head in agreement. "Okay," she said. "The news isn't good. The tumors have not shrunk. In fact, they've grown a little. That explains why your pain has increased. We can try a different chemotherapy regimen. At this point, that is all I can offer."

"Will a different regimen shrink the tumors?" Jack asked. He was trying to concentrate on the facts rather than his emotions. Once his heart processed what his brain had heard, he wouldn't be able to talk. He tightened his fingers around Pat's hand.

"It's possible."

"What's the percentage?" Pat asked.

"Less than ten percent, I'm afraid," Dr. Wright replied.

"What are the other options?" Pat wanted to know.

"There aren't any."

"When can we start this new regimen?" Jack asked, clinging to that last bit of hope.

"Today, if you'd like. It would only take an hour, and Pat has rebounded very well from her last treatment."

"No," Pat said. She said it in a low tone but it was a firm *no*. The firmest *no* Jack had ever heard. He could feel her words as well as hear them.

Dr. Wright didn't quite grasp Pat's statement so clearly. "I'm not sure I understand," she said.

"It's very simple, Doctor," Pat told her. "I want to stop treatment. I want to go home. And I want to enjoy every minute that I have left. I don't want to spend my last days being poked and prodded and ravaged by chemotherapy."

Nobody said a word. Jack could hear himself breathing. And he could feel his heart breaking.

THIRTY-SEVEN

Pat lived for another three months. Most days, after she took her pain medication, she was alert and pain free. She took short walks with Jack in the morning after breakfast and spent her afternoons on the front porch watching the traffic on the Okalatchee.

Jack's Uncle Bill started showing up every morning around breakfast time. Pat got a kick out of him. Even though he was eighty-seven, Uncle Bill had a strong, thick, rich voice and perfect diction.

"Good morning, young man," he'd say to Henry, as though he had stepped to center stage. "And how is the young lady of the house?" he'd ask Pat. The way he said it forced her to smile whether she felt like it or not. It was like having Shakespeare come to the house for coffee.

Jack was always the afterthought. He would simply get a "Hello, nephew." Jack didn't mind one bit. He enjoyed Bill's presence as much as everybody else. It made them feel like a family.

Pat and Jack didn't say much on their morning walks. They just held hands. Pat brought peanuts for the squirrels. They'd stop on the way and sit and drink some water and smile at each other and enjoy each moment, squeezing it for everything it was worth.

In the afternoon, Henry would join Pat on the porch for a while. Her eyes were going bad, and Henry had taken to reading books to her. They were halfway through *Cross Creek*, by Marjorie Kinnan Rawlings, but it was going slowly. Pat kept having him go back and read her the final paragraph at the end of the first chapter before he could pick up where they had left off the day before.

"Read it to me, Henry," she'd say. "Just one more time." And Henry would open the book to page fourteen and read:

> *Folk call the road lonely, because there is not human traffic and human stirring. Because I have walked it so many times and seen such a tumult of life there, it seems to me one of the most populous highways of my acquaintance. I have walked it in ecstasy, and in joy it is beloved. Every pine tree, every gallberry bush, every passion vine, every joree rustling in the underbrush, is vibrant. I have walked it in trouble, and the wind in the trees beside me is easing. I have walked it in despair, and the red of the sunset is my own blood dissolving into the night's darkness. For all such things were on the earth before us, and will survive after us, and it is given to us to join ourselves with them and be comforted.*

"That is so beautiful," she would say when he was done, and then he would find their place from the previous time and continue reading.

One day she stopped him before he finished the chapter he was reading. "That's enough for today, Henry. I'm tired." Henry closed the book and started to get up to help her into her bedroom. "Sit down here next to me, Henry," she said.

"Yes ma'am." He had cared about her before he met her, so it was no surprise to him that his feelings for her had only grown deeper.

"You don't have to feel guilty, Henry."

"Ma'am?"

"About living."

"I'm not sure I understand."

"C'mon, Henry, we haven't known each other long, but we know each other well. You feel guilty because you were spared, and I'm not going to be."

Henry didn't answer. He rubbed those huge hands of his, and his broad, muscular shoulders tightened as he tried to fight back the tears.

"That's just the way it is, Henry. God has plans for me elsewhere and for you here. So promise me you won't feel guilty anymore."

Henry hesitated, collected himself. "I promise," he finally said.

"Even when I'm gone."

"I promise," he said again, his entire body shaking.

Charlie came down from New York every other week like clockwork. She and Pat would sit on the porch and drink tea and chat. Every once in a while the conversation turned serious.

"Would you do something for me, Charlie?"

"Sure, Pat. Anything."

"Sometime down the road when you think it's appropriate, I want you to tell Jack you and I had this conversation. Tell him I want him to go on with his life and live it to the fullest. And tell him…" Pat hesitated for a minute. This was not something she had planned to say, but she knew, sitting here with her old friend, that Charlie would deliver the message. "Tell him that if somebody had told me that I could live to a ripe old age if I gave up the last few years I've had here in Bass Creek with him, I would choose to die tomorrow rather than do that."

Pat almost couldn't get the last words out. Both she and Charlie started crying. They held each other for several minutes.

"That is so beautiful, Pat. Why don't you tell Jack yourself?"

"I can't, Charlie. There are certain things we can't talk about even at this point. It's too hard."

Pat had a different conversation with Jack. It was toward the end, when she was bedridden. He was sitting beside her, trying to put on a game face.

"It's going to be fine, Jack," she told him. "I know it now. I can feel it. My people are going to come to get me. When that happens, when they finally come, I'll let you know. I'll give you a signal." Jack didn't know what she was talking about. He just held her hand and kept his eyes from her view.

"You're the one who first told me it was going to be all right," she said with a weak smile.

He gave her a surprised look, forgetting for the moment to hide his tears.

"That's right. It was you. That day out on the river when I was worried about the cormorant. You said, 'Things that happen in nature are meant to be.' You remember that?"

He nodded.

"That's when I knew. Coming here to Bass Creek—finding our special place. It was all about learning that I was a part of it—nature. And this is simply meant to be. I'm going somewhere, Jack, but I won't be gone."

She took his head to her breast and held him.

They were all there the day Pat slipped quietly away. Uncle Bill usually went home after breakfast. Henry always left Pat's bedroom when Jack entered, not wanting to interfere with their time together. This day, however, Uncle Bill stayed all day, and he and Henry and Jack and Charlie never left the room. They said the rosary—something Bill hadn't done in forty years—several times. And they sang Pat's favorite songs and hymns. They were standing around the bed singing the Beatles' tune "All You Need Is Love" when Pat opened her eyes and caught Jack's—and winked. Then she closed them for the last time.

It took Jack several minutes to realize that was the signal.

PART TWO

THIRTY-EIGHT

New York City, June 14, 1999

Sal Paglia selected his lucky yellow tie with the red stars for the first day of Benny Avrile's murder trial. It looked great with his dark blue shirt and tan summer suit. Sal was sure that Spencer Taylor, the chief assistant district attorney, and his deputy, Norma Grier, would both be decked out in dark suits and that Spencer would wear a red tie. It was the courtroom uniform—stilted and predictable. That just wasn't Sal's style. He was flamboyant, spontaneous, and totally unpredictable. At least, that's the way he saw himself.

The past six months had gone far beyond even Sal's expectations. He'd had six hearings, one a month, and he had invited the press to each one, just to keep the case in the public eye. After each hearing he would perform his usual court-jester routine on the courthouse steps, saying the most provocative things he could think of. He inadvertently struck pay dirt at the very last hearing when he declared that the state of New York should not have a death penalty because it was barbaric. Sal, of course, didn't believe a word of what he was saying. He had always been a firm believer in the death penalty.

The Republican governor, Matthew Palmer, who never missed a chance to make some political hay, took issue with Sal's statements about capital punishment. He knew that many New Yorkers' attitudes about the death penalty had changed, and he had been looking for the opportunity to exploit the issue. Sal had given it to him.

"If this man is convicted, I promise you," Governor Palmer told the people of New York in response to Sal's diatribe, "that he will be promptly executed."

Suddenly Benny Avrile's murder trial was front-page news again.

Uh oh! thought Sal. *Maybe I've bitten off more than I can chew.* He soon dispensed with that negativity, however, when he realized how much publicity his fight with the governor was engendering. Business immediately started to boom at his law office. Poor Hazel didn't have time to play even one game of solitaire. She had to answer phones and do real work. There were many days when Sal watched Hazel curse Luis Melendez under her breath for walking through the front door of Sal's office and ruining her life.

The pressure's on, Sal thought. *But what's the downside? I'm not the one who might be executed.*

All the preliminary skirmishing was over. It was finally trial time. The press was in a dither over it. Was Benny going to be the first person executed in New York in fifty years? Governor Palmer didn't let up either. He scheduled a press conference the very first morning of the trial, to renew his pledge to execute Benny immediately when he was convicted. It didn't matter that the execution might not take place for another ten years. Hype was hype.

Despite the gauntlet laid down by the governor, Sal was confident as he stepped into the elevator on the fifth floor of his apartment building to head for the courthouse and his rendezvous with destiny. *Maybe after this I'll buy another house—bigger and better than the last one. I'm never getting married again, though. I ain't gonna give this one up.*

Sal's confidence stemmed from tempered expectations. He wasn't looking for victory. He knew Benny wasn't going to get off—that was a little too much to hope for. But he did have a shot at saving him from the death penalty, which would be considered a victory by most observers in the know and would enhance his reputation. He had Dr. Donald Wong all set to testify as an expert on Benny's behalf, *and* he had some new evidence that would definitely surprise the state.

All this was going to turn his life around eventually. He only owed

Beano Moffit about thirty thousand, which would be chicken feed once he got rolling again.

Sal leaned back against the rear wall of the elevator and started reading his notes for the opening statement. It was his routine to write out the opening statement in longhand and practice it several times in his skivvies in front of the full-length bathroom mirror. When he felt confident he had it down, he reduced it to an outline. He was reading his outline when the elevator door opened on the third floor and someone stepped in. Sal didn't even look up. When the door again opened at the lobby, Sal started to walk out, his head still buried in his notes. He felt something cold pressed to the base of his skull. Before he could react, he heard a noise, like a pop. His whole head was burning and his legs went limp. He tried to stay up but couldn't. Then everything suddenly turned calm and peaceful. He was unconscious before he hit the floor.

The shooter stepped over the body, which was lying half inside the elevator and half out, turned, and fired two more shots for certainty.

THIRTY-NINE

Miami, October 1999

I t had been a long day, and Jack Tobin was tired. He'd been on his feet for hours presenting evidence to the Florida Board of Professional Responsibility, and he still wasn't done. It wasn't unusual for him to be on his feet all day. Hell, he'd had trials that lasted months. But this fatigue was different. This was emotional fatigue. This was ripping open a wound that had not yet healed, a wound that was festering with infections and pus and all sorts of bad things. This was, in every sense of the word, gut-wrenching.

Now Jack was making his summation to the board.

"As you know, I have been before you many times in the past on the other side of this issue—representing physicians—so I have literally seen both sides. The evidence I have put before you today shows, I believe, that Dr. Hawthorne is unfit to continue practicing medicine. I have presented to you four other instances where Dr. Hawthorne missed the diagnosis of ovarian cancer even though the patient exhibited classic symptoms of the disease. Many individuals never have symptoms. That is why it is often referred to as the 'silent killer.' These five women, however, all had multiple symptoms—abdominal pain, fatigue, bloating, and weight loss—over an extended period of time. Only one of these women, Ms. Eliot, survived, and in that case, where the diagnosis was missed for a precious eight months, the positive outcome was considered a miracle. She told you that herself earlier today. In the case here before you, the diagnosis was missed for more than nine months, and when the proper diagnosis was finally made, it was too late. The cancer had metastasized into multiple organs.

"One blood test could have revealed the problem. An ultrasound could have confirmed the diagnosis. In every one of these five situations, this doctor did nothing. Early detection was the only real chance these women had.

"Everybody makes mistakes, ladies and gentlemen, but when you do it in life-and-death situations and you do it consistently, there have to be severe repercussions. That's why I'm asking you to take Dr. Hawthorne's license."

It was short, sweet, and to the point. And more important, it was devoid of emotion. If Jack had let his emotions enter into the presentation, there was no telling what would have happened.

Dr. Hawthorne's attorney, Ken Cooper, now had his opportunity to present the doctor's side. As Jack sat down, Ken stood to address the board.

This was not the setting where these gentlemen usually worked. They were trial lawyers, and their arena was the courtroom. This administrative hearing was in a ballroom at the San Juan Capistrano Hotel in downtown Miami, and the "court" consisted of a panel of about thirty physicians and other professionals who were going to pass judgment on Dr. Hawthorne's professional future.

Ken did exactly what Jack expected him to do. He pointed out to the board that the symptoms of ovarian cancer are the symptoms of so many common ailments. "It is not a deviation from the normal standard of care not to jump to the conclusion that everyone who has persistent stomach pain or bloating has ovarian cancer. If that were the case, doctors would spend their days sending people to have diagnostic testing, from ultrasounds to CT scans. That's the type of medicine that is already driving up medical costs." After that, Ken read from portions of the five expert depositions that he had submitted earlier as evidence. "Five of the most prominent physicians in this area and in the country have told you that Dr. Hawthorne did not deviate from the usual standard of care. That is evidence you cannot ignore."

It was a good argument, and it was the argument Jack would have made and *had* made many times before, but Jack still had an almost uncontrollable desire to get out of his seat, grab Ken Cooper by the throat, and squeeze as hard as he could. The only reason he didn't was that Ken was a longtime friend who was only doing his job. He also knew that Ken—like himself when he'd represented physicians, delusional as he may have been—actually believed what he was saying. He wasn't so sure about the doctors at the large, elevated, U-shaped table in front of him.

It was Jack's turn for rebuttal. He stood and put his hands in his suit jacket pockets, something he had never done in his entire career as a trial attorney. He took a deep breath to relax. His heart was in his throat. *Maybe I should have gotten someone else to do this. Maybe I'm too close to the situation.* But it was too late now. He had believed nobody else could make the case like he could. Maybe he was right. Certainly nobody else could have felt as strongly about it as he did.

"Ken made a good argument," he began. "He always does. Ken is a good lawyer. He comes prepared. When I handled these cases—and as you know, if you're going to represent physicians in medical malpractice lawsuits, you're going to represent them in administrative hearings as well—I did exactly what Ken has done. I presented the testimony of the best experts in the country. That is why I gave you evidence of *actual cases* where people have lost loved ones or, as in Ms. Eliot's case, where someone almost lost her life—all under Dr. Hawthorne's care. So what's it going to be? Are you going to rule in favor of people, or are you going to rule in favor of the experts?"

There was much more he wanted to say, but he knew instinctively that it was time to sit down and shut up. They had the point. They were either going to buy it or they weren't. As the discussion proceeded around the U-shaped table, Jack quickly got his answer. Most of the doctors and other professionals on the panel quickly adopted the opinions of the experts while expressing their heartfelt condolences to the families of the victims of the good doctor's care. Their chairman, Dr. Robert Green, summed it up well:

"Our hearts go out to you family members who have lost loved ones. However, sometimes doctors can do everything possible and people still die. I believe that's what happened in this case, and that's what our experts have told us."

Jack wanted to puke. He'd been present at numerous such proceedings in the past but felt like he was going through it for the first time, because now he was one of those family members and the case involved the death of his own wife. *How could I have been so blind for so long?* he asked himself as he sat there listening to men and women who liked nothing more than the sound of their own voices supporting the system that fed them so well.

One of the newer and more naïve members of the panel actually had a question for Jack. "Why haven't you filed a lawsuit, Mr. Tobin? If your case has merit, you could present it to a jury of ordinary people."

To his credit, Ken Cooper did not object to Jack's answering the question. He could have successfully argued that the evidence stage of the hearing was over and that the lawyers were no longer allowed to speak. But he didn't.

"Well," Jack replied, remaining seated, "it's a simple question but a complicated answer—an answer I've thought about a great deal. The only thing civil suits can do is compensate people with money. There is a great deal of propaganda in this country right now about those malpractice suits: it talks about greedy trial lawyers tricking juries into awarding huge sums of money and poor doctors having to pay high insurance premiums. The doctors have jumped in bed with the insurance industry, and it remains to be seen who will get the top position in that little affair. On the other hand, many lawyers have abused the system. The people who have been intentionally excluded from this discussion are the victims, because they have no power.

"I don't need money. And I don't want this discussion to be about all that crap I just mentioned. I want it to be about people and how they've been harmed by this doctor. If you want to limit lawsuits, then you have to discipline your doctors. You can't have it both ways. That's criminal in my mind."

"Mr. Tobin," Chairman Green said as soon as Jack finished, "I understand you've had an unfortunate loss, but that is no reason to make accusations and use inappropriate analogies."

Jack only heard the first part of the sentence. He exploded from his chair. "Did you just call the death of my wife—her name was Pat, by the way, in case you don't have it on your cheat sheet up there—did you just call her death 'an unfortunate loss'?" Before the stunned doctor could respond, Jack was at him again. "How about if I come up there and wring your skinny little neck? What adjective do you think your colleagues would supply for that loss?"

"You're out of order, Mr. Tobin," the chairman shouted.

"Out of order? You think I'm out of order? I'm not out of order. This is out of order." Jack threw himself over the table that was in front of him and started toward the chairman, who looked like he was about to wet his pants and with good reason. Jack was a hell of a lot bigger than he was.

As he started forward, a huge hand reached out, grabbed him by the shoulder, and pulled him back. The shoulder and arm attached to that hand wrapped themselves around Jack's body.

"Hold on, brother," Henry said soothingly. At the same time, four uniformed security officers were moving toward them. Henry spoke to them as calmly as he had spoken to Jack.

"Hold on now," he said. "Me and Mr. Tobin here were just leaving. I assure you, you don't want to get in our way."

Perhaps it was the way he said it, or perhaps it was the size of the man—they could see how firmly he held Jack—or perhaps it was the look in his eyes. Whatever it was, the guards stopped in their tracks. Henry and Jack left the ballroom unimpeded.

Jack was in a rage, oblivious to his surroundings. Henry didn't let go until they were in the parking lot. Even then, he stood between Jack and the entrance to the hotel.

"Don't worry, Henry," Jack told him. "I'm not going back in. I've said all I'm going to say to those people."

"If it makes you feel any better, Jack, people like that never listened to me either."

"C'mon, let's get a beer," Jack said.

"Sure thing," Henry replied.

*   *   *

Not long after Henry regained his freedom, Jack had filed a claims bill with the Florida state legislature requesting that the state of Florida compensate Henry for the seventeen years he'd spent on death row. Henry and Jack were invited to a hearing before a legislative committee of state senators and representatives. Jack had witnessed enough closing arguments by plaintiffs' lawyers in his years as an insurance defense attorney to know how to uncork the tear ducts of even the most jaded politicians. By the time he was through telling the story of Henry's near-execution, there were very few dry-eyed members of the committee left. They awarded Henry three million dollars.

Henry was forever grateful to Jack. After Pat's death, he stayed at the home in Bass Creek for a couple of months before buying his own place in Miami. However, he still came out to Bass Creek to spend the weekends.

Henry had made a promise to Jack to work with him on his death penalty projects in any capacity he needed. Henry knew how to do legal research, and he could investigate in places Jack could never go. He could even serve as a bodyguard if necessary. His performance at the San Juan Capistrano proved that even when he was outnumbered, people did not want to mess with Henry Wilson.

Jack was on his fifth beer when the melancholy set in. Henry was used to it.

"It's been a year, Henry, but it's like I lost her yesterday."

"A year isn't very long, Jack, when you love someone as much as you loved Pat."

"Yeah, but I can't seem to get on with things. It's like I'm stuck in place. If Pat were here she'd give me a good swift kick."

"I was stuck in place for as long as I can remember, Jack. You'll come out of it soon. I can see the early stirrings already. Dr. Green was part of that. I can still see his face as you started toward him."

That got a smile out of Jack.

Maybe Henry's right, he thought. *Maybe I am coming out of it.*

FORTY

Langford Middleton was intelligent and ambitious. He was also passive and indecisive, but those qualities didn't show up on his résumé. On paper, Langford looked like he had it all—undergraduate degree from Princeton, law degree from Columbia. He was equally impressive in person, standing a little over six feet, two inches tall with a full, thick head of brown hair, a strong jaw, sharp features, and a booming baritone voice. He was the fourth generation of a prominent New York family. His mother was a professor at City College, his father a Park Avenue doctor like his father before him and his father's father.

The powers that be at the Wall Street firm of Stockwell, Pennington, Morris, and Jewel fell in love with Langford Middleton, his résumé, and his pedigree when they met him on a recruiting visit to Columbia. He was everything they were looking for in a young trial lawyer. So they offered him a job with a six-figure income, which Langford graciously accepted.

Like the other associates, Langford spent the first few years of his career in the library, researching and writing for the partners. His work was acceptable in the sense that he laid out the problems and presented the research. However, time after time, Langford failed to provide the partner he was working for with a decisive conclusion as to legal precedent or a definitive strategy on how to proceed. Even though he was transferred from partner to partner over the years, nobody seemed to notice that Langford was not living up to the expectations the firm had for its associates. He had an affable, easygoing manner about him, and in his brief appearances in court at motion hearings he was generally impressive. He even did okay sitting second chair in a few trials. Consequently, when his five years were up, Langford was offered a partnership, which he again graciously accepted.

When he had his own case files, Langford's character flaws gradually revealed themselves to even the most myopic observer. He wouldn't move cases along to trial, and he failed to make settlement recommendations to clients for fear that they might consider him weak-willed. He was billing okay, but he wasn't turning cases over. Five years after becoming a partner, Langford was bewildered and befuddled and buried under a truckload of cases, old and new. He avoided clients' calls, and they started to complain to the managing partners, who finally took notice and decided to do something. But what? Langford was a partner, and he came from a prestigious New York family. It would be both embarrassing and expensive to jettison him.

"I think we need to make him a judge," Richard Stockwell told the other senior partners at a management meeting.

"A judge?" Howard Pennington said disbelievingly. "How the hell can he be a judge? Judges have to make decisions. He can't decide what type of knot to put in his tie in the morning."

"Nobody knows he can't make a decision but us and our clients," Stockwell persisted. "Besides, he looks like a judge. He's got that hair and that voice."

"He may be central casting's ideal choice," Frederick Morris added, "but this isn't Hollywood. We're talking about a real judge."

"Come on, Fred," Bennett Jewel, the remaining member of the Big Four, weighed in. "We've got a bunch of nincompoops up there right now masquerading as judges. This has been done before. Grady, Scott, and Anderson put that fool Justin Wennington on the bench just to get rid of him."

"Okay, okay," Fred Morris replied. "Let's assume we were going to make him a judge. How would we go about doing it?"

"It's very simple," Dick Stockwell added. "We start putting Langford out there as the face of the firm. We'll put him on bar committees, have him attend all social functions, and let him make the charitable and political contributions for the firm in his own name. We'll divvy up his cases among the other partners so he doesn't cost us any more bad publicity. It'll take a year or two, but when a position comes up for appointment, with his name and face out there and our political connections, he'll be a shoo-in."

"What if he doesn't want to go along?" Howard Pennington asked.

"Oh, he'll go along," Dick Stockwell replied. "In case you haven't noticed, Howard, Langford doesn't like to work very hard. We can sell this new job to him real easy. A year or two down the road when he doesn't have any cases, he won't have much choice in the matter."

The plan worked like a charm. Two years after the plot was hatched, Langford Middleton, in just his twelfth year of practice, was appointed a judge in the civil trial division of the New York State Supreme Court.

Lawyers who appeared before Judge Middleton learned early on that they were not going to get a speedy resolution of their case. The judge didn't like any pressure coming his way. Motion hearings with difficult legal issues were taken under advisement and the attorneys, after waiting months for an answer, usually reached their own resolution. He didn't like trials at all, and he would lean hard on lawyers to reach a settlement. Complaints were made about him. For years nothing ever came of them, until a decision was finally made to transfer him to the criminal division to force him to try cases. Judge Middleton was in his fifteenth year on the bench, having just been transferred to criminal, when Benny Avrile's case was placed on his docket.

Warren Jacobs, the district attorney, was furious when he heard Langford Middleton had been assigned the Avrile case. He discreetly tried to get it transferred to someone else, to no avail. He had to give up the effort or risk exposure and charges of judge-shopping. With no other avenues to pursue, Jacobs resorted to the direct approach. He went to see Judge Middleton personally.

"I want to get directly to the point," Jacobs told the judge when they had dispensed with the amenities and were seated in the judge's chambers. "I want you off the Avrile case."

The polite, insincere smile on Langford Middleton's face vanished. "For your information, Counselor, I want off this case as much as you want me off. Unfortunately, you're stuck with me."

The truth was that Langford was finally under the gun. He had tried to get rid of the case as soon as it had been assigned to him. He didn't want that kind of publicity. The Judicial Qualifications Commission told him in no uncertain terms that the case would not be transferred and that he was being watched.

"Well, if I'm stuck with you, Judge, let me give you fair warning. This case is going to be tried, and it's going to be tried on time. No delays—none of your usual crap to get the parties to settle. My ass is on the line here, and if you fuck around with me, I'm going after you."

Langford Middleton was shocked. He didn't know if Warren Jacobs was aware of the pressure he was receiving from his own superiors. He just knew he was being backed into a corner. Still, he couldn't let Jacobs get away with such talk.

"Counselor, do you realize I could have your license for this?"

"Cut the crap, Judge. There's nobody in this room but me and you, and I don't think you want to get into a pissing contest with me. You just remember what I said and know that I am dead serious about this. I will bury you."

Having said his piece, Jacobs got up and walked out before Langford had a chance to say anything else.

Judge Middleton took Warren Jacobs's threat to heart. There were no delays. At precisely nine a.m. on the anointed date for trial, June 14th, Spencer Taylor, Norma Grier, and the judge were all in court ready to proceed, as were selected members of the press. The rest of the media were outside on the courthouse steps. The courtroom was full of spectators as well. Benny was downstairs in a holding cell. The only one missing was Sal Paglia. At 9:25, the judge called for Spencer and Norma to follow him into his chambers.

"Do you have any idea where he is?"

"No sir," Spencer replied.

"When was the last time you talked to him?"

"Friday afternoon. He was all set to go."

The judge called Christine, his secretary, on the intercom. "See if you can get Mr. Paglia's office on the phone."

Hazel answered on the second ring. She had just gotten into the office. Knowing Sal was going directly to the courthouse, she hadn't seen any need to get to work on time. Her game of solitaire could wait, and so could the clients.

"Law office of Sal Paglia," Hazel sang into the phone while she continued to play the game she had just started.

"This is Judge Middleton's secretary. Is Mr. Paglia in?"

"No," Hazel answered. "He was going directly to court this morning."

"Well, he's not here."

"Something must have happened," Hazel responded. Sal was a lot of things, but he was always on time to court. "I'll call his apartment and call you back."

The phone rang only once at Sal's apartment. "Hello," answered a voice Hazel didn't recognize. It was a woman, which could definitely explain things.

"Who is this?" Hazel demanded.

"Detective Sarah Hingis," the voice answered. "Who is this?"

"Detective as in police detective?" Hazel asked.

"That's right. Now who is this?"

"Hazel Reece. I'm Mr. Paglia's legal secretary. He was supposed to be in court this morning but he didn't show. Is something wrong?"

"Yes, Hazel, something is very wrong. Your boss has been murdered." Detective Hingis saw no problem in letting Hazel know about Sal's demise, although she made sure that she didn't provide her with any details about the murder. At this stage everybody, including Sal's secretary, was a suspect.

Hazel couldn't believe what she was hearing. *Murdered? Sal?* It took all her strength to call the judge's secretary back and deliver the news.

When Christine told him of Sal Paglia's untimely death, Judge Middleton could do nothing but cancel the trial and return Benny to prison.

For a fleeting moment, when he learned that the trial had been put off, Warren Jacobs considered the possibility that Langford Middleton had finally gone too far to avoid his obligations as a judge.

FORTY-ONE

Henry wasn't the only one looking after Jack. Charlie had been down to visit a few times since Pat's death. She was a little more direct with Jack, especially on her last visit, which was just a few days after Jack's performance at the San Juan Capistrano Hotel. Jack was driving her back to the airport when the conversation started.

"Jack, you have to snap out of this funk you're in."

"I know what you're saying. I just feel so lost and so sad. You were close to Pat. How do you deal with the loss?"

"This may sound strange to you, Jack, but I feel that she's still with me. I talk to her all the time."

"Really?"

"Yeah. I mean, she doesn't talk back to me or anything like that. I don't want you to think I'm crazy. I just feel her presence. I can't explain it any better than that."

"I wish I felt it."

"You will. Have you been to your special place since you spread her ashes there?"

"No."

"Why don't you go? See if it helps you."

"Maybe I will," he replied.

The next morning, Jack put on a T-shirt and his jogging shorts and went out for a run. It was his first time out since Pat's death. He headed along the river trail that he and Pat had often taken. It was still dark, and the moon was full in the east. The cool October air gave him a little chill at first. But he soon warmed to his task. He felt remarkably good, although his pace was slow. It was rush hour on the river as the fishing boats headed out to the big lake. After only a few minutes, Jack took a deep breath and exhaled. *I've missed this*, he thought.

He remembered his first visit to Bass Creek on a fishing trip. He had instantly fallen in love with this podunk little town in the middle of nowhere. It was the combination of the river and the slow pace of life and the untouched beauty of the surrounding countryside. He had resolved that very day to retire in Bass Creek. Pat had loved it too. When she came there to live, all the planets seemed to have aligned. It just didn't last very long.

Three miles later he was back at the house, where he kicked off his sneakers, took off his shirt, and jumped into the pool. His stroke was as smooth as ever as he ticked off thirty laps. He could have swum longer, but he stopped. *No sense overdoing it*, he told himself. *You'll feel it tomorrow morning.*

After his swim, he took stock of himself in front of the full-length mirror in the bedroom. He hadn't gained much weight during the layoff, mainly because he'd stopped eating at the same time he stopped working out. *I just need to tone up: three miles for two weeks, and then I'll up it to five. Half a mile every day in the pool. I'll be in shape in no time.* Just then he thought of Charlie and the conversation they'd had the day before. *Tomorrow I'm going out on the river.*

He showered and dressed and headed to the Pelican for breakfast. It was a walk of a mile or so—nothing in Bass Creek was too far—and was one of the few pleasures he had these days. Bass Creek was an old town and many of the homes were run-down, but there was a depth to it, a sense of history. Its essential character hadn't changed in over a hundred years.

The Pelican was a classic diner, an old railroad car complete with aluminum façade and neon sign. Tony and Hannah, a Polish couple from Chicago, had bought the place a couple of years before. Time had eroded the shine on the outside, but Tony polished the façade regularly and made the old place as appealing as possible to the casual passerby. There was a long counter facing the front door as you walked in and booths to either side. Hannah kept the interior spotless, although the plastic covering the cushioned booths was held together here and there with duct tape.

Throughout the downtime of the past year, the diner had always been a wonderful little respite for Jack. It was where his Uncle Bill hung out.

It hadn't taken Uncle Bill long to find a friend after he moved from St. Petersburg. He met Eddie the same day he moved to town. Eddie was seventy-eight, a retired Army supply sergeant who never forgot his calling. His pockets were always full of watches and pens, assorted jewelry, old coins—you name it—that he had traded for or secured in some other way unknown to the average man.

Eddie and Bill were like the odd couple: always together and always arguing about something or other. Jack got a kick out of listening to them. Jack would usually sit at the counter and talk with Hannah. On this particular morning, Eddie and Uncle Bill were sitting at the booth behind him, carping at each other.

"I had three wives," Eddie was telling Bill, "and none of them could cook."

"I had five," Bill countered, his deep voice sounding like Moses addressing the Israelites.

Eddie ignored him. "I did all the cooking,"

"I had a wife in San Diego," Bill mused. "One day I told her I was going out to get a paper. Never did go back."

"People pay good money for this type of entertainment," Jack told Hannah at the counter.

"Yeah, well, if somebody pays us good money, they can have the place *and* the entertainment," Hannah replied.

"I was good to my wives," Eddie went on back at the booth.

"Didn't do you any good," Bill offered. "They still left you."

The two old men were certainly amusing, especially for Hannah, who was obliged to be there. Jack was a different story. *Why*, Hannah wondered, *is a vibrant, talented man like Jack spending so much time at our place?*

*   *   *

Jack rose before dawn and threw on a pair of shorts and a T-shirt. For some reason he grabbed the Yankees baseball cap hanging on the bedpost and put it on. He always wore a hat when he was out on the water, but not this hat. This hat was Pat's. She had been a Yankee fan her whole life, back to the Mickey Mantle days. She and Jack had often kidded each other as to who was the bigger Yankee fan. Jack, like so many boys his age, idolized the Mick. He just couldn't believe that Pat, a girl, could possibly have the same affinity.

He set out on the river in the dinghy, maneuvering through the already brisk traffic heading to the lake until he came to his turn. He hesitated for a moment before steering the little boat under the brush and into the cove where he and Pat had spent so much time. He hadn't been there since he'd spread her ashes over the water almost a year before. He didn't know why exactly. They had always gone together. Maybe he wanted to keep it that way. He wasn't sure.

Nor did he know what he was doing there that morning. He parked the boat in the middle of the inlet and waited for the sunrise.

As the crickets ceased their symphony and the silence set in, a brisk wind began to pick up. Jack could tell a storm was coming fast. In an instant, the normally placid lagoon was ruffled by the rush of heavy winds as thick black clouds raced across the sky. This was not the place to be in a small boat. Jack moved to start the engine. As he did, a gust of wind blew his cap off—Pat's cap. He saw it drifting in the distance. Going after it at this point would be dangerous; visibility was starting to fade, and the wind was whipping the water. Still, he had no choice. Just then an osprey swept down and scooped it up in its talons. Jack's heart sank, but as the osprey flew over the small boat it let go of the cap. It floated down and landed in the water right next to the boat. Jack simply leaned over and picked it up. When he had it in his grasp, he looked up and saw the osprey hovering high above. Then it disappeared into the darkness.

FORTY-TWO

I don't need you to babysit me anymore," Jack told Henry that Friday night when Henry showed up for the weekend. "I can take care of myself."

"I know you can," Henry replied, surprised by Jack's feistiness but reassured by it as well. "That's not the reason I'm here. You know, Pat was right. This place gets in your bones. Besides, I like to fish."

They spent most of their weekends fishing out on the lake in the Sea Ray. Henry usually piloted the boat on the trip out while Jack prepared the fishing gear.

"Not too many black folks driving a boat like this," Henry had remarked one morning when he was getting looks from some of the other boat pilots on the river.

"They would really be envious if they knew you could buy a whole fleet of these boats." Jack laughed.

"Yeah. They'd probably vote all those legislators out of office if they found out where I got the money."

"I don't think so, Henry. I think most people would think you deserved the money."

"That's where you and I differ, Jack."

The following Saturday the weather was bad and they decided not to go out on the water. Jack was in the kitchen eating and Henry was reading a book in the living room when the doorbell rang.

"I'll get it," Henry yelled as he headed for the door.

A short, stocky, middle-aged man was standing there. He was dressed a little too warmly for the weather.

"Can I help you?" Henry asked.

"Yes, I'm looking for Jack Tobin. Am I at the right address?"

"Yeah, you are," Henry told him. "Why don't you come in?"

The man followed Henry from the foyer to the living room. "Have a seat," Henry said, motioning to the couch. The man had no sooner sat down than Jack walked in. He stood up to introduce himself.

"Jack Tobin?"

"Yes."

The man stuck out his hand, a smile on his face. "I'm Luis Melendez."

Jack didn't recognize the name. "What can I do for you, Mr. Melendez?"

"A long time ago you offered to help me, and I didn't take your offer. In a way, I think I'm still paying for that decision. So I decided to come and ask for your help."

"I'm sorry, Mr. Melendez, I don't remember you. I try to remember all my former clients, but your name doesn't ring a bell."

"Oh, I'm not a former client," the man replied.

Jack was totally confused. "Then how do we know each other?"

"Do you remember the Lexingtons football team when you were a teenager?"

"Yes, of course," Jack replied, still puzzled. "I played for them."

"So did I," the man said. "I went by the nickname Rico back then."

Jack studied the man's face. It took his brain a few seconds to race back thirty years. He remembered Rico, the tough, skinny Puerto Rican who had taken him under his wing. He looked at the man in front of him. Time had not been gracious to Rico.

He extended his right hand and touched the man's shoulder with his left. "Rico, is it really you? God, it's been so long. I'm sorry I didn't recognize your name right away. I've been in a little bit of a funk lately. Sit. Sit. Can I get you some coffee?"

"Sure. Just a little milk, no sugar. Thanks."

"I'll get it," Henry told Jack. "You guys obviously have some catching up to do."

They were already back in the sixties when Henry brought Rico's coffee to him. Jack was sitting next to Rico on the couch.

"I remember that championship game like it was yesterday," Jack was telling Rico. "That kick!"

"Yeah. Jimmy Walsh came through for us, didn't he?" Rico replied.

"*You* came through for us, Rico. You created the new kicking team. You taught me to be a holder in, what, two weeks?" Rico didn't say anything.

"You know, Rico," Jack continued, "I took a lot of stuff I learned in that season with me in my life—stuff you taught me. Things like hard work, never giving up, always staying focused. I wanted to thank you a million times, but I never knew where you were."

"I was a lot of places, Jack, some of them not such good places."

"Well, you're here now, so I can finally say thanks."

"You're welcome, Jack. But I didn't come here for that."

"I know," Jack replied. "It sounds like you've got a problem, Rico— I mean Luis. Why don't you tell me about it."

Luis looked over at Henry, who was sitting across from him, and then back at Jack.

"It's okay," Jack said. "Henry is my investigator. You can say anything in front of him that you say to me. We're a team."

"Are you the guy Jack saved from death row here in Florida?" Luis asked.

"Yes, I am," Henry replied. "How did you know about that?"

"I read an article in the *New York Times* about Jack and your case. That's kinda how I eventually came to look for Jack."

Henry nodded. He'd brought the article to Jack's attention soon after his release. It was in the *New York Times Magazine*, and Jack's picture was on the cover. Under it was the caption, "The Lone Ranger— the lawyer who fights for the condemned." The story was all about Jack and his career, but a significant part of it covered Henry's case. There was even a picture of Henry and Jack sitting at counsel table when they appeared before Judge Fletcher. Henry remembered Jack's remark at the time: "Great. Now I'm going to have all kinds of people knocking on my door."

Luis Melendez had been the first one to knock.

"It's my son," Luis continued. "He's in a New York jail, charged with murder."

"Your son? Murder? Knowing you, Luis, that's hard to believe."

"Well, unfortunately, I wasn't the person you knew for many years of my life, Jack."

Luis told Jack and Henry all about his life after football. "When Floyd was killed, I fell apart. I was angry. I felt guilty. If I had kept my mouth shut and if I'd let you help us, maybe we could have gotten out of going to Vietnam. Anyway, I was still in 'Nam, so I was scared too. I started smoking dope and eventually shooting heroin."

Luis told them he had met a girl when he came back to the States, also a heroin addict, and how they'd hooked up and eventually had a kid—Benny.

"I don't know how we did it, but we were together for two years after Benny was born. Then it fell apart completely. She just disappeared. It took me another ten years to get clean. Then I tried to find her and Benny. Her mother finally told me that Benny had been taken from her by the state and she eventually died of an overdose. Still, I couldn't find Benny—until I saw his picture in the paper."

"Didn't you look in the foster care program?" Jack asked. It was the same question Benny had asked.

"Not at first. It's hard to explain. Once you've been in the system—and I spent a few years in prison—you don't even think about asking questions of the state for fear they'll start looking at you again. When I got my feet under me and had enough confidence to go look, it was too late. Benny was gone."

"Have you talked to Benny—explained these things to him?"

"I've tried, Jack. But Benny apparently had a horrible experience in foster care and he blames me for it."

"I know about that experience," Henry added.

"So what can I do for you, Luis?" Jack had an idea, but he wanted to hear it from Luis.

"My son's attorney was murdered about six months ago, on the day of trial. The trial was held up while the state tried to determine if the murder had anything to do with his representation of Benny. They finally decided that he was probably killed by a loan shark named Beano Moffit. Although they haven't arrested Moffit or even charged him, they've reset my son's trial. And a public defender is representing him. Jack, I came to ask if you would consider being my son's lawyer."

Jack didn't answer right away. There were several things he needed to bring up, and he wanted to sort them out in his head before speaking.

"Luis, I'm not a criminal lawyer. My background is as a civil defense lawyer. I represented insurance companies. This second career I have is as an appellate attorney representing people like Henry who are on death row. I know how to try a case, and I now know criminal law thoroughly, but here's the distinction: criminal lawyers represent anybody who comes in the door. I only represent people who I believe are innocent. Is Benny innocent?"

"I don't know. It looks pretty bad though."

Jack started to respond, but Luis continued talking.

"You gotta understand this, Jack. I owe this boy. I wasn't there for him when he was a kid. His mother wasn't there for him. If he'd had a mother and a father behind him, he wouldn't be where he is now."

"You're probably right, Luis, but he is where he is now. And if he's a murderer, there's not a whole lot I can do for him."

Luis's shoulders sank, and he dropped his head. For a moment Jack thought the man was going to cry. He hated being so direct, but he truly didn't want to represent a murderer.

"Luis, what if he is guilty? I don't want to put a murderer back on the street, even if he is your son, and I don't think you do either."

Luis didn't lift his head. "I just thought I could give him another chance at life," he said. "I've had that second chance. I've got a business now—I'm a framing contractor. I thought I could take Benny into the business and teach him the trade."

"You wouldn't be able to do that if he's a hardened criminal, Luis."

"He's not," he said looking up at Jack. "I've seen him and I've talked to him. He's a lost soul, but he's not a hardened criminal."

"How long were you with him?" Jack asked.

"Five minutes maybe, but I could tell."

Jack knew it was wishful thinking. He wanted to help Luis, but representing a murderer would be against the principle he'd established for himself.

Henry, who'd been listening intently to every word, jumped in. "Maybe what you could do, Jack, is hold off making a decision until you look into the case. You could learn all the facts first."

Jack was annoyed at Henry's interruption. He knew Henry was probably identifying with Benny—their childhoods were certainly similar. Henry did have a point, though. Maybe he was being a bit premature.

Luis kept his eyes focused on Jack.

"That's a good idea," Jack finally said. "I'll look into the case before I make a decision. But if the evidence clearly shows that he's guilty, Luis, I'm not going to be your man. Do you understand?"

Luis stood up, elated. "Yes, yes, I understand. I can give you a few thousand to get started. And I can get some more."

"Put your money away," Jack told him. "This isn't about money. Let's see what we can find out, and we'll go from there."

FORTY-THREE

A week after Luis's visit, Jack flew to New York with Henry.
"Why do you want me to go along?" Henry had asked when Jack first extended the invitation. "You probably don't remember this, but I was in prison for seventeen years. I don't like to fly."

"Well, you are my investigator, and it will probably be a good thing to check out the place where the murder occurred. Besides, I'm going to have to make a decision while I'm there, and since you've already interjected yourself into that process, I want you to be with me and help me."

"I don't know about that," Henry replied.

"Yes, you do, Henry. You're going to give me your opinion anyway, solicited or unsolicited. I'd just like to have it beforehand. Sometimes you see things I don't."

"All right then," Henry sighed, still not overly enthusiastic about the trip.

Jack contacted the public defender's office before they left for New York and made arrangements to review Benny's file and meet with the attorney handling the case afterward. He and Henry spent most of their first full day in the city poring over the police reports. At four o'clock that afternoon, they met with Assistant Public Defender Bruce Sentner. Bruce was in his late forties, a short, slight, balding man who had spent his entire career at the public defender's office. He appeared to be genuinely excited to meet both Jack and Henry.

"I've read about you, and I'm aware of your work," he told Jack as they shook hands. "It's a pleasure to meet you."

"It's a pleasure to meet you too," Jack replied, a little embarrassed by Bruce's effusiveness.

"And Henry, your story is inspiring to those of us who work in this business. We'd like to get it right at the trial stage, though."

Henry just grunted. He'd made his peace with Wofford Benton, but public defenders still weren't his favorite people.

"I have to admit I'm a little perplexed," Bruce said, turning to Jack again. "I thought you only did death penalty appeals."

"Benny Avrile's dad is an old friend of mine," Jack explained. "Besides, I haven't taken the case yet. I'm just looking into it."

"Well, fire away. I'll be glad to answer any of your questions if I can."

"Why don't you just give us your overall analysis."

"Off the record?" Bruce asked.

Jack wondered for a moment what record he was talking about. Then he remembered that government workers were all paranoid. It was an institutional disease.

"Off the record," he replied.

"Benny's guilty. Or at least, he's going to be convicted."

"You're sure?"

"I've been doing this for twenty-five years, Jack. I'm as sure as I've ever been. He was at the scene. He had a motive—robbery. The witnesses against him are solid. He doesn't have an alibi or any other defense that I'm aware of. I've been concentrating my efforts on a plea, but Sal Paglia, his prior attorney, pissed the governor off so badly that nobody will even talk to us about a plea."

"So the case has to be tried?"

"Yeah. It's set in three weeks, and there won't be any continuances. Somebody lit a fire under the judge's ass. Before this case, you couldn't get to trial with this guy. Now he's as hot to trot as the state."

"Do you have Sal Paglia's records?"

"No, but I have everything he had, I'm sure."

"I did see the report of Dr. Wong when I read your files. It was pretty convincing."

"Let me tell you a little bit about Dr. Donald Wong, Jack. He's been around for a while. Excellent credentials. There was a time when ev-

erybody was using him. And that was just it. He got the reputation—
and I'm sure you've heard this term before in the civil arena—of being
a "whore." Whoever paid him got the opinion they wanted. About
five years ago, prosecutors stopped using him, so all his opinions for
the last five years have been for the defense. And I'm telling you, no
matter how heinous the crime, Dr. Wong is there with a reason why
your client didn't do it. The state's got a dossier on him that would fill
this room. You put him on the stand and they'll rip him a new asshole
for about four days—excuse my French. I'm not saying his opinion is
bad—he always has great charts and stuff—but he's a powder keg that
will ignite that jury."

"Why was Sal Paglia using him, then?" Jack asked.

"I don't know for sure. Sal didn't often represent people on trial for
murder. He may have used Wong years ago and simply may not have
known how Wong's reputation had deteriorated. I can tell you this—
the state was salivating over the prospect of cross-examining Wong."

"So I take it you wouldn't recommend that I get involved in this
case, and you definitely wouldn't recommend using Dr. Wong as an
expert?"

"I wouldn't let Wong come within a hundred miles of the courthouse, but if you can get his exhibits, I'd use them. Like I said, he's always got great charts and stuff. In this case, I'm sure he's diagrammed
the whole murder scene, especially how and where the bullet struck,
since his opinion is based on that information. All you need to do is
get somebody a little more credible to provide the same opinions using
Dr. Wong's exhibits.

"As for the case itself, I'd be happy if you took it off my hands.
Frankly, in my opinion, it's going to hurt your reputation."

Jack stood up to leave. There was no sense taking any more of the
man's time. "Thanks, Bruce. I appreciate your candor. I'll have an answer for you very soon."

"My pleasure, Jack."

Henry waved good-bye as he followed Jack out of the office.

"You were awful quiet in there," Jack commented as they walked
across the street toward the subway.

"I didn't have anything to say."

"At least, not in front of him, is that it?"

"That's about right, Jack."

"So what do you think?"

"I think that Mr. Sentner was a little too sure of himself. He's got Benny convicted already. I think that happens all too often in the public defender's office. I imagine that same conversation happened when I was coming up for trial."

"I don't know. I understand your position, Henry, considering your own personal experience, but the evidence against Benny is pretty substantial. I think he's right about this Dr. Wong too. I've seen experts like him skinned alive during cross-examination."

"I imagine you did some of that skinning yourself, Daniel Boone," Henry said with a sideways look at Jack, who cracked a smile.

They met Charlie that evening for dinner at an intimate little Italian restaurant on the Upper East Side called Pinocchio. When Jack called to tell Charlie they were coming to New York, she had insisted that they stay with her.

"I've got two extra bedrooms and I won't hear of you staying anywhere else," she'd declared. Jack couldn't say no but mentioned that he couldn't speak for Henry. When he brought up the invitation later, Henry told him he had relatives in Harlem and he wanted to get a chance to stay with them if possible.

"Just be ready. She's going to bring it up as soon as we sit down," Jack said as they walked into the restaurant.

Sure enough, after they had all kissed hello and were seated, Charlie got right to the point. "Are you going to stay with me, Henry?"

"I'd love to, Charlie," Henry began, "but I have an aunt who lives in Harlem, and I've only met her once. She's my mother's younger sister, and I've already made arrangements to stay with her. I want to find out a little bit more about my mother. Besides, we don't eat the same food as you folks. There's only so much of this stuff I can take."

Charlie laughed. Henry had totally disarmed her.

It was a wonderful dinner. Henry and Jack entertained Charlie with their stories about weekends on Lake Okeechobee. Afterward, Henry hopped a cab uptown while Jack and Charlie took a leisurely stroll to her apartment between Lexington and Park Avenues. She lived right in the heart of the neighborhood where Jack and Pat had grown up.

"Did Pat tell you this was our old neighborhood?"

"Of course she did."

"It's changed a lot. It used to be blue-collar. Nobody I know could live here anymore."

"Yeah, that's what I've heard. The only working people left are the ones who live in rent-controlled or rent-stabilized apartments."

"It's the same all over New York. This city has lost some of its soul."

"You're probably right, Jack. I don't know. I'm originally from Indiana."

"So is everybody else," Jack replied. "Not from Indiana, I mean, but from someplace else. The people who were born and raised in Manhattan are gone."

"Pat took me to some of your old hangouts. They seem the same."

"The difference is there are only a few of them left." Jack realized he was sounding like an old curmudgeon. He decided to change course. "Maybe we'll stop at the Carlow East one night this week," he suggested.

"I'd like that."

They walked in silence for half a block until Charlie popped the question she'd been meaning to ask all night.

"So, have you been thinking about dating?"

Jack stopped in his tracks and looked at her. "Of course not," he replied.

"Well, you should be, Jack. It's time."

"How do you know it's time, Charlie? Is Pat talking back to you now?"

"Very funny, Jack. Actually, this is something she talked to me about before she died. She asked me to tell you when the time was right that she wanted you to go on and live a full life in every respect. I think this is the right time."

They started walking again.

"Well, I don't," Jack finally answered. "I don't know if it will ever be time."

"Just be open to it, Jack. That's all I'm saying. You're too young to become a dried-up old prune."

That got a laugh out of Jack. "All right, Charlie. I'll try and be open to it. I'm sorry I jumped all over you like that."

"Does that mean we're still on for the Carlow East?" she asked.

"We're still on for the Carlow East."

Jack tossed and turned all night, wrestling with the decision of whether to represent Benny or not. He and Henry met for breakfast early the next morning.

"I can't do this, Henry," Jack said after they got their coffee.

"Do what?"

"Represent Benny. I'm convinced he's guilty. I'm trying to seek justice for people who aren't guilty. I'm not trying to get guilty people off."

Henry didn't answer right away. He simply took a deep breath and gathered his thoughts. "Jack, you know I love you," he began. "You saved my life. But you need to expand your view of justice. It's not black-and-white. It's multicolored, and the different shades are very subtle. Your friend Luis was railroaded into the service to fight a war that, by the way, just about everyone now agrees was unjust. And the state put Benny into a foster-care program that was nothing more than legalized child abuse."

"I hear you. But should I try to get a murderer off because he had a bad childhood? Is that what you're saying to me?"

"Not at all. I'm just saying that justice means Benny is entitled to his day in court. Neither you nor anybody else should prejudge him. He should get the best defense he's entitled to and the state should be required to prove its case—nothing more, nothing less."

"What if I get him off and put a murderer back on the street? That's the part I can't get past."

"All right, let's work on that. How do we resolve that dilemma?"

"I don't know, Henry. That's what kept me up all night. I'd really like to help Luis."

"Let me make a suggestion. Let's go see Benny. We can get a feel for him just like you got a feel for me on that first visit. Let's find out where he lived and talk to people who know him. If in the end it's pretty clear that he's a violent, dangerous person, then we walk away. But if he's not and this murder charge appears to be an aberration, then you take his case and give him the best defense you can, which means you make the state prove its case beyond a reasonable doubt."

Jack looked at Henry. It was a reasonable compromise, and it appeared that Henry had taken a long time to think it out. He'd probably done some of his own tossing and turning the night before.

"You think he's innocent, don't you?" Jack asked.

"Not necessarily, Jack. I think he's entitled to a presumption of innocence—something I never had."

"All right, Henry, we'll talk to Benny. If he doesn't appear to be a violent criminal and we can verify that independently, then I'll take his case. The rest is out of my hands."

FORTY-FOUR

The next day they rented a car and drove to Ossining Correctional Facility in Ossining, New York, about an hour and a half from the city. Jack had called ahead and made arrangements to see Benny. He was an expert at cutting through the prison red tape and expediting things; he'd spoken directly to the warden.

After they signed in and went through the normal procedure of being searched, the prison guards led them to a private visiting room. The guards were clearly keeping an eye on Henry, probably figuring that a man that size didn't need a weapon to orchestrate a prison break.

Henry wasn't feeling all that comfortable either. Walking through the prison gates and hearing them *clang* shut behind him sent chills up and down his spine. For a moment he felt like running, but he steeled himself. Henry knew that Benny's fate actually depended on him. Even though Jack had experience dealing with death-row inmates, he didn't really know how to get behind the almost impenetrable wall of a guy living in the prison system.

Benny Avrile was no longer the fast-talking, pot-smoking flimflam man he'd been a year ago. At five feet, eight inches and slight of build, the young, fairly handsome Benny had been a sight for sore eyes to more than a few inmates who thought it would be easy to make him their bitch.

Benny had known what was coming. He'd heard enough horror

stories over the years from ex-cons—none of whom ever admitted to being molested—to realize that he was literally going to have to fight for his ass. It wasn't going to be the first time, however, and his experience as a foster kid had given him at least some preparation. Back then when his back was to the wall, Benny had always come out swinging. He adopted the same attitude the day he walked through the prison gates. If somebody even looked at him wrong, he hit him and hit him again and kicked him in the balls and bit him and head-butted him and didn't stop until the guards pulled him off. The next day he'd do it all over again, constantly the aggressor, never waiting for somebody to make a move on him. He talked to nobody. If somebody talked to him he hit him and hit him and hit him. He was put in solitary a few times and got beaten up by the guards, but nothing stopped him. Eventually he didn't get the looks anymore. He'd been tagged as crazy and was left alone.

Now Benny the crazy man was led into the room where Jack and Henry were waiting. Two guards were with him, and he was handcuffed. When they'd seated him, the guards left the room and waited right outside, where they could still see through a window in the door.

Henry knew that once Benny was convicted his accoutrements would change. He'd have leg and waist shackles as well as handcuffs, and the guards would never leave the room. Henry also saw the look of the animal in Benny's eyes, a look he had seen many times.

Jack started the interview.

"Mr. Avrile, my name is Jack Tobin. I'm a lawyer. Your father has asked me to look into your case and, if possible, to represent you in your upcoming trial."

"So you're here to check me out to see if you really want to do it," Benny growled.

"Something like that," Jack answered.

Benny was conducting his own assessment. Jack certainly looked a lot more competent than Sal Paglia, but looks could be deceiving. He was probably another flunky that his father got for a bargain-basement price. But who was the big black guy? He certainly didn't look like a lawyer.

Henry read his mind.

"I'm Henry Wilson, Benny," he said. "I spent seventeen years on death row in Florida before Jack got me released last year. He's the real deal, in case you're wondering."

Benny turned to Jack to respond. "If you're the real deal, my father must be paying you a hell of a lot of money."

"This isn't about money," Jack told him. "I knew your father when we were teenagers. I have a great deal of respect for him."

Benny rolled his eyes. He didn't know it, but he was on the verge of burying the only hope he had left.

At that moment, Henry decided to take over. "Benny!" he said sharply but not very loudly, and he waited for Benny's eyes to meet his. "My mother was a heroin addict," he began, keeping his gaze fixed on Benny. "She used to bring these guys home who beat the shit out of me every day. I was six years old when I found her dead by a creek near where we lived. I was put into the foster system, which was as bad as any prison I was ever in. I had my own bout with drugs and everything else on the street, and I despised my mother for the life she'd given me. I never even knew my father. But when I was strapped to that gurney and they were about to put my lights out forever, all I thought about was seeing my mother and hugging her and telling her I understood because I had my own demons. You hear what I'm saying?"

Benny nodded. Henry had tapped into something that he didn't believe anybody else understood.

"Your father," Henry continued, "had *his* own demons. He was drafted into a war he knew nothing about and he lost his best friend in the process—which drove him to heroin. We could talk about how he got there just like we could talk about how we got there. That part doesn't matter. What matters is that he picked himself up and he fought his way back and now all he wants to do is help you. Yeah, he feels guilty, and he should feel guilty. He's doing something about it, though. He's had a second chance, and he wants you to have one. You've got to get past your hate and let him—and us—help you."

Henry stopped talking but continued to look directly into Benny's eyes. It was a challenge. Henry was waiting for some straight talk back.

Benny didn't speak right away, but there was no mistaking the emotion in his eyes and on his face.

"I got past it once—the hate," he finally said. "I'd wanted to kill them both, but then I let it go. It all came rushing back when I saw him again. This ain't exactly the best place to sort out your feelings, if you know what I mean. I hear you, though. And I know you're right. It's just gonna take me some time to get there."

"I'm with you," Henry replied. "One other question: is there a bar you used to hang out in?"

"Yeah, Tillie's."

"Does the bartender know you?"

"Tillie's the bartender. Yeah, he knows me. Why?"

"I'll tell you the next time we see you." Henry looked at Jack to see if there was anything else he wanted to talk about. Jack shook his head. Henry stood up, reached across the table, and shook Benny's hand.

"You were awfully quiet in there," Henry said to Jack as they were walking to the car. It was exactly the same comment Jack had made after their visit to Bruce Sentner, the public defender.

"Touché!" Jack replied. "Actually, there was no room for me in there. You two were in your own world. You get it now, Henry, don't you? If you hadn't come on this trip I would never have seen that other side of Benny. I'm not convinced yet, but if I'd been by myself today I'd be heading for the airport now."

"You're probably right," Henry replied. "Now, I think we should pay a little visit to Tillie."

FORTY-FIVE

Jack had a general idea from reading the police files where Tillie's was—general in the sense that he knew it was in the South Bronx. They looked up the address in the phone book but had to stop a couple of times on the way to get directions from people on the street. By seven o'clock that evening, they were sitting at the bar, talking to Tillie.

"If you guys can hang on a few minutes," Tillie said after they had introduced themselves, "I'll be off the bar and we can sit in the back and talk." So Henry and Jack each ordered a club soda and waited for Tillie to get off. The six other people in the bar looked at them like they had some sort of disease. One by one they stopped looking, however, when Henry returned their stares.

Fifteen minutes later, Tillie led them to a table in the back so that they could talk freely.

"So one of you guys is gonna represent Benny?" he asked, just to make sure he had it right.

"It's a possibility," Jack replied. "We're kind of in the investigative stage."

"How do I know that you are who you say you are?"

"You mean are we cops or something?" Jack suggested.

"I don't wanna seem like an asshole or anything, but the thought had crossed my mind, yeah."

"Do I look like a cop?" Henry asked. "Besides, we're not going to ask you about anything that could hurt Benny. If we do, then you can refuse to talk to us. We just want to get a little flavor of who the guy is. He gave us your name."

"All right," Tillie said. "I don't know if I can help you that much, but I'll tell you what I know."

"Fair enough," Henry told him.

"Benny is a street guy," Tillie began. "He don't own nothin'—at least nothin' of value. He lived in one of those condemned buildings. He's never had anything going for himself. Never could keep things together, you know what I mean?" Henry nodded. He knew exactly what Tillie meant. "I know he's a thief," Tillie continued, "but in a lotta ways Benny's harmless. This is a violent neighborhood, but it never rubbed off on Benny. Not that I could see, anyway. He's a character. To tell you the truth, I miss him."

"He's charged with murder, you know," Jack pressed.

"Yeah, I know, but I figure that's a trumped-up charge. Some big shot was killed, and Benny's the fall guy."

"There are eyewitnesses who put him at the scene," Jack added.

"I don't know anything about that," Tillie said. "But I'll tell you this. The cop who arrested him—he arrested him right over there by the pool table. I was here. Benny and me were playing pool at the time. Anyway, this cop told Benny that he was arresting him for something he didn't believe Benny did. And he told Benny to clam up—not to talk to anybody until he had a lawyer. Now, that's a cop talking, and a cop who knows Benny real well. That's why I'm saying he's a fall guy."

"What's this cop's name?" Jack asked.

"Joe Fogarty, but that ain't gonna do you no good. He ain't never gonna admit he said those things."

"Is that good enough evidence for you?" Henry asked on their way out.

"If it's true," Jack replied.

"What do you mean, if it's true?"

"I mean, Tillie is Benny's friend. He's going to say things to help Benny. Do you think a jury would believe him without some corroboration?"

"Maybe not," Henry admitted. "But I believe him, and I've been a street person."

"You're not a disinterested party anymore, Henry. You're on Benny's side one hundred percent. Maybe more. I just need something more."

"Where are you going to get that? The cop isn't going to talk to you."

"Maybe not. But I can try."

Jack dropped Henry off in Harlem on the way back to Charlie's. They agreed to meet for breakfast the next morning.

Jack wanted to make a decision about whether to represent Benny before they left New York. When he arrived back at the apartment, Charlie was waiting for him, anxious to hear about the events of the day. Jack put her off for a few minutes. He had to call an old friend right away.

Frankie O'Connor picked up the phone on the second ring.

"Frankie?"

"Yeah," Frankie answered hesitantly. Nobody called him Frankie anymore.

"Frankie, it's Johnny Tobin. How are you doing?"

"Johnny! Long time no see. Where are you?"

"I'm in the city. Actually, I'm in the old neighborhood."

"How long are you going to be in town?"

"I'm not sure. Maybe a couple more days."

"You know, some of us get together at the Carlow on Thursday nights. I'm off on Fridays. It's one of a hundred bad things about being a cop—you rarely get weekends off."

"I'll come down. I was planning on going to the Carlow anyway. Listen, I need to ask a favor."

"Shoot," Frankie replied without hesitation. They hadn't set eyes on each other since Mikey's funeral several years before, but that didn't mean anything to Frankie. Johnny was an old friend.

"I'm trying to get in touch with a cop."

"I'll help you if I can, Johnny, but there are twenty-five thousand cops on the force now. If he's an old-timer, I'll know him. Still, I'm not sure I can help you."

It was an unwritten code, and Jack was well aware of it. Frankie wasn't going to give out any information about any cop until he called the guy, filled him in on the situation, and got his permission to do so.

"I know what you mean, Frankie. The guy's name is Joe Fogarty."

"Oh, I know Joe. He came on a few years after me. Tell me what it's about and I'll give him a call."

Jack filled Frankie in on Benny's case and told him all about the conversation with Tillie. He didn't tell him who Benny's father was just yet. He wanted to let the situation play itself out.

Frankie hesitated. "I don't know, Johnny. You know I'd do anything for you personally. But this would put Joe in an awkward position, and I don't want to do that. Why are you getting involved in this case anyway? Nick Walsh was the lead detective, and Nick's a legend in the department. This guy is guilty."

"He may be, Frankie. I'm just trying to decide whether I should represent him or not." Jack sensed the moment was right. "His father is an old friend of mine. And yours too."

"Who?"

"Do you remember Rico who played with us on the Lexingtons?"

"The skinny Puerto Rican kid who taught you how to play cornerback?"

"That's the one."

"Sure, I remember him. He was one tough cookie. He and Floyd got a raw deal too. Being a cop, I think about what happened to them from time to time. This Benny kid is his son?"

"Yup."

There was a pause on the other end of the line. Then Frankie said, "I'll give Joe a call and tell him about the situation, but it'll be up to him if he wants to talk to you or not. Just remember, Johnny, if he confirms what he said to Benny and the higher-ups downtown find out about it, they'll be writing him up for spilling his coffee."

"I hear you, Frankie. I won't do anything he doesn't want me to."

"By the way—and this is really strange—there's another connection between this case and the Lexingtons."

"Oh yeah, what's that?"

"Do you remember Jimmy Walsh, the kicker?"

"Of course."

"Well, he was Nick Walsh's younger brother. That won't get you anywhere with Nick, though. He's strictly by the book. It's just kinda interesting."

"Yeah, it is," Jack replied.

"I'll tell you something else that should make the hair on the back of your neck stand up."

"What's that?"

"Nick investigated the murder of this Benny kid's last lawyer. Someone blew his brains out. Nick said it was a mess. Watch yourself, Johnny."

"I thought they decided there wasn't any connection."

"They couldn't find a connection, but they never solved the murder either."

Half an hour later, just as Jack was winding up telling Charlie about the day's events, Frankie called to let Jack know that Joe Fogarty would be at the Carlow East on Thursday night.

FORTY-SIX

We're meeting with Joe Fogarty tonight at a local bar," Jack told Henry the next morning at Pete's, a local greasy spoon in the old neighborhood.

"How did you arrange a meeting overnight?" Henry asked.

"You've got to know the right people, Henry. I'm a man with connections."

"I guess you are."

"Listen, we're going to show up about eight. It will be the three of us. I already promised Charlie I'd take her."

"You don't need me for this one, Jack. Cops and I don't get along anyway. I'll just take the family out for dinner."

"Are you sure? This is pretty important."

"I'm sure, Jack. You can handle this one. What else do you have planned?"

"I thought after breakfast you and I would go down to the murder scene to see where the eyewitnesses were and things like that."

"That's a good idea."

"And then I'm going to prepare my stipulation for substitution of counsel."

"Good. You're already anticipating that Fogarty is going to confirm what Tillie said. I like that."

"I figured you would."

"Are you licensed in New York?"

"Oh yeah. I took the bar exam here more than twenty years ago. I always thought I'd practice here. I don't know how to find the court-house yet." He laughed. "But I will."

Frankie O'Connor was still a leader of men thirty-plus years after he played for the Lexingtons. Although he barely finished high school, Frankie rose to the rank of lieutenant in the New York City Police Department. He could have been a captain but turned the job down.

"You get too high in this department, you can't smell your own shit stinking," he'd explained to a friend. That was Frankie. He didn't want to get too far away from the rank and file—too far away from his roots. Not too many lieutenants could call a detective like Joe Fogarty and arrange a meeting where he'd be explaining why he'd violated department rules. Frankie could do it because Joe trusted him. It was that simple.

Jack had been back to the Carlow East a few times since the old days but they had been random visits. Nothing could have prepared him for this night. It was a journey back in time. His old friend Norm Martin was behind the bar. Although they hadn't seen each other in years, Norm recognized Jack as soon as he walked in the front door.

"Hey Johnny, how ya doin'?" Norm greeted him as if the two men had had lunch together that very day. The only difference was that they both leaned across the bar and hugged each other.

"Good, Norm. I'm doing good." He almost forgot to introduce Charlie. "This is my friend Charlie. She used to work with Pat."

Norm shook hands with Charlie. "Nice to meet you, Charlie," he said. "Pat was a great lady. Jack, we haven't talked since Pat passed. I'm real sorry for your loss."

"Thanks, Norm. I appreciate it. Where's Frankie? Is he here?"

"Yeah. He's down at the other end of the bar with everybody else."

The Carlow looked almost exactly the same as it had thirty years ago, except there were a few more televisions for the sports fans, and fake Tiffany lamps hung from the ceiling illuminating the bar. In the old days, people liked being in the shadows. The other noticeable change was the clientele. Thirty years ago this Irish bar had been full of Irishmen—until the Lexingtons came along. Now it was a mixed crowd.

The "everybody else" Norm had referred to were all people Jack had grown up with. His good friend Chris Dennehy was there, along with Tony McKiernan, Joe Powell, Kathy Tripptree, and Lynn Schultz.

Chris gave Jack a big hug.

"What are you doing here?" Jack asked.

"We all come on Thursday night," Chris explained. "It's Frankie's night off. We've been doing it for years."

Jack introduced Charlie to everybody.

"I can't believe you know all these people," Charlie whispered to Jack as the introductions went on and on.

"I went to kindergarten with most of them. You see Joe Powell over there? He was my first friend in the whole world. His mother used to take us fishing in Central Park. You know where Rowboat Lake is?"

"Where they have the rowboats? I didn't know they called it that."

"That's what we called it. We used to catch big carp in there. We were so small we could barely hold them."

Eventually Jack left Charlie chatting with his friends and made his way over to Frankie, who was sitting at the end of the bar with a few guys who looked like cops. Frankie had gained a few pounds since the Lexington days, but he still looked fit. He stood up and gave Jack a big hug.

"Johnny, how's my rich and famous pal? You haven't forgotten where you came from, have you?"

"I wouldn't dare, Frankie. Not while you're still alive." That got a laugh out of everybody. Frankie introduced him to the other guys sitting next to him, one of whom was Joe Fogarty. Neither Frankie nor Joe—nor Jack for that matter—gave any indication that this meeting was anything more than a chance encounter.

Jack had a good time that night reconnecting with his people, all of them regaling Charlie with stories of the old days. At about eleven o'clock he felt a poke in his back. When he turned around, he saw Joe

Fogarty heading for the door. Jack excused himself and followed Joe outside.

Joe walked up Lexington Avenue and turned at the corner. Jack followed. When he reached the corner, Joe was about twenty yards up the street sitting on a stoop smoking a cigarette. Jack walked up to him.

"I trust Frank with my life," Joe said. "We've known each other for a long time. He trusts you, and that's why I'm talking to you. Here are the ground rules, though. After tonight, we never had this conversation. I'm answering some questions for whatever reason you need them to be answered, but I will never admit at any time that I told you what I'm about to tell you. Do you understand?"

"I do," Jack replied.

"Understand something else too. If my superiors, other than Frank, even suspect that I talked to you, my career is over."

"I understand."

"Then ask away. But make it quick."

"A guy named Tillie, I'm sure you know him, said that you told Benny to clam up when he was arrested. He said you didn't believe Benny committed the murder he was being arrested for. Is that true?"

Joe Fogarty didn't answer right away. He seemed to be mulling the words over in his head before he spoke. "I've been rousting Benny for years. I know he's a two-bit punk and a thief, but he's never been violent. When Tony Severino called me and asked me to pick Benny up for this murder, I didn't believe it. This was a high-profile guy that got shot, and I figured Benny might have been a fall guy—in the wrong place at the wrong time. So I told him to keep a lid on it."

Joe took a long drag on his cigarette. "I didn't know anything about the murder investigation at the time and I still don't. I worked with Tony Severino for years. He's a good detective. And Nick Walsh is one of the best homicide detectives this department has ever had. If they think Benny is guilty, then that's it. I said what I said based on my instincts at the time. Any other questions?"

"Do you think Benny could murder somebody?"

"I think anybody could murder anybody given the right circumstances. It wouldn't be Benny's first choice, but I wouldn't put it past him. Like I said, he's a criminal. Anything else?"

"Nope. Thanks for the info."

"Sure." Joe tossed his cigarette into the street as he walked past Jack back toward Lexington Avenue. He turned left at the corner and headed away from the Carlow East without looking back.

"I'm going to take the case," Jack told Henry at breakfast.

"Really?" Henry said. "So Joe Fogarty confirmed what Tillie said?"

"Who's Joe Fogarty?" Jack replied.

"I gotcha. Well, I'm glad you made the right decision, Jack."

"I'm not so sure it's the right decision."

"I don't understand."

"Well, my source didn't give Benny the Good Housekeeping seal of approval. I've still got my doubts about him. But like you said, he deserves a defense."

"Speaking of which, Jack—now that you're Benny's lawyer, just how are you going to defend him?"

"That's the part I haven't figured out yet."

After breakfast, Jack called Bruce Sentner and told him of his decision.

"I've got a stipulation for substitution of counsel prepared. If you can be available to sign it, I'll file it today. Can you have the file ready?"

"Jack, this is government," Bruce responded. "We don't usually work that fast. However, since it's you, and you're taking this file off my hands for God knows what reason, I think we can accommodate your request."

His second call that morning was to Luis.

"I've decided to represent your son," he told his old friend. There was a long pause. Jack could tell Luis was trying to get his emotions in check.

"Thank you, Jack," Luis finally replied. "I'll never forget this. I'll be indebted to you forever."

"Don't thank me yet, Luis. And don't get your hopes up too high. I can't change the facts. All I'm doing is agreeing to give Benny the best representation I can. He may still be convicted."

"I know all that, Jack. I also know you're putting your reputation on the line. I'm trusting God on this one. God brought me to you."

Jack wished he had that kind of faith.

"Luis, do me a favor, will you?"

"Sure, Jack. Anything. You name it."

"Go visit your son."

"Do you think he'll talk to me?"

"I think it's worth another try."

"Okay, I'll do it."

On Saturday morning, with Benny's file in hand, Jack and Henry left for the airport. Jack couldn't wait to get back to Bass Creek.

FORTY-SEVEN

Jack and Henry pored over Benny's file on the flight back, and Jack kept reading through the police reports at home that evening until a vague picture of what happened started to form in his mind. Still, he had lots of questions he couldn't answer. He shared his bewilderment with Henry, who came over on Sunday morning to work with him.

"I've read this file over and over again, Henry, and things just don't make sense."

"Take me through it, Jack. Slowly."

"Okay. Do you remember the credit card incident?"

"Yeah. Carl Robertson's girlfriend, Angie, reported a credit card missing."

"My hunch is that Benny was the guy at the bar that night who tried to hit on Angie. Actually, he wasn't trying to hit on her at all—he was stealing her credit card."

"Very good, Jack, you're starting to think like a thief."

"Don't give me too much credit. I'm going to get lost here very shortly. Okay, Angie was at the bar that night with this Lois Barton woman, the one she was having an affair with."

"Yeah, I remember. That was the best part of the whole story."

Jack ignored Henry's feeble attempt at humor. "Lois then followed Benny out of the bar."

"Yeah. So?"

"So, I think Lois was part of this robbery and murder of Carl Robertson."

"How do you figure that?"

"Lois was definitely setting Angie up—pumping her for information about Carl. If you recall, Angie admitted to Nick Walsh that she told Lois about Carl bringing her ten thousand a month."

"That makes sense. She and Benny were probably partners."

"Yeah, but here's what doesn't make sense, Henry. If Lois and Benny were in cahoots with each other, what was Benny doing stealing Angie's credit card? And what was Lois doing leaving Angie and following Benny out of the bar, never to be seen again?"

Henry didn't answer right away. He had to think about that one for a minute. Jack was right. Things didn't seem to make sense. "They probably weren't partners when Benny stole the credit card. Lois probably saw Benny lift the card and followed him out of the bar and sometime after that they decided to team up to do this robbery. That's the way criminals meet sometimes."

"You know, Henry, I thought about that. Here's what bothers me, though. This is a one-man job, and it's not a hell of a lot of money. Why cut somebody you just met into a job you had been setting up?"

"Maybe the robbery was Benny's idea," Henry offered. "Maybe she just told him about Carl and the money, and he came up with the rest."

"Possibly," Jack said pondering. "But that's not Benny's M.O. A robbery like this was a little out of his league. And Lois had to be thinking about the robbery all along. She wasn't pumping Angie for information without some sort of plan."

"Yeah, I think you're right," Henry replied. "I'm just offering possibilities."

"And why, if this was a simple robbery, did Benny shoot Carl?"

"I don't know."

"And where was this Lois on the night of the murder?"

"You're batting a thousand, Jack. I don't have a clue as to that one either."

Jack still wasn't through asking the questions that were bouncing around in his brain. "And why did the police all of a sudden stop looking for Lois Barton?"

"I think I can answer that one. They had Benny, and they had a

pretty airtight case against him. If they kept looking for her and didn't
find her, a good lawyer like you could blow a lot of smoke with any
new evidence they came up with about her. My guess is that they won't
even mention her when they present their case against Benny."

"And dare me to bring her up."

"Exactly."

"Because if I bring her up, what good does it do me? Benny is still
guilty, even if he had an accomplice."

"I don't know what to say, Jack. There're a lot of things that don't
add up, and I don't think we'll ever find the answers."

"Wait a minute—aren't you the one who got me into this?"

"Well, yeah, but I didn't necessarily think you were going to be
successful. I just wanted Benny to have the benefit of your representation."

"Thanks a lot, Henry, I appreciate that."

"No problem, Jack."

Jack spent Sunday afternoon at his office preparing a subpoena for
Carl Robertson's estate to produce his entire financial records for the
five years prior to his death. It was a fishing expedition. He had no
idea what he was looking for or what he might find. It was just
standard procedure to gather as much evidence as possible. He also
subpoenaed Carl's telephone records for the last six months of his life.
According to the police reports, Angie had mentioned a telephone
call and Carl's writing two words, *Gainesville* and *breakthrough*, on
a notepad. Maybe the telephone records would tell him something.
Again, it was a long shot.

As well as the subpoenas, Jack also prepared a motion asking
the court to enter an order requiring Carl Robertson's estate and
the telephone company to produce the information immediately. He
needed as much time as possible to have an expert go through the
records, process it all, and tell him what it meant. Bruce Sentner
had mentioned that Judge Langford Middleton would not continue
the case until a later date under any circumstances, so Jack couldn't
ask for a delay. He could request records, however, and when the

parties balked, protesting that they couldn't produce them on such short notice, he could let the judge arrive at the obvious conclusion that a short delay was needed. There was more than one way to skin a cat.

As he was wrapping up his very long Sunday, Jack received a call from Charlie.

"Are you sitting down?" she asked.

"No. Why?"

"Guess who is on the front page of the *New York Times*, the *Daily News*, and the *Post*?"

"Who?"

"You, my friend. Somebody got word of the stipulation for substitution of counsel you filed on Friday and notified all the papers. It's big news that a man with your reputation is representing Benny. The *Post* headline was the best: 'The Lone Ranger Rides Again.'"

"Oh, Jesus."

"The game is on again," Charlie continued. "Having somebody like you on board has stoked the fire. The governor just gave an interview on television reiterating that he will accept nothing less than the death penalty in this case."

"Well, I guess there won't be any plea bargaining."

"I think you're right about that."

"By the way, Charlie, I've got a couple of things I want to run by you. I'm probably going to be up next week for an emergency hearing on some documents I need."

"You can stay here, no problem. Like I told you, you and Henry can make my home your headquarters for the entire trial."

"Thanks, Charlie, but that wasn't my question."

"Go ahead, Jack."

"I'm requesting some financial and telephone records, and there is a possibility that I might need to have a large amount of data processed in a short period of time. I don't think the parties will be able to produce the material, and I think the judge will probably delay the trial. But the possibility exists that he won't."

"Just what are you getting at?"

"I may need an expert to go through this material on a moment's notice."

"And you want me to do it?"

"Yes."

"Why didn't you just say so? I'll put in for vacation time right away. I may not use it, but we'll be ready."

"Charlie, you're the best."

"I'm glad you're starting to finally realize that."

FORTY-EIGHT

The first thing Monday morning, after his run and swim, Jack faxed his motion to the judge and the DA. Things were about to heat up. For the first time since Pat's death, Jack felt the blood racing through his veins.

Afterward he stopped at the Pelican for breakfast, sitting at his usual place at the counter. Bill and Eddie were the only other ones there.

They were back on their wives again. It was like a soap opera. You could miss two weeks and pick up right where you left off.

While he and Hannah were chatting, a tall, attractive woman who looked to be in her mid-thirties walked into the diner and sat at the counter two spaces away from Jack. Hannah went over to take her order.

"Coffee?" Hannah asked.

"Yes, please," the woman replied. "And could I see a menu?" Hannah handed her a menu and went to get the coffee.

"I'll have two scrambled eggs, home fries, and some whole wheat toast," she said when Hannah returned.

Behind them, Uncle Bill stood up from the booth where he had been sitting. "I think I'll go outside for a smoke," he announced, certain that everyone wanted to know this information. He'd started smoking in the Navy and never given up. Jack had considered launching a personal campaign to get him to stop but decided against it. At eighty-eight, quitting might be more hazardous to Bill's health than continuing the deadly habit.

Eddie followed Bill outside to continue their daily conversation about nothing in particular. Hannah headed to the front of the restaurant to wait on a couple who had just come in, leaving Jack alone at the counter next to the young woman.

"Just passing through?" Jack asked. "I haven't seen you around here before."

"No," the woman replied, turning toward him. "I'm actually here on vacation."

"Really?" Jack asked, genuinely surprised. "You don't look like a fisherman, and we don't get too many vacationers hereabouts these days other than fishermen."

The young woman smiled shyly. She had short blond hair, brown eyes, and smooth, coffee-toned skin. "I'm in sales," she said. "I've passed through here a few times on my way to Miami, and it looked so peaceful. I'm tired and need a rest, so I thought I'd come here."

"Where are you staying?"

"At the Bass Creek Hotel."

"Good place. They have a fine restaurant too. If you're looking for a little variety there's a Mexican restaurant on the other side of town called La Taqueria. They've got great food."

"I'll keep that in mind," she replied. "Thank you."

She was pretty and nice, and for a brief moment Jack considered inviting her to dinner. He dismissed the thought immediately.

"Well, I've got a busy day ahead of me. Nice to meet you," he said as he stood up to leave.

The woman remained seated but extended her hand. "Nice to meet you too," she replied. "My name is Molly, Molly Anderson."

Jack took her hand. "Welcome to Bass Creek, Molly Anderson. I'm Jack Tobin."

He waved good-bye to Hannah as he walked out of the diner.

Jack spent the rest of the day at his office, coordinating a time for an emergency hearing on his motion and trying to track down Sal Paglia's file on Benny. It took most of the morning to find out what lawyers would be representing Carl Robertson's estate and the telephone company at the motion hearing, which was set for that Friday afternoon at three o'clock.

The effort to find Sal's file turned out to be futile.

"We sold the practice to Paver, Morrison, and Gould. They took everything," Glenn Story, the lawyer for Sal's estate, told Jack when he inquired. "Richard Gould was the partner who presided over the sale and transfer."

"What's the name of the file?" Gould asked when Jack finally got him on the phone.

"*State v. Benny Avrile*," Jack replied.

"All right, I'll check it out and call you back."

Gould didn't call back until four o'clock.

"I'm sorry to tell you this, Mr. Tobin, but we don't have the file."

"Do you know where it is?"

"No, and you probably won't ever find it. Mr. Paglia's office was vacant for a couple of months before we bought the practice. It had been broken into and ransacked. We had a master list of all the files. The Avrile case was on that list, but we never found it."

"Were there other files missing?"

"About five in all. We made a police report, but nothing came of it."

"Was anything of value taken in this break-in?" Jack asked.

"Oddly enough, no," Richard Gould answered. "There were valuables in there, paintings and knickknacks and the like—things that could have been sold on the street."

Jack was immediately suspicious. He decided to call his resident expert on petty crimes and criminals—Henry.

"Do you think somebody might have been looking for Benny's file?" Jack asked after he had told Henry all about his conversation with Richard Gould. "And what specifically were they looking for? And if Sal knew something and it was in that file, could that have been the reason he was killed?"

"Hold on, Jack. One question at a time. Wasn't Sal killed by his bookie?"

"Nothing's been proven."

"I think you might be jumping to conclusions. Everybody in that neighborhood knew Sal was dead five minutes after he was shot. As I recall, it's not the best part of town. Of course some crackheads are going to break into his office if they know it's empty. But they're not looking for files or paintings or anything like that. They're looking for money or something they can turn into money quick."

"What about the file? Benny's file was missing."

"So were several others. They ransacked the place. I'm surprised they only took or destroyed five files. I think you're overreacting a little."

"Maybe you're right."

FORTY-NINE

For some strange reason, Jack felt compelled to have dinner at La Taqueria that night. He arrived around seven. Molly was already there, sitting at a table for two under the *Tips up, Aspen, Colorado* sign. She waved to him when she saw him standing by the front door.

Lisa, the owner, saw the wave. "Looks like there's an empty seat at that table, Jack," she said to him, looking over at the seat across from Molly.

"It looks that way," Jack replied. "I'd better check it out." He walked over to Molly's table. "Do you mind if I join you?"

"Not at all," Molly said with a smile.

Rose was their waitress. She didn't look happy to see Jack sitting with another woman.

"Can I get you something to drink?" she asked rather perfunctorily.

"I'll have one of those." Jack pointed to Molly's margarita.

It was a lovely first dinner. Jack had two quick margaritas to calm his nerves. After that, he listened while Molly told him about her work. He noticed that she didn't say much, if anything at all, about her personal life.

She was a regional manager for a pharmaceutical company headquartered in New York City. Her territory was the entire Southeast, and one week a month she traveled to different areas to visit her sales force.

"When I decided I needed a break, I had already been here in Florida for a week, and I'd passed through Bass Creek two days before. It was the first place that popped into my mind," she said.

"So you're looking for seclusion, and your first night somebody invites himself to dinner," Jack replied.

"Nonsense, Jack!" she protested. She looked very pretty in a brightly colored sundress. "I'm enjoying the company."

After dinner he walked her back to the Bass Creek Hotel. It was a lovely clear night. The moon was three-quarters full and a slight breeze was blowing.

"It must be so nice to live in a place like this. It's such a far cry from New York City," Molly said.

"There's still room," Jack replied.

"You know how it is, Jack. New York is where the money is."

"I hear you. Not much industry in Bass Creek, and frankly, I hope it stays that way."

They were standing in front of the hotel now. Jack said good night and started to walk away.

"I'll see you at breakfast tomorrow," Molly yelled to him.

"I'll be there."

Jack finished his run rather quickly the next morning and skipped the swim altogether. Bill and Eddie were already at the Pelican when he arrived, sitting in a booth toward the back. Jack sat at his usual spot at the counter.

"Are you going to be around next winter?" Eddie asked Bill.

"What kind of a question is that?" Bill asked.

"I was just wondering because I have a nice winter coat I want to give you."

"Well, the only place I'd be if I wasn't here next winter is six feet under, and you know that," Bill replied.

"I didn't mean it that way."

"Well, you tell me where I'd be if I wasn't here next winter," Bill persisted.

Eddie just smiled. "I guess you'd be gone."

"That's what I'm talking about," Bill replied. "What kind of question is that to ask anyone?"

Eddie looked over at Jack. "Jack, help me out here, will ya? I just want to tell him I have a nice winter coat for him."

Just then Hannah set down Jack's coffee and a bowl of oatmeal with raisins—his regular breakfast. "Eddie," she interrupted before Jack had a chance to reply, "you said it. Now you have to live with it." Hannah always took Uncle Bill's side.

"But I just wanted to give Bill a coat," Eddie pleaded.

"And you can't give a coat to a dead man," Bill put in grumpily. "That's what you were saying."

Jack couldn't tell if Bill was serious or not. Bill liked to toy with Eddie. "I don't think he meant anything by it, Uncle Bill."

"You don't think so, Jack?"

"No."

"Okay then. Yes, Eddie, I plan on being around next winter, but no I don't want a coat from you. Who knows where you got it from? Jack, do you know the other day he bought a shirt from a bum on the street? I mean, right off the man's back!"

"It was a nice shirt," Eddie protested. "I washed it five times."

Just then Molly came in the front door. She was dressed in blue shorts and a white tank top. Jack couldn't help but focus on her lithe figure as she walked down the aisle between the counter and the booths and sat right next to him.

"Good morning, Jack."

"Good morning, Molly. How are they treating you over there at the hotel?"

"Very well, although I haven't tried their breakfast yet. I prefer the atmosphere right here."

"So, what big vacation plans do you have today?" Jack asked after Molly had placed her order.

"I was thinking of taking a ride over to the east coast. It's less than an hour from here, isn't it?"

"It sure is. Are you sick of Bass Creek already?"

"Absolutely not. I just thought I might like to spend a few hours at the ocean. As a matter of fact, I know this may sound a little forward, but I was thinking of asking you to come with me if you weren't too busy."

Jack felt a shiver of apprehension. "I'd love to," he told her. "Unfortunately, I've got some work to do."

Molly was clearly disappointed. "At least let me take you out to dinner tonight since you paid for me last night."

Dinner was okay. Dinner he could handle. "That would be great. Where would you like to go?"

"How about the hotel? Everybody says their steaks are good."

"They are. How about I meet you there at, say, seven?"

"Excellent!"

Neither one of them had noticed that all other conversation had stopped as Bill, Eddie, and Hannah—who had lingered within earshot after bringing Molly's order—all eavesdropped on their conversation.

Having surrendered to dinner once again, Jack made his exit.

When he arrived at the office, Jack immediately called Dr. Donald Wong in San Francisco.

"He's very busy," Dr. Wong's secretary told Jack. "I'll have to ask him to call you back." Jack provided the incentive for a prompt return call.

"Would you tell him that Jack Tobin called? I'm the new attorney on the Benny Avrile case. He might have seen the story about the case in the *New York Times* on Sunday. I want to find out if he's still interested in being an expert for us."

Jack had taken Bruce Sentner's opinion about Dr. Wong to heart. He had no intention of using him as an expert. The documentary evidence the doctor had prepared—the charts and diagrams—were another story altogether.

His ploy worked. Mentioning the *New York Times* got Dr. Wong's attention. If a big-shot lawyer was representing Benny Avrile, then there was more money to be had in the way of expert witness fees. Dr. Wong called Jack thirty minutes later. They arranged to meet in San

Francisco to discuss the case and go over the exhibits the following Saturday.

When he hung up the phone, Jack typed a letter to Dr. Wong confirming the meeting and also requesting that the good doctor have all the exhibits ready for him to see. Finally, he confirmed that Dr. Wong had already been paid six thousand dollars for his services to date. He finished with the words, *If there is anything in this letter that we did not discuss or is inaccurate, please notify me immediately.* He then sent the letter next-day delivery before calling Henry.

"We're going to New York on Thursday night and San Francisco on Saturday morning."

"For what?"

"I'll brief you on the way."

"You're sure you need me?"

"I'm sure."

"You know I hate to fly. I've already been to New York once."

"I know. I was with you."

"You're sure? All the way to San Francisco?"

"Especially San Francisco."

The restaurant at the Bass Creek Hotel was like a slice of Old Florida. The oak paneling looked and felt like it had been there since the days of Andy Jackson. The ornate bar was made of oak as well, as were the tables and the floor. The chairs were leather. The long-stemmed fans hanging from the twenty-foot-high ceiling added to the atmosphere. It had once been a place where the upper crust convened, and it held a little of that feeling still.

"I love this place," Molly told Jack when they were seated.

"It's been here a long time," Jack said. "Years ago, this was *the* place for a steak and a good cigar."

"A man's place," Molly replied. "All you need to do is look around to see that."

The waitress took their drink order. Jack had Wild Turkey neat. He never drank bourbon except when he was in the bar or the dining room at the Bass Creek Hotel. It was a bourbon type of place. Molly had white wine.

"So, how was the beach?" Jack asked.

"Oh Jack, it was terrific. It was a beautiful day. I spent the whole afternoon bodysurfing and I'm going back tomorrow."

"I guess your love affair with Bass Creek is definitely over now."

"Not at all. I'll be here until next Wednesday. Jack, why don't you come over tomorrow afternoon and swim with me?"

"I'd love to, but I have to go to New York the day after tomorrow, and I have some work to do before I leave."

"That's the second time you've given me the 'I'd love to but' routine, and we've only known each other for two days. I'm starting to get a complex."

"I guess I could drive over for a few hours, swim, and have dinner and be back here at a decent hour. We don't fly out until Thursday evening."

"Great! How long are you in New York? I'll be back there next week."

"I have a hearing on Friday, then I'm headed for San Francisco."

"I must be slipping. I should have found this information out already. Are you a lawyer, Jack?"

"Yeah, I'm representing a guy named Benny Avrile in New York. It's kind of a high-profile case. You may have heard of it."

"Nope, doesn't ring a bell. I don't usually read about that stuff. If a movie star or somebody in the fashion industry was on trial, I'd know all about it."

Jack laughed.

"It's hard to believe—a handsome man like you and a lawyer to boot. How is it that you're unattached?"

They had come to the tough part. Jack knew that this question would come up eventually.

"I lost my wife to cancer a year ago."

"Oh Jack, I'm so sorry. I shouldn't have pried."

"Of course you should have. It's a natural part of getting to know somebody. It's okay, though, and I'm okay. It's time for me to get on with my life. So, what's your story? A beautiful woman like you vacationing in a small town on her own—that's a bit unusual."

Molly blushed. "Yeah, I guess. I was engaged for about a year to a wonderful man—at least, in many ways he was wonderful. He was just too intense—a workaholic. I have a stressful job, and to come home every night to a man who couldn't relax—it was too much. I had to break it off."

They both sat in silence for a while, thinking about their lost lives.

"I think we need another drink," Jack finally declared as he signaled the waitress.

They relaxed and kept it light after that. Jack had a strip steak and Molly a filet. Afterward they took a walk along the river. It was a clear night once again, and a light breeze was coming off the river. Molly slipped her hand inside Jack's as they walked. His first inclination was to pull away, but he didn't, and after a few minutes he actually began to feel comfortable.

Jack finished up his preparations for Benny's hearing on Wednesday morning and convinced himself that a dip in the ocean would be refreshing. He called Molly's hotel on the way and left her a message that he would be there at two.

The hotel was midsized—five stories high. The lobby was elaborate and expensive-looking, but nothing really fit together. The floor and the walls were marble, while the furnishings and the art had that casual Key West feel. Molly was waiting in the lobby, a big smile on her face. She kissed him lightly on the mouth, took his hand, and led him to the elevators. She pushed the button for the top floor.

The room—it was actually a suite—was spectacular. The floors were marble throughout, even in the kitchen. The sliding glass doors off the living room area opened onto a patio that had a magnificent view of the ocean. As Molly and Jack walked to the patio they were serenaded by the sound of the waves pounding the shore.

"This is quite a place," Jack remarked.

"It's an upgrade. One of the few benefits of working in sales. I love watching the waves roll in. It's so relaxing."

Molly showed Jack where the bathroom was, and he changed into his bathing trunks.

The ocean was everything Molly had advertised it to be. The waves were high but not too dangerous for bodysurfing, something Jack had not done in a long time. He quickly regained the form he had first acquired as a teenager on Rockaway Beach and was soon riding the waves like an expert. Molly was even better. Jack watched as she dove toward the shore ahead of a wave, her long, well-toned arms smoothly and swiftly carrying her along until she caught the wave at its crest and let the ocean propel her forward. She had a perfect body for surfing—and everything else in the universe.

"Let's see who goes the farthest," she challenged him, her smile as bright as her little red bikini.

"You're on."

They started a contest, riding wave after wave. Molly was lighter and beat him every time. She would roll over on her back at the shoreline, watch him still coming in, and laugh in triumph. More than a few times Jack had the urge to sweep her up in his arms.

Afterward they stopped at the tiki bar on the beach.

"Give us a couple of those drinks with the umbrellas in them," she told the bartender.

"To the victor!" Jack toasted her when the piña coladas arrived.

"To the runner-up!" Molly replied, raising her glass.

They stayed at the tiki bar for a couple of hours, talking and laughing about nothing in particular. It had been quite a while since Jack had felt so carefree and alive. They were both a little tipsy when they finally headed for the room to shower and get ready for dinner.

Jack sat on one of the high chairs out on the patio looking over the ocean while Molly took the first turn in the shower. It was already dark outside, and the moon lit up the beach.

"Jack," Molly suddenly called to him from the living room.

Jack turned to the sound of her voice. Molly was standing in the middle of the living room, her figure silhouetted by the light from the kitchen behind her. She had shed the little red bikini.

"I think we ought to skip dinner," she said as she walked toward him.

Jack swallowed hard. She was standing next to him now, and he put his arms around her although he had no idea what he was going to do next. "You know, I noticed today that you ride the waves very well. Were you a surfer in your younger years?" he asked, his voice stuttering.

Molly sat in his lap, her naked skin rubbing up against him. "What an interesting question to ask at a moment like this," she said as she kissed him lightly on the lips.

"I was just curious," Jack replied, still not acknowledging what was happening.

"Well, the answer is no, Jack. I've never been a surfer. I wanted to keep that a secret. A woman has to retain her mystery, you know."

"I guess so," Jack mumbled as she leaned over and kissed him again. This one was longer and much sweeter than the last.

Right then he knew he wasn't going to make it home that night.

FIFTY

Where were you last night?" Henry asked when they were seated on the plane the next evening, waiting for takeoff.

"Why?" Jack asked rather defensively.

"Well, I called you around midnight because I'd forgotten what time we were leaving and I got no answer."

"Maybe I was sleeping."

"Jack, this is me, remember. I know your habits. You could be in a dead sleep and still answer the phone at three o'clock in the morning."

"Well, I was out."

"Out where? There's nothing open at midnight in Bass Creek."

"What are you, my mother or something?"

"You don't have to get so defensive. I was just wondering where you were. You're the one with all these conspiracy theories about people getting murdered. I'm just trying to make sure you're not one of them. You're lucky I didn't come over there last night. I certainly thought about it."

"I'm sorry, Henry. I was in Vero Beach with a woman."

"A woman? Last week you couldn't go on with your life, and this week you're seeing hookers?"

"She wasn't a hooker."

"She wasn't? As of last Friday, I was the only one around here in your life. This is Thursday."

"I met her on Monday."

"Oh? You met her on Monday and you're sleeping with her on Wednesday. Is that what they call a whirlwind romance?"

"What's with all these questions? I'm a grown man, you know. I can run my own life."

"I know you can, Jack. I'm just a little concerned that's all."

"About what?"

"Look, you're a strong person, but you're just a little weak right now in the emotional department."

"You've got nothing to worry about, Henry. This is just a fling."

"A fling? You, Jack Tobin, are having a fling?" Henry raised his voice a little on the remark, and the woman sitting next to them in the aisle seat looked up from her book and gave Jack a distasteful look.

"You're ruining my reputation, Henry," Jack deadpanned.

"All right, all right. Forget I mentioned anything."

Spencer Taylor was perfect in every way. Detective Nick Walsh had referred to him as a peacock: his hair was perfectly groomed to look perfectly natural—there was some kind of gel holding it, but it wasn't noticeable. His suits were impeccably tailored. He was just the right size—about six feet tall—and there wasn't an ounce of fat on his well-toned body. He had perfect diction, and he smiled when he spoke, to let you know how pleasant he was and how much he enjoyed talking to you. The perfect gentleman, he was bright and confident without a trace of arrogance—at least, not that anyone could see on the surface. Even his name had a perfect ring to it—Spencer Taylor.

Prosecutors came in many sizes and shapes, but the good ones were usually either bulldogs or, on rare occasions, smart, smooth, and silky. Spencer was clearly the latter. The bulldogs were normally career guys who really believed in truth, justice, and the American way. Guys like Spencer were filling out their résumés on their way to private practice and a life of representing rich drug dealers, white-collar criminals, and celebrities. Spencer had only stayed this long at the district attorney's office because he thought he had a shot at the top job.

Spencer was delighted when he heard that Jack Tobin was going to represent Benny Avrile. Sal Paglia had been a blowhard and in many ways an easy mark. Jack Tobin was a formidable opponent, at least by reputation, and Spencer relished the opportunity to do battle with him and in the process enhance his own standing.

When Spencer received Jack's emergency motion requesting an expedited production of documents, he immediately called the attorneys for the telephone company and Carl Robertson's estate and invited them to lunch. They met at O'Malley's, a little Irish pub on Worth Street. Spencer was his usual charming self. He had never met Samuel Mendelsohn, the attorney for the estate, or Gary Hunt, the telephone company's counsel.

Before his untimely death, Sal Paglia had bragged to Spencer that Benny's father had paid him twenty-five thousand to represent his son. Sal had even told Spencer how he had talked Luis into refinancing his house to get the money. Spencer had filed the information away, never thinking that it might be useful one day. As he was formulating a plan to thwart Jack's emergency motion, he realized that day had arrived.

"Gentlemen," Spencer said to the two attorneys sitting across from him at O'Malley's. "The district attorney himself wanted to be here today to meet with you, but he was unable to get away. He wants you to know, however, that he considers this case the most important one in the DA's office right now. You are, of course, aware of all the publicity it has received. Mr. Jacobs and I believe that Mr. Tobin has filed this emergency motion in order to delay the trial. We cannot let him do that, and we need your help."

Sam Mendelsohn protested immediately. "He's asked for five years of financial records. Mr. Robertson was a very busy man, even though he was retired. We can't produce that type of information in a week. The judge will have to delay the trial."

"Ours isn't that big a problem," Gary Hunt offered. "Still, it will be very costly for us to get the information that quickly."

"I think we need a game plan for Friday's hearing, gentlemen," Spencer told them. "And I can tell you the judge is not going to listen to 'We can't do it.' The defendant is on trial for his life. He is entitled to this information, even though it is totally irrelevant and isn't going to help him one bit. On the other hand, this case has been pending for a year now. The judge does not want to continue it. I suggest that you fellows go back and figure out how much it will cost in manpower hours to comply with this 'impossible' request. Then, at the hearing, instead of telling the judge that you cannot comply, you tell him how much it's going to cost to comply. You see what I mean? You're giving him an option. I suspect that he'll make the defendant foot the bill and that the defendant won't be able to pay the freight. He spent all his money on his last lawyer. So you'll be getting what you want—you'll just be doing it in a roundabout way."

"That's beautiful," Mendelsohn said. "This Tobin guy won't know what hit him. I'll get the numbers together."

"I'll do the same," Gary Hunt added.

The press was waiting outside the courthouse on the Friday afternoon of the hearing. Henry had decided not to attend, so Jack was alone. As he walked up Centre Street toward the courthouse, a throng of reporters followed, shouting questions as they surged forward. Jack didn't say anything until he reached the courthouse steps. He knew they were looking for some kind of quote that they could then bounce off the governor and keep the war of words going. Sal had been great for that. Jack, however, was not going to play their game.

"Look," he told them, "this is a minor hearing to obtain certain records for trial. I don't expect it to take more than fifteen minutes." He then refused to say anything more and headed into the courthouse.

Spencer Taylor had already given his interview, telling the reporters that the state had no objection to the request. "The state is just interested in seeking justice as quickly as possible."

Spencer was waiting for Jack outside the courtroom.

"Mr. Tobin?"

"Yes?"

"I'm Spencer Taylor. I'm the prosecutor in the Avrile case." Spencer extended his hand and Jack shook it. As he did, he noticed the handsome face, the tailored suit, the perfect hair, and the too-firm grip.

"I recognize your name," Jack told him. "It's nice to meet you."

"I just want you to know beforehand that I don't have an objection to your request. I'm more or less just an observer here today."

Yeah, right! Jack said to himself. *You just want to help.* He smiled at Spencer to let him know he understood.

The Avrile case had been like a dark cloud hanging over Judge Langford Middleton's head since day one. The Judicial Qualifications Commission was watching to see how he handled it, and so was Warren Jacobs, the district attorney. Now that Jack Tobin had entered the fray, the pressure had become even more intense. For all those reasons, Judge Middleton had decided that every hearing, no matter how trivial, would be in open court. He was also determined to get this case to trial on time and to finally repair his reputation in the process. Along the way, there'd been many sleepless nights and frequent trips to the bathroom. *What was it the doctor called it—irritable bowel syndrome?*

He had read Jack's motion and, once again, didn't know what to do.

Promptly at three o'clock, the judge walked into the courtroom. He waved the lawyers to sit down.

"I've read your motion, Mr. Tobin. What do you want this information for?"

"Your honor, the deceased, Carl Robertson, was a very wealthy and powerful man. There is evidence in the police investigation that another person, a woman, may have been involved in this murder. I just want to find out if somebody else had a motive."

"What do you say, Mr. Taylor?"

"It's a fishing expedition, Judge, but I can't argue that it won't lead to discoverable evidence. I just don't know."

"Who are the other people here? Please identify yourselves."

Sam Mendelsohn stood up. "Samuel Mendelsohn, your honor. I represent Mr. Robertson's estate."

Gary Hunt stood up next and introduced himself.

"What's the estate's position, Mr. Mendelsohn?"

"Your honor, we don't object to the production per se. But if we have to produce this material, the earliest we could do so would be a week before trial, and the volume is so enormous it will cost us twenty thousand dollars in manpower hours to compile it. I have cost estimates here from our accountants. Most of the cost will be digging the material out, assembling it, and copying it."

Jack recognized the tactic immediately. When he was an insurance defense attorney, he had always tried to make frivolous lawsuits too expensive for the plaintiffs' lawyers to pursue. These clowns were trying to play the same game with him. One look at Spencer Taylor, who was smiling smugly, told him who the ringleader was. Gary Hunt's figure was five thousand dollars to retrieve the telephone records.

"How do you respond to this, Mr. Tobin?"

"I assumed there would be some cost, your honor. But twenty thousand dollars to produce five years of financials and five thousand for some telephone records is a little ridiculous."

"Your honor," Sam Mendelsohn responded, "Mr. Robertson was a very rich man with extensive holdings around the world. It's all there in that summary I gave you. Nothing is inflated."

"Did you give this summary to Mr. Tobin?"

"Not before this hearing, Judge. We didn't have time."

Judge Middleton liked the argument almost as much as Spencer did. He didn't have to deny the motion, he just had to require the defendant to pay. Best of all, the trial wouldn't be delayed.

"I know you've come in here late in the game, Mr. Tobin, but this case has been pending for a year. I'm not going to deny your client access to these records, but I believe the cost for expediting their delivery should be borne by him. I'm going to grant your motion, but I'm going to make your client pay the twenty-five thousand dollars requested to expedite production if he still wants the records. And I'm going to make him pay it by the end of business today. The records must be available by a week before trial, gentlemen," Judge Middleton told the two lawyers for the estate and the telephone company.

Spencer Taylor's plan seemed to have worked. It had even paid off better than expected. Nobody had thought the judge would require immediate payment.

Jack made one last attempt to get the trial delayed. "Judge, I've got to get an expert to look at these documents and I haven't settled on anyone yet, although I do have somebody in mind." He was trying not to lie outright. "It's going to be almost impossible to get someone, have them review the records before trial, notify opposing counsel, and provide counsel with an opportunity to depose that expert in the time frame we have."

Spencer Taylor had anticipated this argument and was ready for it. "Your honor," he responded, "the state will waive notice of the expert's name, and we will also waive any discovery rights." Spencer was so sure of victory he was eager to erase all Jack's arguments.

"What about witnesses who might arise from this material?" Jack asked Spencer directly.

"We waive notice of them too, although I doubt there will be any."

"Anything else, Mr. Tobin?" the judge asked.

"No, your honor."

"Then my ruling stands."

Jack gave the three lawyers a moment to cherish their triumph. Spencer was smiling from ear to ear, enjoying the fact that he had outmaneuvered and outflanked Jack at every turn.

Then Jack took it all away by pulling out his personal checkbook.

"Your honor, let the record reflect that I am providing two checks to counsel here in open court in the amount of twenty thousand dollars and five thousand dollars to satisfy the court's ruling."

"The record will so reflect," the judge replied. The other lawyers were momentarily speechless—a rare event in any courtroom.

"Nice move," Jack told Spencer as they walked out of the courtroom. "I'm looking forward to seeing what else is in that arsenal of yours."

Spencer Taylor didn't reply. Jack noticed, however, that a couple of hairs on his perfectly groomed head had fallen out of place.

FIFTY-ONE

The fact that a hearing took place made the six o'clock news. The press never understood what it was about, so they simply showed film of the lawyers walking in and out of the courthouse and played snippets of the interviews. Jack watched Spencer Taylor's interview before leaving to meet Charlie for dinner downtown. Henry was again having dinner with his aunt.

Charlie lived on the north side of Eighty-eighth Street in the middle of the block between Lexington and Park. It was January and bitterly cold. Jack pulled the lapels of his overcoat together to shield himself from the wind as he exited the building and started across the street, stepping between two parked cars. As he did so, something—it wasn't a voice, more like an intuition—told him to look a second time to his right. A black car with its headlights off tore out of a parking space and headed directly for him. He was almost in the middle of the street now and became acutely conscious of his mind telling his feet to move. He took three steps as fast as he possibly could and dove over the front of a parked Ford Mustang on the south side of the street just a fraction of a second ahead of the speeding black car. He landed with his hands on the ground and his legs still resting on the hood of the Mustang. His heart was banging madly in his chest. When he finally righted himself, the black car was nowhere to be seen.

It had happened so fast that it seemed unreal. Some people on the street had stopped and were looking at him, but nobody came up and asked if he was okay. It took him a few moments to gather himself. Then he walked to the corner of Lexington and hailed a cab.

He didn't mention the incident to Charlie. They ate in the back room at P. J. Clarke's, and Jack told her about the hearing and gave her the time line for receipt of the financial and telephone records.

"A guy like that, Jack, could have a ton of financial records, both corporate and personal. I might not be able to make a dent in them in a week."

"Well, try to concentrate first on the six months before his death and work backwards if necessary. I want you to see if there are any unusual trends or patterns."

"I'll give it my best shot."

"That's all I can ask for, Charlie."

Jack told Henry about the attempt on his life on the plane ride to San Francisco the next morning, including his sixth sense.

"Sounds like somebody's looking out for you—even though you're having a fling," Henry said pointedly.

"And you should take your lead from that, Henry. The one who's looking out for me wants me to go on."

"All right, all right. I'm only trying to inject a little humor into the situation. Seriously, this attempt on your life probably means that Sal was killed because he found something out. And you may be dangerously close to whatever he discovered."

"It must have something to do with those records."

"And it may not have anything to do with Benny's guilt or innocence."

"I've thought about that," Jack replied. "Carl Robertson may have been doing some illegal stuff and somebody doesn't want that to come to light."

"We're going to have to take steps to protect you and whoever you get to review those records," Henry told him.

"I was going to ask Charlie to do it."

"Maybe you should think about somebody else."

"I'd have to disclose the danger, and who else would do it?"

"Well, you have to tell Charlie too," Henry insisted.

"I know. But Charlie's not going to decline the job."

"Yeah, you're right. We'll just have to figure something out."

"She's okay for now, though. I haven't disclosed my expert yet."

Donald Wong had his offices in Chinatown. The décor in his waiting room was ostentatious and very Chinese, with near-blinding red the overwhelming color. Dr. Wong himself was very American. He was dressed in a Brooks Brothers suit, and he spoke without an accent.

Dr. Wong was very friendly as he greeted Jack and Henry and then escorted them to a large conference room. At one end was a kind of stage area with a very large easel. An exhibit had already been put in place. The other exhibits were all neatly stacked on the floor nearby, and two Chinese men who worked for the doctor were standing next to them.

"Mr. Tobin, you told me that you would like to see the exhibits that I prepared for the Avrile case. I have them here, and I can quickly go through them for you. However, I am strapped for time. We had to move some things around on my schedule to accommodate your visit."

"I understand, Doctor."

Dr. Wong gave them a very fast but professional rundown of the ten exhibits he had prepared. They were all basically artist's sketches of Carl Robertson's skull, showing the angle of entry of the bullet that killed him and the damage to the cranium. They were clear and simple, exactly what Jack needed to illustrate his arguments to the jury. As Wong's men were removing the sixth exhibit and placing the seventh into position, Jack looked at Henry and gave him a nod. Henry excused himself from the room. Dr. Wong looked at Jack.

"You can proceed," Jack told him. "He'll be back in a minute."

Jack had a few questions to ask the doctor when the show was over. While he and the doctor were talking, Henry returned with two other men, who were carrying a large cardboard-and-wood crate. Neither Henry nor the two men said anything. They just started loading the exhibits into the crate.

"What are you men doing?" Dr. Wong yelled.

"Oh, they're loading the exhibits," Jack told him. "I forgot to tell you before we started that we couldn't get the trial continued, so we can't use you but we can sure use your exhibits."

"No, you can't," Dr. Wong yelled at Jack. "Those exhibits are mine. They are my work product. I'm going to call the police right now. You men stop what you're doing!"

"Keep going," Henry told the two men, motioning them to continue.

Dr. Wong shouted something in Chinese, a· ght away four Chinese men rushed into the room. Dr. Wong said something else, and the men moved toward Henry and his two assistants, who were still loading the exhibits.

"Hold it! Hold it!" Jack yelled and moved between Dr. Wong's men and Henry. Dr. Wong's men stopped in their tracks. They seemed to be looking for a reason not to go near Henry.

"Doctor, I have a letter here that I sent you last week confirming that you were paid six thousand dollars for your work." Jack pulled a letter from his inside jacket pocket and handed it to Dr. Wong. "Now, you can call the police and you can set these men on me and my partner, but the bottom line is, those are our exhibits."

"I never let my exhibits leave this office," Dr. Wong shouted. But he didn't tell his men to proceed.

"That may be your practice, Doctor. And you may have gotten away with it up to now. But again, the bottom line is that you were paid for your work by my client. He's going to trial in a couple of weeks, and he needs these exhibits. I'll certainly give you credit for them with everybody—the judge, the jury, the press. I guarantee you, however, that if I walk out this door without them, you will not want to hear what I have to say to every news outlet in the country about you, and you will not want to be in court against me in a civil suit for damages."

Dr. Wong only needed a few seconds to understand the full import of Jack's words. If he tried to hang onto his exhibits, the damage to his reputation and his finances could be substantial. It was a no-brainer.

He motioned his men to move back.

"Take them and get out of here," he barked at Jack.

"That was a pretty convincing speech you delivered just before the fireworks were about to begin," Henry told Jack on the cab ride to the airport. "Did you practice it beforehand?"

"No. I just operate well under pressure."

"Nobody knows that better than me, Jack. I just hope you have some magic left for Benny."

FIFTY-TWO

The week before Benny's trial, Luis took a train to the Ossining Correctional Facility, better known as Sing-Sing. He'd heard about the place all his life. It was where prisoners had always been executed in New York.

Luis had called beforehand to make arrangements to see Benny and to make sure somebody told Benny he was coming. He didn't want to surprise him again; Luis's heart couldn't take it. Jack had called the warden as well and asked that the two men be allowed to meet in a private room. This was the second time Jack had spoken with the warden, and they had developed a bit of a rapport. He pointed out that Benny was still presumed to be an innocent man even though he was already a resident in a maximum-security prison. The warden didn't agree to the request right away; he had to make some calls of his own. He got back to Jack the next day to tell him he'd authorized the private meeting.

Luis was shown in first. The room had windows that looked into the prison hallway. He waited nervously for his son to arrive, not knowing what kind of reception he would receive this time. As he sat, he wondered if it was a good idea to be meeting Benny without some bars between them. Then the door opened and two guards brought Benny into the room. They removed his handcuffs and promptly left. Luis watched them just to make sure they were staying close to the window and could see inside.

"How ya doin?" Benny said pleasantly as he extended his hand.

This simple gesture melted Luis's heart on the spot. "I'm doing okay. I'm a little nervous."

"About being in a room alone with me?"

"Oh no, no—about your trial coming up."

"Oh yeah, that. There's nothing we can do about that. It is what it is."

"Yeah," Luis replied. There was an awkward silence for about thirty seconds.

"Listen," Benny began, "I want to apologize for the way I acted last time I saw you."

"There's no need to apologize," Luis told him. "You have a right to feel the way you do."

"That's just it. I don't feel that way anymore. I've had a lot of time to think in here. And that new lawyer you got for me, Jack Tobin, and his partner, the big black guy, they said some things that made me think a little differently. You had your own shit to go through with the war and losing your best friend—"

"That's no excuse," Luis interrupted him.

"Well, I have no excuses either, Pop. I made a mess of my life too. If the war and losing your best friend isn't an excuse for you, then you not being around isn't an excuse for me. I've gotta take responsibility for my own shit. I've been a pimple on the ass of this world for too long."

Luis wanted to recognize the significance of what Benny was saying—that he was taking ownership of his life. It was the first step toward any type of new beginning. But he couldn't do it right away. For the moment, he could only focus on one word—*Pop*. Luis would polish that word, put it in his pocket, and take it with him from the prison that day. Over the next week as the pressure mounted, he would take it out and listen to its sweet sound and it would relax him. That one word made him a father again.

He addressed everything else a few seconds later.

"Benny, it's a long life. We can stumble and bumble and make a mess of it all and still right the ship in the end. Look at me. I'm drug free. I have my own business. Look at Henry, the big black guy. He was on death row for seventeen years."

"Yeah, I hear ya, Pop." There it was again. "But I don't think I'm gonna be getting any second chances anytime soon. I just want you to know that I appreciate what you're doing for me. And I don't want you to carry any guilt around with you if things go bad in that court-room. I want us to make peace with each other right now."

Luis didn't know what to say. This was what he'd been hoping for for so long. This was a dream he'd thought would never come true. Tears filled his eyes. Try as he might, he couldn't stop himself from crying. Once he started, it was like a dam bursting. Benny went over to console him. The guards at the window took notice of the contact. Benny put up his hand to let them know everything was okay. He held his father until he had no more tears left.

FIFTY-THREE

Back in his office in Bass Creek the next day, Jack called Mike McDermott, a civil trial lawyer in the city and an old high school buddy, to get the lowdown on Langford Middleton. He had to take some good old-fashioned ribbing before he got what he needed.

"Is this the famous Jack Tobin? The one who's all over the newspapers in New York City? Would it be possible for me to get an autograph at some time?"

"You play your cards right, Mike, and I'll see what I can do. Have your people call my people. We'll do lunch and all that stuff. How are you doing?"

"Good, Jack. I'm not so sure about you, though. That's a tough case you've got."

"I hear you. As a matter of fact, that's why I'm calling. I wanted to get the straight poop on Langford Middleton."

"The worst judge you could get, bar none. He just can't make a decision. I'm actually surprised you've gotten this far. He refuses to try most cases. He pressures the lawyers into settling."

"I've heard that about him from the public defender, but that's not the way he's been handling this case."

"That's because he's getting pressure. The wife of one of our associates is an assistant DA, and she says the DA himself went to see Middleton. The DA told Middleton if he even thought about continuing the case he'd go after him. I hear the Judicial Qualifications Commission is looking at Middleton too because of the complaints they've been getting. That's one of the reasons they transferred him to criminal."

"That's why he won't even think about a continuance. Well, at least we're getting a trial. How would you propose that I handle him during the trial?"

"I'm not sure. Like I said, Jack, nobody has had much experience trying cases with the son-of-a-bitch. I know he's sensitive about being appealed, so you may want to imply at every step of the way that you're going to appeal his rulings. That's a backhanded way of putting more pressure on him."

"What about his ego? Does he like to be stroked?"

"He's a really bright guy. He's a little arrogant too. If you can appeal to his intellect you might win him over on a point. The biggest problem you have, as I already mentioned, is the son-of-a-bitch won't make a decision. How in the hell do we get judges who can't make decisions? That's their job, for Christ's sake."

Jack didn't have an answer for that one. He thanked Mike for his advice, and the two men agreed to meet for lunch soon.

"Oh, one other thing, Jack," Mike added. "My office is a stone's throw from the courthouse. Why don't you come down here sometime before the trial starts, and we'll get you a security clearance and a key and you can work out of here. I've got an extra office, a copier, fax, telephone—whatever you need. You can come and go at any time, day or night."

It was a detail Jack had not thought much about. He needed a place to work from, and Mike's office would be perfect.

"Mike, I'm definitely going to take you up on that offer. Thanks again."

FIFTY-FOUR

Jack had returned from San Francisco on Tuesday but didn't call Molly and didn't show up for breakfast at the Pelican the next morning, Molly's last day in town. He assured himself that Henry's remarks had nothing to do with his decision. He just wanted to slow things down a little. Molly had left a note for him with Hannah, and it included her address and telephone number. *Please call me when you're in New York*, she wrote.

An envelope had been waiting for Jack when he arrived home, mailed from New York but with no return address. He'd opened it right away. It was Sal Paglia's autopsy report, complete with gruesome photographs of Sal, his face bloodied, an exit wound in his forehead and two holes in his chest. *Somebody is going to great lengths to scare me out of this case*, Jack told himself. *But it's not going to work.*

He called Henry right away and told him about the package. Henry agreed with his assessment. "They're putting the heat on you, Jack. They're asking you if you want to end up in a pool of blood like Sal."

"Who are 'they,' Henry?"

"Good question: I have no idea, but I'm working on it. Listen, I know I got you into this, so hear me out. I wanted Benny to have a good lawyer, something I didn't have. It shouldn't mean your life, though—especially since he's probably guilty. Jack, you should seriously consider dropping out."

"That's not going to happen, Henry, and don't mention it again."

"That's what I thought you'd say. No, that's what I *knew* you'd say. I had to bring it up, Jack. You understand."

"Yeah, I do. Now let me bring something up. It's your job to protect me, so don't screw up."

On Thursday afternoon, a week and a half before trial and just a few days before they were off to New York for the duration, Henry and Jack decided to take a break and do a little fishing. They anchored out on the big lake. Henry was lounging in a chair at the back of the Sea Ray with a fishing pole in his hand while Jack was in the galley making some Cuban sandwiches for lunch.

"So did you talk to Charlie about someone trying to kill you?" Henry asked.

"Yeah, I did. She's in, no matter what the risk. You know Charlie— nothing or nobody is going to scare her away."

"That's what I figured. Have you found a place to hide her?"

"I think so. Some friends of mine have a lake house in Virginia that's always vacant. They said I could use it." Jack brought the sandwiches out along with two beers from the cooler and sat in the chair next to Henry. The sky was cloudless and the temperature was close to perfect. They hadn't had a fish on the line all day, but neither man cared.

Henry took a swig of his beer. "Have you thought about how to get her to Virginia undetected?"

"Not really. Who would follow her if I haven't disclosed her as my expert yet?"

"You know, I've been thinking about that since you first mentioned using Charlie as your expert. They could be watching the apartment. Obviously they know that's where you stayed, since that's where they tried to kill you. We've got to assume they know you and Charlie are friends. She's a CPA. You need a financial expert. Are you starting to get the picture yet?"

"Oh my God, you're right! I didn't think about that. Has she been in danger this whole time?"

"Probably not. If they kill her too early you can just get another expert. They'll probably wait until she and the documents are together in one place—kill two birds with one stone, so to speak."

"When did you become so damned smart, Henry?"

"I know how criminals think. Why don't you let me take care of getting Charlie out of town?"

"All right."

"She can't stay alone, you know."

Jack stood up, grabbed his pole, and reeled in, then cast the line back into the calm waters of the big lake and sat down again next to Henry.

"Yeah, I've thought about that," he said. "I've got somebody in mind, so I'll take care of that part."

"Why don't you call her tonight and let her know I'll be contacting her?"

"All right."

"Have you made any arrangements for the transfer of the documents?" Henry asked.

"I talked to Sam Mendelsohn, the attorney for the estate, yesterday. Get this: they're bringing the documents in by truck—that's how many there are—and they're going to park the truck in a secure warehouse downtown late Sunday night. I'm going to meet him at the warehouse. Monday morning we can remove the items from the truck and transport them however we want to wherever we want."

"What about the telephone records?"

"They're going to be on the truck as well. The lawyers are working together."

"I'll bet they are," Henry replied. "Listen, let me make arrangements for the unloading and loading."

"Sure," Jack replied.

"By the way, we're going to be staying in Harlem."

"Why can't we just stay at Charlie's apartment?"

"That's where they tried to kill you last time, if you recall. I'm not sure, but I doubt that the people who are trying to kill you know anything about Harlem."

*   *   *

That evening Jack drove to the other side of the lake to visit his friends Joaquin and Maria Sanchez. They lived on a little inlet off the lake and were sitting out on their lanai looking out over the water when Jack arrived. Jack always experienced a brief bout of melancholy when visiting Joaquin and Maria. He and Pat and Joaquin and Maria were married together in a double wedding. Joaquin and Maria's happiness brought home to him in a unique, personal way the depth of his loss. They knew it too and refrained from any displays of affection when Jack was around. Pat's death was an event still too close to everyone's hearts.

Joaquin brought Jack a beer without asking and set up another chair on the lanai. Jack didn't waste any time getting to the reason for his visit.

"Joaquin, I've got to hide a witness in Virginia and I need a bodyguard to watch her. Are you interested?"

"Whereabouts in Virginia?" Joaquin asked.

"I'm not sure of the town. It's up in the mountains on a freshwater lake."

Joaquin was a retired homicide detective and, like so many of his colleagues, still kept up with the major murder stories across the country. He knew all about Benny Avrile's case and who was representing him. "How long is the job and when does it start?"

"It starts next week—Sunday, to be exact. It will probably be for two weeks, three at the max. You'll be paid for three no matter what, and the cabin is yours for three weeks and longer if you want to get some fishing in afterward. You just tell me what you require for a salary."

"Give me some more specifics, Jack."

"I've got an accountant who's going to be reviewing some records for me and testifying. If they find out where she is they may try to kill her."

"Who's 'they'?"

"I don't know."

"The state of New York is on the other side of your case."

"I know, but somebody has already tried to kill me, Joaquin. I can't take any chances with this witness. She was Pat's best friend."

Joaquin looked at Maria. "What do you think, honey?"

"I'd feel much safer if you had backup," she told him.

"I could call Dick." Joaquin was referring to his old partner in Homicide, Dick Radek.

"That's fine with me," Jack said. "I was going to give him a call after I talked to you two anyway."

"Let me call him," Joaquin offered. "He'll have a hard time refusing me. I'll call you tomorrow and give you a final decision."

"Thanks, Joaquin. And thank you, Maria."

On Saturday afternoon at three o'clock, Dorothy Pierce, a tall, husky black woman in her early sixties, knocked on Charlene Pope's door.

"Who is it?" Charlie asked without opening the door.

"Ms. Pope?"

"Yes?"

"Ms. Pope, my name is Dorothy Pierce and I'm Henry Wilson's aunt. You may have heard him talk about me—at least, I hope you have. Anyway, I have a message for you from Henry."

Charlie immediately opened the door. "Hi, Dorothy," she said. "Come on in. It's so nice to meet you. Henry did indeed talk about you."

Dorothy smiled politely but seemed a little distracted. "Thank you, but I can't come in. Could you step into the hallway for a moment?"

It was an unusual request, but Charlie went along with it and stepped into the hallway.

"Close the door," Dorothy whispered. Charlie closed the door. "My nephew is worried about bugs. I think he's been watching too many spy movies. Of course, I haven't been where he's been. Anyway, he wanted me to give you a message. Two black men are going to knock on your door at two in the morning. Their names are Calvin and Mohammed and they won't be saying anything to you. You're simply supposed to go with them. Henry says you can trust these men. Don't pack. If you have a dark running outfit or something, you may want to put that on. Don't turn any lights on before you leave. Just walk out the door. Someone will be waiting for you where you're going and will take care of your wardrobe and your other needs when you get there. Any questions?"

"Where am I going?"

"I don't know, and I don't think Henry wants you to know either. It's better that way. Of course you're to say nothing to anybody about this."

For the first time Charlie was starting to realize that she might be in some real danger. "But my dog. I've got to get somebody to take care of my dog. And I've got to tell my mother I'm going out of town."

Dorothy thought about it for a moment.

"Can your mother watch your dog?" she asked.

"Sure. She does it all the time when I go to Florida."

"Leave me a key," Dorothy told her. "And write down your mother's address. I'll take your dog over myself tomorrow, and I'll explain to your mother that you had to go out of town and you'll call her next week. Anything else you can think of?"

Charlie was bewildered. "I guess not," she replied.

Dorothy handed her a piece of paper. "Before I forget—if you want to talk to Jack, call this number. Don't use your phone for anything. Somebody will give you a phone to use. Okay?"

"Yeah, sure."

"Okay. I'll wait here while you get me your mother's address. Why don't I meet the dog while I'm waiting?"

"Sure," Charlie replied again and disappeared back into her apartment.

FIFTY-FIVE

Dorothy Pierce lived in a tenement on 127th Street off Lenox Avenue. The building was old, the hallway was dirty and dingy, and the neighborhood was nothing to write home about. Dorothy's three-bedroom apartment was contrastingly neat, nicely decorated, and very clean. It reminded Jack—who had arrived there with Henry on Saturday evening—of Frankie O'Connor's old place on Ninety-sixth and Lexington.

Dorothy's children were all grown, but her sixteen-year-old grandson William was living with her. So Jack and Henry had to share a room.

Their bedroom was narrow; the two single beds barely fit side by side with a little space between them. There was a dresser with four drawers, which gave them two drawers apiece. Jack had to hang his suits up in the hall closet. Any room became small when Henry walked into it. This particular one felt like a closet to Jack.

"You and I are getting too close," he said to Henry that first night as they tried to work their way around each other and get into bed.

"All I've got to say is, you better not snore," Henry shot back.

When they first arrived at Dorothy's, there was a young man who looked to be in his mid-twenties standing outside the building. He seemed to be guarding the place. He stood on the stoop mostly and walked up the stairs every fifteen minutes or so. Dorothy's apartment was on the second floor. Another young man was inside the apartment. Henry had simply introduced him as George. He was watching television when Henry and Jack went to bed.

"You're not going to try and convince me that those two guys are just kids living in the building looking for a little extra money, are you?" Jack asked Henry when they were in their respective beds with the light turned out.

"Why not?"

"Because I can tell they're both packing. I didn't see the guns but I know they're there."

"Jack, you're on a need-to-know basis."

"What does that mean?"

"That means I'm not going to tell you everything unless you need to know it."

"It seems like you have an army up here, Henry. And I thought you lived in Florida."

"My cousin Jermaine, Dorothy's son, is a businessman. He loaned me a few of his employees."

"Are some of his employees the ones who are escorting Charlie to Virginia?"

"As a matter of fact, they are."

"That's at least four people. You don't know Jermaine that well. I'm sure he's not doing this for free."

"Maybe not. That's my business, Jack. Remember, I'm the one who got you into this case. I want to make sure I get you and Charlie out in one piece."

"We want to do things the right way though, Henry."

"Is that right? Are the people on the other side—the law-and-order side, the side of *justice* in your eyes—are they doing things the right way? Jack, you do what you do best and leave the rest to me. Trust me. I'm going to stay on the right side of things."

Aunt Dorothy gave Jack some more advice at breakfast the next morning. William was sitting at the table with Henry and Jack. Dorothy was at the stove making pancakes.

"You're all right during the day. There are enough white folks up here now it's not too unusual. You don't wanna be white and walkin' around here late at night alone, though." Henry and William both laughed at Dorothy's bluntness.

"I'm not kidding and you both know it. William, you'd better get off to school."

"Yes ma'am." William finished off the last of his pancakes before standing up, grabbing his backpack, kissing his grandmother, and heading out the door. "Good-bye, Uncle Henry. Good-bye, Jack."

"See you, William. Have a good day," Henry answered. Jack just waved. His mouth was full.

After William left, Henry handed Jack a cell phone and a piece of paper with a telephone number written on it. "Use this phone," he told him. "If Charlie needs you she's going to call on this phone. If you're downtown late and I'm not with you, call and let somebody know when you're on your way home. Don't take the subway—take a cab right to the door. This neighborhood can be dangerous for you for a lot of reasons. And by the way, Charlie has arrived in Virginia safe and sound."

On Sunday evening, Jack and Henry met Sam Mendelsohn at a warehouse just off Fulton Street in downtown Manhattan. The warehouse manager, a man named Hector Fuentes, was also there. They were standing by a large truck that was open in the back and stacked full of boxes. Henry was walking around checking the place out while Jack was being introduced to Hector; Henry wasn't one for meeting people. He became very attentive, however, when Hector started describing the logistics of the transfer.

"You sign the documents over right now to Mr. Tobin," he told Sam Mendelsohn. "And Mr. Tobin, you be here tomorrow morning at nine o'clock. Ask for me, nobody else but me. Bring the documents and a truck and your people, and I'll arrange everything. It will go very smoothly, I assure you."

While they were shaking hands and pretending they actually liked each other, Henry wandered over to the black security guard and struck up a conversation. Ten minutes later, Jack called him to let him know they were leaving.

"This is a setup," Jack told him when they were on the FDR Drive and headed to Harlem.

"How do you figure that?" Henry asked.

"Come on, Henry—this isn't a business transaction, it's a document production. We don't need bills of lading to transfer this stuff. And this guy Hector has to be present at every step of the way? They want to know exactly when this truck is leaving the warehouse, and Hector is the man who's going to give them that information."

"Who are 'they'?" Henry asked.

"I still have no idea," Jack replied. "We've got to figure out a way to get those documents to Virginia without anybody knowing about it."

"Jack, you're actually starting to think like a criminal."

"I'm not so sure that's a good thing."

"It is when you're dealing with crooks."

The next morning at nine sharp they were back at the warehouse. Jack had the transfer documents Sam Mendelsohn had given him and was waiting to present them to Hector Fuentes, who had to be paged. Their own truck was not there yet. Jack looked a little concerned, but Henry informed him that it was still in Harlem waiting for his call to come to the warehouse.

Hector Fuentes made them wait for ten more minutes just to let them know how important he was. Finally he showed up, accepted the documents from Jack, and once again led the way to the truck containing the records.

"Where's your truck?" he asked before allowing them to inspect the contents one final time.

Jack was getting very tired of Hector's demands. "It'll be here in a few minutes," he said. "Just open the truck."

Hector bristled for a moment, then noticed Henry standing right next to Jack. The look Henry was giving Hector assured him that opening the truck would be beneficial for his health.

Hector unlatched the back and swung open the doors. His jaw dropped when he looked inside and saw that it was completely empty.

"What's going on here?" Jack yelled. "Where are the documents?"

"I have no idea!" Hector replied. "They were here last night, I swear. You saw for yourself."

"They're not here now," Jack shouted. "What the hell kind of game are you playing?"

"I'm not playing a game, I assure you. The records must have been stolen. I'm going to call the police myself right now. You can watch me call. You can be here when they come. I'll get the night watchman in here as well. We'll get to the bottom of this." The man was clearly in a panic.

"You'd better," Jack told him. "I need those records today. I don't have any time to hang around here. I'll be back in two hours, and you'd better have some answers for me."

He and Henry got in their rental car and drove off, leaving the bewildered Hector Fuentes scratching his head.

"All right, Henry, tell me how you did it." They were back on the FDR Drive headed uptown.

A smile broke across Henry's face. "I simply negotiated a price with the night watchman last night while you were making small talk with the rest of them. We picked up the boxes at about one o'clock this morning. They'll be at the lake house in another hour or so."

Jack just looked at him. "Are you sure you were just a small-time crook?"

"I was young, Jack. I didn't know my own potential."

Jack smiled. As they drove, he kept running through all the details in his mind. "I don't like the fact that he's making a police report, though."

"Don't worry about it. I'll call in an hour or so and say there was some sort of mix-up and we have the records. They'll know we pulled a fast one, but it won't go any further than that. Remember, whoever is behind this is a hell of a lot dirtier than we are. And that's where your real problem is, Jack."

"I've been a couple of steps behind you for a while now, Henry. I'm not sure what you're getting at."

"Look," Henry replied, "I've been thinking about this over and over—who 'they' are. We still don't know who engineered the plan to follow the records to their ultimate destination. We do know, however, that the attorneys for the telephone company and the estate had to be in on it. What did you tell me about that hearing—that they were in cahoots with the DA?"

"Yeah, so?"

"So the DA may be involved. Theoretically, the estate might have something to hide, and I guess they could be engineering this on their own but I don't think so. This is too coordinated an effort."

"Henry, do you realize what you're saying? You're at the very least implicating an assistant district attorney in a plot to commit murder."

"That may or may not be true. I don't know what the big picture is. I'm just trying to add the facts up as we go along."

"Look, the attempt on my life was right after the hearing to get the records. They want to follow that truck to get to my expert, you said so yourself. How did you put it? They want to kill two birds with one stone. I don't understand. Why would the DA, with such a strong criminal case against Benny, be involved in a murder plot? It doesn't make sense. It's preposterous."

"Do you see it any other way, Jack? Do you see this whole thing going down without the DA knowing about it?"

Jack thought about it for a moment. "Maybe it's not the DA. It could be Spencer Taylor acting on his own. I don't think scruples would get in that guy's way. I'm positive that he orchestrated the last hearing."

"Hopefully when Charlie sorts through those records we'll find some answers," Henry told him. "In the meantime, what do you think the DA will do when he learns that you got the records and he doesn't know where they are?"

"Well, if I was him, I'd try to get this case over before anyone has time to review the records. Charlie couldn't get through all those boxes in a month. If Spencer Taylor plays his cards right, this trial could be over in a week."

FIFTY-SIX

Charlie called Jack at his new number on Monday night to let him know she got the records. "Jack, this house is beautiful, and so is the lake. And Joaquin and Dick are perfect gentlemen. I feel totally secure. Unfortunately, I can't enjoy the house or the lake or the company because I'm buried in paper. Did you see the volume of documents they sent?"

"I did."

"It will take me months to get through this stuff, let alone make any sense out of it."

"Just remember what we discussed, Charlie. Find the telephone records first. I'm really only looking for the last month or so there. With the financials, work your way backward. See if anything grabs you in the last six months to a year."

"I'll give it my best shot, Jack, but finding the telephone records may take a week all by itself."

"Your best is all we can ask for, Charlie."

Jack spent all of Tuesday at Mike McDermott's office working on the case. Mike set him up in a spare office and showed him where the copier and the fax were in case he needed them. Then he left Jack to himself. There was no way Jack could ever repay Mike for his hospitality, but when Mike came to check on him at lunchtime, Jack insisted on treating him to dinner that night.

On Wednesday, Jack and Spencer Taylor appeared before the judge in his chambers for an impromptu status conference. The judge had called them personally, so there was no formal notice and thus no press.

"I just want to get a few things straight and get the preliminaries down before the fireworks start," the judge told them. "We're going to be on center stage for the whole country, gentlemen, and I, for one, don't want to look foolish.

"The press has been hounding me from all corners of the globe. I appreciate the fact that you two have not been stoking the fire. I'd like that to continue. I'm allowing one reporter to represent all the major networks, and one to represent the local stations—they'll serve as pool reporters. The foreign press gets one. The local papers each get one and, of course, the Associated Press.

"There will be no electronic devices of any kind in the courtroom. Cell phones will be confiscated at the entrance. That goes for you gentlemen as well. If either of you needs a computer for this case, let me know now."

"I don't, Judge," Spencer Taylor answered.

"How about you, Mr. Tobin?"

"No, sir."

"I don't want any speaking objections or grandstanding of any kind. You will stand, state your legal objection, and ask to approach the bench. Understand?"

"Yes, sir," they both answered almost in unison.

"Have you seen each other's documents?"

"All but the ones we had the hearing about, Judge," Spencer Taylor responded.

"Mr. Tobin, did you get your documents?"

"Yes, your honor. They were voluminous, however, and my expert has not been able to get through any of them yet. I won't see any documents that my expert will present until the last minute, if at all. I mention that because we have stipulated that the prosecution's inability to see the documents is not an issue."

"I recall that stipulation, Counsel. And I also recall that Mr. Taylor graciously waived any notice of witnesses that might arise from those documents. Is that correct, Mr. Taylor?"

"Yes, your honor."

"How do you want to handle the jury?"

"I'd like to question each juror individually, Judge," said Jack. "And I'd like the courtroom closed for voir dire."

"Any objection?"

"No, your honor."

"When we start the trial, we're going to bring the spectators in an hour early so they will all be seated beforehand. I know this doesn't involve you, but we are going to give tickets out on a first-come, first-serve basis downstairs after the press gets their tickets—I'm going to let them sit in the front rows. There's a limited number of tickets, so if you have anybody that you want to be here, let me know now and we'll give you tickets for every day. Nobody gets in the courtroom without a ticket."

"Judge, I'd like my investigator, Henry Wilson, to sit at counsel table with me when he is in the courtroom."

The judge looked at Spencer Taylor. "Any objection?"

"No, your honor."

"So ruled. Anything else?"

"Yes, your honor," Jack said. "I'd like the defendant's father to sit behind us."

The judge didn't ask for Taylor's comments on that request. "So ruled. Check with the bailiff before we start each day so he or she can make the appropriate arrangements. We don't want any fights to break out over seating."

"Last request, your honor," Jack told the judge. "I want to make sure my client is not handcuffed when he comes into the courtroom. His father is going to bring him a suit every day, and I'd like him to be able to change into it and be seated in court before the jurors are brought in."

The judge again looked at Spencer Taylor.

"No objection, your honor." Spencer wasn't sweating the small stuff. He also hoped he was making points with the judge. Jack was making all the requests and he was just agreeing.

"So ruled. You two gentlemen keep going along like this and we'll be through with this trial in no time."

The hearing seemed to have given the judge confidence.

He was warming up to the idea of being on center stage. Jack thought that was a good development. He needed a strong judge for his plan to work.

On Thursday Jack and Henry had lunch in the city with Luis. The man was so nervous he was visibly shaking. For a moment, Jack thought back to their days with the Lexingtons. Back then Rico was so tough, so hard, so sure of himself. Jack was certain that person was still inside there somewhere. Luis had already lifted himself out of the gutter, but the situation with Benny seemed like it was about to knock everything out from under him.

"How did your visit with Benny go?" Jack asked.

"Great. Great. It couldn't have been better. I owe that to the both of you. Whatever you said to him made him start to see things differently."

"It wasn't me," Jack replied. "It was Henry. He and Benny have traveled some of the same roads."

"It's prison too," Henry added. "If you've got half a brain, it makes you start thinking about things."

"Whatever it was, Benny and I are together now," Luis responded. "I'm just so on edge. I'm so afraid the state is going to pull something in that courtroom that will send Benny to his death." Luis started shaking again. Jack searched for something to say that would calm the man.

"Luis, I told you before, I can't guarantee the outcome of this trial. But I can guarantee you that Benny will get the best day in court he will ever have. Nobody is going to pull any shenanigans in that courtroom. I won't allow it. I'm the Mayor of Lexington Avenue, Luis. And that courtroom is my turf!"

Luis smiled. He remembered the day on a football field many years ago, when he had given that lesson to Jack. He was thankful that his friend had learned the lesson so well. Henry, on the other hand, had no idea what Jack was talking about.

FIFTY-SEVEN

The criminal courts building was a seventeen-story monolith located on Centre Street near the tip of Manhattan Island and within walking distance of the Fulton Fish Market, the South Street Seaport, and Wall Street. The surrounding area was a complex of judicial and government buildings. The civil courthouse was two blocks away, the federal court was on the next block, and City Hall was across the street. The area was always overrun with television cameras and reporters for one reason or another.

For criminal trials, the networks set their little kiosks up on the sidewalk in front of Collect Pond Park, a small park directly across the street from the criminal courts building. Each kiosk had its own lights, its own camera on a tripod, and its own talking head. There were also producers and producers' assistants and runners and plenty of others to give and take orders and to whisper about what was happening and create a buzz that would work itself into a frenzy that could be translated into exciting news for the TV screen.

The press had gotten word that the courtroom would be closed for jury selection, so Monday morning was rather subdued. The kiosks were still being set up and reporters were there to meet the attorneys as they entered the courthouse, with cameramen at the ready to film them. But there were no crowds to speak of, no buzz and no frenzy—yet.

The felony courtrooms were on floors eleven through sixteen. Judge Middleton's courtroom was on the eleventh floor. The walls were covered with maple paneling for the first six feet. It matched the wood of the judge's dais and the attorneys' tables. The rest of the wall up to the thirty-foot ceiling was white and bare. There were four large, modern, ugly lights that lined the ceiling on each side of the room. Overall it was a sterile, cold environment.

The judge's dais was relatively modest for such an imposing place. The witness chair was to the judge's right and the jurors' box to the right of that. The lawyer's rostrum was movable. During voir dire and opening and closing statements it was placed facing the jury. For the questioning of witnesses it was turned to face the witness chair so that the witness would be looking directly at the lawyer and the jury could watch the interplay of questions and answers. The court reporter was also on that side right in front of the judge's dais so as to be able to hear the questions and answers and record them. All other court personnel were on the far left side of the room opposite the jurors. Accommodations were tight inside the bar that separated the judge, the lawyers, the jurors and the court personnel from the rest of the courtroom.

The benches for spectators were behind the bar and were set up on each side of the middle aisle like the pews in a church. Jack counted six rows on each side, each row accommodating maybe eleven people. When the trial started they would be packed in like sardines.

This morning, however, since they were selecting a jury, the courtroom was empty of spectators. Only the judge, the lawyers, and the court personnel were present as each prospective juror was brought in for questioning.

Jack had always felt that the term "jury selection" was really a misnomer. It should have been called "jury exclusion" because the purpose was to identify and exclude anyone with a bias. In order to do that for his part, Jack had to ask the right questions, and in order to ask the right questions, he had already made a profile of his ideal juror. He'd decided that it didn't matter whether it was a man or a woman. He wanted people who were independent and open-minded and who had the intelligence to evaluate the evidence unemotionally and apply it rationally to the appropriate standard. He wanted to eliminate those who saw things in black and white, who never questioned authority, or who had relatives who were career military people or in law enforcement.

So as Jack began the process, to find clues to their personality he asked all the potential jurors detailed questions about their family, their job, their relatives, their thoughts about current affairs, the books they read, and their hobbies. He asked how they felt about the legal system. As an experienced litigator, Jack knew that no matter how good a case you put on, no matter how well you cross-examined the other side's witnesses, if you picked a bad jury you were dead out of the box. Jury selection was the most important part of any trial.

He had a laundry list of questions addressed to the burden of proof. This was where he started conditioning jurors to his case.

"Mrs. Jones, do you understand that the state has the burden of proof to prove its case beyond a reasonable doubt?

"Do you understand what a reasonable doubt is?

"Do you understand that the defendant does not have to present any evidence whatsoever?

"Do you understand that the defendant himself has a constitutional right not to testify?

"How do you feel about that?

"If the state fails to prove its case beyond a reasonable doubt, do you understand that it is your sworn duty to find the defendant not guilty?

"Will you do that if the evidence does not support the state's case beyond a reasonable doubt?"

That last one was particularly important. He had to get that commitment and he had to evaluate each person's demeanor as they gave that commitment. It was an art, not a science, and Jack was an artist.

It took two days of questioning potential jurors before both sides were satisfied with a panel of twelve and two alternates. The process had gone rather smoothly. The lawyers had conducted themselves professionally, and Judge Middleton was continuing to feel comfortable. He swore the jurors in at six o'clock on Tuesday evening.

The fireworks would begin promptly at nine o'clock the next morning.

*　　*　　*

Jack had still not heard from Charlie since their conversation on the previous Monday, so he gave her a call that evening from Mike McDermott's office.

"I've got good news and I've got bad news," she told him. "I found the telephone records. They were tucked away in the back of the last box. I think that was intentional."

"Probably so," Jack replied. He was antsy. He wanted to cut through the small talk, but he knew Charlie needed to have her say. She was the one buried under mounds of paper. "So, did you find anything?"

"Yeah. There was a person in Florida that Carl Robertson was calling all the time. He wasn't in Gainesville, though. He was in a little town called Micanopy. I found thirty-eight calls in the month before Robertson's death—twenty the month before that."

"Do you have a name and an address?"

"Yeah, I do. His name is Leonard Woods and his address is 26 Robin Lane, Micanopy. I called the number; it's been disconnected."

Jack didn't know if this was a break or not. So Carl Robertson had a good friend somewhere in Florida that he talked to a lot. So what? He would have to pursue it, though.

"Where the hell is Micanopy anyway?" he asked Charlie. "I've never even heard of it."

"I checked on that for you too. It's a small town north of Ocala."

"Okay. I'll get Henry on it right away. What's the bad news?"

"I haven't even started wading through the financial records. Where are you in the trial?"

"We've picked a jury. We start opening statements in the morning."

"How long will it take for the state to put on its case?"

"I think they could do it in two days."

"If that's the case, Jack, you'd better hope Leonard Woods has something for you, because I won't."

"I understand, Charlie, but keep at it. You never know what might happen."

He called Henry as soon as he got off the phone.

"We got a name. Charlie says Carl Robertson called a guy named Leonard Woods in Micanopy, Florida. Apparently it's a little ways north of Ocala. The exact address is 26 Robin Lane, and the closest major airport is probably Tampa."

"So I take it you want me to get on a plane and go visit Mr. Leonard Woods."

"Tonight."

"Tonight?"

"That's right. It may be our only lead. Charlie hasn't even touched the financials yet."

"All right. I'll see if I can find a red-eye and get down there. Jack, remember everything I told you. Watch yourself. And be sure to call on your way home so somebody is waiting for you. And take a cab."

"I will."

Jack worked for another hour until his brain was no longer functioning. He wasn't ready to go to sleep, and a drink or two to calm his nerves seemed like a good idea. He reached into his wallet to see how much cash he had and found the note from Molly with her phone number.

Molly answered on the second ring. "Hello?"

"Molly, this is Jack."

"Jack, I didn't think I'd ever hear from you again. How's the trial going? I've been following it a little bit in the paper. You've been doing jury selection, is that right?"

"That's right. You've been paying attention, I see. It's going very well. We finished picking the jury today. Assuming we get through opening statements, the prosecution will start putting on evidence tomorrow. Listen, I know it's late, but would you like to have a drink?"

Molly didn't hesitate. "Sure. Where are you now? I can meet you."

"I'm downtown still. I know you're in the West Village. Is there someplace in between?"

"Yeah. There's a little Irish bar called Colin's Place over on Spring Street, two blocks east of Broadway. I can't remember the cross street. I'll meet you there in fifteen minutes."

Molly was already there when he arrived. She was a sight for sore eyes even though the red bikini had been replaced by a bulky wool knit sweater, boots, and jeans. Jack gave her a big kiss. Molly glowed.

"Here we are in New York City," she said with that familiar sparkle in her eyes.

"Yeah. It's a far cry from Bass Creek, isn't it?"

"They both have their advantages, don't you think?"

"I do. Still, I've been in the city for only a week and I'm already missing Bass Creek."

They chatted for about an hour. It was precisely what Jack needed to relax. He wanted more than anything to invite himself home with Molly, but he knew he couldn't. He had an early morning, and Henry's words were ringing in his ears. After his second beer, he told Molly he had to leave.

"I'll call you tomorrow night. Maybe we'll meet again for a drink."

Molly gave him the kind of good-bye kiss that ensured he would call the next day.

"Good luck tomorrow," she said, her eyes holding the connection between them as he headed for the door.

FIFTY-EIGHT

Jack knew that Wednesday morning outside the courthouse would be different from the previous two days. He hadn't anticipated how different.

George, the bodyguard, drove him downtown in an old Mercedes with heavily tinted windows. George was not a talkative person, and no words passed between them during the trip. He let Jack off on a side street a couple of blocks from Centre Street so that nobody would see how he'd arrived and be able to recognize the car and follow it.

"I'll call you tonight when I'm on my way home," Jack told him before shutting the car door.

"Uh-huh," George muttered.

The crowds were thick, and there was some pushing and shoving when he reached Centre Street. He was carrying his trial briefcase and had trouble working his way through the mayhem. He saw the kiosks all lit up across the street. Several people in the crowd were carrying signs. In the immediate group around him all the signs had slogans against the death penalty. On the other side of the entrance to the criminal courts building the signs were all pro death penalty. The two groups were shouting at each other and chanting in unison like opposing fans at a football game.

The police had erected barriers to either side of the courthouse entrance to separate the crowds and prevent them from entering the building. Somebody in the crowd around him recognized Jack and shouted, "Way to go Jack! Keep fighting for justice." Others picked up the chorus. He shook hands and smiled as he tried to shoulder his way through to the wooden barriers. When he finally got there he yelled to a cop to tell him who he was. Finally a sergeant noticed him, came over, and motioned him to climb under the barrier. He was in the open space now where everybody could see him. The crowd he'd been in was cheering; those on the other side booed loudly. Jack walked up the steps and into the building.

The last week before the trial, when the media was showering its attention on Benny's plight, Jack did not read the newspapers or watch the news. He didn't want or need that kind of distraction, so he had no idea what the media was writing and talking about. Since he'd undertaken Benny's representation, Jack had focused solely on the strategy he was going to use to try to get him off. He'd assumed the high profile of the case came from Carl's status as a wealthy captain of industry. Yes, the governor had been very vocal touting the death penalty, but New York hadn't executed a person in fifty years. The signs and the attitude of the crowd had surprised him. In the eyes of the public, the New York State death penalty was on trial.

As he rode the elevator to the eleventh floor, Jack realized that the public's focus on the death penalty was a good thing. If Benny was convicted, so long as there were grounds for appeal, his case would remain in the spotlight. The public would follow it through the entire appellate process and at every juncture apply pressure on the judiciary. His job was to make sure there would be an issue for appeal in the event Benny was convicted.

Even though Jack was thirty minutes early the courtroom was already full of spectators. Luis was there. Benny had not yet been brought in. Jack took his place at the defendant's table and turned to Luis.

"Remember what I said, Luis. This is my courtroom." Luis smiled nervously to let Jack know he understood.

A court officer approached and whispered in Jack's ear. "Your client is in there," he said, pointing to a door on the right side of the courtroom. "He's changing." Jack walked over to the door and into the room. Luis had brought Benny a new blue suit, a white shirt, a red tie, and black shoes, and Benny was getting into the pants when Jack walked in. Three guards were in the room with him.

"How are you feeling?" Jack asked him.

"A little nervous but fine," Benny answered. He seemed a lot better off than his father. When he had finished getting his pants and shirt on, Jack helped him with the tie.

"You're going to look like one of the lawyers," he remarked. Benny smiled sheepishly. "Seriously, Benny, you look really good. When we go into the courtroom, I want you to stand when everybody stands and I want you to stand up straight. When you sit, sit straight. No slouching. No matter what anybody says on the stand, I don't want you to make any facial expressions, understand?"

Benny nodded.

"As I've told you before, the jurors will be watching you constantly. Even though you won't be testifying, they'll be watching you and sizing you up. An important part of all this is you and your demeanor in that courtroom. Got it?"

"Yeah," Benny answered. "I'm ready."

"Okay, let's go."

Benny followed Jack into the courtroom and Jack showed him where to sit. He took a yellow pad and a pen out of his briefcase and put them on the table in front of Benny.

"You can write things down, even doodle—anything that makes you look attentive. If you want to alert me to something, write it down. Don't talk to me while somebody is testifying because I can't divide my attention. And remember, don't tell me anything about what you did or didn't do on the night of the murder."

"I understand," Benny told him.

They both sat down and Jack started unloading the contents of his briefcase onto the table and readying himself for his opening statement.

Spencer Taylor was already in the courtroom at the table farthest away from the jury. Like most prosecutors, he wanted the scum-sucking, lowlife defendant as close to the jurors as possible. As the trial progressed and Benny's guilt became apparent, he wanted them to have a bird's-eye view of him. Spencer trained his perfect pearly whites on Jack before the jury came in, flashing his best smile.

"Good morning, Counselor."

"Good morning," Jack said blankly.

Spencer's table was all set up. He had a yellow pad directly in front of him and his exhibits stacked neatly on the table. Norma Grier, the deputy district attorney who had assisted Spencer earlier, wasn't there. Spencer wanted the battle to be *mano a mano*, solely between him and Jack Tobin. He was still bristling from the stunt Jack had pulled at the hearing, not to mention the files he'd *stolen* from the warehouse. Spencer wanted to gut Jack in the middle of that courtroom, and he didn't want any help when he did it.

Promptly at nine o'clock Judge Langford Middleton walked into the courtroom, and the bailiff announced the beginning of the proceedings. "All rise!" he bellowed.

Everybody stood up. Jack stole a glance at his client. Benny was standing at attention looking straight ahead. *If only he can stay that way for the rest of the trial*, Jack thought.

"You may be seated," the judge announced. He waited for everyone to settle before delivering his opening remarks.

This was Langford Middleton's moment. The years were starting to show on him. His once-thick brown wavy hair was now gray in spots and almost completely white at the temples, and age lines creased the corners of his eyes. He was still an imposing figure, though, and in his black robes, on this stage, he certainly looked like a judge. Nobody could see that underneath those robes his knees were shaking.

"Ladies and gentlemen," he said in a great booming voice addressing the spectators, "your presence here is a privilege—a privilege that may be revoked at any time. This is a courtroom. It is not a movie theater. It is not a television studio. A man is on trial for his life. You will not root for one side or the other. You will not comment in any way on the testimony. You will sit and observe in silence and, if you cannot do that, you will be removed by court personnel, forcibly if necessary. Do you understand?"

Everybody seemed to nod as one. It was an auspicious start for the judge.

"Counselors, is there anything we need to take up before we bring the jury in?"

"No, your honor," Spencer and Jack answered almost in unison.

"Bring in the jury," he instructed the bailiff.

When the jury was seated, the judge turned to the prosecutor. "Mr. Taylor, you may proceed."

"Thank you, your honor," Spencer replied as he walked to the podium, which was now situated directly in front of the jurors. He was wearing a tailor-made charcoal gray suit, a crisp white shirt, and a lavender tie. His hair was once again coiffed to perfection and his clear, smooth skin was lightly bronzed, probably from a tanning booth. In short, he looked beautiful.

Spencer stood at the podium and made eye contact with each juror. When he started to speak, his words were warm and generous, his smile captivating.

"Good morning, ladies and gentlemen. As you know from jury selection, my name is Spencer Taylor, and I represent the people of the state of New York." He didn't say "*you* the people," but they got the message. "And I am proud to stand before you today in that capacity." The words were a little overdone, but he seemed to pull it off. His blue eyes spoke of nothing but sincerity and conviction.

Jack watched the jurors, especially the women, fall for Spencer and his schmaltz.

When Spencer finally got to Benny's case, he began by describing the victim, Carl Robertson, and his stellar and lucrative career in the oil business. Then almost reluctantly he told them about Carl's "imperfections," that he'd had a mistress whose name was Angie and that he'd brought her money every month and paid for her apartment.

He briefly described what Angie's testimony would be and told them he would also be calling two eyewitnesses, Paul Frazier and David Cook, who lived in Angie's building. They had heard the shot and immediately gone to the window and seen a man leaning over the body of Carl Robertson. They'd later identified that man as Benny Avrile, the defendant.

It was a simple story of motive and opportunity: Benny was there, the motive was robbery, and he'd shot Carl Robertson in cold blood.

"The only question you have to answer, ladies and gentlemen, is this: Does the evidence prove beyond a reasonable doubt that the accused, Benny Avrile, killed Carl Robertson in cold blood? The answer is a resounding yes."

Spencer was driving an express train. His opening had taken only twenty minutes. He hadn't talked about any of the forensic evidence. He didn't need to. It would come up during the testimony itself, clearly supporting the simple, straightforward story he had told the jury.

It was now Jack's turn. Jack had considered waiving his opening and giving it at the start of his defense. But this was a fight, like a boxing match or a gladiator's duel. The jury had seen and heard from Spencer; now they wanted to hear from him. He had a problem, though, and it was a big problem. He still didn't know what his defense was. All he could do was give them what he had at the moment.

In his preparations, two major issues had concerned Jack, the first obviously being the charge of first-degree murder. The second problem was almost of equal importance: the felony murder count. The felony murder rule basically provided that if someone was killed during the commission of a felony, everyone involved in the felony was guilty of murder. Thus, if Benny was attempting to rob Carl Robertson, that was enough for a conviction under the felony murder rule. Felony murder was second-degree murder and not punishable by death.

The governor wanted death. Spencer Taylor wanted death so badly Jack was sure that the man could taste it; anything less than a first-degree murder conviction would be considered a blot on his résumé. Jack hoped to take advantage of that relentless focus to at least dispose of the felony murder count. Then the jury would only have one issue to decide.

He had a plan, but like everything else at this point, it was pretty much a crapshoot.

He stood up and walked to the podium. Jack was wearing an olive green suit, a blue shirt, and a maroon tie. At six two, he was taller than Spencer and appeared stronger and fitter than the younger man. His hair was short and gray and sparse in places, and his face was weathered by age and experience—a good-looking man, but even on his best day nobody would ever have described Jack Tobin as beautiful.

"Good morning, ladies and gentlemen," he began. His tone was pleasant but businesslike enough to let them know he wasn't going to ingratiate himself to them. That wasn't his style.

"You know what I'm going to say to you first off because we discussed it during jury selection. The state has the burden of proof: it has to prove its case beyond a reasonable doubt. That is our system of justice. You all assured me that you would hold the state to its burden. The defendant has a constitutional right not to testify, and he will not in this case. You all assured me that you would honor that right. The defense does not have an obligation to put on any witnesses. You all assured me that you understood that concept. I'm going to hold you to those promises."

Jack paused and looked each juror in the eye.

"Now, what have you heard from the state this morning? I know it's not evidence, but let's assume for the moment that Mr. Taylor is accurately stating his case. A man is shot on a city street at ten o'clock at night and two people look out their window sometime soon after the event and see another man kneeling over the victim and they later identify the accused as that man. Is he just a person who happened to be on that street at that precise moment responding to an emergency situation without thinking, or is he the perpetrator? That is the ultimate question you have to answer. In order to do that, you must ask the following questions: Did anyone see this man stealing money? Did they see him with a gun? If the answer to those two questions is no and there is no evidence of any other connection between the defendant and the deceased, then the state has simply not met its burden and you must find the defendant not guilty."

That was it. Jack's opening was only a few minutes long—much shorter and simpler than Spencer Taylor's. Both men knew the trial was going to be a lot more complicated.

FIFTY-NINE

Henry had another name for Micanopy— two names, actually. He wanted to call it Oakville or, even better, Eerieville. Micanopy was a small little inland town, a slice of Old Florida—an old Florida that Henry didn't think he would have liked too much. Somewhere in the recesses of his brain he recalled that a whole community of black folks had been massacred somewhere around here at a place called Rosewood.

The main street was lined with giant oak trees that formed a canopy over the road. Spanish moss hung from the branches like rotted tinsel. "Eerieville" was just right—and he hadn't even seen the place at night yet.

It was about ten o'clock in the morning. He had flown into Tampa late Tuesday night and stayed at a hotel near the airport. He'd rented a car first thing in the morning and headed north on Interstate 75.

Micanopy was nothing more than two or three blocks of antiques stores, a town hall, and a library. It had that slow feel of the Old South. Henry had no idea where 26 Robin Lane was, so he pulled up next to the only person on the street, an old man who was shuffling along, and asked him for directions.

The old man rubbed his chin and looked to the sky for guidance. Henry was sure he didn't have a clue. After a minute or so the man finally spoke, in a slow Southern drawl that only added to the feel of the whole place.

"Well, you go down this street here a ways," the old man said, pointing back in the direction Henry had come from, "and you go maybe half a mile or so until you see a turnoff on the right. That's Robin Lane. Now 26, I believe, is the third place on the left. That's about a mile down the road." He took another look at Henry and added, "I'd be mighty careful if I were you," and then he turned and shuffled off. *Old South indeed*, Henry thought as he pulled away, shaking his head.

Surprisingly, the old man's directions were very good. Henry found Robin Lane right where it was supposed to be. It was a narrow dirt road not wide enough for two cars, and he took it slowly. After about a mile and a half he'd counted only two places on the left so he decided to backtrack, realizing he'd probably missed the third left. Then he spotted it—a driveway so overgrown with old orange trees and bushes and mangroves that there was barely room for a car to fit. He turned in and kept going for what seemed like forever, the overgrowth scratching the finish of the rental car, until he came to a clearing. Beyond was a two-story wooden house with a wide front porch and a tin roof. A dog was lying on the porch; it didn't move as the car approached. Henry noticed fields behind the house, a barn, and some cattle and horses. He turned to the left and pulled the car up a good distance from the house, mindful both of the dog and of the old man's words. He got out and started walking slowly and cautiously toward the house. He was just about to shout and ask if anyone was home when a single shot rang out. Henry hit the ground.

He lay there for a few minutes not moving. Then he inched his head around slightly so he could see the front of the house. Everything was still, including the dog, who had not moved from his spot on the porch. Slowly Henry stood up and walked around toward the back of the house.

There was an old man in the backyard feeding the chickens. Henry slipped up behind him and put him in a headlock with his left arm, grabbing him around the middle with his right. The old geezer started kicking and flailing his arms.

"Hold on there, Mr. Woods. I don't know what you're thinking, but I don't want to hurt you even though you just tried to kill me. I'm just looking for some information."

The old man kept up the barrage of kicks and punches. "I'm not Mr. Woods," he cackled. "And if I wanted to kill you, you'd already be dead. I just fired a warning. Figured you'd go away after that."

Henry realized he needed to do something to calm the situation. He spun the old man around and hit him with a right cross to the chin. The poor fellow went down like a sack of potatoes. The chickens squawked, but the dog, who was now lying on the back porch, didn't move.

Henry found some rope in the barn, tied the old man's hands and feet, and carried him into the house, propping him up on a ratty old couch near the window. Henry sat down across from him and waited for him to come round.

Finally the old man's eyelids flickered as he started to regain consciousness. He looked around as if lost, then focused on Henry, a flash of anger crossing his face. He struggled briefly against the ropes and then went limp, staring all the time at Henry.

"We can do this the easy way or the hard way," Henry said calmly. "First, I'm going to tell you who I am and why I'm here. Then you can decide if you want to answer my questions."

"I've got no choice, I guess," the old man grumbled.

Henry then told him about Carl Robertson's murder, Benny's murder charge, and Jack's representation of Benny. "I work for Jack Tobin. The reason I'm here is because Mr. Robertson called you thirty-eight times in the month before he died. We want to know why and if there's any connection to Mr. Robertson's death."

"He didn't call me," the old man answered. "He called Lenny."

"You're not Leonard Woods?"

"I already told you that before you slugged me. My name's Valentine Busby. I farmed the land here for Lenny. He left me the house. Lenny Woods is dead."

Henry's heart sank momentarily. "When did he die?"

"Over a year ago back in the summer."

"What happened?"

"He was murdered. A hit-and-run at seven o'clock in the morning right out there on Robin Lane."

"Why do you think it was murder and not an accident?"

"Lenny went for a walk at seven every morning after the animals were taken care of and all the morning chores were done. It was broad daylight. Anybody coulda seen him. Do you know how fast you have to go on a road like that to kill a man? No, it was murder."

"Did the police think it was murder?"

"The police around here don't think, period."

Henry frowned. These two murders didn't appear to be a coincidence.

"Do you know what Lenny and Carl talked about on the phone?" he asked.

"No. I know they were working on something together but Lenny didn't tell me about that kind of stuff. He had a colleague in Wisconsin who I'm sure knew all about it."

"A colleague? What kind of business was Lenny in?"

"He wasn't in any business. He was a professor of microbiology at the University of Florida."

"In Gainesville?"

"Yeah. Right up the road."

"Do you know the name of this colleague in Wisconsin?"

"I sure do. I've got his name and address written down somewhere. If you untie me, I can get it."

Henry figured things were safe enough so he started to untie him. "Now don't try anything funny."

"Tangle with a man the size of you again? I'm not that stupid," Valentine Busby said, rubbing his bruised chin now that his hands were free. "By the way, when was Carl Robertson murdered?"

"September first of last year," Henry said, crouching down to undo the knots on the rope around Valentine's feet.

"That's funny."

"Why is it funny?"

"Lenny was murdered on September second."

Henry almost had a heart attack. He was still trying to process this new information when Valentine dropped another bombshell.

"You know, you're not the first person I talked to about this."

"Really?" Henry replied as he straightened up and helped Valentine to his feet.

"Yeah. I talked to an attorney maybe six months ago. Not the guy you work for. Somebody else. I told him pretty much what I told you, although it was a much shorter conversation. I never heard from him again but after that things got a little creepy. Cars started coming by at strange hours, that kind of stuff. I know it could be my imagination. I'm an old man and all, but that's when I cut off the phone and wouldn't let anybody past that clearing where you parked your car. I'm sorry I fired that warning shot, but now you know why."

Henry wasn't quite ready to accept Valentine's apology so he ignored it. "Was the guy you talked to named Sal Paglia?"

"Can't be certain. I don't have the greatest memory in the world. But yeah, I think that's the guy."

SIXTY

For a moment at the outset of the trial Jack thought Langford Middleton was in cahoots with Spencer Taylor, because he was moving the case along so fast.

"Call your first witness," the judge told Spencer before Jack had arrived back at his seat after finishing his opening statement.

"The state calls Angela Vincent."

The bailiff left the room and came back less than a minute later with a beautiful blond woman dressed appropriately in a modest black dress. The clerk swore her in and she stepped up to the witness chair.

"Please state your name for the record," Spencer Taylor began.

"Angela Vincent," she replied.

"Ms. Vincent, did you know the deceased, Carl Robertson?"

"Yes."

"And could you tell the jury the nature of your relationship?"

"I was Carl's mistress for five years. He set me up in an apartment on Seventy-eighth Street and East End Avenue and he gave me ten thousand dollars a month. He came to visit every Tuesday and Thursday and sometimes on the weekend."

Jack could tell from the detail in Angie's answer and the directness with which she delivered it that she and Spencer had rehearsed her testimony thoroughly.

"Do you know where Carl lived?"

"In Washington, DC."

"And he came to your place every Tuesday and Thursday without fail?"

"Yes."

"How did he get there?"

"Carl had his own jet, so he flew here and then drove to the apartment in a car he kept at the airport."

"And what kind of car was it?"

"A black Mercedes."

"And where did Carl park when he came to see you on Tuesdays and Thursdays?"

"He had a private spot reserved right in front of the building."

"In what way was it reserved?"

"There was a sign that said 'No Parking.'"

"And that sign was visible to the general public?"

"Yes."

"And was the deceased dressed in any particular way when he came to see you?"

"Carl always arrived in a suit. He was very particular about how he looked."

"What did you know about Carl before you began this relationship with him?"

"Well, I knew he was a very nice man. I went out with him on several occasions before I moved into the apartment."

"Anything else?"

"I knew he was very wealthy."

Jack could have raised an objection on the grounds that Carl's wealth wasn't directly relevant to the murder charge before the court, but Spencer was going to get that evidence in one way or another. Hell, the jury probably already knew that part. Objecting would only make Jack look like he was trying to keep something from them. He let it go.

On a related issue, though, Jack was ready to go to the mat. While the fact that Carl was wealthy was sufficient to establish robbery as a motive, it was not in itself evidence that the separate crime of robbery had occurred. The fight over that was about to start.

"Ms. Vincent," Spencer continued, "you mentioned that Carl brought you ten thousand dollars a month. How did he bring it?"

"In cash—one-hundred-dollar bills bound together. He kept it in his left inside pocket."

"And when did he usually bring this money?"

Jack was on his feet immediately.

"Objection, your honor. May we approach?"

"State the basis for your objection, Counsel."

"The question is irrelevant, speculative, and prejudicial."

"You may approach."

Both Jack and Spencer walked over to the judge's dais on the side opposite the jury for a sidebar discussion. The court reporter went with them so she could take down everything that was said.

"I'm not sure I understand your objection, Counsel, so clarify it for me," the judge told Jack.

"Mr. Taylor asked when the deceased *usually* brought the money, your honor. This is not a contracts case. What the deceased customarily did is not an issue. It speculates as to whether he had the money with him that night. In that respect it is prejudicial because the jury could assume without any *actual* evidence that Mr. Robertson brought the money that night. I believe Mr. Taylor could ask the witness if she knew whether the deceased had the ten thousand dollars on him that night. Then I assume the prosecution could establish through other testimony that it was missing after the murder. Nothing else is relevant, your honor."

"I'm not so sure, Counselor. I think it is relevant for the jury to hear that Mr. Robertson was wealthy and that he normally brought ten thousand dollars a month."

"Relevant to what, Judge? Doesn't he have to show my client knew about the money before it becomes relevant?"

The judge looked at Spencer Taylor. "Do you have anything to add, Mr. Taylor?"

"Yes, your honor. Mr. Tobin's argument is ridiculous. That's like saying the prosecution has to show in every case that the defendant knew beforehand how much money was in the victim's pocket in order to prove a robbery occurred." It was a good argument, and it made sense to the judge.

"I agree, Mr. Taylor. I think the question is admissible. However, sometime during your case you're going to have to establish that something of value in excess of five hundred dollars was *actually* stolen from the deceased in order to establish that a felony occurred."

It was exactly the ruling that Jack wanted at this stage of the proceedings. "You may answer the question," the judge told Angie.

"I'm sorry, could you repeat it?" Angie asked Spencer.

"Certainly. When did the deceased usually bring this ten thousand dollars?"

"The first Tuesday of the month."

Spencer Taylor had gotten everything he needed from Angie. He had learned through trial and error over the years only to ask the questions that needed to be asked.

"No further questions."

The judge looked at Jack. "Cross-examination?"

"Yes, your honor, thank you."

Angie was stunning, and she had been direct and honest in her testimony. The jury obviously liked her, and Jack wanted to be very careful not to appear to be the bad guy with her.

"Ms. Vincent, you testified that the deceased usually brought the ten thousand dollars on the first Tuesday of the month, correct?"

"Yes."

"But he didn't always bring it on the first Tuesday, is that accurate?" Jack wasn't fishing. He already knew the answer from the police reports in Benny's file.

"Yes."

"So some months he brought it on the second Tuesday or the third Tuesday or even the fourth Tuesday, is that accurate?"

"I don't believe I ever had to wait until the fourth week."

"So you were always paid by the end of the third week?"

"Yes."

"And within those first three weeks sometimes you were paid on the Tuesday and sometimes on the Thursday, is that correct?"

"Yes."

"And is it accurate that you do not know for a fact whether the deceased had your money, the ten thousand dollars, on him the night he was murdered?"

"That's accurate. I do not know whether he had the money on him or not."

"No further questions, your honor."

"Redirect, Mr. Taylor?"

"No, your honor." Spencer still felt he had won this round and that Jack had essentially scored a meaningless point.

"Call your next witness, Counselor," the judge told Spencer. The express train was rolling again.

As expected, Spencer called Paul Frazier and then David Cook, the eyewitnesses who lived in Angie's building. He painstakingly took them, one at a time, through the night of the murder, their visit to the police station, their assistance in helping the police artist come up with a composite sketch, and their ultimate selection of Benny in the lineup—all setting the stage for the dramatic courtroom identification.

"Is the man you saw the night of the murder leaning over the deceased in the courtroom today?"

Each man when he was on the stand answered yes.

"Would you point him out for the jury?" Both men had pointed directly at Benny, who remained stoically upright and facing directly ahead each time.

Jack had the same cross-examination questions for both men and received almost identical answers.

"How much time elapsed between your hearing the shot and going to the window?"

"I couldn't say for sure," Paul replied. "We were watching television. I don't know what the show was—something makes me want to say it was *NYPD Blue* but again I can't say for sure. We didn't rush because frankly we didn't know it was a gun that went off. I'd estimate it was about ten to twenty seconds."

David's estimate was "about a half a minute or so."

"When you saw this individual you have identified as the defendant leaning over the deceased, did you see him take anything?"

Both men had the same answer: "No."

"How far away were you when you first saw the defendant?"

They both said close to thirty feet.

"And he came toward you and then he saw you looking at him and took off, is that accurate?"

Again they agreed.

"How far away was he right before he took off?"

Paul's estimate was five feet and David's six to eight feet.

"At any time while you were observing the accused on that night, did you see him with a gun?"

Neither said they had.

"Were both his hands visible?"

Paul was definite that they were. David said, "I think so, but I couldn't say for certain."

When Jack finished his cross-examination of David Cook it was four o'clock in the afternoon. The judge noticed that the jury was tired and decided to recess for the day.

"The court will reconvene at nine o'clock tomorrow morning. The jurors will follow Mr. Jennings, the bailiff, who will lead you out and show you where to meet tomorrow so you can avoid the crowds in front of the courthouse. Remember my admonitions to you. Do not talk to anyone, including family members, about this case. Do not read the newspaper or watch the news on television. I'll see you tomorrow morning."

After the judge left the courtroom, Jack approached the court reporter and asked her to transcribe his cross-examination of all three witnesses, as well as the sidebar discussion and the judge's ruling. "I'll need it by tomorrow," he told her.

Jack went directly to Mike McDermott's office to prepare for the next day's proceedings. First he called the company that had shipped Dr. Wong's exhibits from San Francisco and made sure they would deliver them to Langford Middleton's courtroom before nine o'clock the next morning. A little after six, he called Charlie.

"How's it going?" he asked, dreading the response.

"Nothing yet," Charlie replied. "I'm still wading through crap. How's the trial going?"

"Fast. Do you think you'll have anything by tomorrow night?"

"No, absolutely not. It would be more than a miracle if I did."

"Okay, I understand. Go ahead and book a flight for Sunday night. We won't plan on using you until Monday."

"What if he finishes up tomorrow?"

"I'll do something. I've got a motion for acquittal to argue. Maybe Henry will have something for me by then."

About half an hour later Henry called to give Jack a blow-by-blow of his meeting with Valentine Busby, starting with the shooting. He told Jack that Leonard Woods was dead, that he had been killed the morning after Carl's murder by a hit-and-run driver, and that Valentine Busby was certain he had been murdered, although the local police had not ruled it a homicide. It was a lot of information for Jack to synthesize after a long day of trial. Henry wasn't finished yet.

"There's more. Leonard and Carl definitely knew each other. Carl actually visited once. Valentine says that they were working on something, but he doesn't know what. Leonard was a professor of microbiology at the University of Florida in Gainesville."

"So that call Carl got at Angie's apartment was from Leonard, which explains the word *Gainesville* on the message pad. But what was the *breakthrough*? What were they working on?"

"I haven't a clue, Jack. Valentine says there is a guy up in Wisconsin, another professor named Milton Jeffries, who probably knows. I called his number but it's been disconnected. I've got his address, so Valentine and I are flying up there tomorrow. It's the soonest we could get a flight. Valentine's a little out there, but he's not a bad guy. He really wants to find out who killed Leonard."

"All right, keep me posted. I'm starting to get more than a little paranoid, especially after all this new information you've given me. From now on, let's keep the substance of our phone conversations to a minimum. We'll talk about when you're coming and things like that, but no specifics, got it?"

"Sure."

"Do you think you can be back here by Friday? I may not have a witness to put on if the prosecutor rests tomorrow."

"I don't know. I'll do my best."

"I know you will, Henry. Call me tomorrow at the same time."

"Will do. Good luck in court. I wish I had some answers for you."

"Maybe something will still come up tomorrow."

"We can only hope," Henry replied.

Jack's mind was churning. There was clearly a connection between Carl and Leonard's murders, but he had no idea what that connection was or whether it was helpful to his case or not. He would just have to wait until he heard from Henry again and hope that it wasn't too late.

Jack worked for another hour before calling Molly.

"I know it's late. Do you want to meet for a drink?"

"Sure. I'll be at our 'regular joint' in fifteen minutes," she answered. He could hear the smile in her voice.

She was waiting for him when he got to Colin's Place. This time she had discarded the bulky sweater for a tight-fitting turtleneck and jeans. She looked fabulous and gave him a big kiss before he sat down.

"How's the trial going?"

"As good as can be expected. I got everything I thought I could get out of the prosecution's witnesses today."

That was the extent of their conversation about the trial. This brief moment late in the day was Jack's opportunity to unwind. Molly seemed to understand. She kept things light, talking about the latest celebrity sightings and even sports. She was a Yankees fan.

Jack stayed about an hour and had a couple of beers. He could have talked to Molly all night and then gone home with her, but he had to go. Tomorrow was a huge day.

"Molly, you know how much I'd love to spend the night with you."

"I know, Jack. You just do your work for now and we'll take a little vacation afterwards."

He kissed her good night and left while he still had the fortitude to do so.

SIXTY-ONE

Thursday morning's temperature was in the low twenties, and only the staunchest advocates on each side of the death penalty issue were outside the courthouse. Jack had a relatively easy time making his way inside. The transcripts he'd requested from the court reporter were waiting at his table. The reporter was already at her seat, and Jack gave her a nod of thanks. One of the court officers came over to tell him that Dr. Wong's exhibits had arrived and were resting against the far wall behind the court personnel. Moments later, Benny was ushered in through the side door. Today he was wearing a brown suit, blue shirt, dark multicolored tie, and brown shoes. His father, who had taken his place behind Jack, was certainly going to great lengths to ensure his son made a good impression on the jury every day.

Jack turned to Luis. "Nice job. He looks terrific."

Luis seemed much more relaxed. "Tomorrow he's in charcoal gray, like the dandy wore the first day," he said, glancing in the direction of Spencer Taylor, who was dressed in navy blue with a bright gold tie. Jack got a kick out of Luis's moniker. Spencer was indeed a dandy.

Spencer started the morning off with Detective Tony Severino. The testimony began with Tony's telling the jury about his training and experience as a homicide detective. Then Spencer took him right to the murder scene.

"What time did you arrive?"

"I arrived at the scene at precisely 11:11 p.m."

"Were you the first to arrive?"

"No. There were some uniforms there already. The coroner was there, I believe. There was a crowd, and some members of the press."

"Were you the first homicide detective?"

"Yes."

"What did you do when you arrived?"

"I went to the body and gave it a cursory inspection."

"What did you observe?"

"I observed a white male, tall, probably in his late fifties or sixties— I found out later that he was actually in his seventies but he didn't look it. He was wearing a blue suit, white shirt, and maroon tie."

Jack noticed a couple of the female jurors stealing a glance at Benny, who had worn the exact same outfit the day before. He wanted to whack himself in the forehead for missing that detail. It was one of those little things that might tip the balance in a close case. That was the way trials went. You couldn't possibly think of everything. At least Benny wasn't sitting in court today in that outfit. Then even the men would have noticed.

Back on the stand, Tony Severino was continuing his testimony. "He had a bullet wound in his forehead."

"What did you do next?"

"I directed some of the uniforms to tape off the crime scene. You don't want people walking all around there. It can contaminate the evidence."

"How did the police department first learn of this crime?"

"A woman from the neighborhood called it in. Her name was Frances Holloway."

"What did she say?"

Jack was on his feet. "Objection, your honor. Hearsay."

"Sustained."

"Your honor, I'd like to be heard on this," Spencer protested. "May we approach?"

The judge gave Spencer an annoyed look. "Come along," he motioned to the two lawyers.

"Mr. Taylor, when it is obviously hearsay we don't need to come to the bench to make a record."

"I understand, Judge, but I'm not offering it for the truth of the matter asserted."

Langford Middleton rolled his eyes at that one. It was an argument every lawyer tried at one time or another, but it was rarely successful. He let Spencer continue, though. "Carry on, but make it brief."

"Mrs. Holloway merely reported that she heard the shot, came to her window, and saw someone kneeling over the deceased. She couldn't identify him. This evidence was already entered through yesterday's testimony and I don't think counsel has disputed it. I'm only trying to create my time line without having to bring another witness in."

It was a clever way to put it, appealing to the judge's desire to move things along. The judge looked at Jack. "Well, Mr. Tobin?"

"It's cumulative, Judge. He's trying to get a third witness to say my client was kneeling over the deceased without bringing her in."

"I'm going to allow it. If necessary, Mr. Tobin, I'll let you call Ms. Holloway. As it stands, Mr. Taylor has the right to establish a time line with Detective Severino. Objection overruled."

Spencer gave Jack another peek at his perfect teeth as they left the sidebar, smiling broadly as he gloated. Twenty years ago Jack might have gone after him right there in the courtroom, but he had learned to squelch those urges. If it was meant to be, the worm would turn eventually.

Spencer and Tony Severino went on and on for the rest of the morning. Spencer asked Tony about his expertise with firearms. Besides his experience as a detective, Tony was a certified firearms expert, which partly explained to Jack why Spencer called him rather than Nick Walsh as a witness. Spencer might still call Nick, but if the prosecutor was looking to get this case over as soon as possible, probably not. Spencer had Tony talk about the slug that was taken out of Carl's skull and establish the chain of custody from that moment to his appearance at trial. He then introduced the bullet into evidence. Jack had no objection. It was a bullet without a gun. Yes, it killed Carl, but who was at the other end of the gun was the issue in this case. Spencer had Tony describe the bullet in great detail.

"It's a nine-millimeter Parabellum, commonly known as a Luger cartridge," Tony told him. "As you can see, it's not in very good shape. It's distorted. Once a slug like this hits bone, it starts to break up a little."

"Were you able to establish the type of gun that this bullet was fired from?"

"Yes."

"How do you do that?"

"It's a little technical, but I'll try to explain it as best I can. Each gun has distinctive markings in the barrel. They're called lands and grooves. The grooves are cut into the barrel of the gun in a spiral; the lands are the spaces between those grooves. When the gun is fired, the spiral grooving makes the bullet spin so that it flies straight. The heat inside the chamber makes the slug softer and makes it conform to the spiraling and the grooves in the barrel. If the slug is not damaged too badly you can examine those impressions and determine the make and possibly the model of the gun."

"Was the slug that you retrieved from the deceased's cranium in decent enough shape to make that examination?"

"Barely."

"And did you make that examination?"

"I was present when it was done. I'm no longer a full-time firearms examiner, but I was present when this examination was made."

"And did you determine the make and model of the gun that killed Carl Robertson?"

"Yes. It was a Glock nine-millimeter semiautomatic weapon—probably a Glock 17. It's a handgun manufactured by the Austrian company Glock. It has a unique barrel groove, and we could see that in this bullet even though it was distorted considerably."

"What does the term *semiautomatic* mean?"

"It means that the gun can be fired like an automatic weapon—that is, it can fire multiple rounds rapidly—but unlike a true automatic weapon you actually have to pull the trigger each time."

"In this case, from the evidence presented, how many rounds were fired?"

"One."

"How do you account for that with this semiautomatic weapon?"

"The person firing only pulled the trigger once."

"Thank you, Detective Severino, I have no further questions."

"Cross-examination, Mr. Tobin?"

"Yes, your honor." Jack walked to the podium and looked at Tony Severino.

Trials were often won or lost on how an attorney cross-examined key witnesses. In Jack's mind, Tony Severino was a key witness in the case. It was very difficult to make a prosecution witness your own, especially a seasoned police detective who had hundreds of hours of courtroom testimony under his belt. One mistake and the whole process could backfire.

Jack was not a seasoned criminal lawyer, but he understood the art of cross-examination better than most other trial attorneys on the planet. You had to lead the witness down the road without letting him know where he was going—keep the pace up, cut off exits, until eventually he found himself on a dead-end street with no way out. He was about to try to do that with Tony Severino.

"Detective Severino, you told Mr. Taylor that the motive for this murder was robbery, is that accurate?"

"Yes."

"Can you be more specific?"

"We think he stole ten thousand dollars from Mr. Robertson's inside jacket pocket."

"You do concede, however, do you not, that Ms. Vincent cannot say for certain whether Mr. Robertson had that money on him on September 1, 1998?"

"Yes, she said that."

"And there is no other evidence to establish Mr. Robertson had that money on him that night, correct?"

"That is correct."

"There were three individuals who immediately went to their windows after they heard the shot and saw someone kneeling over the deceased's body, correct?"

"That's correct."

"And two of those individuals, Mr. Cook and Mr. Frazier, identified that individual as the defendant, correct?"

"That's correct."

"Ms. Holloway could not?"

"No, she could not."

"Is it also accurate that nobody saw this individual take anything from the deceased's body?"

"Yes, that's accurate." Tony was beginning to look bored. This was all set out very clearly in the police reports that were already in evidence.

"How do you square that with what you just testified to—that he took the money out of Mr. Robertson's inside jacket pocket?"

"He took it before they got to the window and looked out."

"And nobody saw this individual carrying a gun—this Glock 17 that you just told us about, correct?"

"Correct."

"And he certainly didn't drop it at the scene because you didn't find a gun at the scene, did you?"

"No, we didn't."

"And you never found the gun—the murder weapon, is that accurate?"

"That's accurate."

"In your analysis, what did he do with the gun?" Spencer couldn't object to this line of questioning even though it was speculation. He had put Tony on the stand in part to explain how the murder occurred. He would be annihilated in each juror's mind if he now objected that his own witness was speculating on that exact issue.

"He probably tucked it in his pants or a pocket. It's not a particularly large weapon."

"Before the three individuals saw him from their windows?"

"Sure."

"And is it accurate that there is no other physical evidence linking the defendant to this crime—no DNA evidence, no fingerprints, no hair fibers—other than the fact that he was present on that street and was seen kneeling over the victim after he was shot?"

Tony Severino took a deep breath. He didn't want to answer the question. "Do you mean other than the fact that he was the only person in the area when Carl Robertson was murdered?"

Jack didn't waste time arguing with him. He went directly to the judge.

"Your honor, I asked a question that calls for a yes or no answer. Would you instruct the witness to answer the question?"

"Answer the question, Mr. Severino."

"No. There was no physical evidence other than the fact that the defendant was identified leaning over the body moments after Carl Robertson was shot."

"Thank you, Detective. In your analysis of the crime scene, did you assume that the murderer was close to the deceased at the time of the murder?"

"Yes."

"How close?"

"Within a few feet."

"How did you determine that?"

"The witnesses came to the window immediately and he was already kneeling over the deceased. He had to be very close. There was no time to come from somewhere else."

So far it was plausible to think that Benny could have shot Carl, taken his money, and stashed the gun before any of the three eyewitnesses reached their windows and looked out and saw him. Anything else would have been implausible in that short a time. Jack looked at the jury just to make sure they were still awake. They were listening intently; they wanted to see where this was going. Only Jack knew that he now had Tony Severino on that dead-end street.

"The bullet that you showed the jury and that counsel introduced into evidence as exhibit number 6, I believe, was taken from the deceased's skull—is that right?"

"That's right."

"Now, that bullet before it is fired is in a shell casing, right?"

"Right."

"And when it is fired from that Glock nine-millimeter the shell is ejected, right?"

"Yes."

"And it lands in the immediate area where the gun is fired?"

"Usually, yes."

"I'm not sure I understand that answer. It pops right out, doesn't it?"

"Yes, but it could roll away if the surface was uneven or something."

"Was the surface of Seventy-eighth Street and East End Avenue uneven?"

"Not that I noticed, no."

"You searched the immediate area for that shell casing, didn't you?"

"Yes."

"But you didn't find a shell casing, did you?"

"No."

"Did that lead you to any conclusions?"

"Yeah. He must have picked it up."

"Who's 'he'?"

"The defendant."

"Let me see if I understand this. A shot rings out. Three people hear it and go to their windows immediately and they see a man kneeling over the deceased. From their observations, he doesn't have a gun, he doesn't take anything off the deceased, and he's not searching on the ground for an empty shell casing. It is your theory that before all three of those people got to their windows and looked out, he had found the money, taken it and stashed it somewhere on his person, concealed his gun somewhere in his clothing, searched and found his empty shell casing, and also concealed it in his clothing. Is that accurate?"

"That's pretty much it."

"Pretty much it, or is that it? We want to be precise here, Detective. This is a murder trial."

Spencer Taylor finally caught wind of the fact that his witness was floundering.

"Objection, your honor. He's badgering the witness."

"Overruled. Answer the question, Detective."

The objection had given Tony Severino time to think. He tried to squirm out of the trap Jack had set for him.

"There is a possibility that he didn't look for the shell casing and we just couldn't find it."

It was too important a point for Jack to let go unchallenged.

"How many police officers did you have there that night?"

"I don't know exactly. A lot."

"A lot?"

"Yes."

"How many of them searched the area with you?"

"I don't know for sure. Several."

"Is several the same as a lot?"

"I don't know. I don't know. I'd say a lot of officers were looking for that shell."

"You testified just a few moments ago that it was your conclusion that the defendant searched for the shell, picked it up, and put it in his pocket, correct?"

"That's correct."

"Then you said there was a possibility that the defendant *didn't* look for the shell casing and you and your officers couldn't find it, right?"

"Yes."

"Are you changing your opinion here today in court, Detective Severino?"

The jurors were on the edge of their seats waiting for the answer. Even the judge was leaning over watching the witness intently.

"No. I'm not changing my opinion."

"And your opinion was that the defendant took the time to look for the casing, found it and put it in his pocket?"

"Yes."

"Because you and a lot of other police officers combed the area and no shell casing was there, right?"

"That's right."

"No further questions, your honor."

"Redirect, Mr. Taylor?"

"Yes, your honor."

Spencer Taylor knew his witness had been beaten up pretty badly. He didn't want to make things worse on redirect by going back over the same ground, but he did have one point to make.

"Detective Severino, what did both Mr. Cook and Mr. Frazier tell you the defendant did when he saw them?"

Both Cook and Frazier had already testified to these facts in court, so Jack couldn't object on the basis of hearsay.

"He fled."

"He fled from the scene of the crime?"

"Yes."

"No further questions."

It was lunchtime when Tony Severino slithered from the stand and the judge recessed the proceedings. Jack stayed in the courtroom to go through Dr. Wong's exhibits in detail. He knew the coroner was probably coming up next, and he wanted to be ready. Luis stayed with him.

"You were right, Jack," Luis said. "This is your courtroom. You owned that man today. I don't know why I ever doubted you."

"Don't get your hopes up too high, Luis. We still have a long way to go. Trials can turn on a dime—it's the nature of the beast."

Jack had subpoenaed all the prosecution's witnesses before the trial started as a precaution. It was a habit he'd gotten into a long time ago as a civil defense attorney. He'd sent along a letter telling them that if they called and left a number where they could be reached during the day, they wouldn't have to appear in court the first morning that testimony began and hang around potentially for days until they were called. Everyone always rang—the incentive was too great not to. The number Jack had given was Dorothy's, Henry's aunt.

Jack phoned Dorothy—who among other things was doing an excellent job as his temporary secretary—and asked her to get in touch with Nick Walsh and tell him to be at the courthouse at nine o'clock the next morning. If Spencer rested at the end of the day and Henry wasn't back with witnesses, he needed a warm body to put on the stand. Maybe Nick Walsh would give him something he didn't expect. Frankie O'Connor had told him that Nick was a legend in the police department. Joe Fogarty had said he was one of the best homicide detectives the department ever had. He was Tony Severino's partner. Yet Tony never mentioned his name during his entire testimony. *Why?*

Leland Pendergast had been the coroner of the City of New York for twenty years. He knew every politician in the state and walked and talked with an air about him that suggested power and influence. His favorite attire were expensive, custom-made suits that padded his shoulders and tapered his waist—efforts on his part to hide most of the fat on his beefy, six-foot frame. He couldn't hide his face, though, and those thick jowls.

Leland Pendergast strode confidently into the courtroom on the afternoon of the fourth day of Benny Avrile's murder trial and took the stand. Spencer led him through his extensive and very impressive qualifications before honing in on the substance of his testimony. Not surprisingly, Spencer spent very little time on how the murder had occurred and the cause of death. Their little tragic opera was all about photographs, twenty in all—extremely graphic pictures of the bloody corpse. Each image was six feet tall and three feet wide, and Leland Pendergast stood in front of each one with a pointer—like a teacher leading a classroom discussion—explaining its significance to the jury.

Jack objected to each photograph, initially on the grounds of prejudice and eventually on the grounds that the evidence was cumulative and prejudicial.

"Judge, how many photographs does the jury need to see to understand that Carl Robertson was shot in the forehead? The prosecution is just trying to inflame the jury," Jack argued at sidebar. But his objections were overruled.

The jurors were horrified. Some of the women were moved to tears. At the end of his testimony, Leland Pendergast finally gave the only opinion that mattered. The cause of Carl Robertson's death was a single bullet wound to the head. It took him two and a half hours to get there.

Sitting in the front row behind Jack and his son and watching the juror's reactions to the pictures, Luis understood what Jack meant about a trial turning on a dime. The pictures weren't the only bad turn. Benny, who had been silent and stoic throughout the trial as Jack had directed him, was visibly moved by the pictures. Try as he might, he couldn't help himself. Tears rolled down his cheeks. The jurors saw the tears and wondered if they were tears of guilt.

Jack saw the tears too. There was nothing he could do about them. He had to concentrate on taking a pound of flesh from Leland Pendergast. As he rose to begin the cross, something in his mind clicked about a piece of evidence whose significance he had not understood until that very moment.

Before taking his place at the podium he walked over to the easel facing the jury, removed the last of the grisly pictures, and placed it facing backward on the far wall with the other exhibits so it would not be a distraction during his cross-examination. Mr. Pendergast was going to have to get through cross on his words alone.

"Were you at the scene of the crime?"

"No."

"Was somebody from your office there?"

"Yes."

"Who was that?"

"Dan Jenkins."

"And is Dan Jenkins a licensed pathologist like yourself?"

"Yes."

"And has he testified in court before?"

"Yes."

"In murder trials?"

"Yes."

"Has he ever been disqualified for any reason?"

"Not that I am aware of."

"Who did the actual autopsy?"

"Dan Jenkins—with my supervision, of course."

"We'll get to that. The autopsy report that you've been talking about, state's exhibit number 10—did Dan Jenkins sign that?"

"Yes. And so did I."

"Is it your practice to sign every autopsy report?"

"Yes. I am responsible for every opinion that comes out of my office."

"And that signature of yours on this autopsy report, is that a stamp?"

"Yes, it is."

"Is the stamp for convenience so you don't actually have to sign all the autopsies that are done by your staff?"

"Yes."

"How many autopsies does your office do a year?"

"Thousands. This is New York City. We are very busy."

"So you don't read and approve every autopsy report before it comes out of your office, do you, Mr. Pendergast?" This was where Jack expected the big lie. He wasn't disappointed.

"I try to. I'm sure some slip by."

"You said Dan Jenkins did the autopsy with your supervision, correct?"

"Yes."

"How long has Mr. Jenkins been with your office?"

"Around ten years."

"Does he need supervision to do an autopsy?"

"Absolutely not. What I mean by that statement is that I supervise the work of all my people."

"You weren't present when Dan Jenkins did the autopsy of Carl Robertson, were you?"

"I may have walked in and out of the room a few times."

"Do you specifically recall if you did or not?"

"No, I don't."

"So you don't have any firsthand knowledge of the findings in this autopsy report that you have been testifying about all afternoon, is that correct?"

Leland didn't answer right away. Instead, he made one of the most amateur and devastating moves a witness who is trying to appear impartial can make. He looked over to Spencer Taylor for help. Spencer looked down at his notes.

"Is that correct?" Jack prompted.

"Yes, but as an expert witness I can testify about the findings of others, especially my staff."

Jack had taken enough wind out of Leland's sails. It was time to get down to specifics. He was debating whether he should even use Dr. Wong's exhibits at this point. There had to be a reason Dan Jenkins was not on that stand. Maybe he would save the exhibits for when he called Jenkins himself.

"In your opinion, Dr. Pendergast, was the assailant close to the deceased when he shot him?"

"Yes."

"How close?"

"Not point-blank but very close."

Jack wanted to ask him how he'd arrived at that conclusion but he refrained from doing so because Leland had given the exact answer he'd wanted. "I've reviewed this autopsy report and I noticed that there was—I'm not sure how you put it—a protrusion at the rear of the cranium, is that accurate?"

"Yes, it is."

"Is that where the bullet struck the back of the cranium?"

"Yes, that's correct."

"Now, did you or Mr. Jenkins measure the angle from the entry wound to this protrusion in the back of the cranium?"

"Yes, we did."

"And why would you do that?"

"To determine the trajectory of the bullet. It's not always totally accurate, because sometimes the trajectory is thrown off by other obstacles in the body."

"How about in this case? Do you think the trajectory was accurate?"

"Yes, I do."

"And what was the trajectory of the bullet?"

"It was almost a straight line from the forehead to the rear of the head. There was a slight upward angle."

"Are you aware of how tall the defendant is?"

"Yes, I am." Leland smiled when he gave the answer as if he suspected Jack would be surprised by his positive response. That told Jack that they knew where he was going and were ready for him. He kept going anyway.

"How tall is he?"

"Five feet eight."

"And Carl Robertson, how tall was he?"

"Six feet four."

"At close range, if a five-foot-eight man shot a six-foot-four man, wouldn't the trajectory be straight up with the bullet hitting the top of the cranium rather than the rear?"

Leland smiled again. He'd obviously been waiting for the question. "Not necessarily, and certainly not if the taller man was looking down at the shorter man. Say they were having a conversation like 'Give me your money' or something like that. Then the trajectory would be at a straight angle, just like we found."

That last opinion did in all of Dr. Wong's wonderful graphs and charts. Jack had considered Leland Pendergast's explanation as a possibility; he had just hoped that the state had been overconfident and not done its homework. Now he was out on a limb with no place to go, and Leland Pendergast was all puffed up and confident again.

Jack decided he had no choice but to try the new theory that had just come to him. "Doctor, is it accurate that a bullet loses its velocity the more distance it travels?"

"That's hard to say with any definiteness. Velocity depends on a lot of things—the type of gun and the type of ammunition being the two most important factors. I don't know as I sit here what the speed per foot was of the ammunition fired from the Glock that was used. That's not my area of expertise. However, the longer the distance, the more resistance the bullet encounters in the atmosphere, and eventually it starts to lose a little steam—so I would agree with your proposition in general, but I don't think you can gauge the loss of velocity with any accuracy. If the target is in the range of the gun as it obviously was in this case, the job gets done, no matter what the distance."

It was a confusing answer, and Leland probably meant it to be so. Jack ignored the explanation completely.

"Is that a yes, Doctor?"

"Yes, I'd agree with your proposition in general."

"Would a gun fired, say, at point-blank range or very close be more likely to pass through the skull?"

"Not really. The skull is very durable. That's where we get the term 'hardheaded.'" There was a laugh from a few members of the gallery. Some of the jurors smiled as well. The judge wisely let it go. "I don't believe that a Luger Parabellum, the bullet that was used, fired from a Glock nine-millimeter would penetrate the skull no matter what distance it was fired from. Just look at how beat up this bullet was."

Jack had what he wanted. It was time to bring Leland down a few pegs again before he let him go.

"When was the last time you actually performed an autopsy rather than simply supervising your staff?"

Leland didn't answer right away. "Maybe five years ago."

"How long has it been since you did autopsies on a regular basis as part of your job duties?"

"Ten years, I'd say."

"No further questions, your honor."

It was almost five o'clock when Leland Pendergast sashayed off the witness stand. The judge dismissed the jury and cleared the courtroom. He wanted to talk to the lawyers alone and get a sense of where they were and when they expected to be done with their cases.

"I may have one or two witnesses, I may not," Spencer told the judge. Jack took that statement to mean that Spencer would be resting his case first thing in the morning.

To his credit, Judge Middleton didn't buy off on Spencer's dodge. "Come on, Mr. Taylor, you know if you're going to rest tomorrow or not."

"I really don't, Judge. There's a possibility I might rest first thing in

THE LAW OF SECOND CHANCES 345

the morning. If I do call more witnesses, they'll be brief. I'm not going to go back over ground we've already covered."

"Good," the judge replied. "Because I'm not going to let you." Jack liked the judge's attitude. In spite of everything he had heard, up to now Langford Middleton had run this trial as well as anybody could have. Jack hoped he would continue in that vein.

"Mr. Tobin?"

"Yes, your honor?"

"Be prepared to start your case tomorrow."

"Yes, your honor. I also have a motion I would like to argue after the prosecution rests."

"I figured you would. Okay, gents, I'll see you in the morning."

Jack caught the court reporter on the way out and requested the transcript of his cross of Tony Severino. He then called Dorothy and gave her another witness to call—assistant coroner Dan Jenkins.

SIXTY-TWO

Henry and his new cohort, Valentine Busby, had driven to Tampa early Thursday morning and boarded a plane to Chicago, from where they would head to Madison, Wisconsin. It was a bumpy flight, and Henry had been so nervous he was sweating.

"This is nothing," Valentine told him. "When I was in the Army we used to fly overseas in those big transports. They never flew around storms back then. I thought I was going to die at least a dozen times, and I'm still here."

Valentine's pep talk didn't do much for Henry, who hadn't felt better until the plane touched down in Chicago. They rented a car and arrived in Madison three hours later, finding Milton Jeffries's house with little difficulty. Things seemed to be going well—until a woman in her mid-fifties answered the door and told them that Milton Jeffries didn't live there anymore.

"My husband and I bought the place last year. We're both professors at the university, and so was Milton. He retired just before he sold the house. He didn't tell us where he was going. To be honest, he was a little weird about it. If you go to the administration building on campus, they may have a forwarding address."

"Thank you, ma'am," Henry said graciously. "We'll do that."

Milton Jeffries hadn't left a forwarding address with the school, so Henry went to the biology department and started knocking on the doors of faculty members and asking if they had any idea where their former colleague could be. At the fourth door they met Harvey Nelson.

"I don't have any idea," Harvey told them after Henry explained who he and Valentine were and that it was quite literally a matter of life and death. Harvey was an affable fellow in his mid-forties, with curly brown hair that stopped just a few inches short of his shoulders. Henry could tell he was trying to be helpful. "To tell you the truth, Milton's retirement was a shock to everybody. He really loved his work. Then all of a sudden he was gone—no forwarding address, no nothing. They had to scramble to get somebody to take his classes."

"Is there anybody who might know where he went?"

"Unfortunately, no. He was pretty much of a loner. I was probably his closest friend in the department, but we weren't really that tight. We went fishing together a few times. Hey, wait a minute—fishing. Milton loved to fish. He had a cabin out in the middle of nowhere at a place called Castle Hill Lake. He invited me up a couple of times. He had to give me directions to the cabin or I never would have found it. I think I still have them in my computer, if only I can remember what I saved them under. It's a long shot, but he might be living there."

"That would be great if you could do that," Henry replied.

"No problem," he told them. "Come on in and sit down. It may take me a few minutes." Harvey went to his desk and started searching on his computer. "Let me see, maybe it's under *Milton* or *Milton's cabin*," he muttered to himself as he stared at the screen. "Nope. Let's try *cabin*. Nope. I need to get these files organized better," he said apologetically over his shoulder before turning back to the screen. "Let's go over to *fishing*. Nope. How about *directions*, Harvey?" Henry gave Valentine a sidelong look. "Aha! Here it is: *Directions to Milton's house.*" He opened the file and scanned the lines of type. "Yup, this is it," he said, turning to Henry and Valentine with a look of satisfaction on his face. "I'll just print it out for you. Let me see, where is that *print* command..."

A couple of minutes later the directions were printing out. "It takes about an hour and a half to get there," he told Henry as he handed him the paper. "If you left now, it would be dark by the time you got there. You don't want to be driving up to somebody's house after dark in that neck of the woods, especially if you're not expected. Besides, I can almost guarantee you'll get lost. I got lost in the daylight."

Henry knew all about the hazards of arriving unexpectedly. He stole another, sharper glance at Valentine.

Valentine just shrugged his shoulders. "People don't like being surprised," he muttered.

They thanked Harvey and left.

"What do you think?" Henry asked as they were walking back to the car. "If we went now and found him, would Milton Jeffries be as ornery as you?"

"My guess is yes," Valentine replied. "He's a man who was spooked by something, and he's probably still spooked. If you came up to my house in the dark you might be dead now. It's been a long day, it's freezing out, and in case you haven't noticed, we're not properly dressed for this weather. I think we should get a hotel room and get a good night's sleep and start out fresh in the morning."

"I guess you're right," Henry replied. "We'd probably get lost anyway."

Henry called Jack at six-thirty as planned and gave him a brief, almost cryptic summary of the day's events, remembering Jack's concern about revealing too much over the phone. He didn't mention any names or where they were or where they were going the next day— just that getting to New York by Friday was not going to happen.

"Sorry about that, Jack, but we've just had a little trouble with, um, directions."

"I understand, Henry. Just let me know when you have a better idea."

"Will do. How are things at your end?"

"Not bad. I was hoping to have you back here tomorrow, but I think I'll be okay for now," he said, thinking to himself that he'd definitely have to put at least one of the prosecution's witnesses on the stand.

Jack worked for another hour before calling Molly. It was a routine now. She didn't even bother to say hello.

"Are you ready?" she asked when she picked up the phone.

"I'll be there in ten minutes," Jack replied.

Molly looked radiant once again. Her cheeks were red from the cold, which made her even more desirable to Jack.

"How'd it go today?" she asked as usual.

"Pretty good," Jack replied. "We made some good points, and we haven't even started our defense yet."

Molly changed the subject. This was relaxation time. "So, where do you want to go on vacation?" she asked.

"Didn't you just come back from vacation?"

"Yeah, but I can always take a Friday and a Monday to fly to London or something like that. I'm management, after all."

"London would be nice. But how about Aruba or Jamaica or somewhere like that? I need to warm up these bones."

Molly laughed. "I'm flexible. Aruba would be fine. How about next weekend?"

"Sounds great. The trial will definitely be over by then. I'll need the break."

"So will I," Molly replied. "I've got to go out of town tomorrow until next Tuesday. We're having one of those business conventions."

"That's a vacation too, isn't it?" Jack chided.

"I wish. I'll be giving talks all weekend."

"I won't see you after tonight until next Tuesday?"

"I'm afraid so," she said, looking at him with doe eyes.

"I'll miss you." Jack really meant it. He was starting to count on their little rendezvous every night. Molly knew how to get him to relax.

"I'll miss you too, Jack."

Friday morning was another frigid day, with the thermometer hovering in the teens. Very few spectators were braving the elements outside, although the courtroom was as packed as it had been the two previous days.

Luis was in his usual spot. "How are you feeling, Jack?"

"Good. How about you?"

"Pretty good. The coroner didn't hurt us too bad, did he?"

"No, Luis. He may have helped us. It all remains to be seen."

Jack didn't want to give Luis false hope, but he was feeling pretty confident. Just then the guards brought Benny into the courtroom. He had the charcoal gray suit on with a blue striped tie and a white shirt.

"Benny, you look better every day," Jack told him.

Benny smiled. "It's all my dad's doing," he said, turning to look at his father. Luis beamed.

Across the aisle, Spencer was pacing as he waited for the judge's appearance. Jack noticed that he was excited and smiling. Something was up.

Promptly at nine, Langford Middleton walked into the courtroom. After giving his daily sermon to the spectators, he turned to the lawyers.

"Is there anything we need to take up before we bring the jury in?"

Spencer stood up. "Yes, your honor. May we approach?"

Langford looked puzzled. A sidebar when there was no jury in the room was a little unusual, but Jack was pretty sure he knew what was going on: the dandy had something he didn't want the spectators to hear yet.

"Come on," the judge said impatiently. "What is it?" he asked when they were standing in front of his dais.

"Your honor, the police department got an anonymous tip last night. We believe we've found the gun that killed Carl Robertson."

Jack had been expecting trouble, but even so, he was shocked. He was relieved that Spencer hadn't announced it in open court because Luis probably would have had a heart attack right on the spot. He couldn't think about Luis now; he had to concentrate on the problem at hand. How he responded could be crucial to the case.

After a slight pause to savor the bombshell he had dropped, Spencer continued. "The police have the gun in custody, your honor. They picked it up this morning. I've spoken to one of the department's ballistics experts—his name is Pete Ingram—and he says he can do all the necessary tests today to determine if this is in fact the murder weapon. He also says he could meet with Mr. Tobin late this afternoon to answer questions. I'll need a one-day delay to handle these matters, but I can be finished on Monday."

This was the fly in the ointment Langford Middleton had dreaded. So far he had handled everything. Now Spencer Taylor had to drop this in his lap. He looked at Jack.

"Well, Mr. Tobin?"

Jack cut right to the chase. "Judge, I'd like to make a motion for a mistrial. My client's due-process rights would be violated if these proceedings continue. This trial has been pending for a year. Now, all of a sudden, after four days of trial, a gun appears. In addition, your honor, I don't have the opportunity to get my own expert. We are at a total disadvantage."

Jack knew this was the moment to make a record for appeal. If Langford didn't grant his motion and give him time to get his own expert, Jack would have a better-than-average shot at overturning a conviction on appeal. At the moment, that was looking like Benny's best hope.

Langford Middleton didn't reply right away; he was trying to think of a way to keep the whole thing from falling apart. His stomach was grumbling.

After a long few moments he looked at Jack. "We don't have to make a decision today on your motion, Mr. Tobin. We'll let Officer Ingram do his tests, and you can meet with him and talk to him. Who knows? He may not be able to say this gun is the murder weapon. I'll tell you this, Mr. Tobin: the people of the state of New York have rights too. They have a right to see that justice is served, not delayed. If Mr. Ingram determines that this is the gun that killed Mr. Robertson, I'll want to hear this opinion outside of the presence of the jury before making my final decision on your motion. Now, is there anything else?"

"Yes, Judge," Spencer Taylor replied. "I am requesting that you enter an order releasing prosecution's exhibit number 6—that's the bullet, your honor—to Detective Severino so that he can deliver it to the state's ballistics expert."

"So ordered. Anything else?"

"No, Judge," they both answered.

The lawyers returned to their tables and the judge addressed the spectators. "Ladies and gentlemen, some new matters of evidence have come up, as they often do during trials of this nature. We are going to have to recess for the day. We will resume promptly on Monday morning. Please leave the courtroom now in an orderly manner."

He called the jury in next and gave them the same speech. The judge then left the courtroom.

Spencer walked over to Jack, who was huddled with Luis and Benny. "Call me at three o'clock this afternoon," Spencer said, cutting in. "We can probably set up a meeting with the firearms guy at that time." Jack nodded curtly, and Spencer turned and left.

Only Jack, Benny, Luis, and Benny's guards now remained in the courtroom. The guards gave them room to talk.

"What happened?" Luis asked.

Jack looked at Benny. "I don't want you to say anything during this conversation. Just listen." He turned back to Luis. "They think they found the murder weapon."

"They think?"

"They have to test it. That's the reason for the delay."

"This is bullshit. They've had this all along. They just waited to spring it on us."

"Hold on there, Luis. We don't even know if it's the gun."

"Do you think their expert, a police officer, is going to say it's not the gun, Jack? Come on."

"But he has to give reasons, and we can attack his reasons."

"It doesn't matter, Jack."

"What do you mean, it doesn't matter?"

"Look me in the eye and tell me that if they have the gun Benny has any chance of getting off."

"Luis, the gun doesn't really put them in a better position. They had the bullet. Now they have the bullet and the gun. Who shot the gun is the issue."

"I don't trust these people, Jack. There's more to this, you watch. The dandy has something else up his sleeve."

Jack felt it too. Spencer was holding something back. They would have to wait until Monday to find out what it was. "You may be right, Luis. We'll just have to deal with it as it comes—make our objections for the record and keep fighting."

Benny sat silently through the whole exchange, but his expression spoke volumes.

SIXTY-THREE

Henry and Valentine set out early Friday morning for Castle Hill Lake, stopping first at the local Wal-Mart to buy winter coats. It was freezing cold, and the roads were icy. Valentine turned out to be very good at directions and they found Milton Jeffries's cabin without too much trouble; it was right on the lake. Unfortunately, the door was locked and nobody was home.

While Henry tried the windows, Valentine walked around to the back porch that faced the lake and did some investigating of his own. Henry caught up with him out on the dock. The lake was frozen, and there were some fresh snowmobile tracks leading from the dock.

"It snowed here last night, so those tracks have to be fresh," Valentine told Henry. "Which means he left this morning. Who knows where the hell he went?"

"Damn!" Henry exclaimed. "We should have come last night."

"We never would have found this place last night, Henry, you know that. We'll just wait."

"That's a big lake out there, Valentine. He might be gone for days."

"Unless he's got a cabin out there on the ice or a honey on the other side of the lake, he'll be back today. He'd freeze out there overnight."

"We're going to freeze here," Henry replied.

"Let's just go find a place to eat and we'll come back from time to time and check on the place."

*　*　*

At four o'clock that afternoon Jack met at a downtown office with Pete Ingram, the firearms expert who had analyzed the newfound gun. Jack had anticipated that Spencer Taylor would be present during the conversation. He never expected to be able to question the prosecution's expert alone. Spencer had to be extremely confident.

Pete Ingram got right to it. "They told me to tell you everything, so here it is. The gun they found is a Glock 17 semiautomatic. All the serial numbers were filed off, so we couldn't tell where it was purchased or who purchased it. You probably know how we test a gun to see if it was used in a crime, but I'll tell you anyway." Jack smiled and nodded encouragement for him to continue. "It's very simple. We load the gun with a cartridge or bullet of the same make and type as the one found at the scene. We then fire the gun into a soft material, retrieve the slug, and compare it under a microscope with the slug found at the scene to see if the lands and grooves match. I assume you're familiar with those terms?"

Jack nodded again and said, "Yes, thanks. So what did you find?"

"I could show you the slides, but it's easier if I describe it. I can tell that the slug from the crime scene is from a Glock. Their grooves are unique, and there's enough there for me to determine that. But I can't compare the slugs. The one found at the crime scene is too distorted. Thus, I can't match that slug to the gun that was found."

Jack couldn't believe his ears. The system actually did work. He started to smile but caught himself. Now was not the time to relax. Spencer Taylor might have other surprises up his sleeve.

Henry called Jack that night.

"How's it going?" Henry asked.

"Not well. They supposedly found the murder weapon yesterday."

"You're kidding me! A year later, in the middle of trial, they find the gun? That's a little convenient, isn't it?"

"It sure is, but I think we can deal with it. Have you got anything?"

"Are you sure we should do this over the phone?"

"Stick to the ground rules we talked about and we'll take the chance. I really need some good news."

"Well, the good news is we found our man. The bad news is, he won't talk to us. We waited for him to come home all day, and when he finally arrived, he wouldn't talk to us. This guy is really spooked. He knows something, and I'm not sure what it is. I think we're dealing with something that's way over our heads, Jack."

"We can't think about that, Henry. Listen, you've got until Tuesday. Stay there and keep trying to get him to talk. If you find out anything, get here as fast as you can. At that point, don't call me or tell me when you're coming or what you've got—the risk would be too great that they'd try to stop you. And keep an eye on that Busby guy. He may be our only hope if nothing else comes up. See you Tuesday morning."

"I'll be there."

Jack called Charlie right away. "Got anything yet?"

"Nothing."

"Well, we've got an extra day. Don't call me before you come. I don't want to know when you're coming or where you're staying. We can't trust the phones anymore. I'll see you in the courtroom on Tuesday morning at the latest, and you can give me anything you've got then. It's the criminal courts building, 100 Centre Street, eleventh floor. And have Dick and Joaquin escort you—I don't care what the cost is. All right?"

"We'll be there."

SIXTY-FOUR

It had warmed up a little, and by Monday morning the temperature was into the low thirties. But that wasn't the reason the sidewalks were jammed again. Spencer had leaked the discovery of the gun to the press over the weekend, and it had made front-page news in all the papers.

Jack could tell from his first sight of Spencer Taylor in the courtroom that the prosecutor still had a few surprises in store for him.

"Mr. Taylor, as I stated on Friday, you can call your next witness outside of the presence of the jury," Judge Middleton told Spencer after he had entered the courtroom and the proceedings had begun for the day.

"Before I call that witness, your honor, I would like to call the police officer who found the gun so we can establish a time line."

"All right," the judge said and spoke directly to the bailiff. "Bring the jury in."

After the jurors were seated, Spencer rose from his place at the prosecution's table and announced his next witness.

"The state calls Detective Joseph Fogarty, your honor."

As the bailiff brought him in, Joe Fogarty avoided looking at Jack. Only when he took his seat in the witness chair did they make eye contact.

Spencer had Joe give his name, rank, precinct, and all the other preliminaries as quickly as possible. He was clearly anxious to get to the meat.

"Officer Fogarty, tell the jury what you did at approximately eight o'clock on Friday morning."

"Well, I got a call at home about seven that morning from downtown. They told me they had received an anonymous call the night before. The person said he knew where the gun used in the Carl Robertson murder was located. He said the gun was in an abandoned building where Benny Avrile lived in the South Bronx, behind a loose brick in the wall. So they called me."

"Is that all the person said?"

"As far as I know." It was all hearsay, but Jack wasn't going to object and give Spencer the opportunity to parade about five more cops into the courtroom.

"Why did downtown call you?"

"I've known Benny for about five years, maybe longer. We used him for information."

"He was a snitch?" Spencer spat the words out.

"Yeah."

"Did you know where he lived?"

"Yeah, I knew the building and that he was on the fifth floor."

"So what did you do?"

"I immediately went up there and searched for the loose brick. It took me about fifteen minutes. I pulled the brick out and there was the gun."

Jack was furious. He had felt in his bones that Spencer Taylor was holding something back. Now he knew what it was. Spencer spent the rest of his time establishing the chain of custody from the time Joe Fogarty picked the gun up until it appeared in court that morning. He offered the gun into evidence.

Jack was on his feet. "May we approach, your honor?"

"Come on," the judge replied.

Jack was still so angry when he reached the judge's dais that he could hardly speak.

"Judge, there is no evidence that this was the gun that was used in the murder," Jack said. "Therefore, it should not be admissible."

The judge didn't even ask Spencer Taylor to comment.

"I agree with Mr. Tobin. At this point, there is no concrete evidence to establish that this gun is the murder weapon. You can try and do that with your next witness, Mr. Taylor."

It was a small victory, but as he walked back to counsel table, Jack realized he had made a major mistake not objecting to Joe Fogarty's testimony before the man said a word. He should have demanded that Fogarty also testify outside the jury's presence. Now, even if he got the gun excluded as evidence, the jury had heard that a Glock 17 had been found where Benny lived. There was an old saying in the law: "You can't unring a bell." The jury could be instructed not to consider the evidence, but they had already heard it. Spencer Taylor had snookered him.

"Cross-examination, Mr. Tobin?" the judge asked when the lawyers had returned to their seats.

"Yes, your honor." Before he stood, Jack glanced at Benny, who was staring straight ahead, expressionless. Then he turned to Luis, who was looking at the floor, shaking his head back and forth. Luis had predicted these last-minute tricks, and Jack had told him not to worry. Now Joe Fogarty had linked the gun and the bullet to Benny. Jack walked to the podium and faced Joe Fogarty.

Jack recalled the promise he had made to Joe as they sat on the stoop around the corner from the Carlow East. But that was before either one of them knew that Joe was going to be one of the star witnesses for the prosecution. So what was it going to be? Honor his promise to a man he didn't know, or defend his client with every weapon he had? At that moment he also remembered that Frankie O'Connor had trusted him not to betray Joe.

Joe Fogarty was sitting on the witness stand rubbing his hands together nervously. Jack saw the look of fear in his eyes.

"Detective Fogarty, you said you knew the defendant, Benny Avrile, for five years or more, is that accurate?"

"Yes."

"And he lived in a condemned building?"

"Yeah, that's accurate."

"And when you got information from him, did you pay him?"

"Sometimes."

"Getting information like this is a part of law enforcement, isn't it?"

"Yes."

"An essential part?"

"I'd say, yes."

"So Mr. Avrile was assisting law enforcement in a way?"

"Yes."

"If you knew where Mr. Avrile lived, were there other people in the neighborhood who also knew?"

"I'm sure there were. It wasn't a secret."

"Did the place where the defendant lived have a door that you could lock?"

"No."

"Anybody could get in there?"

"Sure."

"Had you been up there before?"

"Yes. After Benny was arrested, I took a team of forensic people up there and we searched the place entirely. I didn't know about the hiding spot behind the brick, though."

"A few moments ago Mr. Taylor took you through the chain of custody from the time you picked this gun up until you brought it into this courtroom. Chain of custody is a procedure you follow in every case, isn't it?"

"Yes."

"And that is to ensure that evidence is not tampered with, stolen, or replaced, isn't it?"

"Yes."

"So you can walk into this courtroom and account to the jury for every moment that a piece of evidence has been in your custody, correct?"

"Correct."

"And when a piece of evidence is collected, it is marked and entered into a logbook and placed in the property room or evidence room at the police department, correct?"

"Yes."

"And the evidence room is guarded at all times?"

"Yes."

"But this gun was in an open and unguarded room in a condemned building, correct?"

"Yes."

"And there was no chain of custody *before* you retrieved it last Friday morning, correct?"

"That's true."

"Can you tell the jury as you sit here today whether it was there for a year or a day before you retrieved it?"

Spencer Taylor wanted to object, to throw Jack off his rhythm, but he couldn't—he had no grounds.

"No, I can't say how long it had been there," Joe Fogarty replied.

"Now, the anonymous person who called the police on Thursday evening and told you where the gun was located obviously knew about the hiding place behind the brick, correct?"

"Yes."

"Was the gun tested for fingerprints, do you know?"

"Yes, it was. Nothing came up."

"Did the gun have any serial numbers so you could trace who purchased it?"

"No. The serial numbers had been filed off."

"In the five years that you knew Mr. Avrile, did you ever see him with a gun?"

"No."

"Do you know whether he owned a gun?"

"No."

"Was he ever involved in any type of violence to your knowledge?"

"No."

"You were the officer who arrested Mr. Avrile, correct?"

"That's correct."

"Did he resist in any way?"

"No."

"Did he have a gun on him at the time?"

"No."

This was the spot. Jack had the questions on the tip of his tongue. *Did you tell Benny to clam up the day you arrested him? Did you tell him to clam up because you thought he was being railroaded because some big shot had been killed and the brass downtown needed a sacrificial lamb? Did you meet with me? Did you tell me the same thing?* Joe was shifting again nervously in the witness chair.

"No further questions, your honor."

Joe looked at Jack and held his gaze for a moment. His hands went still and his shoulders visibly relaxed. Jack merely turned and walked back to his table.

"Redirect, Mr. Taylor?"

Spencer thought about it for a moment. He had what he needed, and Jack hadn't made any dents in that. "No, your honor."

When Joe Fogarty had exited the courtroom, Judge Middleton explained to the jurors that they once again had to be excused while he took up some legal matters with the lawyers. Jack noticed that some of them looked disgruntled. After they had filed out, the judge addressed the prosecutor.

"Call your weapons expert, Mr. Taylor."

"The State calls Officer Peter Ingram."

Pete Ingram was almost as forthright and honest in his direct testimony before the judge as he had been with Jack in his office, except for one important opinion that he had failed to mention at the meeting on Friday afternoon. Spencer Taylor did the prompting.

"Mr. Ingram, do you have an opinion as to whether this gun found at the defendant's living quarters was the gun used to kill Carl Robertson?"

"Yes."

"And what is that opinion?"

Jack objected but was overruled.

"I cannot say for certain that this was the gun from looking at the slug alone, as I have already testified. However, considering the fact that the defendant was at the scene at the time of the murder; that the slug was fired from a Glock semiautomatic; and that a Glock 17

semiautomatic was found at the defendant's premises—it would be
my opinion that this gun was probably the gun that was used to kill
Carl Robertson."

Jack had only a few questions for Pete Ingram.

"Officer Ingram, you cannot through any type of scientific examination link the gun that was found last Thursday to the slug that was
taken from Carl Robertson's skull, correct?"

"That's correct. The slug is too deformed."

"And you would agree that there was no chain of custody for that
gun from the time of the murder until this anonymous tip was received by the police department on Thursday night?"

"That's correct."

"So you cannot say with any degree of certainty when this gun was
placed behind the brick wall at the defendant's residence, can you?"

"No."

"So somebody could have heard from the testimony in this very
courtroom that a Glock 17 was used as the murder weapon and
planted the gun as late as last Thursday in the defendant's residence
and then called the police anonymously, couldn't they?"

"That's possible," Pete Ingram replied. "But I don't know of any
evidence that suggests that scenario happened."

"Thank you, Officer Ingram. No further questions."

Spencer Taylor had no redirect. It was now up to the judge whether
Pete Ingram was going to testify before the jury or not and whether
the gun was going to be admitted into evidence.

"Mr. Tobin, would you state your objection for the record?"

"Yes, Judge. I would reiterate my objection that this witness was a
complete surprise, and I would add that this type of testimony is the
most dangerous form of speculation there can be. An anonymous call
out of thin air more than a year after the murder, no chain of custody,
and now, opinions based on that house of cards. We're talking about a
man's life, Judge. This testimony is too prejudicial and speculative to
be admissible. And for the record, I renew my motion for mistrial. If
this evidence is inadmissible, Officer Fogarty should never have been
allowed to testify."

Judge Middleton didn't even ask for a reply from Spencer. He gave his ruling as soon as Jack was finished.

"Based on the facts that Mr. Avrile was present at the crime according to eyewitnesses, that the slug found in the deceased's body was from a Glock semiautomatic, and that a Glock 17 semiautomatic was found at the abandoned building where Mr. Avrile resided, I am going to rule that Officer Ingram can testify about his opinions to the jury and that the gun, the Glock 17, is admissible evidence. Mr. Tobin, you can make your arguments to the jury at closing as to the weight they should give to this evidence. Bring in the jury."

Jack had wanted Langford Middleton to be strong and definite in his rulings, and he was doing exactly that.

While the bailiff went to get the jury, Spencer Taylor had a few choice words for Jack. "You told me you were looking forward to seeing what else I had in my arsenal. Now you know."

Jack didn't respond. He was afraid there might be another murder if he did.

After Pete Ingram's testimony before the jury, the state rested its case and they recessed for lunch. Jack expected some retribution from Luis at the lunch break—a little "I told you so." He got none of it. Luis spoke to him as the guards were taking Benny out and the courtroom was emptying.

"You are amazing, Jack, how you hang in there. No matter what they throw at you, you keep your cool and get what you can from the witness. No matter how this turns out, my son has had the best lawyer there is." He then left the courtroom with the few remaining stragglers from the crowd.

When the afternoon session began, the judge addressed Jack.

"Mr. Tobin, are there any matters we need to take up before you start your defense?"

"Yes, your honor, I have some motions to argue at this time outside the presence of the jury."

"You may proceed, Mr. Tobin."

Jack stood up. His argument was going to be short and sweet and direct.

"Your honor, my motion is directed to all counts of the indictment. The state has simply not met its burden. In particular, I want to address the felony murder count."

Jack was signaling the judge. He had to make his record for appeal, but at the same time he wanted to let the court know that there was a real basis to dismiss the felony murder count.

"Your honor," Jack continued, "I am handing you and counsel for the state excerpts from the testimony of Angela Vincent, Paul Frazier, David Cook, and Detective Tony Severino. I have highlighted the appropriate questions and answers. As you can see from Detective Severino's testimony, the assumption was that the defendant stole ten thousand dollars from the deceased. However, both eyewitnesses said that they didn't see the defendant take anything, and Angela Vincent said that she didn't know whether Mr. Robertson had the ten thousand on his person that night. In short, your honor, there is no evidence of a robbery. Therefore, the court should grant the motion for acquittal on that count."

The judge didn't have any questions. He looked to Spencer Taylor for a reply. Spencer had connected the gun to Benny, and he had Benny kneeling over the victim at the time of the murder. The jury had all the evidence they needed to convict on the charge of first-degree murder, which had been his goal—and that of his bosses— all along. He made a halfhearted counter to Jack's argument on the felony murder charge.

Langford Middleton didn't know why Jack was even wasting the court's time with this motion. His client was about to be convicted of first-degree murder. He had a point, though, and he had the evidence, and the state didn't seem to care.

"The court is going to grant your motion as to the felony murder count, Mr. Tobin. I find that there is insufficient evidence that the deceased was killed during the commission of a robbery. I deny your motion as to all other counts of the indictment. Are you ready to call your first witness?"

"Your honor, with all the delays we have had in this case, it has been difficult to schedule my witnesses, especially since most of them are coming from out of town. I would like to begin promptly at nine o'clock tomorrow morning."

"Very well, Mr. Tobin. This court is dismissed until nine a.m. tomorrow."

Jack followed his usual procedure and went to Mike McDermott's office for a couple of hours to prepare for the next day's testimony. He didn't know who was going to show up or what they were going to say. He prepared open-ended questions, hoping for the best. At seven-thirty, he hopped in a cab and headed uptown. His original plan was to go straight to Aunt Dorothy's apartment and get to bed, but he decided to stop at P. J. Clarke's for a beer or two. He needed to unwind.

The first beer didn't do the trick, nor did the second. He had succeeded in getting the felony murder count dismissed, but Benny was on the verge of going away *at least* for the rest of his life. That reality weighed heavily on Jack's shoulders.

SIXTY-FIVE

The Tuesday-morning newspapers universally praised Jack for his tough, thorough cross-examination of the state's witnesses the previous day. However, the consensus of every reporter was that Benny was going down. It was cold, rainy, and windy when Jack stepped into the back seat of the old Mercedes to have George drive him to the courthouse downtown. His head was buried in his files during the entire trip. Luckily, he didn't have time to read the newspapers.

The courtroom was packed and buzzing. Luis was keeping a stiff upper lip. He patted Jack on the back when he arrived at counsel table and sat down. The guards brought Benny out a few minutes later. Benny's face was drawn, as if he hadn't slept. The reality of what had occurred in the courtroom the day before was written all over his face. He looked like a condemned man.

A few minutes before nine, Jack looked to the rear of the courtroom and saw Dick Radek and Joaquin Sanchez standing against the back wall. The guards wouldn't have let anybody else do that: they were showing deference to the badge. Jack nodded at both men. He was visibly relieved to see his old friends, people he could trust—and had trusted—with his life. Just then, Henry walked in. Jack motioned for him to come to the bar.

"You can sit at counsel table with me if you want," he told him.

Henry was dressed in blue jeans, a flannel shirt, and a leather jacket. He didn't feel like sitting on the other side of the bar with the lawyers and the court personnel. Hell, even Benny had a suit on. "I'll stand in the back with your cop buddies, if you don't mind," he told Jack.

"That's fine. How many witnesses do you have for me?"

"Two," he said, handing Jack a folder. "Charlie is ready to testify as well."

"Great! Great job, Henry," he said, opening the folder.

The judge walked into the courtroom just as they were finishing their conversation. Jack returned to his place and quickly started flipping through the few pages of notes and other documents in the folder; Henry moved to the back of the room and stood with Dick and Joaquin. Nobody told him to sit down.

When all the spectators and reporters had risen and were seated again, the judge addressed Jack.

"Call your first witness, Mr. Tobin."

"The defense calls Mr. Valentine Busby."

The bailiff left the room and returned seconds later with Valentine Busby. The old man looked fairly presentable in a pair of black slacks and a short-sleeved white shirt that he and Henry had bought in Wisconsin. Valentine raised his right hand, took the oath, sat in the witness stand, and stated his name for the record.

"Where do you live, Mr. Busby?" Jack began, still sneaking a glance at the notes.

"I live at 26 Robin Lane, Micanopy, Florida."

"Do you live alone?"

"Yes, I live by myself."

"And what do you do in Micanopy?"

"I'm a farmer."

"Did you always live at that address alone?"

"No. I used to live with a man named Leonard Woods. I actually worked for Mr. Woods. I lived in an apartment attached to the main house. Mr. Woods left me the house when he died."

"Was Mr. Woods a farmer too?"

"No. He was a professor of microbiology at the University of Florida in Gainesville, which is about twenty miles up the road from Micanopy."

"Do you know if Mr. Woods knew a man named Carl Robertson?"

"Yes. Leonard had known Carl for about five years. They were working on something together."

"Did you know Carl Robertson?"

"I met him once. He came to the house to see Leonard about a year and a half ago."

"Do you know what they were working on?"

"I haven't a clue. There's a man in Wisconsin who knows. He was also a microbiology professor and a friend of Leonard's. His name is Milton Jeffries."

"Now, you were approached about this case by my investigator, a man named Henry Wilson, is that correct?"

"Yes."

"Was he the first person who contacted you about this case?"

"No. A man named Sal Paglia called about six months ago. I told him that Leonard knew Carl and that they were working together on something, pretty much exactly what I told Henry—Henry Wilson, your investigator. And, of course, I told him that Leonard was dead."

"How did Leonard die?"

That was enough for Spencer Taylor. "Objection, your honor. This entire line of questioning is totally irrelevant."

The judge looked at Jack, who responded, "Judge, the next two witnesses will establish the relevancy, I assure you."

Jack could tell he had piqued Langford Middleton's curiosity. "I'll allow it," the judge announced. "Make it quick, Mr. Tobin."

"I will, your honor." Jack turned his attention back to Valentine. "How did Leonard die?"

"He was struck by a hit-and-run driver."

"Was the driver ever caught?"

"No."

"Tell the jury the circumstances of the hit-and-run."

Spencer Taylor was on his feet again. "Your honor, this is totally irrelevant."

"I assume that is an objection, Mr. Taylor? Overruled. Mr. Tobin, my patience is running thin."

"Yes, your honor, I'm almost done."

He didn't have to ask the question again. "He was hit on Robin Lane at seven in the morning," Valentine answered. "Robin Lane is a little dirt road that is very bumpy. Most cars can only go ten miles an hour on it."

"And when did this take place?"

"As I said, seven o'clock in the morning. It was on September 2, 1998."

Someone in the gallery let out a loud gasp, and there was a general murmuring. Obviously those who were following the case closely had picked up on the fact that Leonard Woods was killed the morning after Carl Robertson was murdered.

Judge Middleton banged his gavel for the first time in the entire trial. "Silence!" he bellowed. "If you want to talk, leave the courtroom. If you talk here again, you will be removed." The murmuring stopped.

"No further questions, your honor."

"Cross-examination, Mr. Taylor?"

Spencer Taylor looked like he wanted to beat Valentine Busby over the head, but Busby was a dangerous witness, and there was nothing to gain by cross-examination. So far, he had just raised a coincidence. The defense still had a long way to go to connect the dots. "No questions, your honor."

"Call your next witness, Mr. Tobin."

"The defense calls Ms. Charlene Pope."

Charlie was looking her professional best in a blue business suit, and she gave Jack a warm and encouraging smile as she sat in the witness chair. Jack first took her through her qualifications, then started in on the significant portion of his direct examination.

"Ms. Pope, were you hired by me to do anything in this case?"

"Yes, I was."

"And what were you asked to do?"

"You asked me to review the last five years of financial records of Mr. Carl Robertson to see if there was anything in those records that might shed some light on why he was killed. You also asked me to review the telephone records of Mr. Robertson for the same reason."

"Did you review the telephone records?"

"Yes."

"Was there anything in those telephone records that appeared to you to be unusual?"

Spencer Taylor was on his feet again. "Objection. The question is vague."

"Sustained."

Jack tried again. "Had Mr. Robertson been in contact with anybody in particular before his death?"

Charlie answered right away before Taylor could object again. "Yes. In the month before his death he called Leonard Woods thirty-eight times. He called him twenty times the month before that." The murmuring started up again, but it stopped immediately when the judge raised his gavel.

"Proceed, Mr. Tobin."

Now it was time for Jack to venture into the unknown and ask Charlie questions he didn't know the answers to.

"Were you able to determine from the financial records if Mr. Robertson was working on anything in particular before his death?"

"Yes." Charlie turned and looked at the jury like a seasoned expert would. "You have to understand something. Mr. Robertson was a very rich man, a multibillionaire, a conglomerate unto himself. About five years ago, Mr. Robertson started buying up gas stations across the country. He owned at least five in every major city in the United States and at least one in every city with a population of more than a hundred thousand people."

Spencer Taylor interrupted as Charlie was about to continue. "Your honor, what Mr. Robertson did with his money before he died is totally irrelevant to why we are here today."

Jack couldn't believe Spencer had made such a statement in open court. Besides being contrary to the judge's specific instructions, it was the type of statement that could come back and bite him later on.

"Mr. Taylor, I warned you and Mr. Tobin about speaking motions. Approach the bench."

When they got to the sidebar, the judge addressed Jack, not Spencer

Taylor. "Where is this going, Mr. Tobin? It's starting to sound like a wild goose chase."

"It's not, your honor. Milton Jeffries is here, and he will tell the court what Carl Robertson and Leonard Woods were working on when they were killed. I have a witness after that who will relate it all to the murder before this court."

While the judge was thinking, Jack was hoping like hell he wouldn't be asked what Milton Jeffries was going to say, because he had no idea.

"All right, Mr. Tobin. I'm going to give you some leeway because your client is on trial for murder, but if you don't connect the dots I'm going to strike all these witnesses' testimony. And if Mr. Taylor wants it, I'll give him a mistrial. Do you understand?"

"Yes, your honor."

"Proceed."

Jack walked back to the podium. "You were talking about the gas stations, Ms. Pope."

"Yes. In addition to the gas stations, Mr. Robertson was buying trucks—tanker trucks for gasoline as well as eighteen-wheel hauling trucks. He had a very large fleet at the time of his death. He also had constructed and tooled four large manufacturing plants—in the Northeast, Northwest, Southeast, and Southwest—and he was in the process of hiring people to work in those plants."

Jack was doing everything he could to dampen down his own raging curiosity. He knew from his cursory look at Henry's folder that Milton Jeffries was the payoff to everything Charlie was setting up. At the moment, though, he didn't even know if Charlie was done. He looked at her intently and caught an almost imperceptible signal in her expression.

"Thank you, Ms. Pope. No further questions."

"Cross-examination, Mr. Taylor?"

"Yes, your honor." Spencer walked to the podium and glared at Charlie.

"You put a lot of time in on this, Ms. Pope?"

"Yes I did."

"And how much were you paid for your services?"

"I wasn't. I did it for free."

"Free? And why is it that you devoted your time for free?"

"Because Jack Tobin is a friend of mine."

"Oh! And did Mr. Tobin tell you that he needed you to find something in those records that he could use to get the defendant off?"

"Yes. If something was there."

"If something was there? Let me ask you, then—do you know what Mr. Robertson was doing with all these gas stations and trucks and factories?"

"No, I don't."

"You don't. You don't even know what this so-called evidence you found for your friend means, is that what you're telling this jury?"

"Yes."

"No further questions."

"Redirect, Mr. Tobin?"

"No, your honor."

"Call your next witness."

"The defense calls Mr. Milton Jeffries."

Milton Jeffries was a tall man with a thick moustache and glasses. He wore a brown tweed jacket, and he looked like the stereotypical professor. Jack took as little time as possible over the preliminaries; he could tell the judge was losing his patience.

"Mr. Jeffries, did you know Leonard Woods?"

"Yes, I knew Leonard for many years. He was a colleague. We both taught microbiology—I at the University of Wisconsin, he at Florida. It's really a small community. We'd meet at seminars a few times a year, exchange information, that sort of thing."

"There has been some testimony about a project he was working on before his death. Do you know anything about that?"

"Yes, I do. I helped him a little bit on it."

"Do you know who Carl Robertson is?"

"Yes. He was Leonard's partner in the project."

"Can you tell the jury what that project was?"

"It's a little complicated, but I'll try. Leonard had created a bacteria—cloned it, actually. This bacteria could break down biomass in a unique way—a way that had never been done before. Let me explain what biomass is. It's basically the garbage of the environment—farm waste such as corn stems, cobs and leaves, sugarcane residues, rice hulls, wood wastes, and other organic materials."

Jack could see Milton starting to drift off into that scientific no-man's land. He needed to bring him back.

"What was the purpose of this bacteria breaking down this biomass?"

"That's the exciting part. The bacteria can break down these waste products into ethanol."

Jack didn't understand, and he knew the jury didn't either. He had to ask the question even though he was fumbling in the dark.

"So?" he asked.

"So, before this breakthrough, ethanol could only be made from high-value materials such as cornstarch and cane syrup, using yeast fermentation. In other words, the ethanol was more expensive than regular oil and the supply—corn and sugar—was limited. Leonard's process created a virtually unlimited source for ethanol, and he wasn't depleting the food supply. He and Carl calculated they could sell it for about $1.40 a gallon. They figured they could replace half the automotive fuel in the United States with this new fuel."

Jack's brain was firing with connections. It all made sense now: *Gainesville* and *breakthrough*, the relationship with a microbiology professor—and the high stakes that had somehow led to more than one murder. Henry was right. They *were* dealing with something way over their heads.

Milton Jeffries wasn't through. "Leonard perfected his process just before he was killed. He was about to apply for a patent. Carl was going to start production—get the trucks rolling, so to speak—the day of the application. Carl had the factories in place and had acquired the gas stations so they could be on the market literally before anybody knew they existed."

"They could be in business overnight?"

"Exactly! And that's the only way they figured they could be in business at all. There are some powerful interests in this country that they expected would try to stand in the way."

"And that's when both of them were killed."

Spencer Taylor finally woke up. "Objection. Speculation."

"Sustained."

Jack didn't need an answer. It wasn't a question—it was a statement.

"No further questions, your honor."

"Cross, Mr. Taylor?"

Spencer Taylor seemed almost reluctant to get to his feet. He sat in his chair with his head down without responding to the judge.

"Mr. Taylor?"

Spencer raised his head at the second inquiry. "Yes, your honor." He stood, walked to the podium, and snarled at the witness. "Mr. Jeffries, you knew both men were dead a year and a half ago, correct?"

"Yes."

"Have you said anything to anybody about this during that year?"

"No."

"You didn't say anything until Mr. Tobin found you in Wisconsin and enticed you to fly back here to tell this wild story to the jury, is that correct?"

"It's correct that I didn't tell this story until now. It's not a story, though. It's fact. And I have the research to prove it."

Spencer ignored Milton Jeffries's last sentence. "I have no further questions of this witness, your honor," he said in as dismissive a manner as he could muster.

They broke for lunch after that. Under any other circumstances Jack would have wanted nothing more than to have lunch with Dick, Joaquin, Henry, and Charlie. He still had work to do, however, and lunch was a luxury he could not afford. Milton and Charlie's testimony had presented the jury with an alternative theory about why Carl was murdered. But Spencer still had Benny at the scene and Benny with the gun. Jack could see him belittling the defense's "conspiracy theory" during his closing: *The defense has given you nothing but wild and unsubstantiated theories. You also have the facts before you, ladies and gentlemen, facts you can get your arms around.* Jack knew he needed to deal a blow to Spencer's facts. That was what he was hoping his final witness would accomplish, but it was a very, very risky move that could easily backfire.

When he was trying civil cases as an insurance defense attorney, he had a mantra that he followed religiously: *Pigs get fat. Hogs get slaughtered.* It meant that you didn't try to go too far if you already had enough evidence to make your case. You never called a witness who could kill you—unless you were desperate.

Those were the rules for civil cases where, if you made the wrong decision, your client paid a lot of money. Here, the wrong decision could very well cost Benny his life.

Jack didn't make his final decision until the jurors were seated and the court was ready to proceed.

"Call your next witness," the judge told Jack.

"The defense calls Detective Nick Walsh."

Nick followed the bailiff into the courtroom wearing a plain and rather undistinguished brown suit. He swore to tell the truth and took the witness stand, appearing to be as comfortable as if he were sitting in his own living room. Jack noticed and wondered if Nick was so relaxed because he knew he was going to blow the defendant out of the water.

"Detective Walsh, you were the lead homicide detective investigating the Carl Robertson murder, correct?"

"Yes."

"And you made the decision to arrest the defendant for that murder, correct?"

"Yes."

"And what is the standard to make an arrest?"

"Probable cause."

"And that is a different standard from 'beyond a reasonable doubt'?"

"Yes, it's a much lower standard. We arrest when we feel there is a reasonable basis to do so."

"Do you stop investigating when you arrest someone?"

"No. At least, not usually."

"Now, I want you to recall your first interview with Angela Vincent, Carl Robertson's mistress. Do you remember that?"

"Yes."

"Ms. Vincent told you that Mr. Robertson got a phone call two weeks before his murder, is that accurate?"

"Yes."

"Was there anything significant about that phone call to you?"

"Well, Ms. Vincent said that Mr. Robertson was excited about the call and he wrote down two words on a notepad, *Gainesville* and *breakthrough*."

"Did you know at the time what those words meant?"

"I didn't have a clue."

"Did you think they were important?"

"Everything in an investigation is important."

"Did you ever find out what those words referred to?"

"No."

"In your second interview with Ms. Vincent, she told you about a woman named Lois Barton whom she'd met not long before Carl Robertson was murdered, correct?"

"Yes."

"And is it correct that she was having an intimate relationship with this woman?"

"Yes."

"What did she tell this woman about Mr. Robertson, if anything?"

"She basically told her everything—the days that he came to visit, the ten thousand dollars he brought her every month. She even told her when he brought it."

This was the tricky part. This was where Walsh could go off on the supposition about Benny and the mysterious Lois Barton being partners. Jack had already gotten rid of the felony murder count, but any hint of a partnership and Benny was almost certainly sunk in the eyes of the jury.

"Was this Lois Barton a suspect?"

"Yes."

"Did you ever find her?"

"No." The crowd started murmuring. Judge Middleton rapped his gavel on the dais and, like trained dogs, they stopped.

"I assume, then, that your investigation continued after the defendant was arrested, is that correct?"

"No, that's not correct."

"No? Is there a reason why you stopped looking for this woman?" Jack was in that proverbial no-man's land again. He had no idea what Walsh was going to say.

"I was told not to."

Jack felt that statement was worth repeating. "You were told not to?"

"Yes."

"By whom?"

"By my superior, Assistant Chief Ralph Hitchens."

"What were the circumstances that caused Assistant Chief Ralph Hitchens to tell you to stop your investigation?"

"He just called me in his office." Nick Walsh looked right at Spencer Taylor. Jack thought he saw a smile cross the detective's face for a split second. "Mr. Taylor was there," Walsh continued. "They told me I was off the case and that the investigation was closed." Nick hadn't been asked who was present: he didn't have to offer Taylor's name up, but he recalled the meeting in Hitchens's office well. He remembered Taylor's arrogance. *Payback is hell*, he said to himself.

His offer did not go unnoticed by Jack. Nick Walsh appeared to be helping him. He continued his questioning.

"Mr. Walsh, you also investigated the murder of Sal Paglia, is that correct?"

"Yes."

"Who was Sal Paglia?"

"He was the defendant's lawyer before you."

Spencer Taylor was on his feet. "Objection, your honor. Relevancy."

"I was thinking the same thing, Mr. Tobin," the judge said. "Where is this going?"

"I was just about to ask Mr. Walsh that question, Judge."

"Ask it, then."

"Mr. Walsh, are there any similarities between the murders of Sal Paglia and Carl Robertson?"

"Yes, there are. They were both murdered with a Glock nine-millimeter semiautomatic weapon, and they were both murdered execution-style with one shot to the head."

"Did you ever determine who killed Mr. Paglia?"

Spencer was on his feet again. "Objection, your honor. Relevancy. We can only try one murder at a time."

It was a speaking objection, but the judge let it go. "Overruled. He has established the relevancy, Counsel. Answer the question, Detective Walsh."

"No, the murder of Sal Paglia is still unsolved."

"Did you recover the slugs that were used?"

"Yes."

"What type were they?"

"Nine-millimeter Parabellum, or Luger, standard grain."

"Are they similar to the bullet used in Mr. Robertson's murder?"

"They are the same."

Jack now knew who had sent him Sal Paglia's autopsy report. "Where were the slugs that you recovered?"

"One was lodged in a concrete column. That was the head shot. There were two other shots that were imbedded in the floor."

"So there were three shots?"

"Yeah. The way we figured it, the initial shot was at point-blank range to the back of the head. That was the fatal shot. After that, the killer put two slugs into the body for insurance."

"And you're saying they all passed through the body?"

"Yes. You shoot a person with a Glock using that type of ammunition at close range and the bullet is going to pass through unless it hits a bone or something and shatters." That statement directly contradicted the testimony of the coroner.

"The bullet in Carl Robertson's murder was lodged in the back of his skull, is that correct?"

"Yes."

"What does that tell you?"

"That he probably was not shot at close range. At close range the bullet would likely have passed through the skull."

"Have you tested the slugs from Sal Paglia's murder to see if they came from the gun that was recovered last week?"

"No. We really couldn't because the slugs were too distorted."

"How about the shell casings?"

"We never found the casings."

"Did you look?"

"Oh, yeah."

"What did you conclude must have happened to the shells?"

"The murderer picked them up. This was a hallway outside an elevator. If the murderer didn't pick them up, we'd have found them."

"Does that happen often that a murderer stops and picks up the shell casings?"

"No. It's a sign that somebody is taking their time. They are very deliberate. It's the sign of a professional."

"Why would picking up a shell casing be important?"

"Because the shell casing can be matched to a gun. If the slugs are distorted, you won't be able to match the gun and the slug. If you had the casing, though, you could."

"Is that another similarity between Carl Robertson's murder and Sal Paglia's—the fact that no shell casings were found?"

"Yes."

"Thank you, Detective. I have no other questions."

"Cross-examination?" the judge asked Spencer Taylor. Jack wondered if Spencer had the balls to go after Nick. Of course, at this point he obviously had nothing to lose.

"Yes, your honor," Spencer replied. He was livid. He wanted to rip Nick's throat out. He had never seen a cop give that kind of testimony in a criminal case.

"Detective Walsh," Spencer began, "you were the lead detective on this case, weren't you?"

"Yes."

"So it was your decision to arrest the defendant and charge him with the murder of Carl Robertson?"

"That's correct."

"This woman you talked about, is it accurate to say that you considered her an accomplice in this murder?"

"That was a possibility we considered, yes."

There it was—the connection that Jack feared most.

"A possibility?" Spencer asked.

"Yes. We had no evidence linking the two. It was no more than a supposition."

"I want to talk about the bullet for a moment. Are you telling this jury that the defendant could not be the shooter because the bullet did not pass through the skull?"

"No, I'm not saying that. I don't have that kind of expertise. All I can say is that I would expect the bullet to pass through the skull if it was fired at close range."

"That would be speculation on your part, then?"

"Yes."

"And you would defer to the coroner's opinion as to what occurred in this case?"

"Yes."

Spencer had actually scored a point. He decided to quit while he was ahead. "No further questions, your honor."

"Redirect?"

"No, your honor," Jack replied.

Nick Walsh stepped down from the witness stand.

"The defense rests, your honor." It was four o'clock in the afternoon.

"Do you have any rebuttal, Mr. Taylor?"

Spencer wanted to bring the coroner back on to rebut Nick Walsh's testimony, but it was too dangerous. Besides, he had done okay with Nick on cross. "No, your honor," he said.

"All right. I think we'll adjourn for the day and have closing arguments in the morning."

*   *   *

Luis left the courtroom immediately after Nick and caught up with him in the hallway by the elevators.

"Mr. Walsh," Luis said. Nick turned and looked at him questioningly. "I just wanted to thank you for your honesty in that courtroom. It may have saved my son's life."

"It's my job to be honest," Nick replied.

Luis expected that would be all, but Nick lingered. Luis could tell he wanted to say something else.

"You know, my younger brother Jimmy died a few years ago," Nick began. "He had his own war with drugs. There weren't too many positive things in his life. That kick in that championship game was one of them. He took it with him always, talked about it all the time. He also talked constantly about a guy named Rico who made it all happen. So I guess I want to say thank you to you too."

Luis was speechless. He hadn't even realized Nick knew who he was. The two men shook hands warmly and then parted.

Jack took Dick, Joaquin, Henry, and Charlie out to a steak house that night. He invited Luis, but Luis was still too nervous about the outcome to eat. The trial certainly was not over for Jack either. The verdict was always in doubt until the jury delivered it. But these people had put their lives on the line for him and this cause, and he wasn't letting them get out of town without showing his appreciation.

Even though Henry had just met Dick and Joaquin, they were all getting along famously.

"We've been talking, Jack," Dick said, "and we've decided that being your friend is very dangerous to our health."

"Yeah, I know," Jack volleyed back. "But look at the benefits—a couple of weeks on a beautiful lake in the Virginia mountains, travel to Wisconsin and New York City, free steak dinner." They all laughed.

"Next time we're actually going to swim in the lake," Charlie added.

They were seated in a private little spot in the back of the restaurant. Jack had ordered a couple of bottles of wine, and the waiter poured. Jack stood to offer a toast. He surprised himself by getting a little choked up.

"You all went beyond the limit for me, and for Benny and Luis. It's something that words cannot do justice to. I cherish you all."

"Hear, hear," Joaquin added as they all clinked glasses.

The steaks were delicious. They drank and laughed until a little past midnight. Then they went their separate ways.

The courtroom was packed the next morning, and speculation was running rampant. Would Jack Tobin's strong presentation be enough to carry the day, or had the jury already decided Benny was guilty before Jack even started his defense? There was a theory among lawyers that the first side to score a blow was usually the winner. Jack didn't endorse that theory. He gave jurors a lot more credit than that.

Spencer Taylor was first up. The obvious frustration that he had displayed in court the day before had vanished. He was back to his old self, making eye contact with each juror and flashing that winning smile as he thanked them for their attention and service.

"You are the backbone of our system of justice," he reminded them before jumping into the substance of his argument.

Spencer's closing was no surprise to Jack. He took the jurors back to the night of September 1, 1998: "A shot rang out. Three people ran to their windows and saw Benny Avrile standing over the fallen Carl Robertson."

It was at this point that Spencer diverged from the anticipated script.

"They say that a good lawyer can get you off even if you are standing over the body," he told the jurors. "That's what the defendant is banking on. He hired the best. And now you have heard a tale—a tale that takes you away from what happened on September first and strings together fractured pieces of information and forms a conspiracy, all designed to make the defendant a free man. Don't get sucked into this fantasy, ladies and gentlemen. Stick to the facts. Stick to what you know. If you do that, you will find the defendant guilty of this crime."

It was Jack's turn now. He stood in front of the jurors and didn't say anything for about thirty seconds, then began in a calm and even tone. "You all promised at the beginning of this trial to do several things. You promised to keep an open mind until all the evidence was in. And you promised to follow the law, which means holding the state to its burden of proof. These are not arbitrary rules in a contest between two opposing parties. These are fundamental laws that come from our Constitution. We sometimes forget that part of the great American experiment was to protect the rights of the innocent at all costs. That is why a man is presumed innocent until he is found guilty in a court of law. It is here in this courtroom that truth is decided. Hype goes out the window. Blustering will not withstand vigorous cross-examination.

"So what has the evidence shown? It has shown that the defendant was at the scene. Period. It has shown that Carl Robertson was attempting to fundamentally change American life—to wean us off oil overnight. It has shown that Leonard Woods was his partner in that endeavor and that Mr. Robertson and Mr. Woods were killed nine hours apart. Mr. Paglia, Mr. Avrile's former lawyer—who apparently learned about the plan while trying to defend his client—was killed execution-style with the same type of gun and bullets that killed Carl Robertson. These facts didn't come from me, ladies and gentlemen. They came from that witness stand. The last witness you heard in this case was a twenty-year homicide detective who told you that Mr. Robertson's murder, a bullet right between the eyes, was not done from close range because the bullet would have passed through the body. It had all the earmarks of a professional murder—the same as Sal Paglia's.

"He also told you there was another suspect, a woman, who had an affair with Carl Robertson's mistress and learned all about Mr. Robertson and his comings and goings. When the defendant was arrested, however, the investigation came to a screeching halt and the police stopped looking for this woman. She was never apprehended and, as you well know, she was forgotten. The prosecution never mentioned her.

"Mr. Taylor has asked you to ignore these facts and convict Mr. Avrile simply because he was there. You cannot do that and live up to the promises that you made."

Spencer Taylor took advantage of the opportunity for rebuttal, but he didn't say anything new. The judge then charged the jurors with the law they had to follow, and they retired to deliberate. As he watched the jury file out, Jack thought about Langford Middleton. The judge had kept control of the trial throughout. His rulings were dead-on. He had faced his demons and conquered them. Perhaps this would be the turning point for a man who still had the potential to be a great judge.

Luis was on the verge of losing it completely. He hugged his son before the guards took him away and almost broke down.

"You're going to be a free man soon," Luis told him.

"It doesn't matter, Pop," Benny replied. "What matters is that you were here for me all the way." He looked at Jack, who was standing next to Luis. "And I got a better defense than I deserved."

The jury was out for two hours. Both sides interpreted that as an optimistic sign. "Members of the jury, have you reached a verdict?" the judge asked when they had filed back into the courtroom.

"Yes, we have," the foreperson, a middle-aged woman, answered.

"Is it unanimous?"

"Yes it is, your honor."

The foreperson handed the verdict to the bailiff, who handed it to the judge, who read it and passed it over to the clerk to publish.

"The defendant will rise," Langford Middleton bellowed.

Benny stood up. Jack stood with him.

"Madam Clerk, publish the verdict."

The clerk stood up and read the verdict. "We the jury find the defendant, Benny Avrile, not guilty."

Benny immediately turned to his father. The two men held each other and let the tears fall. Jack just watched. It was all the thanks he needed. He was certain now that Rico was back and would take Benny under his wing and teach him finally how to navigate the field of life—how to carve out his own turf and protect it. Benny was going to be fine.

Jack looked to the back of the courtroom where Henry was standing. Henry gave him a thumbs-up. Jack returned his gesture with a smile. They had made the decision to fight this fight together. Nothing more needed to be said.

SIXTY-SIX

On Wednesday night, Jack met Molly at an Italian restaurant in the West Village. He was a little late, as usual, and Molly was waiting for him outside in the cold. She was dressed warmly in a knit cap and Navy peacoat over jeans and black boots. She looked good. She always looked good.

"My client's father, Luis, recommended this place," he told her as the maitre d' seated them. "He said the food is great."

The restaurant itself was not much to look at. It was small—maybe twenty tables. The walls were pale yellow and hung with painted landscapes of the Italian countryside. The place was clean, and each table had a white linen tablecloth.

"It's very quaint," Molly commented as she took off her peacoat, revealing a black wool turtleneck that accentuated her fine figure. About ten minutes later, Luis and Benny walked in.

Luis saw Jack and Molly and headed toward their table with Benny in tow. Jack saw him coming and started to stand.

"Don't get up," Luis told him. "We're not staying. I left my credit card here the other night and I just came in to pick it up. We've got reservations elsewhere."

Jack stayed seated. "Luis Melendez, I want you to meet Molly Anderson."

Luis took Molly's hand graciously. "Pleased to meet you," he said.

"And that's his son Benny behind him." Benny did not come forward. He stayed behind his father and nodded to Molly. She remained seated and nodded back.

As they headed for the exit, Benny turned and gave Jack a thumbs-up. He was not smiling. Molly saw it and understood.

She had come to this dinner to break off the relationship in a natural way so there would be no lingering suspicion. Her excuse was going to be the geographical distance between them. She had planned a short speech, and she had wanted to make it before they ordered dinner. Her plan had been foiled, however, and she no longer needed to give an explanation. It was simply time to go.

"Jack, I just remembered there's something I have to do. I'm sorry. It completely slipped my mind. I've got to go."

It was Jack's turn to understand. "You're not even going to give me the chance to lay it out for you?" he asked.

Molly stood up. "I'm not going to sit in this restaurant after what just happened."

"You don't need to worry about Benny coming back or anything like that. Luis and I made sure that wouldn't happen before we set this up. They're gone."

"Sorry, Jack, I can't take your word on this one. If you want to, you can walk with me."

Jack called the waiter over and handed him a fifty. "We have an emergency. We have to leave."

"I understand, sir," the waiter replied, bowing slightly.

Outside the restaurant, Molly sidled up close to him. "Don't worry, Jack, I'm not going to molest you in public," she said as she undid the middle buttons of his overcoat and ran her hands over his chest, then his stomach and his groin. She then bent down and checked his ankles and all the way up his legs. Jack didn't move.

"I'm not wearing a wire," he told her.

"I know," she replied. "Now we can talk." They started walking down the street again as if they were taking a moonlight stroll. "When did you find out?"

"I didn't know for certain until tonight, when Benny gave me the thumbs-up. I had my suspicions before that. Every night during the trial when we met, you only asked me one question about what was going on, and then you went on to something else. Pat would have grilled me for hours."

"I'm obviously not Pat."

"I know, but it just seemed that if you were that interested in me, you would have been more interested in what I was doing. Then I thought about when we first met. I was on the front page of the New York papers on Sunday, and you conveniently walked into the Pelican diner on Monday morning and sat a stone's throw away from me. By Wednesday, we were having an affair. That's pretty quick work."

"You're jumping everywhere, Jack. I'm not following you."

"You're following me fine, Molly, or whatever your name is. We don't need to pretend anymore. You used Angela Vincent; you used Benny; and you used me. Where was I? Oh, yes, after I went back and traced the steps of our relationship and realized it was a setup all along, I knew that you or somebody who worked with you was in court every day following this case as closely as the most conscientious reporter. All you really needed to know at the end of the day was how I perceived things. You knew I'd never tell you my strategy. So every night, you'd simply ask me how it was going.

"You had an idea Spencer's case was going south on Thursday night. When I confirmed it, you decided to help the prosecution along with the anonymous tip about the gun."

"Just being a good citizen," Molly replied.

Jack couldn't believe how calm she was. She probably had a gun in her pocket and could blow him away at any time.

"Not exactly, Molly. After the trial was over, Benny and I talked. On the night of the murder you gave him a *revolver*, which means that you had to switch guns at his place before calling the police. It also explains to me how the murder occurred. You had gotten close to Angela Vincent in order to find out about Carl's habits so you could kill him. Benny just happened to fall into your lap. I figure you got the idea the night he stole Angela's credit card. You knew Leonard Woods was going to be killed around the same time Carl was. If one of the murders looked like a robbery, nobody would ever connect the two. So you en-

ticed Benny with the promise of a ten-thousand-dollar score, and then
you pretended to trip and fall so that Benny had to take center stage.
You gave him the *revolver*, told him it had a hair trigger and not to
shoot under any circumstances, and then you filled his head with cocaine. When Carl got out of his car, you were across the street and you
shot him right between the eyes. You even had Benny believing he was
the murderer. It was *almost* perfect."

"What do you mean 'almost'? It was perfect."

"Not any longer. Now Benny can tell his story. Angela can identify
you, and there's a bartender in the Village who Benny believes can finger you as well."

"Finger me as to what, Jack? A woman who was with Benny and
Angela and eventually you? And that gets you where? The state already has enough egg on its face. It's not going to prosecute me for
anything, even if your theories had any merits."

"You may be right."

"I am right, Jack. Knowing you, if I wasn't right the police would
have picked me up already. You wouldn't wait until after dinner to report what you know."

Jack refused to acknowledge that she was right. He also refused to
get angry at her attitude. He wanted some answers.

"At least Carl's plan won't be thwarted," he told her.

"That's where you're wrong, Jack. In the year and a half since Carl's
death, all his gas stations have been purchased out of his estate, as have
his factories and his trucks—so his grand plan is over even though the
existence of a formula has been revealed."

"How come you didn't get rid of Milton?"

"We didn't know about him. Besides, the existence of a formula
means nothing without the financial backing, and Milton won't get
that. He won't even try."

"If the trial didn't matter, why did you kill Sal?"

"It didn't matter a year and a half later. Six months ago, everything
wasn't in place. And Sal made the mistake of finding out about
Leonard Woods's relationship with Carl and the close proximity in
time between their deaths. He wasn't able to put things together like

you were—and I have to tell you, Jack, you did an incredible job against overwhelming odds—but Sal had to go. It gave us an additional six months."

"You keep saying 'we.' Who do you work for?"

Molly looked at him and smiled. "You've already gotten more out of me than any man or woman alive. Now you want to know who I work for?"

"There's no harm in asking."

"Oh, yes, there is. If I gave you names I'd have to kill you right after I told you. Here's the general answer: I work for the powers that be— the people who get things done in the world."

"The government?"

Molly shook her head. "The people who run the government are like the officers of a corporation. I work for the owners."

"You're not going to tell me any more than that, are you?"

"No."

They were at the corner. She stopped and looked at him, her hands in the pockets of her peacoat. Jack figured she had the gun in there. "Good-bye, Jack," she said, knowing there would be no polite exchange of kisses.

"You know, you're really good at your job, Molly. There were times there that I thought we had something going on between us."

"We did, Jack, we did. If we hadn't, you wouldn't be standing here."

She turned and walked away.

EPILOGUE

A month after Benny's trial, Jack was back in New York for a visit. He met Frankie O'Connor for breakfast at Pete's. Frankie brought along a friend, Nick Walsh. The two men shook hands. Throughout the entire investigation and Benny's trial, Jack had never spoken with Nick Walsh except on the witness stand.

"I asked Nick to join us for breakfast, Jack. He wanted to personally pass along the results of the information you provided to us."

Jack had given Frankie Molly's telephone number, hoping it would be useful to the police in some way. Apparently, Frankie had turned the information over to Nick.

"She obviously ditched the phone when the trial was over," Nick began. "However, I was able to persuade her phone company to give me the last month's billing records. They were very interesting."

"Who was talking to her?" Jack asked.

"One of my personal favorites," Nick replied. "And as I understand it, one of yours as well—a little peacock named Spencer Taylor."

"I'll be a son-of-a-bitch," Jack replied. "He was in on it all the time."

"I don't get a hard-on for too many people," Nick added. "But I'm going to love watching this guy go down."

"Do you have anything specific on him yet?" Jack asked.

"Not yet," Nick said. "I've just been watching him. There was, for sure, a boatload of money involved in a deal like this, and sooner or later I know he'll be spending it."

"That could take a long time," Jack replied.

Nick just smiled. "Yeah, it could. However, Taylor just booked a flight to the Caymans. I strongly suspect he wants to see his money and count it. I'll be there when he does." Jack looked at Frankie, who was smiling as well.

"That's beautiful," he said.

"Once we catch him, he'll start squealing like a pig," Nick continued. "We won't ever get to the people on top, but maybe we can cut a few legs off and make them think twice the next time."

"It's a constant battle," Frankie added.

Back in Bass Creek later that same week, Jack lifted his head from the pillow and glanced at the clock on the nightstand next to his bed. It was 5:35 a.m. He rested his head back down for a moment and took a deep breath before swinging his legs over the side and sitting up. Ten minutes later, he was out the front door, dressed only in running shorts and a T-shirt.

This was his time now, the early morning when nothing stirred except the night owl and the crickets, and the moon and the stars were on center stage. He followed his and Pat's familiar path into the woods, armed with his flashlight. Five minutes into his run in the deepest foliage, as a possum ran across his path and almost sent him reeling, he heard her voice in his head: *Keep that flashlight up so you can see where you're going.* He smiled to himself. Maybe it was an illusion. Maybe he was just plain crazy. It didn't matter, though, because it was his own personal craziness, a warm feeling in his heart that he didn't share with anybody. Nor was he troubled that she had seen him with Molly. In all probability there would be others. Pat was above that now—a spirit devoid of human frailties, unburdened by time and space—free at last.

NOTE TO THE READER

In case you think Henry Wilson's story in Part One of the book is a little too far-fetched to be real, it is loosely based on a true story—the case of Florida inmate Juan Roberto Melendez. You can find numerous articles about Juan Melendez on the Internet, including the actual opinion of Judge Barbara Fleischer granting Mr. Melendez a new trial.

The breakthrough biotechnology mentioned in the book is also true. Lonnie Ingram, a professor of microbiology at the University of Florida, perfected this technique and patented it. Chuck Woods, a reporter for *The Palm Beach Post*, wrote an article on May 5, 2005, in which he quoted Mr. Ingram as saying this new biomass technology could make ethanol at $1.30 a gallon. (That estimate has probably changed in the last few years.) The article also stated that half the automotive fuel in the United States could be replaced with this new technology. You can read more about this on the Internet as well.

ACKNOWLEDGMENTS

My greatest joy has always been my family, and I have been blessed in that regard.

My three children, John, Justin, and Sarah, are my anchors. We have always been there for one another. John's wife, Bethany; Justin's wife, Becky; my children's mother, Liz Grant; my five grandchildren, Gabrielle, Hannah, Jack, Grace, and Owen; and my great-granddaughter, Lilly, make up the rest of my inner circle. The next band of that circle is my brothers and sisters: John, Mary, Mike, Kate, and Patricia, and their significant others, Marge, Tony, Linda, Bill, and John. You form a unique bond when you grow up in a railroad flat in New York City with your mother and father and five brothers and sisters. My siblings have always kept my feet firmly planted on the ground. I also have an extended family of aunts, uncles, cousins, nieces and nephews, in-laws, close friends, and three godchildren, Ariel, Madison, and Nathaniel, and two great-godchildren, Annalyse and Juliette, whom I love dearly.

I'm thrilled to have a new publishing home at Center Street, and I'm grateful to publisher Rolf Zettersten, associate publisher Harry Helm, and my editor Kate Hartson, for their enthusiasm for my work. Kate's advice and expertise have been invaluable to me throughout my career. Kate is the reason I am a published author. She has been my mentor from the very beginning, and she also happens to be my sister.

Kate's assistant, Lauren Rohrig, has been a joy to work with and has helped greatly in the publishing process. I would also like to thank

Andrea Glickson, director of marketing, and Shanon Stowe, publicity director. And I'm excited to be working with the Hachette sales team, especially my good friend Karen Torres.

Thank you to the staff at Center Street for the outstanding layout and cover design of this book and especially to designer Tina Taylor.

Larry Kirshbaum has always given me tremendous support. I'm so grateful to Greg Tobin and Bob Somerville for their early editing. Emily Hill has taught me, and is still teaching me, how to promote my books on the Internet.

I owe a large debt of gratitude to many friends who have read my work and provided me with their honest analyses and opinions. I am tempted not to name names because I'm concerned that I might forget someone. But, having filed that disclaimer, I'm going to give it a shot.

Patty Hall, Dottie Willits, Kay Tyler, Robert "Pops" Bella, Peter and Linda Keciorius, Diane Whitehead, Dave Walsh, Lindy Walsh, Lynn and Anthony Dennehy, Caitlin Herrity, Gary and Dawn Conboy, Gray and Bobbie Gibbs, Teresa Carlton, Linda Beth Carlton, Kerrie Beach, Cathy Curry, Dee Lawrence, Ron DeFilippo, Urban Patterson, Stephen Fogarty, Brian Harrington, Paul Hitchens, Nick Marzuk, and Richard Wolfe.

If you liked *The Law of Second Chances* be sure to pick up James Sheehan's nail-biting legal thriller THE ALLIGATOR MAN due out October 2013.

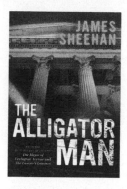

"As a writer, Sheehan, a former trial lawyer, bears comparison to Scott Turow: his books are noteworthy not just for their intricate plotting but also for their literary finesse."

—*Booklist*

THE ALLIGATOR MAN is what they're calling the dead guy in the supposed open-and-shut murder case, because pieces of his clothing have been found in the swamp, but things aren't as they seem.

When Miami defense attorney Kevin Wylie returns to his small Florida hometown to represent William Fuller, the only suspect with a solid motive and damning evidence against him, he's up against a tough fight. But Kevin reunites with his dad, legendary trial lawyer Tom Wylie, and together they build a strong case to take to the courtroom. THE ALLIGATOR MAN is a story of greed, anger, love, and redemption, and two powerful trial attorneys who fight to the end—and risk everything—for the truth.

CENTER
STREET

An excerpt from

THE ALLIGATOR MAN

PROLOGUE

Billy Fuller had spent his whole adult life as an employee of Dyna-tron, a major energy company located in northwest Florida, until the company folded and he lost everything. He had two recurrent nightmares that left him constantly tired and on edge and haunted him during the daylight hours as well. This night he was dreaming about his wife, Laurie. It was always the same dream.

He's sitting in the chair by Laurie's bedside, watching her as she lies there with her eyes closed. Dark, hollow sockets harbor those eyes, her cheeks are gaunt, her body ravaged by disease.

Her eyes open. She turns as she always does to where he is sitting and smiles. At that moment, she is so beautiful to him. He wants to cut his wrists open and give her every drop of the good, clean, healthy blood that flows through his veins.

"Come here," she says, and Billy comes to her and kisses her on the lips.

"I love you," he says.

"I love you too, honey."

He sees a faint twinkle in those deep-set eyes. He wants to reach in, pull it out, and make it light up her whole body. He wants his life and his wife back. This time he wants a happy ending.

She raises those thin arms, arms that are black-and-blue from the IVs. They are part of her beauty too. She puts her hands on Billy's shoulders.

"My body's tired, Billy. I'm going to have to leave it soon. I can't fight anymore," she says. "I need you to be strong for the kids."

"Don't say that, honey. There's still time. There's still hope. I need you. I can't do this alone."

"Yes, you can. I'll help you. Part of me will always be with you."

"I don't know."

"You'll have to trust me on this one, sweetheart," she says, closing her eyes. "I'm so tired."

Billy puts his hands to his face then and weeps. *No,* he says to himself. *No.*

The sound of his own voice shouting those words wakes him up.

His other dream was about his best friend, Jimmy Lennox. Jimmy had stood with him through Laurie's hospitalization despite his own personal setbacks. He'd been Billy's lifeline.

Billy is sleeping. The phone rings in the middle of the night. He doesn't want to answer it. He knows. But he is compelled to get out of bed and pick up the phone.

"Hello."

"Billy."

"Hi, Jimmy."

"Billy, I just want to tell you how much I appreciate your friendship and all you've done for me."

"What are you talking about, Jimmy? It's me who should be thanking you."

"Billy, I can't take it anymore."

"Take what? What are you talking about? We can take anything, you and me."

"I'm sorry, Billy. I really am."

"Jimmy, Jimmy, don't hang up. I'll come over. I'll be there in a minute. We'll talk this out."

He hears the click.

He runs out of the house. Calls 911 on his cell phone as he jumps in his car and races over to Jimmy's house. "Come on, faster," he yells at the car as he presses the accelerator to the floor. Finally, he reaches Jimmy's apartment. The door is unlocked. He walks in and sees Jimmy on the living room floor, his arms and legs splayed out, the phone in one hand, a revolver in the other. Blood oozes from his right temple. His left leg is twitching.

"Oh my God! Oh my God. Hang on, Jimmy."

He kneels down, opens Jimmy's mouth, breathes into it, presses down on his chest. Does it again. And again ... until the police and paramedics arrive and pull him off.

"No. No," he yells as they drag him away.

Then he wakes up in a sweat.

ONE

Gazillionaire Roy Johnson was, among other things, a lush. Every night somewhere between ten and eleven, Mighty Roy would get a bottle of red wine from his wine room, walk outside into his enormous backyard garden, and sniff his various, expensive tropical flowers. Then he'd sit in his overstuffed chair, drinking by himself until the bottle was empty and he'd have to get up and get another one.

He'd screwed a lot of people over to get to that position in life.

Johnson had been the CEO of Dynatron, a major energy company in the United States and overseas that employed over twenty thousand people. In his heyday he'd dined with kings and queens and heads of state, including the president. A little over a year ago, over a period of three months, Dynatron stock fell from seventy-five dollars a share to fifty cents and then to nothing as the company slipped into bankruptcy.

Roy was not around for that debacle, however. He'd long ago cashed out to the tune of a hundred million dollars.

His employees were there, though—to the bitter end. Their pension savings had all been converted to Dynatron stock before the collapse, and the fund had been frozen so they could not transfer their assets to other securities.

No word or combination of words could capture the collective havoc inflicted on those people. In addition to their jobs, every employee lost his or her retirement and health insurance. Some lost the ability to hope; some lost their spouses and families; others took their own lives.

None of that seemed to bother Johnson as he sat in his garden chair gazing at the stars. When he was good and soused, Mighty Roy and his bottle would take a walk on Gladestown Road, a two-lane road that was the only entry and exit into Gladestown, the little town where Roy had chosen to build his kingdom.

After Dynatron collapsed, the feds determined it had inflated the value of its stock for several years through a series of sophisticated accounting procedures. The chief accountant pled out to a three-year sentence. Mighty Roy claimed no knowledge of wrongdoing, and so far there was no evidence linking the slimy bastard to anything. That was it. Millions of investors screwed, twenty thousand employees decimated, or worse, and one guy got a three-year sentence. Case closed.

Or maybe not…

He was walking down the road with his bottle in his hand. He loved this sleepy, little town with its clear moonlit skies. There were no lights on the road, no traffic, and no other signs of civilization. The only sound was the croaking of the gators who resided in the swamps that surrounded the narrow asphalt strip. There were hundreds of them down there, he knew, and they could smell him for sure as he walked along. It was such a narrow, artificial line between safety and danger, life and death. He laughed out loud as the thought struck him.

A gator could shoot out of the swamp at any time and grab him. Hell, they crossed the road all the time. Others had disappeared. Maybe it was him, the smell of him, that kept them at bay. Fear. Irrational fear. He loved it.

He turned and started back toward home, staying in the middle of the road, mindful of the fact that if he slipped by the shoulder and fell, he would have crossed the line. There would be no hesitation then. They would be on him in a heartbeat, and to them he would become just another piece of meat.

He heard the engine behind him, saw the road light up from the head-

lights, and moved to the left side of the road, paying careful attention to where the asphalt ended and the swamp began. It was a little strange for a car to be out here at this hour of the evening, but he wasn't worried about the car. There was plenty of road for the car. His fuzzy brain didn't detect the sound of the engine increasing speed, didn't notice until it was too late that the headlights were focused dead center on him. The car hit him without attempting to stop, propelling him into the murky darkness. There was a splash as his body hit the water, immediately followed by a thousand other little splashes as the creatures of the night raced each other for a piece of the unexpected evening meal.